Against All Odds

CONTENTS

AGAINST ALL ODDS

C.W. FARNSWORTH

CHAPTER ONE

AIDAN

"Who is Brooke, and what are we doing tomorrow night?" Hunter Morgan asks me.

"Huh?" I say, glancing up from my phone.

Hunter spins his coffee cup toward me so I can read the black Sharpie scribbled on the brown paper sleeve.

Can't wait for tomorrow night! XO, Brooke. A phone number —hers, I'm guessing—is scrawled beneath the message.

"Oh. That one must be mine."

My best friend raises one eyebrow. "You think? Thought it tasted too sweet."

I added *one* of those little sugar packets.

"Get your own next time," I retort, taking the coffee from him and nudging the other cup closer with my elbow. "Thought this one tasted bland."

Now both of Hunter's eyebrows do that annoying judgmental lift. "What the hell crawled up your ass, Phillips?"

"Nothing," I mutter, right as our third roommate Conor walks into the kitchen.

1

Hart is whistling, which is even more annoying than Hunter's expressive eyebrows.

As long as I've known the guy, he's been serious and focused. Sure, I've seen him let loose, but only when he's physically incapable of playing more hockey. For the past few weeks he's been uncharacteristically depressed, lazing around in sweatpants and sighing a lot. Ever since his trip to Seattle last week, he's as cheerful as could be, right when I could really use a reliable wingman and drinking buddy.

He was a wet blanket our entire trip to Vail, refusing to do anything except snowboard and mope.

And now he's in a committed relationship and so happy about it, he's *whistling*.

It's weird to witness.

"You headed out?" I ask as Conor grabs his Holt Hockey windbreaker off the back of a kitchen chair. The entryway to our house, where you would normally store coats, is piled high with hockey equipment.

"Yeah. Going to Harlow's, then to PeeWee practice."

I stand, deciding to grab a yogurt. "That's great, Hart. Coach will be thrilled you're going back to basics."

Hunter snorts, the sound audible over the slam of the fridge closing.

Conor just shakes his head. He's harder to rile up than he used to be. Probably a side effect of getting laid on a very frequent basis. Since we share a wall, I have a good idea of just how often that is.

"*Do Not Answer* is calling you, Phillips," Hunter tells me.

I don't glance toward the spot on the table where I left my phone. "Is the name not self-explanatory?" I ask, ripping the flimsy top off the yogurt with more force than is necessary before tossing it in the trash can.

"Wow, you're touchy. Just letting you know."

I should apologize to Hunter for snapping at him, but I shove a bite of yogurt into my mouth instead.

My dad figured out I blocked his number and threatened not to send this semester's tuition check unless I started taking his calls. So I unblocked him, but was petty enough to change his name in my phone and I haven't answered a single time.

I'm sure I'll have another pissed-off voicemail from Lincoln Phillips very soon.

My mood sours even more.

"You're not coming back here before going to the rink?" I ask Conor.

Hart shakes his head.

"Are you going back to the rink later?"

We're almost at the end of winter break. Spring semester— our *final* semester—starts Monday. Conor's taken advantage of the calmness on campus the past couple of weeks to fit in extra skates most days. I'm surprised he's at home right now instead of out on the ice.

Another head shake. "I'm busy later. And I thought we talked about you not being my schedule secretary, Phillips."

I groan. "I'm not asking to be nosy. I just need a ride to the rink later. I'm supposed to meet with Coach."

"You're meeting with Coach today?" Hunter asks, suddenly interested in the conversation. "Why?"

I shrug. "Dunno. He texted me after practice yesterday, asking to meet today."

"Weird." Hunter glances at Conor, who's pulling on his jacket. "Did you get anything? I didn't."

Hart shakes his head a third time, then looks over at me. "I can drop you off at the rink on the way to Harlow's."

3

"I'm not supposed to meet Coach until five," I tell him. "My balls will be frozen by then."

Hart heads for the hallway, obviously eager to leave. "Fine. See you guys later."

I finish my yogurt, toss it in the trash, and then follow Conor.

His car is already gone by the time I get my boots on and walk out our front door.

The January wind rips right through the flannel I'm wearing as I approach my truck, parked next to Hunter's green SUV. My *useless* truck, as I discovered when I tried to go out last night. A fourth Washington winter appears to have been too much for it.

Despite my silent prayer that the issue magically resolved itself overnight, the engine doesn't so much as click when I press the button that's supposed to turn on the truck.

I press my forehead to the cold steering wheel, swear under my breath, and then climb out of the driver's seat.

I know nothing about cars. I'll have to call a mechanic to come tow it to a garage to get looked at.

Hunter is still sitting in the same spot at the table when I reenter the kitchen, his legs stretched out so far I have to step over them to get to the other chair.

"Didn't start?" he asks without looking up from whatever book he's reading.

Hunter was home last night when I discovered my truck is currently useless.

Conor wasn't, but he didn't even bother asking why I wanted a ride. Lately, if it isn't related to hockey or his new girlfriend, it's off his radar.

"Nope." I sigh.

He nods toward my coffee cup, then smirks. "Call Brooke. Bet she'll give you a ride."

My hungover memory of the blonde who served me and some

4

of the guys coffee earlier is vague, but yeah, she probably would. I barely remember what I said to her or what the hell we're supposed to be doing tomorrow night. I was distracted and exhausted this morning. Still am, actually. And ever since winter break, it's been harder not to compare every flirtation to that night in the hot tub. To keep interest, when they've all been lackluster in comparison.

"Can you drive me?" I plead. "At quarter of five?"

Hunter raises one of his damn eyebrows at me again.

"*Please*," I add. After experiencing how fucking freezing it is out, I have no interest in walking. "Or let me borrow your car?"

"I've seen you drive, Phillips. You're not borrowing my car."

"Then give me a ride. I brought you coffee, remember?"

"You mean the *bland* coffee?" Hunter is annoyingly good at holding a grudge.

"Better than *no* coffee."

"You didn't even bother to keep track of the cups, Phillips."

"We fixed that issue, remember?"

Hunter heaves a sigh. "Fine. But only because I left my favorite sweatshirt in my locker at the rink."

"Thank you." I grab my phone and coffee off the kitchen table, then head upstairs.

———

When Hunter and I walk into the lobby of the rink, the chatter of young, excited voices is literally bouncing off the walls.

I've never really gotten why Conor volunteers with the local PeeWee team. He's by far the best player at Holt, could easily have played for a Division I school, and I know he must get frustrated by the talent discrepancy between himself and other guys on the ice, myself included.

Spending time around little kids still figuring out the basics sounds like it would be ten times worse. But seeing the awed, admiring expressions of the kids passing us with miniature hockey bags slung across small shoulders, most of them escorted by a parent, makes me smile.

I still remember my first exposure to hockey—a pro game when I was eight. My older brother Jameson chose not to go, so it was just me and my dad. Plus the man my dad was trying to purchase a company from. The only reason that detail sticks in my head is because it's why my dad opted for rinkside seats, so close to the boards I could reach out and touch the players.

From the first second those big, hulking guys appeared, speeding across the ice effortlessly, I was hooked.

And now I'm one of those big, hulking guys, at least in these kids' eyes.

It's a strange realization, one I'm not entirely sure how to feel about. Kind of like I already peaked and kind of like I should have been lifting weights last night instead of doing shots. Half-nostalgia, half-regret.

"Never thought I'd see the day," Hunter says, shaking his head slightly as we pass through the lobby and the rink comes into view.

Hart is out on the ice, which is nothing new. He often stays late after our practices, so it's no surprise he'd do the same after coaching kids, which isn't much of a workout. What *is* new is that he's not alone out there. The flash of Harlow's red hair is impossible to miss against the white backdrop.

"Me neither," I agree.

Conor getting a girlfriend was not on my bingo card for this season. He didn't have the same reputation I do, but he definitely enjoyed his single status. Him getting serious about a girl, especially right before hopefully winning the championship he's been chasing since freshman year, was a surprise.

I feel like I could take some credit for the happy couple we're watching. Up until I all but forced him to a few months ago, I'm not sure if Hart had ever said a single word in Harlow's presence.

You'd never know that, looking at them now.

I might miss having him around lately and the wild nights when we would go out and let loose together, but I'm also relieved.

I've been worried how Conor might handle the end of the season. If we don't win a championship, if he doesn't get a call during free agent season, if this is how his career ends, I'm relieved he'll have Harlow. That his world is no longer exclusively centered around hockey. I'm happy for him.

Conor spots us walking along the boards and steers Harlow this way. And I do mean *steers*. I'm not sure you could call what she's doing skating.

Since I've never seen Harlow look anything except in total control and completely at ease, I can't help but grin at the sight of her clinging to Conor like he's the only thing anchoring her from a twenty-foot drop.

"Hey, Harlow." Hunter is the first to speak when we meet at the home bench, and I shoot him a skeptical look. He was the one who had doubts about them, who told Hart he was losing focus and a relationship would be a mistake.

I was the one who not only engineered their first conversation but also encouraged Conor to reach out to Harlow over break. Partly so I didn't have to deal with his sulking, but it should still count.

That's Hunter, though. He's never afraid to share his opinion. He's also quick to move on and mind his own business.

"Hey, guys," Harlow says.

Her cheeks are noticeably red for her only exertion being pulled around on the ice.

Conor looks at her with a soft expression that I'd never seen him wear before recently. Harlow glances at him, her cheeks growing redder, and I realize she's not flushed from skating.

I should probably buy more earplugs. The honeymoon phase appears to still be in full effect.

"What are you guys doing here?" Conor asks.

"I'm meeting with Coach. I mentioned it earlier, remember?"

Conor shakes his head.

I roll my eyes. Our conversation was only four hours ago. "I asked you for a ride. You were 'busy' later."

"I *am* busy," Hart tells me, resting an elbow on the boards.

I'm tempted to roll my eyes again. Busy skating in slow circles. "Yeah, yeah, looks like you've got Boyfriend of the Year in the bag. But Hunter's my new favorite best friend, because he actually drove me here."

"I left my favorite sweatshirt in my locker, actually," Hunter says.

"Eyesore broke down?" Conor asks.

His disdain for my truck's color is consistent; I'll give him that. He's been ragging on the red shade for years.

I sigh. "Yeah. I don't know what's wrong with it. Guess I need to call a garage and get them to take a look at it."

"I'll text you the name of the place I used," Conor says. "They did a good job."

"Great, thanks. See you guys later." I start toward the locker room, knowing how much Coach hates tardiness.

Hunter follows me, heading straight for his locker and pulling his sweatshirt out. I continue toward Coach's office.

"Hopefully this won't take long."

Hunter nods. "If it does, I'll just ditch your ass here to walk home."

This meeting could last four hours, and he'd still be sitting here when I walk out. He and Hart are two of the most loyal guys I've ever met.

I suck in a deep breath before knocking on Coach Keller's door. The letters spelling out his name are peeling and worn, evidence of how long he's occupied this office.

Year after year of disappointing seasons, something Conor is determined to change. We've only lost one game this entire season. Holt has the best record in our division, meaning there's a good chance we could actually win a championship in March.

"Come in," Coach calls.

I turn the metal door handle that's rubbed shiny from use and walk into his office.

It's small and sparsely decorated, which isn't much of a surprise. It matches the locker room and the rest of the building, which I'm pretty sure is a decade older than I am.

"Take a seat, Phillips," Coach tells me, nodding to the two chairs across his desk.

The patterned plaid is faded and worn. One of the cushions has a rip sagging open on the side. I choose the chair in slightly better shape, glancing at the bare walls and the two picture frames on the desk as I settle into the seat. They're turned away, so I can't see the photos, but I'm surprised they're there at all. Coach has never struck me as sentimental. At the end of each dissatisfying season, he's told us to look ahead, not back.

I wonder what he'll say after our final game this year. If we don't win a championship, odds are Coach K will never get one.

My elbows dig into my thighs as I lean forward, resisting the urge to bounce my knee. Maybe other players have gotten called in here for conversations before, but I never have. If Coach wants to talk to one of us, he usually has us stay a few minutes late after practice. I have no clue why I'm here or what to make of the fact that he asked me to come.

"So…what's up, Coach?"

Coach Keller sighs, shutting the open binder in front of him, setting his reading glasses on top of it, and then leaning back in his swivel chair.

Its loud squeak is the only sound in the small space for a minute.

He sighs again. "You failed Statistics last semester, Phillips."

I freeze, dread trickling through me like icy water.

Failed. Not even a D. *I fucking* failed.

"Passing that course is a graduation requirement for all Business majors." He pauses. "And failing a class puts your GPA below what you need to play, according to the athletics committee."

I'm still frozen, processing.

No one would call me a star student, but I've never flunked a class before.

Fall semester grades get posted over winter break. But I haven't bothered checking mine—or logging into my school email—because *break* is supposed to be a vacation from all the boring parts of college. I figured I'd gotten a mix of Cs and Bs like I usually do.

"So I'm off the team?" It's a small miracle I manage to choke those words out past the panic lodged in my throat.

I'm not chasing a pro career like Conor is.

I'm not as fast or as focused as Hunter is.

But I love playing hockey. Love being part of a team and the high of winning we've been experiencing a lot lately. Hockey is the one thing I put *some* effort into, as opposed to the none I normally give everything else. And I care about helping Hart get his championship. It's practically all he's talked about since freshman year, and this is his last chance. The thought of being seated on the bench, stuck watching those hopes die, makes me feel sick to my stomach.

"No," Coach Keller answers, and I take a breath for the first time in what feels like forever. "But you are on probation."

I exhale, my muscles finally relaxing. I've been on some sort of probation most of my life. With my parents or with some authority figure. It's a warning; that's all.

"Professor Carrigan has agreed to let you retake the final exam once the season has ended. Provided you pass that, you'll still be able to graduate with your year."

My posture slumps further. I lean back in the chair, relief replacing fear. Even if I fail the final again, I'll still get to play in the championship, assuming we get that far.

If I flunk out of college after that, it'd have the silver lining of horrifying my image-obsessed family. I can only imagine what kind of story my parents would spin to explain how a Phillips ended up degree-less. Even if they cut me off, I could continue crashing with Hunter and Conor until graduation, minus having to go to class, which I barely do currently. I'll have full access to my trust fund after my birthday in August, unless my dad decides to take that too. And if he does, I'll find a job somewhere doing...something.

Coach is still studying me, and I'm worried I might look *too* relieved.

Quickly, I rearrange my expression, aiming for remorseful and appreciative. He talked to Professor Carrigan for me, set this whole deal up.

Honestly, it's surprising. Appreciated, but surprising. Usually, Coach is a big fan of consequences. If anyone's late to practice, we all skate suicides. That kind of thing.

"Okay. Thanks," I say.

Coach's serious expression doesn't waver. "Professor Carrigan seems to think your grade was a result of poor motivation, not an issue comprehending the material."

I fight the grimace that wants to appear. The material was dry, and Professor Carrigan is an older woman with an uninspiring teaching style. I'm not looking forward to a round two, that's for damn sure. Unfortunately, I have no other option.

"I'm just not great at math. I'll study harder this time."

"I'm sure you will, Phillips. Since Professor Carrigan is making a notable exception to her normal policy, I assured her you would be a dedicated student."

Quickly, I nod. "Yeah, I will be."

"I'm not leaving that up to chance. So, I've set up a tutor for you. You'll meet with her once a week to review materials from Professor Carrigan and prepare for the final."

A tutor? A *female* tutor? After three and a half years on this campus, I know that means my tutor will either be too nervous to talk to me or too busy flirting to focus on math. Neither bodes well for me passing the retake.

"That's really not necessary—"

"You're not in a bargaining position, Phillips. Take the deal— or you're off the team."

"I can pass on my own."

He says nothing, just stares me down. It's intimidating as hell and a look I recognize from practice whenever one of us deviates from his directions.

It means *I'm the coach, so we do it my way.* And he's right; I'm not in any position to challenge him.

I swallow. "Fine. Uh, thanks—for setting the tutor up."

"I arranged for you to work with my daughter, Phillips."

This time, my swallow is more of a gulp. *He did* what?

"Your daughter goes to Holt?" I ask.

I had no idea Coach had kids, let alone a college-aged one. He doesn't wear a wedding ring or talk about his personal life. As far as I noticed, he's never had family members show up at a game— just like me. Honestly, he gives off more bachelor vibes than family man.

I glance at the photos on his desk again.

"She's a new student, but she's more than qualified to help you," he tells me.

I'm betting he wanted to say *overqualified* instead.

And she's a new student...so a freshman? I'm having a hard time picturing Coach raising a shy geek smart enough to tutor for a senior-level class. But I keep my mouth shut tight this time.

Coach continues talking. "This is serious, Phillips. Any funny business, and you're off the team. The deal with Professor Carrigan goes away and you're back to needing to retake the entire course to graduate, which means you won't graduate on time. And I don't think I need to talk you through what will happen if I hear you're treating my daughter with anything less than total respect. Understood?"

I nod so quickly I must look like one of those bobblehead dolls. "Understood, sir."

"Good. Professor Carrigan will be in touch with you soon about the tutoring schedule. Go study or eat or do something that won't make me regret helping you."

I nod again, then stand. Hastily, I head for the door.

Glance back, once my hand is on the handle.

"Thank you, Coach," I tell him.

He's already refocused on his binder, probably preparing plays for our next game. But he looks up and nods, hopefully hearing the sincerity in my voice. I close the door behind me, the weight on my chest a lot heavier than when I walked in.

If I had to describe Coach using one word, it would be *fair*.

I respect him a hell of a lot more than my own father. But it's always been obvious to the entire team that Conor is his guy, understandably so.

Hart wasn't officially named captain until last season, but he's always been the unofficial one. The player everyone—including Coach—looks at to lead.

Coach probably would have done this for any guy on his roster.

I'm not used to having faith put in me, though, and certainly not from someone *I* respect.

People expect fun from me, not leadership. Expect me at parties, not to see me studying in the library. Expect a grin from me, not the grim line my mouth is pressed in as I approach Hunter. He's sitting on the bench in front of his locker, reading a paperback. He doesn't glance up until I clear my throat—twice.

"Let's go," I tell him, heading toward the door connected to the tunnel that leads to the ice and then veering right in the direction of the parking lot.

I need some fresh air. To breathe. To think.

"Slow the fuck down, Phillips," Hunter calls after me. "It's not like you can go anywhere without me."

The reminder chafes.

I need Hart to send me the name of the garage he used as soon as possible so I can get back to having my own mode of transportation. I could walk, I guess, but the weather here is usually cold, raining, or both. Maybe the only thing I miss about living in LA.

"So?" Hunter asks once he's caught up. We're outside, crossing the mostly empty parking lot. "What'd Coach want?"

"To tell me I flunked a class last semester."

"You *what?*" Hunter's normally deep voices flies alarmingly high.

"Relax, it's fine. I can still play. I just have a few tutoring sessions to get through."

I sound calmer than I feel. It's not great, but it could be worse. I think.

"Will you still graduate?"

"Dunno. I'll see how smart Coach's daughter is. I have to pass a retake at the end of the season."

Hunter stops walking right in the middle of the parking lot. "What about Coach's daughter?"

"She's my tutor," I tell him. "I guess she's some kind of freshman math whiz. The professor agreed, so whatever."

"Coach's daughter—a freshman—is the tutor who's going to keep you on the team and help you graduate college?" He shakes his head, then mumbles something that sounds suspiciously like *God help her* as he starts walking again.

"I'm not an idiot, Morgan. I just didn't think I needed to study for the final."

Hunter snorts. "That does make you an idiot, Phillips."

"Just don't tell anyone, okay?"

"Which part?"

"Any of it. I don't want the guys thinking I'm about to get kicked off the team, and I don't want Hart riding my ass about partying less. If I didn't study for the first final and got an F, a few study sessions should put me firmly in C territory."

"Like I said, you're an idiot."

"Just keep it to yourself." If anyone will, I trust Hunter to. He's the thoughtful member of our trio, while Conor and I tend to be more impulsive.

Hunter shakes his head again but agrees. "Fine."

CHAPTER TWO

RYLAN

The brakes of the old SUV squeak as the tires stop rolling. A definite downside of living in a damp climate—everything rusts.

"You're sure this is the right place?" my dad asks, turning off the car. He leans over the center compartment to peer at the exterior of the brown house critically, his tone dubious.

"Anthony," my mom chides, hitting his arm lightly.

"I was just checking." My dad tugs the keys out of the ignition, then spins them around one finger. "It looks a little…old."

"It has character," my mom says, ever the optimist to my dad's crusty pessimism.

She glances over her shoulder, winking conspiratorially at me crammed in the backseat with all my boxes of belongings.

My chest constricts like it's being squeezed by a rubber band as I smile back at her.

This is a moment I should have shared with my parents two and a half years ago. Instead, I was selfish and stubborn, insisting that Boston University was my dream school despite being thousands of miles away from home and lacking the free tuition Holt offers to its employees' children.

All they could afford was one plane ticket. My mom helped me pack; my dad drove me to the airport. They never got to see my dorm room in person, much less helped me move into campus housing. Only visited Boston once, during sophomore year, and it was an uncomfortable visit thanks to my ex.

But this is a new year and a new semester.

A fresh start, and I'm trying to leave all my regrets in the past.

"This is it," I say. What little of the exterior I can see through the piled boxes on the seat next to me matches the photos online.

Aside from the fact that those were taken in summer, on a rare sunny day. Today is damp, gray, and cold.

But the house is not a dorm filled with underclassmen, thankfully.

And despite the two askew shutters on windows facing the road, unfortunate choice of paint color, and the overgrown bushes on either side of the front door, it doesn't look *that* bad.

I was lucky to find this place advertised on a student forum. It's a four bedroom of all juniors, one of whom is going abroad for the spring. I'm taking her room.

Setting aside my apprehension about living with three strangers, it's significantly better than living at home with my parents or in a dorm. Plus, it's only a couple of blocks from campus. A huge bonus since I don't have a car.

I climb out of the backseat of my parents' car, tugging the zipper of my down jacket a couple of inches higher so it rubs against the underside of my chin and blocks more of the January wind.

I grab my backpack out of the footwell and heft it over one shoulder, then lift a box out of the backseat before heading toward the front door. Balancing the heavy box while hitting the doorbell with my elbow is a challenge, but I manage.

A smiling girl with light-brown hair cut into a bob answers the door. Since I stalked all my future roommates on social media over winter break, I recognize her instantly. Chloe Ellis.

"Hi! You must be Rylan. I'm Chloe."

I nod and smile, relaxing some as I register her friendly expression. She seemed sweet when we texted back and forth about the available room, but in person always feels different.

"I am. Nice to meet you, Chloe."

Chloe steps aside, beckoning me inside the warm house.

"Dakota and Malia aren't home right now, but you'll meet them later," she tells me. "Do you need help carrying anything in?"

"I think we're good, thanks." I glance over my shoulder as my mom and dad step into the house, each carrying a box. "These are my parents, Miriam and Anthony. Mom, Dad, this is Chloe, one of my roommates."

"So nice to meet you, Chloe," my mom says warmly.

"Hello," is my dad's gruff greeting. He immediately goes back to studying the house carefully.

Unfortunately, I favor my father's more reserved personality. Whenever I try to emulate my mom's openness, I feel fake.

"Your room is this way!" Chloe spins and heads deeper into the house.

I follow, glancing around as I walk. The first floor is open concept, a kitchen with an attached living room to the left and dining room that's been repurposed into more lounge space to the right.

Everything is clean and neat, which will make my mom happy. And nothing looks in a state of disrepair, which should reassure my dad some.

Rather than start up the stairs, Chloe walks down the hallway to the right of them. I follow her, take another right, and end up in my new bedroom.

The wooden floor creaks as I cross the threshold.

Cream, bare walls. A double bed pushed against one wall, a desk and a dresser against the other. There's a closet, which I wasn't expecting. And two windows, one facing the backyard and the other the hedge that separates this lot from the neighbors.

To my surprise, I love it.

Even empty, it feels much homier than anywhere else I've lived since moving out of my parents' at age eighteen. I can picture myself living here.

"The bathroom is at the end of the hall," Chloe tells me. "You'll share with Dakota. Malia and I are upstairs. Both of those bedrooms have their own bathrooms." Her expression turns apologetic. "Dakota and Emily drew the short straws in August."

"It's fine," I tell her. "I'm used to sharing a bathroom with more than one person, so that sounds luxurious."

Chloe's expression becomes even more animated, which I didn't think was possible. "I want to hear all about what London was like. I've never been out of the country and would love to—"

"Oh, honey. This is perfect!" My mom appears in the doorway, beaming around the small room as she stacks a box on the dresser. My dad is right behind her, looking cautious but less concerned than when we first arrived.

"I'll let you get settled," Chloe says. "I'll be upstairs, so just holler if you need anything."

"Great, thank you," I tell her.

"I'm going to grab another load from the car," my dad says, shuffling back out of the room after Chloe.

My mom opens the box she carried in and starts pulling items out. "Go help your dad. I'll start unpacking."

I agree easily. I'd never tell her, but I spent last semester living out of my suitcase. My dorm room in Boston never looked that settled either. And I didn't unpack anything except the essentials staying at my parents' over break, knowing I was about to move here. Having all my stuff settled—for me—sounds wonderful.

I walk back down the hallway, heading for the front door. I pause when I hear a bang from the kitchen. Chloe said she was heading upstairs, so maybe one of my other roommates is home?

Nope, it's my father squatting in front of the sink.

"Dad!" I hiss. "What are you doing?"

He startles and stands, a guilty expression on his face. "Checking to make sure there was a fire extinguisher in the kitchen," he tells me. "Lots of landlords don't bother following the code and rely on the tenants, even if they're college students."

"Is there one?" I ask, because that's easier than focusing on the lump in my throat.

My dad fussing over the house, my mom arranging my room.

The anxiety I've been carrying around, dreading the start of this semester, is slowly being replaced by relief. I'm proud of myself for leaving Boston, for finally admitting I wasn't happy there. I'm tired of the guilt I've felt about choosing Boston in the first place. And a little grateful for it, right now, knowing it's making me appreciate my parents that much more.

"Yes," he answers.

"Good." Straightforwardness has always been my dad and I's love language. He wouldn't know what to do with a sappy thank you any more than I'd know how to deliver one. He coaches hockey players and only smiles on special occasions.

According to my mom's doctor, I was supposed to be a boy, which is how I ended up with my unique name, a variation on the family name they planned to give me. And I might not have been the son my dad was expecting, but we've always shared a special relationship.

One I didn't realize how much I missed until I returned home.

It was easier, when I was thousands of miles away, to put emotional distance between me and my parents in my attempt at total independence.

"Do you need to check the plumbing and the fuse box too, or can we finish unloading the car?" I tease.

My dad chuckles as he bends down to close the cabinet beneath the sink. "When did you get grown-up enough to know what a fuse box is?"

"You should be asking who taught me what a fuse box is, and the answer would be you. Just like we went over how to change a tire and drive stick shift."

Another gruff laugh. Then, to my surprise, he tells me, "I'm proud of you, Rylan. I know transferring will be an adjustment."

I force a smile in response, trying to ignore the way the knot in my stomach tightens. I'm glad I transferred, but it doesn't make starting over at a new school suck any less. "It will be fine. I grew up in Somerville, remember?"

"Of course I do, honey. But that's different than going to college here. I want to make sure you're—"

"I'm excited, Dad. It will be great."

A hopeful statement I've repeated to myself so often, it almost sounds genuine now.

He nods, but I'm not sure he believes me. "I set something up…something I need a favor from you to make happen."

I raise one eyebrow, thoroughly confused. The last favor my dad asked of me was to lift the wipers on the car last week when it was predicted we'd get snow. And he didn't look nearly this serious then. "Okay…what did you set up?"

"One of my players—"

I groan. "Dad…"

My only interest in hockey is the polite kind I've feigned for my father. I sit through watching games with him because I know it makes him happy. But those are professional athletes playing. Hockey involving guys I'll never meet, not peers.

Wanting to avoid the uncomfortable dynamic of being the coach's daughter factored into my decision not to enroll here as a freshman, if I'm being honest. And so, *of course*, I'm starting at Holt while interest in the hockey team is at an all-time high. When I went to the campus bookstore yesterday to pick up my textbooks, two girls were there buying Holt Hockey sweatshirts.

I'm happy for my dad. He deserves the attention and recognition for turning around what's been a historically terrible team.

I'm less than thrilled for me.

But if Holt is anything like my last school was, there's not much overlap between interest in mathematics and sports. I'm hoping most of my new classmates won't care that my dad coaches the hockey team. If I get really lucky, maybe they won't even know Holt has one.

My dad scratches his chin, his expression a mixture of sheepish and stern. "One of my centers failed Statistics last semester. He needs to pass that class to graduate. I talked the professor into a retake after the season ends, which keeps him eligible to play as long as he follows through on the prep. He's smart, just unmotivated. And doesn't take a damn thing seriously. I needed a tutor who won't take any bullshit." The brown eyes I inherited warm. "You can handle Phillips."

"Dad, I haven't even started my *own* classes here yet. I'm not sure I can—"

He nods. "I know, I know. But it's only for one hour a week. The university has a tutoring program you'll get paid through. And…" He rubs his chin again. "I might be old, but I'm not senile yet. Despite my best efforts, I'm aware my boys attend—if not host—most of the parties on campus. I know you don't study every hour of every day. It might be good for you to branch out and meet some new people. Phillips, in particular, is a real social butterfly, from what I hear behind the bench. Boys think I'm deaf."

I snort, then sigh.

This is undeniably a low point, having my dad worried enough about my social life that he's recruiting his players to help me make friends here.

Uncomfortable proof that he and my mom are more concerned than they've acted since I returned to Somerville. I was sparing in the details I shared about the break-up with Walker last year. There wasn't much to say and even less that wasn't shameful. Walker was simply the last strand holding me in Boston. And as soon as it was snipped, I realized it was a string I should have cut a lot sooner. At least he had the decency to cheat on me *before* the transfer deadline.

Looking back at the first two years of college, I don't have much to show for it. I got good grades at an excellent school. I dated a guy who turned out to be a waste of time. Convinced myself his friends were mine, until they promptly deserted me after we broke up. London wasn't the special experience I was hoping for, either. More like moving my melancholy to a new city. The closest friend I made was another American student, Jess, and I've only talked to her once since leaving Colorado. She invited me to visit her family's place after the holidays.

I left Somerville at eighteen thinking I needed to, to grow. Now I think that maybe the location doesn't matter as much as my willingness to explore.

My dad is still waiting for an answer, and I'm not sure what to tell him. He's trying to help me, and I want to help him. It's the least I can do, after how understanding he and my mom have been about me reversing my stubborn decision and transferring.

But...my plan was to steer as clear from the hockey team as possible. Avoid being labeled as the coach's daughter and whatever stigma comes with it. Committing to tutoring a player will make that impossible.

"I can't be the only math major at this school, Dad. There must be someone else who can help."

His expression falls a little bit, lines of worry webbing out from the corners of his eyes. "I wouldn't be bothering you with this if I didn't think you were the best option, honey."

I study my dad more closely. Most people would miss the hint of desperation threading through the words; I don't. I can read my dad better than most. Maybe because we're similar in so many ways.

And I realize this is about more than me making friends or earning some money.

"What year is he?" I ask.

"He's a senior."

"And a center?"

"Yes."

My dad's hockey career ended after a college injury. He took a job coaching at Holt when I was five as a way to stay close to the sport that was his first love. I saw the disappointment on his face at the end of each hockey season until I turned eighteen. He's chased a championship for sixteen years. This season is his best chance of getting one. The team has only lost one game—a feat that's basically unheard of in college hockey and that's receiving a lot of attention even at the Division III level.

What my dad isn't saying? He thinks he needs this player to win.

And he doesn't ask for empty favors. My dad supported me

leaving Washington to attend what I thought was my dream school. Whatever small part I can play in his dream of getting a trophy, it's the least I can do.

"Statistics?" I ask. I got an A in Stats freshman year.

"Yes. And one hour a week. That's it."

"Okay," I agree.

"Thank you, honey."

My mom appears, her forehead creased with confusion as she looks at us standing in the kitchen. "What are you two doing in here?" she asks. "Isn't there still a bunch of stuff to carry in from the car?"

"Working on it," my dad and I say at the same time.

He glances at me. Winks.

There's a flicker of warmth in my chest, appearing like the strike of a match lighting. It feels good to be in sync with my dad, to know I'm helping him.

But I spend the next ten loads trying to forget what I just agreed to.

CHAPTER THREE

AIDAN

I lean to the left, gingerly. "I think Pierce broke a rib with that last hit."

Hart appears unconcerned I could be seriously injured, squirting some Gatorade into his mouth as he watches the third line run through the drill we just completed. "Tape it."

I stretch to the right. Wince. "I was thinking a massage."

Some painkillers to help with my aching ribs and pounding head would be nice too.

I knew going out with Sampson and a few other guys last night was a stupid idea, but dumb decisions are kind of what I'm known for.

"And a nap."

"I'm not waiting for you next time," Conor tells me.

Since I'm still car-less, I had to rely on Hart to drive me to practice today.

Him banging on my bedroom door with his hockey stick early this morning is partially responsible for my headache. The rest of the credit goes to tequila.

"You can skip the lecture. You weren't even home when I got

back."

"I spent the night at Harlow's," he tells me. "Drove home to eat breakfast and get changed before practice."

Dammit. Had I known that, I definitely wouldn't have gone out last night. "Tell me next time, so I know to skip the earplugs."

"Don't be so dramatic, Phillips." Conor swallows more orange liquid, then glances at me. "You're louder than I am. We shared a wall in Colorado too, remember?"

"That was only for a few nights." I reach out, grabbing a bottle. My mind immediately jumps to the brunette in the hot tub as soon as Conor mentions Colorado, and I really need to stop thinking about that night. It's not like I'll ever see her again, and it's made my hookups of late seem dull and empty. "And at least I have the decency to keep it out of the house here."

"I'm not sure the girls you fuck in random places at parties would describe it as *decency*, Phillips."

I swallow some Gatorade, annoyed this bottle is also filled with orange. My least favorite flavor. "They know what they're getting," I say, then take another drink.

I'm practically a campus attraction at this point. Library, coffee shop, student center, guy who guarantees a good time. I never say anything about more than one night and I never bring girls back to my room.

It's exactly how I like my life: simple and uncomplicated. College is supposed to be about enjoying yourself—the window between being controlled by your parents and entering the real world with responsibilities.

Hockey is the one responsibility I allow to cut into my social life. Our schedule is only going to get more intense with playoffs creeping closer.

Plus, I'm going to have to start *studying* soon.

I grit my teeth at the unpleasant reminder. At least Hunter has kept his mouth shut like he promised. The lecture I received from Conor about how I spent last night on the way to practice this morning would have been way worse if he knew I failed a class last semester.

"You ever think about dating?" Hart asks me casually.

I cough mid-swallow. I have to clear my throat twice before I can respond. "*What?*"

"It's more than just steady sex, you know. Having someone to talk to…who always has your back… I didn't realize what I was missing out on before."

I shake my head, smirking. "You heartless asshole. *I* was your pillar of support long before you pulled your head out of your ass and noticed Harlow Hayes."

Conor laughs once, sounding unamused. "*Noticing* her wasn't the problem."

"She is super hot," I agree.

Hart elbows me, right where my ribs are aching from my collision with the boards earlier.

"Ow!" I glare at him.

"Get your own girlfriend."

I snort. "Never gonna happen," I tell him.

Too forcefully, because it prompts a curious head tilt.

"Never?"

If the faded scars on my heart haven't healed by now, I'm not sure they ever will. And even if they do, the sting of betrayal is a lasting lash.

I think Conor has an idea there's someone in my past, probably from something I said while drunk, but he's never explicitly asked me about it. And he's certainly never suggested I *date* before.

"Why would I? I have you and Morgan for sappy shit and I

can fuck anyone I want without forced small talk or holding hands in a movie theater first. Win-win."

Conor shakes his head. "You haven't told me or Hunter what *sappy shit* has been bothering you for the past couple of months."

I look away, at the ice. "It's nothing," I say, same as every other time he or Hunter have asked me what's going on.

Nothing they can fix, at least. I'd rather remain in denial as long as possible, and talking about it means I can't pretend it's not happening.

Hart sighs.

Coach Keller's whistle cuts through the cold air.

Conor pops his mouthguard back in, stands, and climbs over the boards onto the ice. If the first line is up, that means I only have a few minutes left on the bench.

I stretch to the left again, wincing. Whether or not my rib is actually broken, I have a bad feeling it'll bruise. And the only upside to having a purplish blotch on my side is that girls seem to find it sexy. Most act like I'm a war hero returning from active combat if we hook up after I've recently taken a nasty hit. But even that sympathy isn't worth the annoying ache until it heals.

The whistle sounds. I stand, swearing under my breath when I experience the sharp stab of pain along my ribs.

It was a sophomore defender who took me out, too, which is just embarrassing.

I should be faster. Should be sharper.

And my hangover isn't entirely to blame. My head is all over the place. I'm stressed about school—the seriousness of what's at stake in the Stats class. Dreading the engagement party that's creeping up closer and closer. I'm still dodging my dad's calls like it's a sport, but I'll have to talk to him eventually.

Problems I temporarily solved last night by getting drunk and hooking up with a blonde whose name I already forgot.

Today, I'm paying the price.

The blades of my skates scrape as I move into position for the drill we're running. The frozen surface is marred, the ice carved and covered with sprays of shavings from the past hour. Today's practice has been brutal.

Dean Zimmerman, the assistant coach, sends a puck to Ace Carter, my right winger, to start the play. Carter enters the zone first, me and Tyler Yarrow, my left winger, trailing slightly behind him so we don't trigger an offside call for crossing the blue line before the puck. Carter passes to Yarrow. Yarrow circles, then passes to me.

I miss, the puck whizzing an inch past my waiting stick. I hustle after it as fast as my aching side and hungover muscles will allow.

My maximum speed is too slow. Andy Pierce, who's responsible for my throbbing ribs, reaches the puck before I can and sends it straight out of the zone.

Another sharp whistle pierces the cold air.

I swear under my breath as I skate back to the bench and take a seat next to Conor. He says nothing, which is worse than anything he could have commented. His silent disapproval saturates the chilly air, suffocating me. I hate disappointing him. Hate worrying I'm the weak link letting down the team. And the more I worry about it—about everything that's weighing me down—the more tempting an escape sounds.

Grow up, Aidan, is what my dad would say if he could see me slumped on the bench right now. And he doesn't even like hockey. Couldn't care less how many passes I miss.

The fourth line finishes the drill, and Coach blows his whistle for a final time.

"That's it, boys. See you tomorrow."

I'm pissed and relieved. That was a terrible fucking way for me to end practice, but I'm so exhausted I'm not sure I could have made it through another shift.

All I want is a hot shower, a cold pack, and to be relaxing in bed.

Everyone hustles off the ice, except for me.

I skate slowly, irritation about missing that pass dulling the throb of my side a little.

"Phillips."

I pause, reluctantly, just past the bench. Coach Keller is standing with Coach Zimmerman, the two of them comparing notes on a clipboard.

Coach Zimmerman heads toward the opposite end of the bench.

Coach Keller stays put, rubbing his chin as he studies me. "Did you hear from Professor Carrigan?" he asks.

I nod. "She emailed me."

Short and to the point, letting me know my tutoring sessions would be taking place on Tuesday evenings, and to meet my tutor on the first floor of the library.

I'm obviously not her favorite student.

Wonder why.

"Good."

Coach doesn't mention the whole *your tutor is my daughter* aspect of it, which is a relief. Considering I actually need to pass this class, I'm grateful to him for interceding and ensuring that I have a tutor who a.) knows what she's talking about and b.) I won't hook up with.

Coach continues to study me, and I resist the urge to fidget under his scrutiny.

This is the one and only way in which he reminds me of my father. A commanding presence with the ability to wield silence like a weapon.

"Break is over, Phillips," he tells me. "Seems like you could use the reminder."

I nod, running my tongue along the backs of my teeth.

Technically, break for anyone playing a winter sport ended two weeks ago. We've had daily practice and a few games while most of campus was still off enjoying themselves. But as of tomorrow, classes resume. My final semester of college will start, and I don't feel any closer to figuring out the next phase of my life than I did when I committed to attending Holt.

It seems like everyone else already does. Or at least has *some* clue.

I'm not sure exactly what Conor will do if he doesn't get signed as a free agent, but he's majoring in English and, unlike me, gets straight As. Hunter is majoring in Political Science and is waiting to hear back from the graduate programs he applied to. Jack Williams is moving back to LA to join his family's accounting firm. Robby Sampson just got offered a job as a market research analyst.

Basically, it feels like everyone except for me has some sense of what they want to pursue, and I somehow missed out on how that gets decided.

But that's not Coach's problem, and I'm trying to pretend it's not mine either. Semi-successfully.

"Just an off day," I tell Coach, assuming he's referring to my pathetic performance during practice today.

Another few seconds of uncomfortable appraisal, then he nods. "Go shower, Phillips," he tells me, then calls, "Dean! Meet me in my office so we can go over those plays again."

I take the dismissal, stepping off the ice and stomping along the rubber mats that lead into the locker room. It's in its usual state of chaos, guys pulling off their gear, guys leaving the showers, guys headed into the showers.

I keep my head down as I walk straight toward my locker.

My mood is the same dark one that's fueled by a thundercloud I can't seem to shake lately.

It started following me around in November, when Jameson proposed to Parker. When I realized the shit between my brother and my ex wasn't just sticking around, it was becoming permanent. And got worse when I realized my dad's lectures had a kernel of truth to them. Jameson is only eighteen months older than I am. He's got a job track that will lead all the way to future CEO and he's got the wife lined up. His entire life—personal and professional—is decided.

There's no part of me that wants my whole life mapped out that way.

But it's emphasized how blank my future is. Not only lacking direction, but *any* paths at all.

"Big plans tonight?" Cole Smith asks as I take a seat in front of my locker to unlace my skates. His is right next to mine. "I heard last night was pretty wild."

"My big plans are to sleep."

Cole laughs. "With who?"

"An ice pack, probably. Pierce fucked up my ribs."

"Sorry, Phillips," Andy calls from across the room.

The kid sounds genuinely remorseful, so I resist the urge to flip him off.

Not Pierce's fault I'm slow and unfocused.

I finish pulling off my gear and head for the showers.

Holt's athletic facilities are not what anyone could call new or luxurious with a straight face, but they're clean and well-maintained. The white tile is scrubbed so clean that it gleams under the overhead lights as I find an open stall. The plastic dividers are a half-hearted attempt at privacy, since you can see right into them and most of us walk to and from the showers naked. The humid air dampens everything, so it's not worth wearing or carrying clothes in here unless you want to change twice.

I rinse off, soaping my hair and watching the white suds wash down the drain before shutting off the water and grabbing a clean towel.

The school must have bought some new ones, because they're less threadbare than they used to be.

I rub it through my hair, wrap it around my waist, then head back into the main section of the locker room. A lot of the guys have left, my chat with Coach slowing my post-practice progress down.

I check my phone, my stomach hollowing when I see the new voicemail from *Do Not Answer*.

I press play and tuck the phone between my ear and shoulder as I pull on a clean pair of sweats. Might as well see if there's any variety in his pestering.

"Aidan, it's your father. I'm very disappointed by your behavior. Your brother's engagement party is only a couple of weeks away and I expect you to—"

Nope.

I pause the message, then delete it and toss my phone into my hockey bag.

My dad doesn't need to worry I'll show up and cause a scene. All I want is to get in and out of there as quickly as possible. The only reason my family cares about me showing up is that my absence would be noticed, and they don't want to have to answer any questions about it.

"You failed a class?"

I turn toward Conor's voice, belatedly realizing it's just me, him, and Hunter left in the locker room.

I glare at Hunter. "Way to keep your mouth shut, Morgan."

He shrugs. "Hart asked me what your meeting with Coach was about. I hate lying."

I shouldn't have mentioned my meeting with Coach in front of Conor.

I figured Coach was trying out something new, talking to all the seniors before playoffs start or something. Had I known the real reason, I wouldn't have mentioned anything about the meeting to him or Hunter. I already had to deal with Morgan's judgy eyebrows when I went out last night. Now I'll get disapproval from Hart too.

"Don't blame Hunter," Conor says. "He told *me*, not the entire campus. And I should know, as your captain."

I scoff.

"And best friend," he adds.

I snort. "*Absentee* friend would be more accurate."

Conor sighs. "I'm sorry the trip to Colorado sucked, okay? And I know I've been spending a lot of time with Harlow lately—"

"Which is fine," Hunter interrupts, frowning at me.

Great. Now I feel guilty.

Harlow stole all of Conor's attention that wasn't attached to hockey long before they officially started dating.

But Hunter is right—Conor's happiness is nothing I should be criticizing him for. What I should be doing is explaining to my two best friends why I'm in such a shitty, short mood lately.

Except it's not a conversation I'm ready to have. And if anyone gets that, I think Conor might.

Up until a couple of weeks ago, he'd never mentioned his own father or that they're estranged. Maybe one day we can commiserate over our crappy dads, but today isn't that day for me.

"I'm glad you and Harlow worked things out," I tell Conor. "Really. I was the one telling you to fix it with her, remember?

Just…don't dip in because you're worried about me flunking. Coach set up the thing with his daughter. It'll be fine."

Conor's gaze sharpens. "What thing with Coach's daughter?"

I glance at Hunter, who's focused on tying his sneakers. Fuck, I should have known he'd be sparing with details. Of the three of us, Morgan is by far the least chatty. And he probably felt guilty telling Conor anything at all when I'd asked him to keep it to himself.

"She's my tutor," I say, yanking on my sweatshirt.

"His *daughter*? Coach has a daughter, and she goes to Holt?" Conor sounds torn between surprise and suspicion that I'm making this all up.

"Apparently. He set it up."

"And she's tutoring you."

"Yep."

"Don't even think about—"

I know exactly where he's going with this. "I'm capable of keeping my dick in my pants, Hart."

"News to me," Hunter mutters.

Not my fault he's usually home when girls come looking for me, whereas Hart is always out.

It's common knowledge on campus where the three of us live. It's not like I'm handing out my home address after every hookup.

"If you say so." Conor also sounds dubious.

"I won't touch her."

I might be generally unreliable, but they can trust me on this.

I've never hooked up with a freshman. Certainly not a math nerd.

And even if she was neither of those things, she's Coach Keller's daughter.

In other words, off-limits.

CHAPTER FOUR

RYLAN

The annoyingly cheerful chime of my alarm wakes me up.

I reach out and hit the *Snooze* button, feeling like I fell asleep five minutes ago. That might be accurate, actually.

My eyes are dry and gritty as I blink up at the white plaster ceiling of my new bedroom. I only managed a few hours of sleep, up late tossing and turning, worried about what today will be like.

I sit up, untangling the sheets from around my legs before I slide out from under the warm comforter.

The sting of cold floorboards against my bare feet makes me wince as I rush over toward the dresser that contains all my neatly folded, clean clothes. Reminding me to thank my mom—again—for unpacking my entire wardrobe.

First day at a new school.

The thought makes my skin prickle with panic.

I hate starting over. I attended elementary, middle, and high school in Somerville with the same set of people.

Fresh starts aren't second nature to me. And I only know one other Holt student. A girl from my graduating class chose to attend Holt, but I haven't reached out to her since I was accepted as a transfer.

I was adamant—excited—about leaving Washington for college, and my eighteen-year-old self made that obvious. Ending up back here feels like a failure, even though Holt is considered an excellent school and isn't necessarily an academic downgrade.

I focus on even breathing—deep inhales and long exhales—as I walk into the hallway and head toward the bathroom.

Dakota's bedroom door is still shut, so I don't have to worry about waiting my turn. I run through my usual morning routine and then return to my room to get dressed.

I decide to wear a wool-blend miniskirt I bought in London and a cozy sweater. My shoulder-length, dark brown hair is a knotted tangle from my sleepless night. It takes me ten minutes to coax the strands into cooperating, then another twenty to apply a full face of makeup. More than I would normally bother with, but today it feels like armor. Like the more flawless my complexion appears, the more smoothly today will go. I pull on tights, boots, and a jacket, loop a scarf around my neck, and then grab my backpack.

Aside from the occasional creak that's just a characteristic of old houses, there's no sound as I walk toward the front door.

I'm not a morning person. I don't understand why anyone would choose to get up when the other option is to stay under warm sheets. But I had last pick of classes because I was abroad last semester and got stuck with a nine a.m. lecture.

Despite my annoyance with the early hour, the walk isn't terrible. There's something peaceful about being outside with little commotion around you. Makes it easier to think and to relax. The sun is peeking out today, making the walk toward campus a little more enjoyable. The rhythmic thump of my backpack against my spine is almost relaxing, as steady as a heartbeat.

This neighborhood is mostly other Holt students, so there's not much activity yet. No adults rushing to work or kids standing outside waiting for the school bus.

The tree branches overhead are all bare, but the grass is still more green than brown.

There haven't been any snowfalls since I've been back in Washington, my only recent glimpse the drifts in Colorado over winter break. Snow in a major city wasn't the same, more of an inconvenience that led to public transit running even less reliably than usual.

I'm hoping Somerville is due for a small blizzard soon. Nothing is more scenic than seeing the boughs of the pines scattered along the Sound's shore weighted down with glinting white. I've always loved taking photos of snow.

My skin warms despite the slight breeze, thinking of my favorite photo I took in Colorado.

Five minutes later, I'm passing the main entrance of the university, marked with a giant stone sign that's new since I last visited.

Holt's campus is beautiful.

I've seen it before, obviously.

My dad has worked here for most of my life, and Somerville is not a huge town. Local swim lessons were held at the pool here, and I learned to skate on the same ice rink my dad coaches on. The middle school theater production I reluctantly took part in was held in the university's auditorium.

But everything looks different now, passing buildings for the first time as a student. There's a warmth in my chest, a comforting familiarity and an allegiance that never appeared anywhere else I've attended college.

Returning home to realize it has changed, and so have I, is not the terrible feeling I was expecting. And it feels a lot less disjointed than any of my other first days on a college campus.

I still have twenty-five minutes before my first class, so I head toward the coffee shop located next to the student center and bookstore first. Nerves have stolen most of my appetite, but I could really use some caffeine after my sleepless night.

Warm air hits me first when I walk inside the coffee shop, the smell of brewing coffee appearing a few seconds later.

There are a couple of girls chatting with the blonde managing the register, giving me time to scan the chalkboard menu. They're all standard offerings, nothing all that exciting or original. We're past pumpkin and peppermint season, I guess, and a long ways from summer.

I'm supposed to be focusing on positives today, so I take note of the banana nut muffin in the pastry case. My favorite flavor, and showing up to my first class with an empty stomach is probably a bad idea. Math classes are rarely that rambunctious, and I don't want to be the new girl with the growling stomach audible over the professor's lecture.

Once the girls in front of me finish up their conversation, I order a coffee and my muffin. The blonde working the register is cheerful and pleasant, which helps.

So far, everyone I've met at Holt has been incredibly nice. Chloe marked the locations of all my classes on a campus map for me last night. She's by far the most outgoing of my new roommates, but Malia and Dakota are both sweet too.

I pay, take the bag with my muffin, and then head toward the end of the counter.

I'm standing and scrolling on my phone, waiting for my coffee to appear, when there's a sudden burst of activity.

The entire coffee shop seems to perk up, especially the blonde at the register and the brunette working the espresso machine. The barista knocks over an entire stack of paper cups as the sound of loud male voices fills the smallish space.

I glance over at the group of new arrivals, then do a double take.

Not because they're attractive guys—although they are—but because three of the four are wearing Holt Hockey jackets.

This is as strange for me as being on Holt's campus as a student.

The last time I attended a Holt hockey game was back in middle school. I was eleven, maybe twelve at the time. After that, I was too preoccupied by my own interests to go to any games. It just became my dad's job to me, something separate from my own life. My mom still goes occasionally, just to support him, but hockey has always been my dad's thing. Neither my mom nor I are that invested in sports.

All I recall from that game years ago is it was long and boring. I didn't pay attention to much, certainly not the college-aged guys on the ice who seemed awfully old at the time.

It's bizarre, realizing these players aren't just peers, they're guys my dad spends a lot of time around.

In the past few years, they've seen him more often than I have.

I look down at my phone screen before any of them catch me staring in their direction. Let my hair fall forward to shield most of my face, like I have my last name stamped across my forehead and there's some way they'll be able to tell exactly who I am at first glance.

My drink arrives a few minutes later.

I thank the barista and head for the door, passing the group of hockey players. Most of them are busy relaying orders to the blonde, but one glances my way and grins. I smile back automatically but continue walking quickly, not wanting to engage in conversation.

Post-Walker, I'm focusing on myself, not guys. Not that I'm against having some fun, because I'm not, but the bar for that was recently set pretty high. My standards have been reset. And I want simple and uncomplicated. One of my dad's players is not that.

I take my time walking across the path that cuts through the campus green, enjoying the sunshine warming my face as I alternate between sips of coffee and bites of muffin. By the time I reach the brick building that houses the mathematics department —and therefore most of my classes—the bag with my muffin is mostly crumbs and my cup is half-empty. I toss the bag in the trash and climb the steps toward the carved wooden door. Tug at the handle.

Nothing happens.

I tug again.

Nothing.

Check the time on my watch. It's five to nine, and there were some eight-thirty classes on the schedule. None I had to take, thankfully, but there's no reason this building should be locked.

"Try pushing."

I startle at the sound of the unfamiliar voice behind me, glancing over one shoulder at the guy who's appeared. His dark hair is cut short, and he's wearing a pair of tortoiseshell glasses.

Unlike the hockey guys, who were all wearing sweats, he's dressed in a pair of dark jeans and a green sweater over a button-down. More how I'm used to students looking from being abroad. I feel overdressed—all the other girls I've seen on campus so far have been wearing leggings.

I press the handle again, this time pushing instead of pulling. It opens easily, so I step inside, holding the door open for the guy behind me.

"Thanks," I tell him.

"No problem. This is the oldest building on campus, and that door has some old-fashioned lock mechanism. You're not the first person to have trouble with it. The architect who designed the campus was pissed because they changed the design of the other academic buildings so they didn't have to deal with the door again."

I stare at him, not sure what to say.

He grimaces. "Sorry. I work in the Admissions Office showing prospective students around. I know tons of useless facts about Holt's campus." He pauses, pushing his glasses up his nose. "Are you new?"

"Yeah. That obvious I just transferred here, huh?"

He smiles. "Aside from struggling with the door, no."

His gaze dips down, checking me out. He's cute and seems nice.

I shouldn't stereotype, but I doubt he plays hockey—or is on any sports team. He reminds me a little of Walker, unfortunately, with the same slightly nerdy, put together demeanor. Earnest reliability I thought was a good idea. That seemed like a safe bet.

"You're a math major?" he asks.

"How'd you know?"

"Because the only class meeting at nine is Abstract Algebra, and I've never met anyone taking it for fun." He grins. "I'm Theo, by the way. 110 is at the end of the hall."

I follow him.

"I'm Rylan," I say, glancing at the posters on the walls as we pass them.

All senior thesis presentations, I'm assuming. Something I won't have to worry about until the fall.

"That's a cool name," Theo says.

"Thanks."

"So, where did you transfer from?" he asks.

"BU, technically. But I spent the fall abroad at Oxford, so this is my first semester on campus."

Theo whistles. "Oxford. Fancy."

He's definitely getting the wrong impression about me.

Oxford was fancy. I'm not. I was there on a full scholarship that covered tuition and housing. What it didn't cover was eating at the expensive restaurants and buying the designer clothes most of the other girls had the resources for. I found amazing bargains at thrift stores and begged off from most meals, saying I needed to study. Honestly, it was exhausting.

"Rainy," I tell him. "Weather was worse than Somerville."

Theo laughs. "Someone already broke it to you about the weather, huh?"

"A *long* time ago. I grew up here."

He looks surprised. "Really?"

I nod. "Really. Where are you from?"

"Des Moines." He pauses. "Iowa."

I smile. "I know where Des Moines is."

"You're in the minority of people I've met, then."

My grin grows. The more I talk to Theo, the less he reminds me of my ex.

Theo pauses outside of the door numbered 110, gesturing for me to walk in first. I thank him. A rare gentleman.

The lecture hall is smaller than I'm used to. Only three rows of stadium-style seating, ascending from low to high. There are no individual desks, just one long stretch of wood with chairs spaced every few feet.

A middle-aged man with graying hair is sorting through a large stack of papers. About ten students are already seated, several of them greeting Theo and smiling at me. I head toward an open section at the end of the middle row, dropping my backpack on the ground and then leaning down to pull out a notebook and pen.

I'm relieved when Theo takes a seat next to me. I'll have someone to ask questions of if I need to.

A few more students hurry in right as the giant clock above the whiteboard hits nine exactly.

Like it's a cue he was waiting for, the professor looks up, carries a stack of papers toward the front row, and drops them down in front of a girl with curly black hair. "Pass those around, please," he says, before returning to the front of the room.

"Good morning, everyone. Welcome to Abstract Algebra. I've had most of you before. But for those who are new faces—"

I'm pretty sure he's referring to mine, since everyone else seems to know each other.

"I am Professor Nelson. In addition to teaching several classes in the Mathematics department, I am also its chair. Should you have any questions about major requirements or senior theses, I am an excellent person to ask. I hope you all had wonderful winter breaks." He pauses, meaningfully. "And I hope you're all refreshed and ready to focus. The syllabus is going around. We'll start by reviewing that, then reminders on set theory."

I glance at Theo. He smiles.

And just like that, I'm a student at the school I once considered my last choice.

CHAPTER FIVE

AIDAN

I cy air burns my lungs as I inhale deeply, trying to focus on Coach as he runs through our schedule for the rest of the week. It's hard, since my legs feel like limp noodles and I know that Hart will make sure I'm wherever I need to show up this week. The mechanic he recommended hasn't been able to figure out what's wrong with my truck yet, so I'm still reliant on him and Hunter chauffeuring me around like a little kid.

I went hard today to make up for Sunday's shitty performance during practice. It paid off several times, but it also means my muscles are trembling from exertion. I'm in great shape, just not the kind where I can skate as hard as I did tonight and not feel it afterward. Usually, it's a push I reserve for games. But our next one isn't until Saturday, and I felt some pressure to prove to Coach I'm capable of more than I've showed him lately. To make him not regret his efforts to keep me on the team and ensure I walk across the stage in May. To not be the unreliable, irresponsible guy most know me to be.

Coach wraps things up.

Our huddle breaks, everyone skating toward the open door that leads off the ice.

"Gaffney's?" Hunter suggests to my left.

"Fuck yeah," I answer.

The best part of Tuesdays are the half price wings and pints at the most popular campus bar. My tired muscles gain new strength as I imagine taking a bite of crispy chicken and washing it down with a cold beer. Fucking delicious.

I shower and change, then chug a Gatorade while I wait for Conor to finish getting dressed. The only upside of relying on him as my means of transit is that I don't have to stay sober. One pint is my maximum tonight, though. Sunday's hangover is a fresh, painful memory.

Most of the guys end up in the Gaffney's parking lot. Every team I've been part of at Holt has been close-knit, but this year's is exceptional. We're gelled, we're focused, we're electric. Win or lose, I'll be sad to see this season end. It'll be the end of my hockey career, and all I won't miss is the bruising. My side still hurts, but at least I was fast enough to escape any checks today. Once it heals, I'll be back in fighting shape.

I walk inside behind Hart, who suddenly takes off to the right.

I'm confused until I spot Harlow sitting at one of the high-top tables with a group of girls. Conor immediately lays one on her, and it's not a quick peck, more like he's trying to fuse their tongues together.

A few of the guys around me hoot and holler, drawing the attention of anyone who wasn't already looking, which appears to be approximately no one.

I follow Hunter over to the long table we always occupy. Stacey, one of the waitresses, immediately rushes over to take our order. I get my usual—a dozen wings and an IPA—flirting back with her until my full bladder commands me to stand and head for the restrooms.

Clayton Thomas, the star—and I use *star* very loosely—of the basketball team is washing his hands when I walk in.

"Hey, Phillips," he greets, looking slightly nervous.

Probably because he knows who I'm best friends with and is also aware that he's high on Conor's least favorite people list due to some shit he pulled with Harlow. I don't have any issue with Thomas personally, but I'm firmly on Conor's side with whatever happened. Thankfully, working things out with Harlow seems to have mellowed Hart out when it comes to anything off the ice.

"Hey, Thomas. How's it going?"

"Not bad." He grabs a paper towel and dries his hands. "Last home game is next week, which is hard to believe."

"Wow. Just one left?"

"Two, technically. We're playing Edgewood in the first round of the playoffs, and we all know how that'll go."

Yeah. The basketball team is notoriously terrible. I've heard Thomas is semi-decent, but the rest of the team is not.

"You never know."

Thomas snorts. "Right. It's all good. I've got some fun plans for the rest of senior year." He grins at me. "I'll probably see you out."

I grin back. "Yeah, you probably will."

"See you, man."

"See you."

Clayton leaves. I take a piss, wash my hands, and am drying them when my phone starts buzzing in my pocket. I toss the paper towel in the trash and pull it out.

It's my dad.

I suck in a deep breath, then answer. "Dad."

"Aidan." He sounds so surprised, I almost smile.

Obviously, he's become as accustomed to leaving annoyed messages as I've become to receiving them.

"Did you get the plane ticket?"

No *How's hockey?* No *How was your winter break?* No asking about my friends or any part of my life.

"Yeah," I lie.

I mean, I probably did get it. I just haven't checked my email lately, but admitting so will give my dad one more thing to complain about.

"Good."

I take a deep breath, staring at the puddle of water on the counter. "How's Mom?"

"She's doing well. Excited about the wedding."

Yeah, I bet she is.

"School going well?"

"Yep," I lie again.

"I'm getting pulled into a meeting," he tells me.

Bullshit. It's dead silent in the background.

"You called me, Dad."

A beat of silence. "I'll see you soon, son."

He hangs up first.

I scoff and stuff my phone back in my pocket.

———

"I can't wait to watch you play on Saturday," Mariah gushes.

"Thanks," I reply.

There's a flash of confusion on Mariah's face before her expression reverts to sultry.

Usually I'd at least tack on a *gorgeous*. More likely I'd tell her to make a sign for me, or say that I can't wait to celebrate with her after we win.

But I do none of that.

All I needed to do was return to the table after taking a piss, but Mariah is the third girl who's stopped me on the way back from the bathroom.

Each interaction, my annoyance has ticked a little bit higher.

I don't know what the hell is wrong with me. Neither does Mariah, by the looks of it. Ordinarily, this is attention I eat up.

It should be the exact distraction I'm looking for after talking to my dad. Instead, I'm fighting the urge to walk away.

"You've been playing so well this season," she tells me, smiling.

So well is a stretch to describe my performance.

I was better at practice today than I've been skating, but it's a low fucking bar. I've played fine in games lately, but nothing spectacular. The last game I scored in was before break began. If you ask my sore muscles from practice earlier, I forgot what doing more than the bare minimum feels like.

"You okay?" Mariah asks me, and I realize I've just been standing and staring at her, totally spaced out.

"I'm not feeling great, actually."

"Oh, no." Her confusion instantly transforms into sympathy.

"Just a headache. From practice. I should go get some water."

I take off before Mariah can say anything else—or offer to act as my nurse. Normally, it's a hot fantasy I'd be all over. But all I feel like right now is downing a pint, eating some wings, and then heading home to ice the bruise on my ribs. It's been bothering me all day.

The food has already arrived when I finally get back to the table. A perk of being on a championship-chasing team, I guess. The people seated nearby who were here before us and still haven't been served don't even look annoyed.

"Thought you fell in," Hunter teases as I take the seat next to him.

I pull my phone out of my pocket and check my email. Sure enough, there's a new email from my father's secretary. I shut off the phone and set it on the table before replying to Hunter. "Nah. I was just talking to Thomas."

Hunter glances toward where Conor is sitting down the table, aware of the hole in Hart's bedroom wall just like I am. "He start shit?"

I shake my head before grabbing my pint glass and taking a long sip of beer. "We were just talking about the end of his season. They only have two games left."

"Two games? Really?"

"Uh-huh. Unless they make it past first round."

"You mean if Edgewood doesn't show?"

I snort, demolishing a wing in two bites. "Yeah."

"That's gotta be a rough way to end things."

I shrug before picking up another piece of chicken. "He seemed fine with it. Looking forward to the off-season."

Hunter scoffs. He's as competitive as Hart is.

"Tuesdays are the best," Robby says from his spot across the table, reaching for a wing.

"Hell yeah they—*fuck*." I freeze. "It's Tuesday."

Robby laughs. "How many drinks have you had, Phillips? That's what I just said—*shit*!"

I almost upend his beer—and mine—hastily reaching for my phone. I open my school email and scroll through the messages, ignoring Hunter as he asks me what's wrong. Finally find Professor Carrigan's email and confirm I fucked up.

I was supposed to meet my tutor a minute ago.

All day, I've had the niggling suspicion I was forgetting something, and I was.

Fuck. Talk about a terrible first impression.

"I gotta go." I abandon my beer and dinner, grabbing my phone and practically sprinting toward the door.

Only to realize…I don't have a car.

I pivot and rush back over. "Can I borrow your keys?" I ask Conor.

Hart's texting someone on his phone, and from the wide smile on his face, I'm guessing it's Harlow, who couldn't have left more than ten minutes ago. If I wasn't in such a mad rush, I'd tease him about it.

He glances up, frowning. "Why?"

"Because I don't have my truck back yet and I need to get somewhere fast. It's important."

I silently plead with my eyes, close to just shouting that I have a tutoring session for the whole world to hear. If I get kicked off the team, the entire campus will find out anyway.

"Must have been one hell of a tit pic," Robby comments.

"Probably a full frontal," one of the juniors, Jake Brennan, says.

I flip them both off, staying focused on Conor. He reaches into his pocket, pulls out his keys, and tosses them to me.

"Not a fucking scratch, Phillips," he calls after me.

I'm already out the door.

CHAPTER SIX

RYLAN

He's late.

I tap my pen against the wooden tabletop. Glance at the watch on my wrist, each tick of the second hand adding to my irritation.

Phillips is eight minutes and thirty-three seconds late, to be exact.

I feel like a fool, sitting alone at the table closest to the main doors so I can't possibly miss him. Professor Carrigan's email said to meet on the first floor of the library. No one has walked into the library since I arrived—five minutes early—so I couldn't have missed him passing by.

I dragged myself out of my warm, cozy bed and walked here, all for him to not even show up. I have a pile of my own work to get done tonight, which, fine, is my fault for procrastinating.

Not all of my classes from Boston and Oxford fulfill Holt's school-wide requirements. Meaning I'm enrolled in the maximum number of credits possible, which is a hefty course load.

I lean down to grab my laptop out of my backpack. If I'm here, I might as well get some work done.

At least I'll be more productive in the library than I was snuggled under blankets on my bed.

"Hey," a male voice says.

I glance up. Freeze.

For two reasons.

One, the guy standing a few feet from me is *extremely* good-looking. The sort of attractive that immediately makes you pause to take notice. Light brown hair that's either styled or naturally ruly. Green eyes that manage to look shadowed and mysterious, even beneath the harsh fluorescent glare of the library's lights. A tall, muscular frame fills out the sweatpants and lightweight navy jacket he's wearing.

Two, the déjà vu. I've experienced this jolt before, during a cold night on a Colorado mountain.

I know exactly what's underneath his casual clothes.

Memorized that secretive shade of green when it was reflecting the stars.

My thoughts are an endless loop of *Fuck*.

I was never supposed to see him again.

"Alice." Aidan takes the seat across from me, his presence immediately overwhelming the four-person table.

Telling him to call me by my middle name seemed harmless, back when I was sure we'd never see each other again.

At least he remembers me. This would be far more humiliating if he didn't.

He looks surprised to see me, but not the same stunned I am.

What are the fucking odds?

"It's Rylan. Alice is my middle name." I glance down, grabbing my pen off the table and rolling it between two fingers. "I was, uh, that was…"

I can't think straight.

I'm rattled, which I rarely am. Mostly because I don't make

54

reckless decisions that might come with consequences. I make smart, logical choices after weighing my options. And I'm usually surrounded by people who coax the same caution.

Almost a year together, and I can't think of a single time when Walker surprised me. It hurt, walking in on him with another girl. But it didn't surprise me. I think part of me was waiting for it to happen, so I was almost relieved when it did.

When I left Aidan in that hot tub, I never thought we'd see each other again.

That was the whole point. That night was supposed to be an impulsive, thoughtless moment I could look back on whenever my life felt boring and predictable, unblemished.

Aidan, sitting two feet away, is more than a blemish.

He's a blowtorch to the perfect memory. The harsh light of reality, dissipating a fantasy.

I clear my throat. Square my shoulders, trying to look like I'm not tempted to slide under the table into a puddle of embarrassment. "You…go to Holt?"

"Yep. And I'm here to meet my tutor. Rylan Keller."

There's a sudden, sinking sensation in the pit of my stomach as all the pieces click together. "Your last name is Phillips."

It didn't occur to me to look up who the Phillips on the hockey team was before tonight.

I assumed—logically—that we'd never met.

Now, I'm really wishing I had done some research. I could have gotten out of this tutoring arrangement before our paths ever crossed. Had some warning, at the very least.

"Uh-huh," he confirms.

"You're on the hockey team."

"Right again. And you're Coach's daughter."

He doesn't phrase it as a question, but I nod anyway.

Then wait, expecting some worry or panic to appear on his

55

face. It doesn't, which is a pleasant surprise. I would have assumed hooking up with one of my Dad's players would end with them begging me to keep it a secret. Aidan appears totally unbothered by the revelation my father is his coach. It makes me wonder what their relationship is like.

I continue playing with my pen, working hard to hide my unease from my face. "I didn't—didn't know you went here."

I'm assuming the shock on my face when he showed up already conveyed that, but I don't want him possibly thinking I knew who he was that night.

"You're the one who told me you were British."

My face heats. The mysterious, mature persona I strove for that night is crumbling. And…he remembers details, not just me. "I didn't tell you I was British. I told you I went to school in London. Which I *did*."

Mentioning it was a stop before returning to attend college in my hometown didn't seem like relevant information at the time. Didn't fit with the fantasy.

"And now you're here." Aidan's tone is matter-of-fact, no inflection suggesting how he feels about it.

"I grew up here." My tone is petulant. *I was* here *first*, I'm saying.

He smirks. "My condolences."

I fight the small smile that wants to appear. "Somerville's not that bad."

Very rich, coming from me. I fled as fast and as far as I could.

"If you say so."

"You're not from Washington, I'm assuming?"

"No," is Aidan's only response.

I know he doesn't live in Colorado. Jess said the eight-bedroom chalet across the street from her family's place sits empty most of the year. It's why I was adventurous enough to venture into his yard in the first place, assuming no one was home.

I roll the pen between my fingers, refocusing on the present and why we're both here. "So you failed, huh?"

A muscle jumps in Aidan's straight jaw.

Part of me thought his appearance was enhanced by the moonlight and the excitement of encountering him.

No such luck—he's still gorgeous under the library's fluorescent lighting and the lens of my complete mortification.

"I'm bored by numbers," he tells me, leaning back and stretching. His shirt lifts a couple of inches, flashing me the carved V and thin trail of hair that I thought was a myth until I saw him naked.

I swallow, forcing myself to focus on our conversation instead of how annoyingly attractive he is. "Bored by numbers... So, of course you're a business major."

"Means to an end."

"Flunking?"

His green gaze darkens. "Visited any hot tubs recently?"

I tap my pen against the stack of papers Professor Carrigan left for me at the student center, chewing on the inside of my cheek. She too could have given me more of a heads-up, instead of referring to Aidan as Mr. Phillips in our emails.

I'm not sure how much any warning would have helped, though. His presence is...a lot. I don't know how I could have prepared to encounter it again, even if I knew I was going to.

"Did you bring your textbook?" I ask, choosing to ignore his last comment.

The only way I'll possibly get through this is if I switch to pretending that night *was* a wet dream and I'm the only one with any memory of it.

Remorse flashes across Aidan's face, answering for him.

He came unprepared. *Shocker*. Between his slouch and the casual way he taps the table—not to mention why we're here in the first place—it's obvious Aidan doesn't take academics seriously.

My molars grind with the realization I'm stuck with a lazy jock.

He hasn't apologized for being eight-and-a-half minutes late, and I'm undecided if that should be a strike against him as well. He might be handling it better, but he obviously wasn't expecting to see me here either. And I'm the one who lied during our last encounter, even if it seemed harmless at the time.

I pull my copy of the textbook out of my backpack and shove it toward him, along with the first assignment his professor sent me.

"We're going over summation notation and measures of variability tonight. We'll work through a couple of new topics each week, then you'll complete an assignment on it before our next meeting that I'll grade and get back to you. Got it?"

"Got it." He's scanning the paper instead of looking at me, which makes it easier to converse with him.

"Okay, let's start with standard deviation." I open my notebook and pick up my pen. "For the first—"

"I know how to do this," Aidan interrupts. He flips the page over to look at the back. "Know how to do all of these."

I exhale. "I'm trying to make this as easy as possible, okay? You don't need to pretend—"

Again, he interrupts me. "I'm not *pretending*. I know how to do all of these."

"Professor Carrigan picked the topics based on what you struggled with on the final."

He shrugs, nonchalant. "I was more interested in fast-forwarding to winter break than taking a final. Doesn't mean I'm dumb."

"I don't think you're dumb."

Irritating, arrogant, and distracting, maybe, but not dumb.

Aidan picks up the paper again. "Is Carrigan grading this, or you?"

"Uh, me."

Aidan looks up, focusing all his intensity squarely on me. He leans forward, the motion sending a whiff of spicy cologne my way. I resist the urge to inhale deeply, wishing he smelled like stale sweat or body odor instead. Wishing *something* about him was repellant, aside from his lackluster work ethic.

"Let's skip the lecture today, then. If I bring this back next week and I got better than an eighty, you trust me when I tell you it's a topic I already know. If I don't, you can walk me through the entire class for all I care. I'm saving us both time."

I should be relieved. Instead of an hour of his company, it's maybe been five minutes since he showed up.

But instead of pleased, I'm offended he's so obviously trying to get away from me as quickly as possible.

He barely let me get more than a few sentences out, but I don't think I'm that terrible of a tutor. I already looked over the syllabus and I'm confident I know the material well enough to help him pass.

I cross my arms. "Eighty-five or better, and you have a deal."

Aidan flashes me a heart-stopping grin. "Deal."

He leans back and stretches again, then winces like he just got kicked. Shoves the textbook back toward me. "Same time next week?"

"If by *same time* you mean ten minutes late, I'll be leaving after five next week."

"I'm sorry," he says seriously. "I didn't mean to waste your time."

Aidan apologizing strikes me as a rare event.

He's hot, rich, and charming. Any one of those dismisses responsibility.

The combination of all three? I'm guessing he gets away with whatever the hell he wants.

"See ya." He grabs the assignment paper and then strolls out of the library as quickly as he appeared. At least three people turn to watch him leave.

I stare after him too, releasing a shuddery exhale before sinking against the hard back of the chair.

I thought my first one-night stand was a total success.

Turns out it was a complete failure.

Even if Aidan had told me his last name when we first met, I wouldn't have put the pieces together. My dad mentions his players sometimes, but I'm rarely paying close attention. I don't have the roster memorized. I still would have climbed into that hot tub…with one of my father's players. With a guy I'm stuck spending an hour a week with.

What are the odds we met more than a thousand miles from here and end up in the exact same place again?

I shake my head, then start packing up my stuff. I won't be able to focus here, not with Aidan's presence still lingering in the air. The chair he sat in is half-crooked from his hasty exit, the delicious scent of his cologne surrounding me.

I probably won't be able to refocus *anywhere* until I sufficiently freak out about this, but I'd rather not focus from the comfort of my bed.

Chilly air nips at my cheeks as I step outside the library. I bury my hands in my pockets and tuck my chin as far inside my coat as it'll go, my steps hasty as I head for the path past the parking lot that's my quickest route home.

Since I'm trying not to think about it, that night in Colorado is all I can focus on.

It replays in my memory through the filter of the new details I've learned about the guy I was with that night—his last name is Phillips, he's "bored by numbers," and, most importantly, he plays hockey for my dad.

A hot flash of humiliation creeps across my skin, recalling some of the things I said to him. He'd been drinking that night, so hopefully his recollection isn't as vivid as mine is.

Unfortunately, I can recall our entire interaction perfectly. Everything I said. Everything I encouraged—begged—him to do.

At least my embarrassment will keep me warm on the cold walk home.

I'm so caught up in my own thoughts, it takes me too long to notice the tall figure standing near one of the light posts. My heart starts racing, first from fear and then from dread.

Aidan pulls the phone from his ear, then shoves it into his pocket.

His expression is harsh, brows pulled tight and his jaw clenched tight. Whatever he was listening to, it wasn't pleasant.

"I thought you'd left," is all I can think to say.

"Not yet."

I nod. "Okay. Well, night." I debate waving, for some absurd reason, but thankfully opt to keep my hands warm in my pockets. Then turn and continue on the path.

"You're walking?"

I'm too close to pretend I didn't hear him. I glance back. "Uh, yeah. It's not far."

Before I can escape, he says, "I'll drive you home."

I'm surprised by the offer, but don't let it show. "I'm good, thanks."

"Rylan."

All he says is my name, and it stills me into a frozen state. Hearing that voice that I've replayed in my mind like a favorite song say my first name…it twists my insides into knots.

"If something happened to you, Coach K would kill me."

Annoyance sparks as soon as he mentions my father.

"If you're worried about my dad's opinion of you, you probably shouldn't have fucked me in a hot tub," I snap.

Wait for the obvious rebuttal—he didn't know who I was when that happened.

Instead, he asks me, "Do you want to stand here and keep arguing about it, or do you want to get home in half the time?"

If the offer of a ride had come from anyone else, I'd be reacting very differently. It's cold and dark out, and I'm not *thrilled* about walking home. But I'm nervous, honestly, about being alone in a car with him.

Aidan has an effect on me I've only experienced with alcohol, effortlessly washing away my inhibitions. I'm not shy but I can be reserved, especially around people I don't know very well. I don't know Aidan, well or otherwise, but he made me act more thoughtlessly than anyone else has ever managed to.

"Fine," I say.

"Fine, what?"

"*Fine*, you can give me a ride home."

"Lucky me." He grins, then starts walking toward a black SUV.

It's an older model with a couple of dents in the back bumper. Knowing what his family's *second* home looks like, I'm shocked it's what he drives.

He unlocks the car, then climbs into the driver's seat.

62

I round the rear and open the passenger side, staring at the purple sweatshirt flung on the passenger seat.

A horrifying possibility occurs to me. "Do you have a girl-friend?" I blurt.

I assumed not, since he initiated things between us.

But it's possible he's one of those guys who thinks *if they don't ask, don't tell* is an acceptable policy. Finding out I not only have to interact with my one-night stand but that I also might have been the other woman that night would be a real low point to start the semester.

"No." Aidan's tone is short, his expression annoyed.

And I realize there are two ways to take that question. That I just heavily implied he's a cheater.

"Sorry," I mutter.

"Just because your ex was an asshole doesn't mean that I am."

I somehow forgot I'd mentioned Walker to him. At least I didn't say how long it had been since we'd broken up, so he has no clue those scars should be healed by now.

"That's probably Harlow's sweatshirt. This is Hart's ride. I'm just borrowing it." Aidan starts the car. "Check the registration in the glove box, if you don't believe me."

The vehicle we're in makes a whole lot more sense, all of a sudden.

"Why are you borrowing your friend's car?"

"My truck is in the shop."

"What's wrong with your truck?"

"If the mechanic knew that, I'd be driving it."

"Where did you take it?" I ask.

"Dave's Auto. Why?"

"Just curious. Take a left here," I instruct. "It's the brown house at the end of the block, on the right."

He flips on a blinker before taking the turn, which makes me smile for no reason. I assumed he was the type of driver to take stop signs as a suggestion.

"So…you're a math major," he says.

"Yep." My tone is short, because his is more amused than admiring. I doubt he'll come up with any nerd jokes that I haven't already heard before.

"Because…"

"Because I'm good at math."

"I'm good at hockey, and I'm not majoring in it."

I don't state the obvious—that hockey isn't a major Holt offers. "You're *good*, huh? Are you in the top five for scoring leaders?"

The question is a gamble, because I have no clue what his stats are. But my impression of Aidan from our first tutoring session is that he does the minimum and not much more. It sounds like flunked his final because he couldn't be bothered to put much effort into taking the exam. That's not the personality of an aggressive, hungry player who tops leaderboards.

Aidan's silence answers for him, and I wish I'd kept my mouth shut.

Antagonizing or insulting him isn't conducive to getting through this tutoring arrangement as painlessly as possible.

The uncomfortable quiet only lasts a few seconds, thankfully, before the car stops in front of my house.

I scramble to grab my backpack out from between my knees and climb out of the car. "Thanks for the ride."

If Aidan responds, it's not before I've shut the door and started up the walk toward my front door.

CHAPTER SEVEN

AIDAN

Three weeks earlier...

J ameson is lounging on the leather couch when we walk in the front door of the chalet. Immediately, the high of snow-boarding in the sunshine all day disappears.

Annoyance churns in my gut as I watch my brother alternate between sipping from the crystal tumbler he's holding and scrolling on his phone. He only glances up when I slam the door shut behind us.

Conor glances at me, uncertainty written across his face.

I told him my brother might be showing up. I neglected to mention we're more enemies than siblings. Mostly because I didn't think Jameson would actually follow through on his taunt of coming here after the family celebration I skipped.

When Jameson spots Conor, he grins and stands. "Hey! Nice to meet you, man. I'm Jameson."

"Conor. Nice to meet you too."

Hart shakes my brother's offered hand but doesn't give Jameson more than a polite smile.

I've lost track of how many people I've seen fall for my brother's slick charm. I doubted Hart would, but it's still a relief not to see it happen.

After greeting Conor, my brother turns to me. Opening his arms wide and forcing me to interact with him or else make a scene.

"Been way too long, little brother," he tells me, slapping my back as we embrace.

Not long enough.

I force a nod as I step back and unzip my ski jacket. There's a roaring fire in the giant stone fireplace that takes up most of one wall in the living room. I'm sure Jameson called ahead and had the caretaking company build it while we were on the slopes. When it comes to anything except sucking up to our parents or antagonizing me, he's lazy as shit.

"I was beginning to think I wouldn't see you until the wedding."

My entire body goes rigid. But since a reaction is exactly what he's looking for, I force myself to say, "I'll do my best to make that," in the most bored tone I can muster.

Jameson's smile is smug. "Yeah, I'm sure you will."

He knows, just like I do, there's no way my family will let me miss that wedding.

"Your wedding?" Conor asks Jameson.

"Yeah." Jameson chuckles. "We're young, but our parents are thrilled."

"Uh, congrats." Conor looks confused.

He doesn't come from the same world I do, where parental approval is paramount. Where appearances are everything and loyalty is fluid.

"How long are you staying?" I ask.

Jameson transfers his attention to me slowly, the haughtiness he usually aims my way replacing the pleasantness he manufactured for Conor. "Only tonight. I'm needed back in the office urgently for a big deal we're working on."

I suppress a snort. More like his signature is needed to sign off on a deal he played no major part in. He's a figurehead at the company, coasting on my father's coattails. At least Lincoln Phillips earned the accolades people heap on him. My dad might be a self-centered dick, but he's a hard-working one.

Conor clears his throat. "I should go shower. Good to meet you, Jameson."

"Same here. Aidan talks about you all the time. Nice to finally put a face to the name."

I clench my jaw. I've never mentioned Conor, or anything about my life in Somerville, to Jameson.

We stare at each other as Conor heads upstairs.

"Can't believe you actually came."

"Can't believe you skipped Christmas. Mom was crushed."

"I was busy."

"You've never been *busy* a day in your life, Aidan. You fuck around doing nothing. Contributing nothing. You're a Phillips, for God's sake. Grow up."

"Wow. You sound *just like Dad.*"

Jameson shakes his head. "That's not the insult you think it is."

"If I was trying to insult you, Jameson, I'd ask how many hours you've spent on the deal you're rushing back to close."

"Dozens."

I laugh. "Bullshit. You're Dad's lapdog, and he's tossing you a bone and letting you act important."

"You're living off the same money I am. At least I'm *working* for it."

"I'm in college," I respond. "I don't recall you waiting tables at Stanford."

"You only have one semester left. What's going to be your excuse after graduation? I know you're not taking any of Dad's calls. You'll be lucky to get a job at the company."

"I don't want a job at the company."

"What are your other options?"

To that, I have no good answer. If anyone except my older brother had accused me of doing nothing during my college years, I would have laughed and asked them *Can't I put partying on my resume?*

Truthfully, I have no fucking clue what I'll do after graduation. I'm majoring in business because it's what most student athletes choose, and I had to pick something, not because it's anything I'm passionate about.

Jameson gets a call, saving me from answering.

"Hey, Dad," he answers, flashing me a smug grin as his voice inflates with self-importance. "No, I don't have that in front of me, but I can pull it up. One second." His voice gets quieter as he heads deeper into the house. I'm sure he took the downstairs master for himself. "Yes, he's here. Just got back from *snowboarding*."

I roll my eyes, then head for the stairs.

Jameson's presence will be more tolerable after I've stripped off this gear, showered, and helped myself to a stiff drink. Maybe tonight will be the evening I finally talk Hart into having some fun. He's still sulking about Harlow.

Halfway to the stairs, the doorbell rings.

I stop and sigh. I'm not expecting anyone. Jameson probably ordered something, and of course he's off talking to my dad. I spin around and head for the door.

Instead of a delivery person, there's a gorgeous blonde

standing on the doorstep. Full face of makeup with the flaps of her fancy coat wide open, a low-cut sweater showing off her cleavage. She tilts her head to the left and smiles, a couple pieces of her styled hair falling into the exposed valley between her tits.

"Hello there, gorgeous," I drawl. "How can I help you?"

She blushes, twirling a curl around her finger. "I didn't know we'd have company. I'm Autumn. I'm looking for Jameson?"

Just like that, any interest in her dissipates.

He flew one of his side chicks into town. *Unbelievable.* I'm pissed, and the person I'm pissed for doesn't deserve my anger on her behalf.

"Come on in." I step aside so she can walk into the house.

She frowns, noticing the change in my tone, but forgets about it once she's inside. "Wow. This place is absolutely gorgeous."

"No luggage?" I ask.

"Oh. No." Autumn giggles, then pats the expensive purse she's carrying. I bet Jameson bought it for her. "I have the essentials in here. And well…" Her smile turns coy. "I didn't think I'd need many clothes."

The innuendo is impossible to miss.

"Gets cold as fuck here," I tell her.

Autumn's expression twists, like she's not sure if I'm purposefully misunderstanding or if I'm making fun of her. "Jameson didn't mention we'd have company."

"I'm his brother," I tell her.

"*Oh.*" I can see the admiration on her face as she looks me over. Subtle, she's not. A characteristic I usually appreciate, but it's currently annoying me to no end.

"*Little* brother." Jameson appears, his face brightening when he spots Autumn. "So glad you made it, baby."

He kisses her, using way too much tongue, but she seems into it.

"Younger," I say, when they separate. "I'm Jameson's *younger* brother. Nothing littler about me, which any girl who's been with us both knows."

Autumn's expression brims with obvious lust as she looks me over again.

Jameson's face is twisted with fury.

Sure, it's petty as fuck reminding him who slept with his fiancée first.

But he's the one who showed up here, knowing it's where I was spending part of break, and invited the woman he's cheating on my ex with.

"Maybe we could all…"

My dark mood lightens considerably, seeing Jameson's reaction when Autumn suggests a threesome. His face turns an alarming shade of red as she basically announces she's unsatisfied with their sex life.

"The women I fuck are too satisfied to screw someone else," I tell her. "Sorry."

Then I turn and head upstairs.

———

"I'm headed to bed," Conor says, tossing the rest of his cards on the table before shuffling them into one stack.

I groan. "Seriously?"

He's bailed early every night since we've been here. Even tonight, when I agreed to stay in. We grilled steaks and have been playing cards for the past hour.

"Yeah. I haven't been sleeping great." Hart aims an accusing look at me, like it's *my* fault I'm the only one getting laid on this trip.

"You still haven't texted her, huh?"

He stretches, then stands. Avoiding answering my question, just like he's done every time the topic of Harlow has come up. "Night, Phillips."

I sigh. "Night."

Conor disappears upstairs.

I spin my phone around on the table, debating what to do. Jameson and Autumn left a couple of hours ago, and since Conor was around and has that charisma that makes other guys want to seem cool around him, Jameson shared that they're spending the night at the condo downtown instead of just taking off without talking to me like he would've if we were here alone.

Now that Hart has gone to bed, I have the house to myself.

The girl from two nights ago left me her number. I could call her. Or I could watch a movie. Or go to a bar downtown, although that would risk running into Jameson.

I amble into the kitchen, refilling my glass with whiskey. The only upside of Jameson's visit is that I can blame him for any amount missing.

My father insists on buying this brand that costs an obscene amount per bottle. Tastes the same as any other kind I've ever had, but my father has always put a premium on appearances. The only reason I know this bottle's cost is because I looked it up once, back when I was still giving a shit about my father's opinion and buying him birthday gifts.

I walk over to the French doors that lead onto the back deck and step outside. The cold is like a slap to the face, so sharp and bitter it numbs me immediately.

My parents bought this place when I was in elementary school. Back then, I called it the treehouse. I can still see the similarities to one—the exposed wood and expansive decks and the way it's built into the side of the mountain, surrounded by treetops. It used to be my favorite of my parents' properties, until Parker ruined this place too.

I sip some whiskey, the cool liquid warming me as the wind chills me to the bone. It's a bright night, the exterior lights rendered almost entirely useless by the moon. It's a full one tonight, or nearly one.

Stone slabs lead to the hot tub. Steam rises from the surface of the clear water, drifting away toward the snow-capped peaks in the distance.

I stand and sip, watching the vapor drift away and disappear. My cheeks burn from the cold; my throat burns from the whiskey. And I hate how my eyes burn too, evidence of my weakness.

No matter what, I can't seem to escape it. No matter how far I go. No matter how much I drink. No matter how much time passes without seeing or speaking to my family. No matter how many girls I screw. No matter how many goals I score.

It's always just *there*, this feeling of inadequacy and bitterness and resentment and wariness.

Family are supposed to be the people you trust and rely upon.

All mine has ever done is scheme and lie and manipulate.

I'm used to it by now. Still sucks.

I'm half-frozen now, the whiskey all that's keeping me warm. Impulsively, I set the glass down on the side of the tub. Tug off the sweatshirt and joggers I put on after my shower.

Hiss, when the frigid air bites my bare skin. I can practically feel my dick shrinking.

Grit my teeth when I step into what feels like lava.

Yeah, this was one of my dumber decisions.

When Jameson and I were younger—friendlier—we used to lie in snowbanks, then jump in this hot tub. I remember those afternoons as being fun, not this agony I'm currently experiencing as my body adjusts from being surrounded by ten degrees to a hundred.

I take a seat on the stone bench, relaxing into the water. Spread my legs and tilt my head back to stare up at the star-strewn sky, my only movements to reach for the glass of whiskey a few times.

I'm luckier than a lot of people, I know. Staying in a twenty-million-dollar chalet, waiting for my trust fund to kick in. This pity party couldn't have better accommodations.

But money *can't* buy happiness, something the rest of my family seems unable to comprehend. Or maybe they're just too preoccupied putting on their individual acts to notice they're unhappy.

An owl hoots in the distance.

This place is too far away from downtown's commotion to have any soundtrack except nature.

A stick cracks. Followed by a low, heartfelt "Shit" that is not native to Colorado.

I sit up, squinting in the direction of the sound. There's a girl —or woman, I can't tell her age from here—right along the tree-line, less than twenty feet away. Looking down, dark hair curtaining most of her face.

"You good?" I call out.

She doesn't move for a few seconds. Finally, she raises her head. It looks like she squares her shoulders before turning to face me.

I suck in a surprised breath. She's young, but definitely not a child. If I had to guess, I'd say she's about my age.

And she's stunning, even bundled up in a down jacket and wearing one of those knit hats with a pom-pom on top that I usually think look silly. Her skin looks as smooth and pale as the snow I stared at all day, contrasted against the darker color of her coat.

"Yep. I'm good."

I wait, but that's all she says. "What are you doing?"

She waves the phone she's holding toward me. "I go to university in London. Haven't seen mountains in a while, and this place has a nice view."

Nice view is an understatement.

Properties on this side of the slope go for eight figures and stay in families for generations.

I'm entertained by her nonchalance, and unsurprised. Between that comment and the combination of her American accent and British education, it's obvious she's part of the elite group of snobs who love this particular zip code. Probably by choice, instead of my own reluctance.

But I'm not one to look for more than a pretty face.

Not anymore.

"View's better from in here," I tell her.

Her expression doesn't change at the invitation, and it's a thrill I haven't experienced in a long time.

Girls rarely challenge me. They usually throw themselves at me. Willing and eager to please, happy to have my attention for however long it lasts.

"I have a personal policy against climbing into hot tubs with strange men. Maybe next time."

I smirk, appreciating her snark even more than her disinterest. My dick reacts too, stiffening underwater. She's the exact distraction I'm craving right now.

"You're trespassing on private property. I hardly lured you here under false pretenses. Just trying to be a good host."

She glances away, and it annoys me.

I can't see her face. Or read her expression.

"This is your family's place?"

"Yeah. You live around here?"

She must have come on foot. The driveway curves right above here into the garage, so I would have heard a car arrive.

"My friend lives across the street."

I think. "The…Coopers?"

"Her last name is Riley. Her parents bought it a few months ago."

"Oh."

The last time I was here was Christmas, years ago. I'm surprised I even remember the Coopers. I met them once, if that, at a cocktail party my mom threw around the holidays. "Your friend isn't the felony-committing sort?"

I can't tell for sure in the limited light, but I think she rolls her eyes. "I just needed some fresh air. Didn't plan to walk this far."

"What's a few more steps?" I ask, grabbing my glass and taking a sip. I let the tumbler dangle between my fingers, watching her through the glass.

I can't decide if she's considering coming closer or about to walk away, and it's affecting me more than the alcohol. There's a bolt of adrenaline—of intrigue—wondering what she'll do next and not knowing the answer.

Part of it is the fact we're strangers and the uncertainty of night. But the rest is realizing how predictable my encounters on campus have become. How I ordinarily know how the night will end before it even begins. Even the girls I've hooked up with since arriving in Colorado have all followed the same pattern. Buy them a drink at the bar by the biggest slope, trot out a few one-liners, and then we've ended the evening in the king-sized bed upstairs. Satisfying, simple…and kind of boring. Close to a routine after only a few days.

Shock—and satisfaction—spreads through me when she takes a step in this direction rather than walking away.

"I don't have a bathing suit," she tells me.

I smirk. "You say that like it's a bad thing. I'm not wearing one."

Another step. Two. Three. Six.

Then she's standing next to my clothes. Since I'm expecting her to glance down, it's satisfying when she continues surprising me and doesn't.

Her gaze remains locked on mine as she takes a seat cross-legged on the deck. She's dressed for the frigid weather. In addition to her heavy coat and silly hat, she's wearing fur-lined snow boots.

"My ex cheated on me. I haven't been with another guy since."

I appreciate her bluntness as much as the indication she's as interested as I am. I also admire it. Most girls would weave some story about ending things first.

My one and only relationship ended with me being dumped. I know how much it sucks, how easily inadequacy sneaks in. Even if I wasn't so attracted to this girl, I'd want to help her regain confidence.

"I'm a great rebound," I tell her.

She scoffs, then looks toward the mountains I was studying before she appeared. "You were right. The view's better from here."

"I meant the view from *in* the tub, not next to it."

She glances at me. Not at my face, at my dick, which swells further under her scrutiny.

I know I'm bigger than average. Some girls enjoy the challenge, others are intimidated by it. It's an inconvenience, honestly, most of the time. Mainly because it's rarely a girl who's seen my cock before looking at my erection and so it's a topic of conversation every time. A reassurance that yes, it'll fit.

This stranger says nothing complimentary or concerned, which is new.

"Girls usually tell me their name, at least, before checking out my package," I say.

She snorts. "Package?"

"Full one, isn't it?" I wink. "Feel free to keep looking."

"You're the one with your dick out. It's a free country; I can look wherever I want."

"Did you learn that in England?"

She shakes her head, then tilts it back to look up at the starry sky.

I take the opportunity to study her profile up close. Don't bother to look away when she turns her head to the side and catches me staring.

"Alice," she says. "My name is Alice."

"Welcome to Wonderland, Alice." I lift my glass toward her in a mock cheers, then sip.

She snorts, then asks, "Do I have to show you my pussy to get your name?"

I start coughing, whiskey traveling up my nose so it feels like I've inhaled fire. My eyes water immediately.

Alice grins at my reaction, the first smile I've seen. It softens her perfectly symmetrical features, warms some of her icy aloofness.

I play hockey. I've heard—and participated in—plenty of chirping on the ice, and I have no problem talking dirty to a girl. But they don't talk dirty to *me*. They giggle and blush and moan in response to whatever shit spews out of my mouth. I've never met a girl who used *pussy* as part of her vocabulary, let alone in a first conversation.

I take another sip of whiskey, trying to soothe my irritated throat and regain some control over the situation.

Alice stands. For one disappointing second, I think she's leaving. Then her pink pom-pom hat falls to the deck, right on top of my joggers. Followed by her down coat. She's wearing a thick sweater beneath it, but that lands on the ground too. Followed by a thermal shirt similar to the one I wore snow-boarding earlier.

She's wearing a sports bra. Not lingerie or lace, but my cock doesn't care. I can see the curve of her boobs above the stretchy material. The smooth, toned skin of her stomach beneath and the sharp edges of her collarbone under the straps. If I squint, I can make out the raised bumps of her nipples.

Her boots go next, followed by wool socks.

Girl dressed for this walk like it was an Arctic expedition.

The leggings are the last to go before she steps into the hot tub. A pink flush spreads across her skin as she rushes to submerge in the hot water, her dark hair fanning around her as she settles on the bench opposite from me.

"This is nice."

I hum an agreement, studying her through the veil of rising steam as she looks around. At the house, at the woods. Every-where except me. I can't tell if it's a purposeful move or not. If I'm really the least interesting thing to look at or if she's feigning the nonchalance.

When our eyes meet again, there's a jolt. In my chest and in my groin. I'm uncomfortably hard now, my entire body humming with an awareness of her proximity.

Hot tub is a first for me. I didn't think to bring any of the girls I hooked up with earlier this week out here, and this is a luxury the house in Somerville is lacking. Bummer, because a soak would feel amazing after a couple of exhausting hours on the ice.

"How does this usually work for you?" Alice asks me. "You lure a girl in here, then what's your move?"

I raise a brow, then laugh. "It's a free country, remember? I didn't *lure* you anywhere. And…there's no move."

"No?" Her eyebrow arches, and it's sexy as hell.

"This is a first for me."

I can't recall the last time I said that to a girl. If I've *ever* said that to a girl, even on the rare times it's been true.

My dad succeeded in some ways, because I hate admitting weakness. Appearing vulnerable. Or maybe that's just a natural human impulse I've never bothered to fight.

Something about Alice—her unpredictability or her mysteriousness—makes me want to admit it. Encourages me to be different from the smooth player confident of every move. She's sure, and it has me scrambling to keep up.

Alice tilts her head, studying me back. Her fingers swish underwater, creating tiny currents on the surface.

"Does *no move* mean you don't want to fuck me?"

God, her fucking mouth.

Most girls would blush or whisper. Alice tosses *that* out, then continues to create ripples in the water like my answer won't affect her. Like she's already decided how tonight will go and I'd be lucky to have any say in the matter at all.

I grab my glass off the stone side and stand, amused, bemused, and insanely turned on.

Alice's head tilts back against the side of the tub as I push through the water toward her, a bob of her throat when our legs touch her only other reaction.

I take a final sip, then hold the tumbler out to her. There's only an inch or so left. About five hundred dollars' worth of alcohol, probably.

She takes it without hesitating, downing the remaining

whiskey in one gulp. I reach out and grip her left wrist, guiding her hand through the water and between my legs.

Red creeps up her neck when her fingers brush my erection, the first falter in her unaffected facade.

I lean closer, not touching her anywhere else but speaking right next to her ear. "You tell me. Do I want to fuck you?"

Her head turns. And then we're kissing, warm, eager mouths colliding in a kiss that's hotter than the water around us.

She's a lit match, and I'm soaked with alcohol.

Everything ignites, my awareness burning down to nothing except her. My hands land on her hips and then slide down to cup her ass, lifting her off the stone bench and lining up our bodies. Her legs wrap around me as our tongues continue to tangle, her pussy grinding against my cock.

Goddamn, can this girl kiss.

Another thing that's become rote. I kiss girls because it's expected, because it's a step you don't skip even though you both know it's only a precursor to the sex. Kissing is never the part of a hookup that I look forward to. I'm usually planning ahead, trying to decide on a position or unhooking the back of a bra.

Alice is making me forget there's more to come. She sucks on my bottom lip, nibbling gently, and I can't control the groan that spills out. Or the low "Fuck" when her fingernails dig into my back and her boobs rub against my chest, the wet fabric of her sports bra bunching between us.

She's destroying me effortlessly, and it makes me desperate to affect her just as much.

I hoist her up onto the edge of the hot tub. Alice flinches as her ass hits the chilly wood, the frosty air raising goosebumps on her skin. It escalates the challenge, raises the stakes. Not only do I want her to forget all about her asshole of an ex, I also have to contend with frigid temperatures.

"Lie back and spread your legs."

She listens, tugging her sweater under her as a makeshift barrier from the hard wood. Her thighs open, offering me a second look at her underwear.

They're pink cotton and full coverage, which shouldn't be sexier than the scraps of lace I usually see. But they are, because they're soaked and might as well be see-through. The wet fabric clings to the outline of her pussy, offering an obscene view that becomes even more explicit when I pull them down and add her drenched underwear to the pile of our clothes. She's almost completely bare below, only a thin strip of dark hair leading to the spot I'm dying to taste.

I kiss the inside of her knee, her legs opening wider the higher my mouth goes.

"Oh my God," she moans, twisting to her left to watch me.

I smile against her skin, finally reaching the curve of her hip. "You want me to kiss your pussy, Alice?"

Instead of answering, she lifts her hips closer to my mouth. It's a silent challenge, almost, to prove myself.

Without asking, I'm fairly certain it means her cheating ex couldn't make her come this way.

I'm not one of those guys who thinks eating a girl out is an inconvenience. This draws out the anticipation even more. And even when I'm not the one getting off, there's a thrill to holding all the power. To watching the girl beneath me react to my touch.

And I've never been more determined to see someone moan and turn incoherent. I don't just like doing this, I'm fucking good at it. Not cockiness—fact.

Alice cries out as soon as my tongue touches the bundle of nerves above her opening, scooting toward me as her hand slides into my hair so she can pull my face closer. The needy whimper breaks the charged silence around us, and makes me even more adamant about making her scream. I swirl my tongue, then suck again. Her legs open even wider, giving me as much access as possible. My lips move to the inside of her thighs, kissing the soft skin there.

I could draw this out longer. Continue admiring *this* view and tease her until she's begging for release. But it's freezing and as satisfying as seeing her casual attitude crumble is, it's only making me more uncomfortable. My dick is so hard it's painful. Regardless of what happens with her next, it's going to need some attention. So I suck her clit into my mouth again, not wasting any more time.

Maybe things ended with her ex a while ago, and she's just craving an orgasm from someone other than herself.

Maybe she's as caught up in this as I am—the silent woods and the steaming water and the feeling that we're the only two people who exist in the world right now.

I don't really care why, as long as she keeps riding my face and making these eager whimpers that send hot bursts of lust thundering through me.

I trail my tongue lower, finding her opening and circling it with my tongue. Alice is soaked, and it has nothing to do with the hot tub. I can taste her, something musky and unique that drives my own desire higher.

She's the furthest thing from unaffected.

She's begging now, loudly, even though I haven't stopped touching her. Rocking against me, her entire body taut and searching. Her firm grip in my hair is almost as painful as my straining cock, which is desperate to replace my tongue.

I lift a hand out of the water, the cold air instantly chilling the drops clinging to my skin. Push two fingers inside of her, working in and out of her tight heat as my tongue moves higher.

Alice comes with a shouted cry, her entire body going rigid

before she's spasming and shuddering with the force of her release.

Then slips back into the water with a shudder, a slight, satisfied upturn to her pouty lips.

A few seconds later, she yanks off her sports bra and tosses it onto the deck where she was just lying.

Her tits are perfect. Full and firm, the swells barely breaking through the surface of the water. I'm already regretting not pulling her bra off myself before going down on her. It's not like the wet spandex was doing much to keep her warm.

She tilts her head back, totally wetting her hair. "Fuck, that was good."

I know she came; I felt it. But the satisfied hum to the words is the best ego stroke I've gotten in a while.

"You're welcome."

She laughs, a light, genuine sound that fizzes through me like a sip of champagne. Warms me more than the lingering whiskey. "I showed you my pussy."

I run my tongue along my lower lip, savoring her taste. "I remember."

"So…what's your name?"

Now, I laugh. Without a doubt, this is the weirdest, most memorable introduction to anyone I've ever had. "Aidan."

"Aidan," she repeats.

"Yep. Alice and Aidan. We're adorable."

There's a shift on her face. A flash of some expression I can't read before it's quickly snuffed out.

She reaches out, fisting my throbbing dick.

I groan in relief, fresh frissons of arousal racing through me. Her grip is perfect, tight and sure as she works her way down my length. Brushes my balls, making my hips jerk.

"I have condoms…but they're all inside." I say the words cautiously, not sure how far she's interested in taking this.

I would be happy with a hand job. At this point, after tasting her and seeing her come, just having her here and naked, I could come from a few strokes.

Her hand releases my cock, which is not the response I was hoping for.

Alice reaches for her jacket, grabbing one sleeve and pulling it closer until she can reach the pocket.

A few seconds later, she tosses a foil packet toward me. I'm so surprised I almost miss catching it and let it sink into the steaming water.

I don't question why she's carrying a condom around in her winter coat. I just send up a silent prayer of gratitude that she was as I tear it open with my teeth, then grit them as I rise out of the water to roll it on.

"Come here and bend over."

She complies as quickly as she did last time, aware of the same thing I am—it's fucking freezing outside the water.

I line the head of my cock up with her entrance and push in slowly, grunting as I watch her stretch to accommodate me.

As soon as I've bottomed out, I let us both slip beneath the water again. Alice keeps her grip on the stone edge, moaning as I start to steadily thrust in and out of her.

My hands skate up her ribcage and reach around, finally getting to touch the soft mounds of her breasts as I drag my tongue along the line of her shoulder.

I think I'm having an out-of-body experience, pleasure suffusing everywhere. It feels like a privilege to touch her. A victory to be fucking her.

"Are you thinking about your ex?" I ask.

"No. Are you thinking about yours?"

Rather than deny what's either a lucky guess or an astute observation, I answer honestly. "She never would have had sex in a hot tub."

"She's missing out."

I chuckle, reluctantly letting go of one of Alice's breasts so I can massage her clit again. "So is he. You're so fucking *tight*..." I curse as she clenches around me, sending a jolt of electricity up my spine.

She's close.

I'm *praying* she's close, because I'm barely hanging on and I pride myself on following a *ladies first* policy.

I wish we were in a bed, where I could kiss and lick and explore every inch of her sinful body without worrying about one or both of us getting hypothermia. And I also can't imagine this tryst taking place anywhere else, the contrasts of the freezing air and the steaming water a different kind of aphrodisiac than anything I've ever experienced before.

I've fucked a lot of women.

Alice will be the only one I ever have sex with in a hot tub.

I'll never be able to do this again without thinking of her. The floral notes that must be from her shampoo or perfume. The way she meets every stroke, taking me as deep as she can. The breathy sounds she makes as her pussy tightens around my cock.

And then—*thank God*—she's coming.

I let go with a long groan, my dick twitching and expanding as I fill the condom.

The sweet, satisfied warmth of an orgasm spreads through me, my vision turning blurry for a few seconds as the euphoria remains. As I realize I'm *still* coming, and so is she.

By the time I pull out, I'm breathing heavily and blissed out. Sluggish and satisfied. Everything is moving slower, so it takes a few seconds for me to register that Alice is moving away. Climbing out.

She doesn't bother with her bra or underwear. Just tugs on her leggings, socks, and sweater, followed by her hat, which looks silly with her dripping hair.

"You don't have to leave," I say, standing so I can tug the condom off and tie the end. I toss it on the deck, then sink back beneath the hot water.

"Yeah, I do. This was fun. Thanks."

I huff an unamused laugh.

This was fun. Thanks?

I've never been that cold, even if the sex was bad. And I felt her come—both times. The sex was *not* bad.

But I've never asked a girl for more. Even with Parker, she was the one who pushed a relationship. Part of why it stung so badly when she ended it and acted like I was the one who tied her down.

If Alice wants to leave—which she clearly does, based on how quickly she's pulling on her coat—that's her call.

"Yep. *You're welcome.*"

She doesn't laugh this time, just starts lacing her boots.

I wish I had more whiskey out here. Instead, I alternate between looking at the mountains and sneaking peeks at her as she finishes getting dressed.

Maybe this is about her ex. Maybe she *was* thinking about him. Or maybe she's freaking out about moving on. I experienced that with the first girl I slept with after Parker. It felt wrong being with someone else for the first time in a long time.

Nothing an endless series of flings didn't fix.

She adjusts her hat, then glances at me.

Fully dressed, the only evidence of what just happened her wet hair and the used condom by her left boot.

"Bye, Aidan," she says, then turns and walks down the two steps. Heads toward the spot where I first saw her.

In a matter of seconds, she's gone, disappeared into the woods that surround the periphery of my parents' property.

I close my eyes, enjoying the lingering euphoria of the best orgasm I've ever experienced.

"Bye, Alice," I tell the night.

CHAPTER EIGHT

AIDAN

"Phillips!"

I exhale, then circle back. My jaw works a couple of times. I know I should've passed, but it's not like I missed.

"Yeah, Coach?"

"Pull a move like that on Saturday, and I might just swap you and Hart. Excellent work." Coach whistles. "Next."

I skate back toward the bench in a state of shock.

On any other Division III team, I'd be on the first line. Except my teammate and best friend happens to be a center who could have easily played for a Division I program and secured that spot freshman year. There have been times when Coach has shifted around the lines, usually because someone was sick or injured. I've played on the first line, had my name announced over the loudspeaker. But it was never because of *me*. Nothing got switched around because I was playing so well that change made logical sense. It was always other forces.

Conor is one of the best players in college hockey, period.

And I resigned myself to being his supporting act a long time ago, I guess.

I enjoy playing hockey, but I don't eat and breathe it the way Hart does. Hell, the main reason that I've put half the effort into the team that I have is *for* Conor, wanting to help him get his shot however I can.

I've never played for myself. To push myself. To see what I'm capable of.

So I underestimated selfishness.

I didn't realize how much caring how *I* performed would affect my playing.

"Holy shit, Phillips," is the first thing I hear once I'm seated on the bench.

"What?" I glance over at Conor, then squirt some Gatorade into my mouth.

Blue today, thankfully. Best flavor.

"That was the best goal I've seen you score." He pauses. "*Ever.*"

"Is that your way of telling me I normally play like shit?"

"No. It's my way of telling you to keep doing whatever you're doing."

I hide the grimace that wants to appear, taking another sip of sports drink instead.

Sure, I'll continue getting insulted by our coach's daughter. I've scored four goals during today's practice because *You're good, huh? Are you in the top five for scoring leaders?* has been on an endless, annoying loop in my head recently.

I'm not in the top five.

I'm a center. Scoring opportunities are easy to come by. But I've always deferred to my wingers, setting them up for the shot rather than taking it myself.

Because I don't want the individual responsibility.

Because I'd rather operate as one part of the whole, encouraging a winning outcome but not caring about directly contributing to it. I'm always hoping for a win, but never hungry for it. We win as a team, we lose as one too. Look up team player in a dictionary, and you'll find me.

But this morning? Every damn time I went to pass, I heard Rylan's voice taunting me in my head.

Pretty soon, the guys will be calling me a puck hog.

I shouldn't give a single shit what Rylan Keller thinks of my stats.

Plenty of girls have provided commentary about my hockey career, and I never paid any attention to most of what they were saying. And that was all positive, gushing about my mediocrity, praise which should matter more but actually affected me less.

I didn't think anyone would notice that I was playing better than usual, not just working harder, and instead it seems like everyone has.

For the rest of practice, I keep hearing comments about how well I'm performing.

Comments that are compliments, and that's exactly how I should be taking them. But I'm on edge for a whole bunch of reasons, so I mostly absorb them as reminders of the ways I've fucked up.

Williams tells me that was a great goal? *I failed a class last semester and might not graduate with our class.*

Yarrow heads for me first because I sent him a perfect assist? *I ruined my relationship with my parents because they supported my brother dating my ex.*

Coach nods approvingly after my shift? *I fucked your daughter in a hot tub, sir.*

It's a different sort of relief when practice ends. Instead of the shame of a poor performance, I'm eager to escape the congratulations.

I leave the locker room as quickly as possible, swearing under my breath when Conor calls my name. I pause to let him catch up as we exit the lobby.

"You don't have class until ten, right?" he asks me.

Yeah, I'm regretting posting all of our course schedules on the fridge right about now.

"Right. I was going to get some work done in the library," I tell him.

Conor nods approvingly, which manages to make me feel even shittier.

Because I was more like going to go sit and continue to freak out about how the tutor keeping me on the team and helping me graduate is the brunette I hooked up with over winter break. How she *also* happens to be our coach's daughter.

It's rare I remember details. Most of the girls I hook up with are part of an endless series of weekend nights. And they usually happen after a couple of drinks, in a closet or a dark bedroom.

Go to a party, get drunk, hook up has been my Friday and Saturday night motto for a long time.

Fun.

And predictable.

Rylan—or Alice, the name she lied to me about—was unexpected in every way.

I remember everything about that night. What she said. What she looked like naked. The sounds she made.

How hard I came.

My tutor was supposed to be a mousy freshman I wasn't the least bit attracted to.

I don't know how I'm supposed to focus around Rylan. Not only do I know a lot about her I shouldn't, she's gorgeous.

"Phillips?"

I glance at Conor. "What?"

"You good?" He's frowning at me.

"Yeah. Just tired. I didn't sleep well." I yawn for effect.

More like I tossed and turned all night, alternating between incredulity at the terrible luck of having hooked up with my tutor a few weeks ago and irritation about her dig about my stats. Who the hell knows what Coach told her about me when he set this tutoring arrangement up. I'm an average player with a tendency to cause trouble. There's not much else to say. And Coach obviously isn't trying to get in my pants, so he has no reason to embellish my mediocrity the way the girls on this campus do. I'm sure he gave Rylan a cut and dry assessment of me.

Again, I shouldn't care.

And again, I *do*.

I didn't tell Hart anything about the girl I hooked up with in the hot tub in Colorado. He was in such a shit mood that trip I figured rubbing in my incredible sex life was unnecessary. And now, I'm relieved I never said anything. Makes me feel a tiny bit less guilty for accidentally fucking our coach's daughter.

Rylan didn't tell me anything that night to suggest our paths could cross again. No mention of Holt or Somerville or even hockey. As far as I can tell, it's pure fucking coincidence that we met in Vail and both ended up here three weeks later.

Getting boarded from behind was less of a surprise than walking into Holt's library, a building I've been in maybe twice before, and seeing Ali—I mean, Rylan sitting there.

I don't know what the hell I'm supposed to do if I run into her around campus. Ignore her? Say hi to her? This is new to me, and the two guys I would go to for advice about dealing with a hookup are going to ream me out for doing the one thing I said I wouldn't do. I doubt either Hunter or Conor will care I had sex with Coach's daughter *before* knowing she was Coach's daughter, not after. Same result.

Conor ends up coming to the library with me, so I put a

half-hearted effort into actually getting some work done. Hart is an A student but his studiousness has never rubbed off on me. We've never studied in the library together before, and watching him smother his irritation as a series of girls come over to hit on him slash wish him luck in our next game is a welcome distraction from thinking about Rylan.

Of course, it's hard to forget about her when I'm working on the assignment she gave me. I wasn't lying—I remember how to do everything that's part of this assignment. I check it over twice, just to make sure, but I'm confident enough is correct to tilt our deal in my favor.

I've considered going to Professor Carrigan and asking if I can retake the test this week, instead of waiting until the end of the season. If I actually study for a couple of days, I'm fairly confident I can pass it without going through the weeks of tutoring with Rylan. It solves the problem of interacting with her and also will mean I won't have the retake hanging over my head for weeks.

But if I *don't* pass? Then I'm fucked for graduation, and I'll be kicked off the team.

It's a gamble, which I normally have no issue taking.

These stakes are high, though.

And as uncomfortable as working with Rylan will be, I'm not accustomed to letting a girl affect my life. I do whatever I feel like, and they accommodate me. There's a prickle of annoyance, realizing I'm letting her dictate my decisions, just like she did the night we hooked up. Stubbornly, I don't want to be the one who admits defeat and avoids her.

I've eaten up all the time I had until my first class working on this *one* assignment, meaning I still have a pile of other work to finish later. Short of ten-page final papers or group projects, I don't think I've ever put this much effort into any homework before.

So you failed, huh?

It's practice all over again. I memorized every judgmental insult she tossed my way, I guess.

I say goodbye to Conor—his earliest class is at eleven, lucky bastard—and then head in the direction of the building that houses the Business department. I leave my headphones on, using them as an excuse not to talk to anyone as I walk across campus.

My mood is a shit one—again. Lately, it feels like that's been an endless stretch. And it's not just my family, as much as I love to blame them for everything. It's realizing some of their criticisms are valid. I have absolutely no clue what I'll do after graduation in May, and even if though that's still months away, I know it'll be here before I know it. And that's assuming I *do* graduate, which is no longer any guarantee. The girl who's supposed to be my guarantee happens to hate—or at least strongly dislike—me. Rylan sprinted from Hart's SUV like it was on fire after I drove her home the other night.

I just need to refocus. Keep my head down and get my work done this week. I'm sure the sophomores will throw a party on Friday night. I'll have a couple of drinks, hook up with a girl who *isn't* Rylan Keller, and be in fantastic shape for Saturday's game.

Hell, if I play anywhere close to how I performed during practice today, there's a good chance I'll break my no-scoring streak.

I'm one of the last to enter my Leadership in Organizations class, which is no surprise. If it's not hockey-related, I tend to run a few minutes late.

Honestly, I would probably run a few minutes late to hockey if I didn't live with Hart, who thinks his role of captain requires military-like precision when it comes to time-keeping.

I settle into a seat in the back row, flashing a grin at a girl in the row in front when she looks back at me and smiles.

She blushes before quickly looking away, and I'm weirdly irritated by the coyness on her face when she glances back a minute later. The cat and mouse game.

I bet Rylan would hold eye contact.

The thought is random and unwelcome.

So what if her boldness was an anomaly? That I was as attracted to her forwardness as her body?

She's. Off. Limits.

And…it's not like her reaction to finding out we attend the same college was happiness. Or any suggestion we should hook up again, this time on dry land.

Fucking figures, the one girl I'm interested in fucking again is, at best, indifferent to the idea. *Un*interested would probably be more accurate. Pretty sure Rylan Keller thinks I'm an unmotivated, brainless jock. And she's not entirely *wrong*, which bothers me even more than her judgment. If you look at my hockey stats and my grades, I don't have anything impressive to show for my college years. I highly doubt any potential employer is going to ask how long I can do a keg stand for or my best pick-up line, and those are the only skills I've put any significant effort into improving.

Class begins with a couple of questions from students about the syllabus.

Our homework from the first class was to review it. There's a red stain on the third page of mine, proof I shouldn't have skimmed it while eating spaghetti last night.

I partially zone out as the professor doubles down on her *no technology* policy, citing several papers that conclude laptops are a distraction and welcoming anyone who disagrees to write an essay with at least ten academic sources. That shuts up complaints fast. The food policy gets challenged next, which is when I start doodling hockey pucks in the margin of my notebook. Literally all I've written for this course so far.

By the time the professor gets through the syllabus questions, there are only forty minutes left in class. I send out a silent *thank you* to the kid who spent ten minutes clarifying her office hours. That was the one topic the professor totally indulged.

Today's topic is inclusive leadership, and how to include *I* in *we*. Seems ironic, considering my selfishness during practice earlier. I take careful notes on the lecture, grab the reading packet for next week's class when it gets passed around, and am overall a model student for maybe the first time in my life. I don't even look when the girl sitting next to me leans down to grab her water bottle out of her backpack over and over again, her shirt gaping forward every damn time.

The professor ends class at exactly eleven twenty, which makes me like her even more. Nothing worse than professors pretending not to pay attention to the time on the clock so they can squeeze in some extra material to add to the final.

The girl in front of me glances back a couple more times as everyone rushes to pack up.

Usually, I'd hang around, waiting to see if she approached me. Come up with a few compliments, maybe invite her to the party on Friday night.

Instead, I'm one of the first people out the door.

CHAPTER NINE

RYLAN

There are two impatient knocks on my door. A pause, then a third.

I toss my pen down and stretch, my cramped muscles crying out in relief. I've been sitting in the same crouched position for longer than I realized.

"Come in," I call out.

"Hey!" Chloe waltzes in like she's visited my room a thousand times before instead of just twice, taking a seat on the edge of my bed and bouncing on the mattress.

In the week I've known her, I've learned that's just Chloe.

I'm not sure she's encountered a situation she's uncomfortable in. Everything gets taken in stride, and it's an attitude I'm striving toward as well.

Hot guy I hooked up with over winter break happens to be the same hockey player I'm stuck tutoring?

No biggie, it happens.

Chloe glances at the notebook open on my desk and makes a face. "You're doing homework?"

I'm assuming the judgment is because it's Friday night. My roommates all seem to care about school, which is a nice change. I've lived with multiple people who have made a point to mention how much time I spent bent over a textbook. To ask what exactly I'll do with a math degree. To wonder if I know how to have fun. In five years, I know who will be laughing. But it still stung every time.

"I was just planning out what I need to get done this weekend," I tell her.

And as pathetic as it sounds, I don't have anything better to do with my time.

I got back from dinner with a couple of girls in my Number Theory class an hour ago.

Showered, changed into sweatpants, and now I'm making a list of assignments due in the next few days so I can prioritize what to tackle first.

This first week went better than I was expecting.

I've yet to feel like I'm drowning in a pool of unfamiliarity, the way I did starting school in Boston and at Oxford.

I like all of my courses and my professors. But school has never been a challenge for me.

Holt isn't huge, the classes much smaller than I'm used to, which has helped getting adjusted and recognizing faces.

But socially, that makes it harder to adjust, not easier. Everyone else on campus already seems to know each other, has formed established cliques. Even the freshmen had a full semester on campus to get settled already.

Theo sat next to me during our Wednesday and Friday algebra class. I've exchanged small talk with at least a couple of people in all my classes this week. I was pleasantly surprised by the dinner invitation after my last class ended earlier. Not everyone feels like strangers the way they were on my first day.

But I'm still the new girl.

Chloe is busy studying the bulletin board above my dresser, which is covered with Polaroids from last fall.

My study abroad program offered a few weekend trips throughout the semester, and my favorites by far are the photos of Scotland. Green fields decorated by dots of white wool. Castle-topped crags. Cobblestone streets.

"You should take a photography class," she tells me. "These are really good."

"Scotland is just pretty enough to make an amateur look talented," I reply, shifting in my chair and tucking a foot beneath me.

Chloe hums, still peering at the photos. "If you say so."

"So, uh, you doing anything fun tonight?" I ask.

I'm not great at small talk. Either I can't think of anything to say or I blurt out something stupid.

Chloe spins around. "That's why I'm here. Get dressed, we're going out!"

I open my mouth.

"Unless you're about to say 'Okay,' save it," Chloe says, holding up a hand like she'll physically prevent the word from coming out. "My older sister transferred after her freshman year, and she had a hard time adjusting to a new campus. You have all weekend to do homework, if you want. Tonight, we're going to a party."

I smile, then open my mouth again.

Chloe raises one eyebrow.

"Okay," I say.

She beams. "Dakota is busy with her boyfriend, but Malia's coming with us. Come into the kitchen whenever you're ready so we can pregame."

"Okay," I repeat.

Once Chloe is gone, I stand, stretch, and start flipping through my closet.

I'm assuming going-out attire here is more similar to Boston than it was in London. I settle on all black—jeans, a silky tank top, and a suede jacket. At least if someone spills beer on me, it won't be visible. Unfortunately, I'm speaking from experience.

I apply some makeup, brush my hair, and then head into the kitchen after taking a couple of deep breaths that don't do much to soothe my anxiety.

Chloe is standing at the counter, mixing a cup's contents with a spoon. Malia is sitting on one of the stools, flipping through songs on her phone.

Both are dressed in jeans and cute tops, so I'm relieved I got the dress code right.

Chloe holds the glass she was stirring out to me as soon as she sees me. "Here, try this and tell me what you think."

I take a cautious sip. "It's good. What is it?"

"Whiskey, lemon juice, and maple syrup. I was going to make mojitos, but we're out of limes."

"And rum?"

"What?"

"Mojitos have rum in them, right?"

Chloe's response is "Do they?"

I glance at Malia, and she shrugs. "I've sampled enough of Chloe's concoctions. I'm sticking to wine."

Concoctions sounds slightly ominous, but I take another sip anyway.

I'm nervous enough about showing up to a party of strangers with two girls I barely know. Doing so totally sober sounds worse.

"Crap, we should go," Chloe says. "Logan just texted me. It's already packed."

"Okay, okay." Malia chugs the rest of her wine in an impressive amount of time, while I down the rest of the glass Chloe gave me.

Maybe it's the whiskey in it I like so much.

The only other time I've had it was…yeah, not thinking about that.

"C'mon," Chloe calls, already heading for the front door. "The faster we walk, the sooner we'll get there. Everyone have keys? Phones?"

"We're walking?" I ask, surprised.

"Yeah, the hockey house is just a couple of blocks away. It'll be faster than ordering a car and no one has to drive home."

My steps slow until I'm barely moving, nothing but those three words registering.

The hockey *house.*

It occurred to me while getting ready that there was a chance whatever party we were headed to could be attended by hockey players. Could be attended by Aidan. Like I already noticed, the campus isn't that big. Aside from the four players I saw in the coffee shop, I'm pretty sure I spotted a Holt Hockey jacket in my Intro to Philosophy class. Avoiding the entire team until I graduate next May isn't realistic, unless I decide to become the antisocial shut-in I turned into in Boston and swore I wouldn't become again.

I'm determined to go out and have fun, no matter how nerve-racking it is. The only way to know more people is to meet more people.

But I didn't think the party we're going to would be taking place at a *hockey house*, where Aidan will very likely be.

I'm dreading Tuesday, our next tutoring session, but I thought I had a few days before facing him again.

And now, I can't think of a single excuse why I can't continue out the door. Except maybe to have another drink for some liquid courage.

"Rylan! Come on!" Malia calls.

My steps speed up again, this time determined.

Aidan Phillips doesn't own this damn school.

Technically, this is home turf for me. He can't accuse me of trespassing this time. If I want to go to a party with my new roommates, I will. I'll get to know Malia and Chloe better, and maybe I'll even meet a guy who will make me forget that night. I'm clearly incapable of shoving it out of my mind myself. It's been three days since I found out his real identity, and I've thought about it triple that. At least.

The light-hearted teasing as we walk down the street is *almost* enough to make me forget about my apprehension. I missed this, the easy banter of inclusion. Ironic—and sad—that I feel less excluded around Malia and Chloe, who've been best friends since meeting freshman year, than I did around Walker's friends or the haughty crowd that made up most of my fellow abroad students.

The tension has totally left my body by the time we reach the end of the block, or maybe that's just Chloe's cocktail taking effect.

Either way, I'm mostly excited as we approach a house with a white clapboard exterior. The walk took less than five minutes.

Whoever Logan is, he or she was right; the house *is* packed.

Once we shove our way through the front door, we take an immediate right. The living room is crowded, clustered groups standing around laughing and talking. The air is thick and warm, flavored by the scent of sweat and vape smoke.

Malia spots some friends and peels off to say hello. Chloe continues into the kitchen, and I stick with her.

Even more people are crammed into here, close to the alcohol, a sea of unfamiliar faces. I can barely see the counters or the cabinets, just a mass of people.

"Want a drink?" Chloe asks once we've pushed through to the center island covered with an assortment of bottles.

More like shouts, really. The music is even louder in here than it was in the living room.

I nod.

At the very least, holding a red cup will make me feel like less of an outsider. I finger the suede of my sleeve, wishing I'd left behind a jacket like Chloe and Malia opted to. Now that we're inside, I can feel the prickle of sweat under my arms and in the small of my back.

Chloe hands me a drink, then starts mixing her own.

I shout "Thank you," then take a tentative sip. It's good. Just vodka and ginger ale, I think. The bubbles almost erase the burn of alcohol.

I relax more, propping a hip against the counter. Slip off my jacket and toss it over one arm, then take a longer pull of my drink.

"Phillips!" someone calls out.

I choke, ginger and condensation burning my throat and making my eyes water.

Fuck.

I cough, then take another sip.

My posture tenses as my heart rate picks up.

My focus remains on Chloe, watching as she adds ice to her cup, resisting the strong urge to glance around the kitchen and look for him.

I have no clue how Aidan might react to seeing me here. Ignore me? Avoid me? Ask me to leave? Point me out to the entire team as the coach's daughter?

I regret the way our last conversation ended, even if I was

right. I checked the team stats, and Aidan is in the solid middle for goals scored this season. But I didn't need to bring that up. I should've kept my mouth shut and stuck with my plan of pretending he doesn't exist unless I'm actively tutoring him. The satisfaction of calling him out wasn't worth the inevitable awkwardness during our next tutoring session or, even worse, tonight.

As his tutor, I can claim to have a vested interest in his grades. How he performs on the ice is my dad's problem.

"Cheers!" Chloe taps our cups together before we both sip.

"Let's go back to the living room," I suggest to Chloe, leaning closer to her so that she can hear me over the loud music.

I'm already getting a headache from the heavy beat and the smoke that the booze won't help.

I steal a look at Aidan as we leave the kitchen. He's easy to spot—talking with a tall guy I'd wager is another hockey player, grinning broadly as he waves his arms around animatedly to emphasize whatever he's saying.

The motion stretches the T-shirt he's wearing tight across his muscular chest, and I'm not the only one noticing the impressive definition beneath.

Everywhere I look, girls are checking Aidan out.

Including Chloe.

"That's Aidan Phillips," she whispers to me as we walk into the living room. "He's the campus playboy. Goes through girls like tissues, but you'll still have to wait in line for a turn. Although…" She smirks. "I've heard it's worth waiting in."

It is, I think, then quickly take another sip to wash away the thought.

I figured Aidan was popular. I didn't realize that meant he'd screwed most of campus.

Skills like his come from a lot of experience, I guess. I'm surprised he even remembered our hookup. Sounds like he's probably been with a dozen girls since.

Do you have to pick between incredible sex with a womanizing player or mediocre sex with a guy you're dating? God, I hope not, but it turns out those are the only kinds I've experienced, so maybe.

And I resent Aidan for shattering the illusion of what I thought sex was supposed to be like, only to turn out to be a notorious ladies' man who is apparently renowned for his bedroom talents. I would have much, much preferred he remained an anonymous memory.

I'm also realizing Chloe does not fall in the category of not knowing Holt has a hockey team and that I should probably tell her my dad coaches the team before it seems like knowledge I was withholding.

We run into a group of girls in the living room that she knows from her nursing major before I can bring it up, and we pause to say hello.

One of them is Logan. I try to focus on remembering the rest of their names, knowing I'll probably only retain a couple of them. It's not as noisy in here as it was in the kitchen, but it's still awfully loud. And I can feel the distinctive warmth of alcohol spreading through me, scattering my focus.

I lose interest in the conversation once all the introductions are complete, since they're discussing people I don't know.

I sip my drink and pretend to be interested in the fireplace.

A few minutes later, there's a fresh wave of activity in the front of the living room.

"That's Conor Hart," Chloe tells me, leaning closer to whisper. "The captain of the hockey team."

I watch an extremely good-looking, dark-haired guy push his way through the crowded living room, headed toward the kitchen. He's holding hands with a stunning redhead, who leans in and says something that makes Conor laugh. It's not until they reach the opening that leads to the kitchen that I realize Aidan has appeared there.

I'm not worried about him catching me staring this time—everyone is looking in that direction. From the way all the attention is focused their way, I'm clearly looking at the popular crowd.

Aidan does one of those guy handshakes with Conor, then hugs the redhead. Conor pulls her back into his body and leans down to kiss her possessively, resulting in a few disappointed sighs around me.

"Dammit," one girl says.

"I told you," another girl replies. "He took her to the banquet."

I guess Aidan wasn't lying about the purple sweatshirt belonging to Conor's girlfriend.

Based on what Chloe just told me, Aidan goes through girls too quickly to end up with any of their belongings in his car.

It makes me feel a lot less guilty for taking off right after our hookup.

Her friends head into the dining room to play a drinking game, but Chloe sticks with me. It turns out I might have hit the roommate lottery, living with her.

Which means I really need to tell her about my dad's job. Thankfully, no one in any of my classes has mentioned the hockey team. But Chloe is clearly interested in the sport—one might say slightly obsessed, considering she's pointed out two players in the short time we've been here.

The team's first home game since I started here is tomorrow.

I'm guessing Chloe will be going, and the longer I avoid telling her about my dad, the weirder it'll be.

"Should we grab refills?" Chloe suggests. "Then go find Malia?"

I glance around before answering, hating that I'm letting Aidan dictate my movements, but also anxious to avoid him.

He's still standing in the opening. Conor and his girlfriend are gone, but Aidan isn't alone. There's a beautiful blonde standing *very* close, her boobs brushing his bicep as she stands on her tiptoes to whisper something to him.

"Um…" I stall on answering Chloe.

Aidan is half-blocking the entrance to the kitchen. There's no way to pass him and remain incognito. And while he's hopefully too focused on the blonde's cleavage to notice anyone walking by, I'd rather not gamble.

"How about we go check out the scene in the dining room instead?" I suggest. "You can have the rest of my drink, if you want."

"No, it's fine. I should slow down, anyway. I didn't drink that much over break. Let's go."

Chloe links our elbows, then starts to pull me toward the dining room.

And I make the mistake of looking at Aidan again, right as he glances this way.

Our eyes lock, and it feels like all the oxygen in the room has suddenly been sucked away. Breathing becomes impossible, my lungs stalling with surprise and uncertainty.

He's about a dozen feet away, and there's at least that many people separating us. But somehow, he captures my full attention as totally as he did that night when it was just the two of us.

I'm expecting his gaze to drop, his attention to return to the beautiful girl by his side.

Instead, he says something to her without looking away from me and then heads in this direction. I focus on Chloe, silently praying he's spotted someone else behind me.

No such luck.

A few seconds later he's here, smoothly cutting us off. Chloe lets out a shocked "*Oh*" before coming to an abrupt stop and forcing me to pause too.

The first time I've seen her speechless, and it's occurring at the worst possible time.

"Hi." Aidan winks at me, which does alarming things to my stomach. Then glances at Chloe. "Hey, I'm Aidan. Nice to meet you."

"Hi. I'm Chloe." Chloe's voice has turned shy and soft, eons away from her usual bubbliness.

And I have a sudden, unpleasant vision of Aidan leaving my house tomorrow morning, fresh from fucking my roommate. Maybe he came over here to flirt with Chloe, and I was just his in to talking with her.

"Having fun?" He's looking at me now. "*Rylan*."

I *hate* how he says my name. Hate how it affects me, specifically. How it seems like I can feel the syllables brushing against my skin. How he's saying so much more than one word.

Chloe glances at me, and I know she's wondering how I know him. Wondering why I didn't mention knowing him earlier.

There's nothing worse he could have said, since having fun is something I'm historically terrible at. For some reason, it feels like he knows that. Can tell that. Depressing, considering he's the person I've let loose most with. Most wasn't enough, I guess.

"I'm helping Aidan out with a math class this semester," I tell Chloe, avoiding his gaze and ignoring his question.

I don't mention it's one he previously failed, since that seems like his own business. I might be confused and irritated about him coming over here, but I'm not that petty.

"Are you a math major?" Chloe asks Aidan.

I cover up the laugh that wants to appear with a snort.

Aidan doesn't look fooled. The question is especially ironic after our last conversation.

"Nah. Business."

"Oh, that's cool. I'm studying nursing."

Aidan nods. "Nice." He glances at me. "See you."

Then he's gone, disappearing into the crowd as quickly as he came over.

Chloe looks to me. "What was that about?"

I shrug, then shake my head. "I barely know him."

That's true, at least.

We make it into the dining room, which I doubt is ever used for eating. Watch several rounds of Flip Cup, followed by a few games of beer pong. Chat with some more people whose names I immediately forget. Drain my cup.

It's almost midnight by the time I tell Chloe I'm headed out. I'm exhausted from forcing smiles and pretending to enjoy myself. Everyone else appears to be having a blast, and everyone else seems to know each other.

I've given up on mentioning London, just saying I transferred from BU if anyone asks. None of the guys who approached me incited a fraction of the effect Aidan's wink had. I hate that that was my metric tonight...but it was. Most were wasted and their main contribution to the conversation was staring at my boobs. I'm not that desperate to replace Aidan Phillips as the last guy I had sex with. Not yet, at least.

Chloe offers to walk home with me, then insists I text her when I'm home after I tell her to stay and have fun.

Definitely hit the roommate lottery. I could have gotten

abducted in Boston, and my parents probably would have been the ones to report me missing.

There are even more people here now than when we first arrived. I have to forcefully push my way through the loud crowd, releasing a relieved sigh when I step out onto the front porch into blissful silence and empty space. The colder air feels nice too.

"Leaving already?"

I spin to the left, my hand flying up to clutch my racing heart. "What the *fuck*, Aidan?"

"What? I'm not allowed to talk to you? That'll make tutoring more challenging." He's alone out here, slouched against the railing that wraps around the porch with his ankles crossed. His eyes roam my body, making my skin prickle with awareness. It's an adrenaline rush, having his full attention on me. A thrill I fight to hide. "I guess we could just make out the whole time."

He's drunk. Maybe. Probably. I don't know him well enough to tell for sure. But he's holding a red cup identical to the empty one I abandoned inside, so I doubt he's sober.

I blow out a long breath as I slide my arms into the sleeves of my jacket, attempting to look unaffected by the prospect of kissing him again. Since I've had two drinks, it's harder than it should be. I watch the tiny cloud of air disappear into nothingness as I zip up my jacket.

"You're not allowed to *sneak up on me*," I tell him. "Scary shit happens to people who aren't six foot hockey players."

"I'm six foot three. And I'm just standing on a porch, Alice."

"*Don't* call me that," I snap.

He smirks before taking a sip from his cup. "What's up with Rylan, anyway?"

"Why's that my name, you mean? Probably a better question for my dad. I wasn't consulted about the choice."

Aidan nods. "Yeah, I'll make sure to ask him before our game tomorrow."

I scoff, then answer his question for some stupid reason. "I was supposed to be a boy named Ryan, after my grandfather. He passed away a couple of years before I was born. Turned out I wasn't a boy, so my parents got creative. It's old English, technically. Means 'land where Rye is grown.'"

"You learn that in London?"

"Yes, actually."

He smiles, looking pleased he guessed right. "Do Brits also bail before midnight?"

"I wouldn't know. Didn't party much there."

"Is that why you left?"

I shake my head, shoving my hands into my pockets. "The program was only a semester. Just delayed the inevitable."

"This was the inevitable?" Aidan asks. His expression has shifted to appear somber and probing, totally different from the playful smirk he was wearing earlier.

I have no clue why he cares. Why he's bothering to make conversation or why he's standing out here alone instead of irritating someone else with his company.

I'm also unsure why I'm still standing here, talking, when I should be halfway home by now.

"Aidan! Aidan!"

I glance at the front walk.

Two laughing girls are stumbling up it, both of them fixated on Aidan.

One is wearing a long fur coat and a pair of heeled boots, the other has a dress on that's partially covered by a leather jacket. Their outfits scream glamorous and mature.

I push my hands deeper into my pockets, second-guessing my

own clothes that now seem plain in comparison. Like casual funeral attire, bleak and boring.

Aidan turns his head toward the girls as they climb the front steps, one corner of his mouth turning up as the girl in the fur coat saunters straight toward him. Her arms loop around his neck, then she smacks a loud kiss on his cheek.

"I missed you over break," she tells him, smiling widely before she steps back and glances at me. "Hi!"

"Hi," I reply, trying to sound as normal as possible.

Not at all insecure or taken aback. She seems nice, and that makes me feel worse for immediately disliking her simply for coming over here. I should be relieved she's occupying Aidan's attention. That the green spotlight of his stare has shifted.

"You coming inside soon?" Fur Coat asks Aidan, trailing her manicured fingers down the center of his chest. "I was hoping we could...hang out."

It's obvious she's suggesting more than talking. I wonder what happened to the blonde he was with earlier. She'd better claim her spot in line fast, before the new arrival cuts in.

"I'll be in soon," Aidan says, not moving from his spot on the railing.

She pouts, but nods. "*Soon*," she emphasizes.

Fur Coat and her friend hurry inside, no doubt freezing in their trendy outfits. I'm not that warm, either, eager to get home and go to sleep.

I take a step toward the stairs, able to leave now that they're no longer blocked.

"I finished the assignment," Aidan tells me. "Got at least a ninety."

"We'll see." It's highly unprofessional of me, considering my job is to help him do well, but I'm hoping he loses our bet.

He smirks like he knows exactly what I'm thinking. "I live across the street, you know."

I raise an eyebrow. "Why would I know that?"

Aidan runs a hand through his short hair. I try and fail not to notice the way his bicep bulges with the motion. "Yeah…I forgot. It's just kinda common knowledge on campus."

"Well, thanks for sharing. I was *dying* to know your address. Next time I leave town, I'll send you a postcard."

He rolls his eyes. "We could go over there and hang out."

I blink at him, totally stunned and more than a little flattered. I'd be lying if I said walking in on Walker with someone else didn't affect my confidence when it comes to sex. Aidan's obvious interest that night—the way he acted like it was as incredible for him as it was for me—is the only thing that's helped heal that wound.

The guy obviously has no shortage of female attention, and he's propositioning *me*.

Again.

"You're seriously asking me if I want to hook up with you?"

Aidan takes another drink from his cup, then lets it dangle carelessly from his fingertips.

There's no confusion or uncertainty on his face, just confidence. He doesn't look wasted, but that seems like the only logical explanation for the turn this conversation has taken.

I thought we'd get through the remaining tutoring sessions with the minimum amount of interaction possible. Not have a conversation at a party that ended up *here*.

"Went well last time," he tells me.

"That was a onetime thing. I didn't know who you were."

"And who am I, Rylan?" he asks, sounding very serious all of a sudden.

Too serious.

Too intense.

Too unlike the carefree playboy he's appeared to be all night. The carefree playboy he *is*, according to Chloe.

I don't like that *I* might be responsible for the switch.

"My dad is your coach," I remind him. "You don't see how that would be kind of awkward for me? For *you*, if he found out?"

Aidan shrugs. "You're an adult. Are you really going to let your dad determine who you hook up with?"

"No, I'm not. And I'm not interested in hooking up with you, either."

Aidan doesn't look the least bit dissuaded. "We already slept together, remember?"

"Thank you for the reminder. It was pretty forgettable."

He grins, and my stomach flips. "You're lying."

He's right; I am.

I've also spent way too much time thinking about that night in Colorado since it happened.

Two things I'll never admit to Aidan.

"You're not my type," I tell him.

That's a truth, at least. Arrogant hockey players—let alone arrogant hockey players coached by my *dad*—have never appealed to me.

His smirk only grows. "Not everyone has good taste."

At least he doesn't bring up Walker again. Historically speaking, he's right about that too. My taste in guys hasn't been great.

"I'm *not interested*," I bite out. "Is that *another* concept you're unable to understand, in addition to anything related to Stats?"

Instead of looking offended, Aidan still appears amused. Where was this tolerance when I mentioned his hockey stats?

"Maybe. We should have our next tutoring date in my bedroom, and you can explain to me what *not interested* means."

I shake my head.

He's tenacious, I'll give him that. If he applied half this much determination to academics, he wouldn't need a tutor in the first place.

"Our tutoring *sessions* will all be taking place in the library."

"Right. I forgot you have a thing for semi-public sex. A bed is too boring for you."

At that, I almost laugh. Before meeting Aidan, my sex life was dimmed lights under the covers. Another thing I have no intention of admitting to him.

"How many girls?" I ask.

A wrinkle forms between his eyes. "What?"

"Since that night we hooked up. How many girls have you slept with?"

Aidan looks away, but not before I catch the spasm of annoyance on his face.

He obviously just realized I've heard the rumors about him. Something I expected him to look proud of, instead of annoyed by. His stats off the ice are much more impressive than the ones on it.

"You have lots of other options," I remind him. "Go flirt with one of them."

I turn and walk away.

Seconds later, the sound of footsteps follows.

I spin back around, staring at Aidan accusingly. "What the hell are you doing?"

He abandoned his cup on the porch. I watch him shove his hands into his pockets. The move emphasizes the muscles lining his forearms, since he's not wearing sleeves.

I guess I find *one* thing about arrogant hockey players appealing.

"Walking you home," he answers.

Why? I want to ask. Why is he extending our encounter? Why is he talking to me at all? I'm not used to being the girl who guys chase. They express interest if it's convenient, if I'm sitting next to them in a class or standing nearby at a party. But no guy has ever walked me home, especially after I just shot him down.

"You're not wearing a jacket," I say, instead of asking for an explanation.

Aidan shrugs. "I play hockey, remember? This is nothing."

"You don't need to walk me home. It's not that late, I live two blocks away, and I have my phone."

"Okay," he says.

"Okay," I repeat, then keep walking.

When the footsteps behind me start up again, I'm not sure whether to be touched or angry. It's sweet, I guess, that he cares about me getting home safely. Except, I'm guessing it's motivated by the same reason as he told me on Tuesday night—my dad. And it pisses me off that he's willing to ignore who my father is if it means getting laid, but refuses to trust I'm capable of making my own choices in other circumstances.

If I didn't feel comfortable walking home alone, I would have asked Chloe or Malia to leave with me. Texted my mom like I did a few times back in high school. Called Campus Security. I grew up in Somerville, and while terrible things can happen anywhere, the crime rate here is extremely low.

I glare at Aidan's stupidly symmetrical profile as he falls into step beside me. Curl my fingers around the house key in my left pocket, not even wincing when the rough metal edge digs into the sensitive skin of my palm.

He walks closer to the curb even though I'm already closer to that side, crowding me until I have to either move closer to the front yards we're passing or risk colliding with him. At first, I think he's just trying to provoke me, but then he says, "Your ex didn't have any manners outside of bed either, huh?" and I realize why he took that spot.

He waited to drive off until I got inside the other night too.

Anyone else, I'd probably find the chivalry charming. Because it's him, it's maddening.

"You are so annoy—"

"Six," Aidan says conversationally, cutting me off.

"What?"

He glances over, his expression unreadable. "You asked how many girls I've slept with since you. Six."

"Oh," is all I can think to say. I have no witty response.

Did I ask him that? Yes.

Was I expecting him to actually *answer*? Absolutely not.

"Higher or lower?"

"What?" I say, again.

"Is six higher or lower than you were thinking, based on what you've heard about me?" His tone is even but there's a flinty undertone, like he's realized I was judging him earlier.

I'm honest. "Lower."

His expression stays neutral as he nods, with the exception of a muscle that jumps in his jaw.

"Which is fine," I tack on, wishing I could just rewind and not ask him anything related to other girls in the first place.

Absolutely none of my business, which I wish is what he'd told me instead of a concrete number.

Aidan snorts.

We're only a block from my house now.

My steps quicken as soon as I spot the brown paint ahead. I've given up on talking him out of walking with me. Now I'm just trying to get this trip over with as quickly as possible.

"What about you?" he asks.

My stomach flips, guessing his meaning but playing dumb and walking faster. His longer legs keep up easily.

"What about me?"

"How many guys have you slept with since we hooked up?"

"Not really any of your business, is it?"

"No, it's not. Who would ask such an invasive, personal question?" His sarcasm is so heavy I can feel it weighting the night air around us.

"Zero," I mutter.

At least that answer shuts him up.

Temporarily.

"Because of your ex?" he asks.

"No. Because I just...haven't."

My personal policy of not having sex with strangers in hot tubs is more of a pattern of not having sex with strangers...ever. At the very least, I've known the guy's last name.

Finally, we reach the edge of my front yard. "Night, Aidan," I say, before heading for the house.

"Night, Rye," he calls after me.

I glance back. "Ry? You gave me a nickname?"

"It's not a nickname. Calling you 'Land where Rye is grown' is just too wordy."

Knowing he memorized the definition I gave him is worse than him simply shortening my name. What happened to him being arrogant and self-absorbed?

"You really didn't need to walk me home."

I should just say *thanks*, but the one word won't come out. I'm fighting any indication he's a decent guy for selfish reasons. He can't be a sex god *and* considerate, or I'll have a much harder time forgetting him.

He shrugs. "I've heard crazy shit happens to people who aren't six foot hockey players."

"Six three," I say.

His grin makes me wish I hadn't mentioned his correction earlier. He's not the only one who paid close attention during our conversation, I guess.

I turn and hurry toward the door.

Not because I'm in a rush to walk away.

Because I'm scared I might do something really stupid—like invite him inside—if I stay.

CHAPTER TEN

RYLAN

C hloe is practically vibrating with excitement as we walk into the lobby of the campus rink. It smells the same as I remember—the chilled air carrying the scent of sweat and steel and buttered popcorn from the concession stand. I inhale deeply, feeling like a little kid again.

I told my roommates this morning that my dad coaches the hockey team. Chloe gave me the perfect opening at breakfast, asking if I was going to this afternoon's game. I told her I was—to support my dad, who's the head coach.

A revelation followed by a barrage of questions, most of which I didn't know the answers to.

Does my dad have a favorite player? *I don't know.*

Does my dad give pre-game speeches like in inspirational sports movies? *I don't know.*

Does my dad think they'll win the championship? *I don't know.*

From the moment Malia parked her sedan in the crowded lot we had to circle twice to find a spot in, I realized this game will be very different from the last Holt hockey game I attended. It's amplified by every step we take closer to the ice, the crowds of people milling about a sea of unfamiliar faces. It reminds me of last night, in some ways. Except the faces aren't just students. There are plenty of families here as well.

Once we're through the lobby and approaching the bleachers that surround the ice, I allow myself to look around more.

There are only a few sections of wood bench visible, most of the stands already packed with enthused spectators. We pass a few girls being herded away from the boards by a campus security guard. His kind but firm "You can't stand here" carries over the din of excited voices echoing through the massive space.

I glance up into the rafters, decorated by a solitary, faded banner from Holt's last championship win. I can't read the year from this angle, but I know it's ancient, predating my dad's tenure by at least a decade.

By most measures, Holt is overdue for a season like this. But sports are unpredictable, unlike math.

I like searching for the right answer.

In sports, you don't know what the outcome will be, and there's never a "right" one.

"Are all the games like this?" I ask Chloe as we sit down, crammed between a group of guys wearing Holt Soccer sweatshirts and two girls with poster-sized signs.

"All the ones I've been to," she replies, pulling her phone out and typing something. "Dakota is here. But she and Mason are sitting with his friends."

"Bummer," Malia says, the sarcastic tone audible over the commotion around us.

I've only met Dakota once, despite sharing a bathroom with her, and she seemed perfectly nice. But I've gotten the sense her boyfriend is not super popular with my other roommates, which Chloe confirms when she glances at me.

"Mason can be a little…unpleasant," she tells me. "Dakota knows we're not crazy about him. But he seems to make her happy, so…" She shrugs a shoulder. "What are you gonna do?"

I nod. If I'd had any real friends in Boston who weren't also his, I'm sure they would have said the same thing about Walker. Hindsight makes spotting people's shortcomings much easier.

The loudspeaker crackles to life, the announcer welcoming everyone to the game and then running through the emergency exit locations. Probably because we're over the building's capacity. Students have started sitting on the stairs now that the bleachers are filled, and more people are still streaming in from the lobby. To watch from where, I'm not sure.

Once the loudspeaker cuts out, pop music starts to play.

Loud cheers echo against the tall ceilings, almost drowning out the song, as blue jerseys begin to appear on the ice, circling the goal at one end.

White jerseys with stripes of green file on at the other end to a chorus of boos and jeers.

Saying Holt has the home ice advantage here seems like a massive understatement. If anyone in the stands came to cheer for today's opponent, they're lost in a sea of blue.

Rather than focus on any of the players warming up, my eyes seek out my dad.

He's standing behind the bench, arms folded as he watches his guys on the ice.

He's wearing a tie and button-down beneath his Holt Hockey jacket, and an impassive expression.

I'm not fooled by the lack of animation on his face, though. That's just my dad—his exterior is usually gruff, measured, and calm. This is his happy place, and there's nowhere else he'd rather be.

I know he's having the time of his life watching his team

warm up, standing expressionless while tapping a folded sheet of paper against his arm. I'm sure he's chewing gum too. As a kid, I used to marvel at the collection of gum wrappers in his glove compartment. It was a running joke for years, that all my dad would want as a gift was a few packs of Trident.

A slightly younger guy dressed identically to my dad sidles up beside him, saying something that has my dad nodding. I'm assuming that's Dean Zimmerman, the assistant coach. I've heard my dad mention his name before but never actually met him. He only joined the team a few years ago, long after I'd stopped attending games.

One of the officials stops at the Holt bench, and my dad leans forward to talk to him.

A couple of blue jerseys skate closer to the bench to listen to the conversation. My dad says something to one of them, and he skates closer, turning so I can see the name and number on the back. *Hart* and *15*. The team captain.

The ref skates toward the visitor's bench next, but the two Holt players remain. My dad steps closer to the barrier between the bench and the ice, beckoning to both Hart and the other player to come closer. They form a small huddle, and I catch a glimpse of the back of the other blue jersey.

Phillips and *34*.

With a start, I realize that's Aidan talking to my dad.

I know they talk, obviously. He's Aidan's coach. They must exchange words.

But it's bizarre to see it happen, to watch the stranger I met in a hot tub and my father having a conversation knowing they've done so dozens of times before.

I came to the game because of my dad.

But I'd be lying if I said I'm not curious to watch Aidan play.

The rest of Holt's players are joining Aidan and Conor, clustering around the bench in a blob of blue.

My dad is talking, the entire team focused on him.

I experience a sudden rush of pride. All of these people are here to watch his players, but they're *his* players. He recruited them. Trained them. Inspired them. Turned this team that no one except him cared about into an attraction that everyone in here is rooting for.

Most of the blue jerseys file off the ice, the bulky form of the goalie and five others remaining. They all face the flag, and the National Anthem starts playing.

Once the song ends, the announcer comes back on the loudspeaker. He starts by announcing Willis, the goalie. Followed by two unfamiliar names who must be the defensemen. "Robby Sampson!" receives a healthy amount of applause. "Hunter Morgan!" gets even more. And then there's a long, deliberate pause before "And your captain and leading scorer...CONOR HART!" is announced.

The noise in the arena hits a new decibel before petering off as soon as the starting lineup for today's opponent, Smithdale, is announced to mostly silence and a few boos.

I scan the bench until I find 34. He's seated but leaning forward, holding his stick with both hands as he looks out at the ice.

I wonder if it bothers Aidan that his best friend bumped him to the second line. His stats aren't Hall of Fame worthy, but they're respectable. And he's a senior. On another team, his name would have just been announced over the loudspeaker as part of the starters.

The official drops the puck in the very center of the largest circle, and the game begins.

I lean forward automatically, trying to gain the best view

possible as I watch the puck bounce off the boards, then get picked up by a white jersey and carried toward the goal guarded by a blue jersey.

Smithdale takes its first shot and misses, thankfully.

Another drop, this one uncomfortably close to Holt's goal. Conor wins the face-off, zipping up the ice so quickly it hardly looks like the other players are moving at all. He takes a shot on goal that the Smithdale goalie saves, and then the lines change.

I search the new numbers on the ice until I spot 34 again. Annoyed when I realize I'm seeking him out, but curious enough I don't look away out of sheer stubbornness. It's not like he'll ever know I'm staring at him.

Aidan's circling by the spot where he'll face off against a white jersey, bent over with his stick resting on his knees.

I frown, wondering if something is wrong.

He straightens when the official approaches, moving into a slightly crouched position opposite Smithdale's center.

The puck drops, sticks clash, and then there's a black blur flying across the ice.

A Holt player traps the puck on his stick and then sends it back to Aidan. His back is turned, so I can't read the name or number on the back of his jersey.

The metallic tang of blood is how I realize I'm biting my bottom lip too hard. Just like I realize I wasn't this invested when Conor Hart's line was on the ice, which was the more probable scoring opportunity.

Aidan has the puck again now.

There's a split-second where he deliberates, a Smithdale defenseman charging toward him.

He decides.

Shoots, the loud sound and flash of the siren announcing the goal before my eyes register the spot of black landed inside the net.

The entire arena erupts, all the blue jerseys on the ice mobbing him. Chloe screams beside me, and Malia is on her feet as well.

"Holt University goal scored by number thirty-four, Aidan Phillips," booms over the loudspeaker. "Assisted by number seventeen, Tyler Yarrow. Time of the goal, three minutes and twenty-two seconds into the first period."

I'm probably the last person in this place to start clapping, shock slowing my reaction.

I was expecting the guy who slouched in the library chair and basically told me he failed because he didn't *feel* like taking a final exam to be the one playing today.

The game resumes at the same quick tempo, Holt now leading one to nothing.

Ten minutes later, Aidan scores again.

I'm stunned as I stare at the ice, watching his teammates congratulate him for a second time as the announcer says, "Another Holt University goal scored by number thirty-four, Aidan Phillips. Assisted by number forty-two, Ace Carter. Time of the goal, thirteen minutes and ten seconds into the first period."

The first period ends seven minutes later, Aidan's two goals the only ones up on the scoreboard. The arena is still buzzing from the explosive start, multiple people around us mentioning Aidan's name.

"Snacks?" Malia suggests.

Chloe nods. "Best part of the game."

We join the line of people slowly filtering down from the bottleneck in the stands, taking the opportunity to go to the bathroom or get food while the Zamboni is out smoothing the ice.

A couple of younger kids are being hoisted up on this side of the clear plastic to watch the machine work, pointing and smiling at the driver as the shavings get cleared off the surface, replaced with a gleaming sweep of water that immediately freezes. A wave of nostalgia hits, remembering doing the same thing with my own dad.

When he first got the job here, my parents just had one car. My mom would drop my dad off for games and practices, and I'd usually come with her. This old building contains a lot of memories I haven't thought about for years.

The concession stand is a popular destination. By the time we reach it, the line ahead of us contains a couple dozen people.

"What a game!" Chloe exclaims. Her cheeks are flushed with excitement.

Malia looks just as excited, nodding in agreement as she reads over the list of offerings on the board above the cashier. All standard rink fare—popcorn, pretzels, hot chocolate, hot dogs.

"Rylan?"

I turn toward the sound of my name, recognizing Isla Yarrow immediately. "Isla! Hey!"

We exchange a quick hug.

"How have you been?" she asks. "You here for your dad?"

Isla and I went to school together, starting in kindergarten. She's the one person from our high school who chose to attend Holt.

It was common knowledge in Somerville that my dad coached Holt's hockey team. But it's strange to have someone know that now, without me telling them.

"Yeah," I answer. "I'm also...I'm a student here now. I transferred."

"Oh, wow. From Boston, right?"

"Right. Wasn't all I was hoping it would be."

"Sorry to hear that," Isla says, her expression sympathetic. None of the judgment I was worried about seeing.

"Thanks. It's been nice to be back."

"We should get together sometime, now that you're back in Somerville," she suggests.

"Absolutely," I reply. "I would love that. I was planning to reach out to you. It's just been a crazy first week."

"I get it. I'll text you? Same number?"

I nod. "Same number."

"Great."

I introduce her to Chloe and Malia, then Isla continues back toward her seat.

"You guys went to high school together?" Chloe asks.

"And elementary school and middle school. She grew up in Somerville, just like me. And started at Holt as a freshman."

A week ago, I would have thought *Like I should have*.

Today, I don't. And it's not because I regret transferring to Holt, because I definitely don't. More that I'm finally accepting I can't change the past and am trying to enjoy the present.

"She seemed nice," Malia says.

"Yeah, she is."

We reach the front of the line. I order a hot pretzel, and we return to our seats right as players are filing back onto the bench.

I chew on the salty, warm dough as my eyes skim over the blue jerseys.

Looking for thirty-four.

I'm irritated with myself, and also making excuses. It's not that we hooked up; it's that I'm tutoring him and he's the one guy I actually know on the team. It's not that I've spent an unhealthy amount of time thinking about him recently; it's that he's been the best player on the ice this game.

Lies, but I tell myself they don't count since they're not spoken out loud.

Aidan's not on the bench.

I scan it twice to confirm.

Then realize…he's already on the ice. That his line is starting this period.

And when he scores for a third time, a few minutes later, I'm not surprised.

This time, I'm expecting it.

CHAPTER ELEVEN

AIDAN

I tug a baseball cap down over my wet hair before climbing out of my truck. I got it back yesterday—finally—and just in time.

The rest of the team is at Gaffney's, enjoying discounted beer and wings.

I should be annoyed I'm missing it. I'm not.

For one, practice since Saturday's game has been uncomfortable. I have no clue how Hart has dealt with this attention for four years, because I've had my fill after four days.

Although it's not so much the attention as the expectations, I guess, and Conor puts those on himself.

He steps out on the ice, determined to score and have an impact on the game.

I'm there for a fun time and hoping we win because of a group effort.

Since Saturday, everyone's been acting like whether we win is dependent on *me*.

Responsibility I don't want, and something I should have considered before pulling a hat trick out of my ass. I've scored a hat trick in a game once before, back in high school. Never in a college game, and not against Smithdale, who we were expecting to be a challenge to our almost perfect record.

I'm extremely nervous about Thursday's game, knowing the expectations that are in place now.

The thing is, nothing about Saturday felt different. I'm not superstitious like some athletes are. I don't have a special pre-game routine and I did nothing unusual before our latest game. I wasn't pissed about anything or riding a high.

I just saw opportunities and took them, and that somehow resulted in me scoring the game's only goals and the guys now referring to me as the team's secret weapon.

A few people call out to me as I walk toward the campus coffee shop, a mixture of hellos and congratulations. A few good games.

At least Thursday is an away game.

If I revert to my usual mediocre performance, there won't be a home crowd to disappoint. Of course, all the people I care about disappointing will still be there.

Like Coach, who gave me an approving, proud smile that had Sampson freaking the fuck out because Coach *never* smiles.

And Hart, who's got trophy-shaped stars in his eyes. He could be after a fourth championship this season, if hockey was an individual sport. It's the rest of us who have let him down year after year. Me delivering a Hart-worthy game takes a lot of pressure off of him. Increases our low odds of getting all the way to the final.

Unfortunately, I have no clue what the fuck happened on Saturday and have even less of an idea how to replicate it.

So I'm hoping another guy on the team will have a great game and no one will notice when I go back to contributing an assist or two but nothing more.

I cover a yawn as I pass the student center, desperate for a jolt of caffeine. I got a shitty night's sleep, since I'm stressed not only about our next game, but also about tonight's tutoring session.

I haven't seen Rylan since the party on Friday, and I'm fucking nervous about seeing her tonight.

As if our first tutoring session didn't go awkwardly enough—realizing the tutor I was absolutely not going to hook up with was a girl I had already slept with was a curveball, to say the least—I didn't avoid her at the party the way I should've.

Not only because she was obviously trying to avoid me, which I should have been grateful for, not peeved by, but because I love a bad decision.

I walked up to her because I was bored. Headed outside because I was feeling restless. Being at that party felt stale and predictable until I saw Rylan there.

My conversations with girls at parties begin and end with flirting.

I don't ask them what their name means.

And I don't fumble through suggesting we hook up, much less at my *house*, where I never bring girls.

I'd had a couple of drinks, received four different offers to fuck upstairs, and I ended the evening jerking off in my room to memories of Rylan in that hot tub.

Again, I love a bad decision. Or five.

Unfortunately, learning Rylan's real name—and her last one—didn't do a damn thing to change the fact I'm wildly attracted to her. I've hooked up with enough women to know this interest isn't common. I don't normally think about a girl unless she's standing right in front of me.

I need to get Rylan Keller the hell out of my head.

Not only is she my tutor and Coach's daughter—she shot me down cold when I suggested we hook up again. I've never done more than the bare minimum, never *chased* a girl, not even with

Parker. Our relationship just evolved over time, changing with us as we grew up together. Parker was always...there. Falling for her was more like sinking, a slow, steady inevitability that made sense. That seemed right. Looking back, I might have confused fate and convenience. And the fact I'm even comparing Rylan to my one and only relationship tells me a whole lot I don't want to know.

I need to get Rylan Keller the hell out of my head...which is going to be challenging considering I *have* to meet with my tutor each week.

I can't avoid her, even if I wanted to.

Because I'm already thinking about her, of course Rylan is the last person standing in line when I enter the campus coffee shop.

She's wearing the same pink pom-pom hat as *that night*, which is a detail I'm surprised I notice and makes our hookup seem more real. Until I walked into the library and saw her sitting there, part of me wondered if that evening in the hot tub was some erotic, whiskey-fueled dream.

Rylan glances back at me, her expression remaining neutral as she registers my arrival.

No *thank you* for walking her home the other night. I've made sure she made it home safely two times now—twice more than I've escorted any other girl.

Regardless of what I told her, it didn't have a damn thing to do with her dad. It was because I wanted to spend more time around her, because there was a tightness in my chest at the thought of some "scary shit" happening to her.

There's also no sign of any annoyance about me hitting on her beforehand, which I guess is a good sign.

And no comment about Saturday's game, which is actually a relief. Who knows if she was even there, but she must have heard about it. The whole campus has been buzzing, not to mention...

she's Coach's daughter. I'm not clear how close they are, but it seems like she would have at least looked up the score because of her dad.

Her total lack of reaction amuses me.

It's the same intrigue I experienced that night we hooked up, trying to figure her out and failing every time.

She went to school in London, but only for a semester. She's smart, but doesn't kiss like any nerd I've ever met. She did her dad the favor of tutoring me, but decided not to attend the university where he works in the first place. She had no problem boldly ogling my dick in the wilderness, but put effort into avoiding me at the sophomores' party like she was scared of what I might say.

"Aidan." Her tone is cool as she finally acknowledges me.

I resist the urge to call her Alice, just to shatter some of that indifference.

"Nice hat," I say, continuing my streak of saying stupid shit around her. "Is it new?"

Her lips press into a thin line. "No."

"Thought I'd seen it before."

The line becomes even thinner.

"Good weekend?" I ask when she says nothing.

"It got better toward the end."

I fight the scoff. *Tough crowd.*

Not that I was expecting anything different from her.

"Does that mean you went to the game on Saturday?"

She pauses before answering, like it's a difficult question. "I wanted to support my dad."

I take that as a *yes.* "Have you been to a lot of games?"

Another hesitation. "No," Rylan finally answers. "I haven't."

"What'd you think?"

Since Saturday, it's been an endless stream of compliments.

I'm genuinely sick of it. But here I am, *fishing*, because she admitted she was there and I want to know what she thought.

Not of the game or her dad's coaching.

Of me.

"That was a sloppy penalty you took at the end of the second. Willis almost gave up a power play goal."

I stare at her, surprised she answered like she knew what I was really asking. I was assuming she'd say that her dad coached well, or she was glad we won.

It *was* a bad penalty that nearly cost Willis his second shutout of the season.

A sloppy play on my part that no one except Coach commented on with a gruff "Watch it, Phillips," when I returned to the bench after my two minutes in the box were up. Everyone else was too busy congratulating me on my goals.

I usually enjoy it when girls talk hockey to me. Those are always compliments.

This is the second time Rylan has insulted me, and I'm as startled and turned on by it as I was the first time. Maybe I should be annoyed instead, but it's hot that she knows what she's talking about. So is her blunt delivery.

"You're right," I agree.

Rylan looks surprised.

"So…you a big hockey fan?" I ask.

She snorts. "No."

"Did you ever play?" I ask.

"For a few years. It wasn't my thing."

"That must have been a bummer for Coach K." I'm teasing Rylan, trying to get her to simply *talk* to me, but when her entire body stiffens, I quickly realize I should have kept my mouth shut. "I didn't mean—"

"To imply that I'm a disappointment to my dad?"

"Yeah. That." I shift my weight between my feet. "I was projecting, I guess."

Her forehead creases, and I wish I could shove the words back into my mouth. Rewind the last minute of our conversation and not mention either of our fathers.

"He's super proud of you," I tell her. "Was bragging about how smart you were in between telling me to make sure I don't fuck this tutoring thing up."

Rylan looks incredulous and a little disbelieving. That her dad actually said that or that I'm…trying to make her feel better, I guess?

I get feeling like your father considers you a disappointment, and I know that's not the kind of man Coach Keller is.

I'm sure he's as proud of his math-loving daughter as he'd be of a hockey-playing son.

"Hi! What can I get for you?"

I've been so wrapped up in Rylan, I've barely noticed the line moving. Suddenly, there's no one between Rylan and the blonde working the register.

The blonde who's talking to Rylan…but looking at me.

I pull my phone out of my pocket and scroll through my messages, avoiding eye contact while Rylan orders an iced coffee. Surprising, considering the temperature out and how she's looked cold almost every time I've seen her.

She was practically shivering on the front porch Friday night. If I'd been wearing a jacket, I would have offered it to her, if only to feel like less of a sleazeball for spending most of our conversation trying to figure out if she was wearing a bra under her black top or not.

"Hey, Aidan!" The blonde beams at me as Rylan steps aside and it's my turn to order.

I force a smile. "Hi."

"*Amazing* game on Saturday," she gushes. "Everyone's been talking about how incredible you were."

I rub the back of my neck. "Yeah, thanks."

She looks vaguely familiar, but I can't come up with a name and she's not wearing a tag on her shirt.

"Brooke, remember? We hung out at the end of break."

A deaf person could comprehend the emphasis she placed on *hung out*; it's *that* heavy. She might as well have just said we fucked.

"Right, yeah." I'm walking the fine line of trying not to be a dick to Brooke while encouraging her to stop talking about us having sex as soon as possible.

For the third time in my life, I wish a girl wasn't flirting with me.

All three times have involved Rylan Keller.

I'm fighting the urge to look over at her, positive this interaction is reinforcing everything she knows about me.

Confused why I care. And uncomfortable, just like I was on Friday night when Sylvie was hanging on to me in the living room and when Lia showed up on the porch.

I've never felt any need to apologize for my behavior before.

Embraced sleeping around as the harmless fun it was with no accountability to anyone.

I'm annoyed I feel ashamed of it now. But I can't ignore the burn of chagrin either.

After paying, I head toward where Rylan is already waiting at the end of the counter.

She's on her phone, ignoring me, and this time I don't try to strike up any conversation. But I'm uncomfortably aware of the awkwardness swirling around in the warm, coffee-scented air.

It feels like any progress I made with Rylan was erased as soon as Brooke opened her mouth.

And I don't get why.

I didn't make Rylan any promises that night. She was the one who took off as soon as we'd both finished. Who turned down my offer of a repeat. Who asked me how many girls I'd been with since, like the answer was any of her business.

Since we re-met, it seems like all she's done is judge me. About my grades and my hockey stats and my body count.

I'm used to judgment. I thought I was impervious to it.

Not hers, it turns out.

"Rylan! Hey!"

I look toward the voice, even though it's her name being called.

A guy wearing glasses is walking this way, totally focused on the brunette beside me. I've never met him before, but I'm guessing he knows Rylan from one of her classes based on his appearance alone.

Rylan slips her phone into her pocket, then tucks a piece of hair behind one ear. "Hi, Theo. How's it going?"

Her voice is warm and friendly, a tone I've never heard from her before.

"Not bad," the guy—Theo—responds. "Just caffeinating up before tackling the Euclidean algorithm problem set."

Definitely a math major, I decide.

Rylan groans. "Not looking forward to finishing that."

"How many have you done?"

"Just the first three," she tells him.

"I'm headed to the library now, if you want to work on it together?"

I'm not sure if Rylan catches the nervous note to Theo's voice, but I do.

He likes her. And I guess nerds show that by inviting girls to do homework with them instead of inviting them into an empty room at a party.

"I can't." Rylan sounds regretful, glancing at me and then quickly away when she realizes I'm looking at her.

I shove my hands into my pockets and focus my attention on the barista, wishing my coffee was ready and I wasn't stuck listening.

"I have a, uh, study thing," she explains.

Would she tell him she's tutoring a failing hockey player if I wasn't standing right here?

Would she say yes to him, if she wasn't stuck tutoring me tonight?

"Too bad," Theo says. The disappointment in his voice is obvious—to me, at least. "Text me if it finishes early."

"Will do," she replies.

He leaves, and Rylan's coffee appears a few seconds later. She picks the cup up but doesn't leave. Not until mine appears too.

Logical, I guess, considering we're headed to the same place to meet up. But I wasn't expecting her to wait for me. Especially with plenty of evidence to support her not wanting to spend her evening around me.

I grab an extra paper sleeve when I pick up my cup, handing it to Rylan as we walk toward the door.

I avoid all the looks aimed at me except hers. People are either staring because of Saturday's game or because I don't really walk around campus with girls. I hook up at parties on the weekends. But around campus? I'm usually with a group of my teammates.

"What's this for?" she asks.

"It'll keep your hand from freezing."

Her "Oh. Uh, thanks" sounds confused.

Not sure what that means, but it's better than indifference or annoyance.

We're both silent, passing the seating area just outside the coffee shop and then starting on the path that cuts across campus toward the academic buildings and the library.

"We can do this another night," I tell her.

"Why?" She sounds even more puzzled, glancing at me with a crease between her eyebrows. It's cute.

"So you can go talk Euclidean algorithm with your math buddy."

I'm kinda expecting her to be impressed I remembered the mouthful that's *Euclidean algorithm*. Instead, when I look over, she appears offended. Her mouth is pressed in another thin line that flattens the pouty lips I spend too much time thinking about. "I don't need Theo's help to do the problem set."

"He doesn't need yours either, genius. He has a crush on you, and you shot him down. Probably did a real number on his poor confidence. Text the guy. Tell him you're free."

I don't know why I'm making a big deal out of this.

Aside from two pathetic reasons. One, if she's dating another guy, then maybe I can stop thinking about her as a possibility, since neither her last name nor the fact she's my tutor seems to be doing the trick. Two, and even more pitiful, because I want to know if he's her type and whether she's interested in him.

"What's her name?" Rylan snaps.

"Huh?"

"The name of the girl you're so eager to skip this tutoring session and go see. Do I seriously need to remind you that hockey and graduating are on the line for you here?"

Now *I'm* offended. "There's no girl. You don't want to tutor me, and you just got a better offer. I can do the assignment and give it to you to grade again."

"I haven't even looked at the first one yet. Eighty-five was the deal."

"I know what the deal was."

Rylan huffs. "You might not take your responsibilities seriously, but I do. I said I would tutor you, and that's what I'm going to do."

She's infuriating. I was trying to be *nice*, to let her focus on her own work and spend time around a guy she liked enough to give him her number. She's acting like I accused her of slacking off.

I bite the inside of my cheek, trying to rein my temper in before responding. "If I didn't take my *responsibilities seriously*, I wouldn't be here."

The rest of our walk to the library is silent.

I'm irritated and she's annoyed, and it bodes badly for the rest of tonight going well.

I'm already stressed about Thursday's game, about keeping my grades up in the rest of my classes, and about going home soon. Having tonight start off so poorly isn't helping with any of it. Neither is the fact my preferred form of stress relief hasn't happened since last weekend because...I don't really know. Some combination of failing a class and playoffs approaching and my family and how I keep comparing other girls to the one walking next to me.

A few people call out to me once we're inside the library. Lots of mentions of Saturday's game and eagerness about our next home one.

I nod or smile back but don't stop to talk to anyone like I usually would.

I follow Rylan inside the elevator without questioning why we're not working on the busy first floor, intent on getting through the next hour as painlessly as possible.

She seems to take anything I say the wrong way, so I might as well say nothing unless it's related to Stats. At least she'll have less to criticize there. I hope. I had Andy Pierce look over my assignment yesterday. He's an Econ major and took a Stats class last semester. Guy jumped at the chance, probably worried I was holding a grudge about the bruise on my ribs that hasn't fully faded yet. According to him, I did know what I was doing.

I'll get through this tutoring session, then head home to tackle the rest of my homework. Hunter and Conor probably won't be back until late. There was talk of going over to Sampson's place after getting food at Gaffney's. I could meet them over there, but I probably won't.

Tomorrow will be busy; we have a dryland practice and a film session before Thursday's away game. And I'm exhausted, the coffee I'm holding doing nothing to wake me up so far.

I take another sip and then exhale, resting my head against the wall of the elevator as I watch the numbers tick higher.

"You okay?"

Startled, I glance over at Rylan. I thought she'd be looking at her phone, not studying me with something that looks a little like concern.

"Yeah. I…yeah." I rub a hand across my face. "I don't know how Hart deals with it."

"Deals with what?"

"The pressure. I had *one* decent game, and everyone's expecting…" I sigh. "Whatever. Never mind."

"It sounds liked you're scared of the expectations."

"I'm not *scared*. I just don't like them."

"Huh," she says.

I resist the urge for one, two, three… "What?"

"I used to fake coming with my ex a lot."

Unfortunately, she says that as I'm mid-sip. I cough three

times to clear the coffee from my throat, and can hear the smile in Rylan's voice as she continues talking.

"That night we hooked up, I didn't fake it either time."

I can't resist saying, "I know."

She rolls her eyes. "You didn't seem surprised."

"I wasn't."

Another eye roll. "That did not seem like a guy who *doesn't like* expectations. It seemed like a guy who exceeded them."

"You're comparing hockey and a hookup? How is that the same thing?"

"I barely know you, but I thought a sex analogy would be most likely to get through to you."

I roll my eyes, fighting the smile. "It sounds like you just wanted to let me know I'm a fantastic lay."

"You knew that already."

Based on her reactions that night, I knew she enjoyed our hookup, yeah. But that's different from hearing it now, a month after. I fight the urge to ask her if *Zero* is still her answer. Like she said, it's none of my damn business.

The silence between us is a little less awkward as the elevator doors open.

We're on the fifth floor, which I've never been up to before. I didn't even know the library *had* five floors.

I don't mention that to Rylan, just trail behind her as she walks over to a table by a window. It faces the campus green, offering a sprawling glimpse at a large section of campus, lit up by the lamps that line the walkways.

It's a nice view.

Not as nice as the one across the table.

I pull out the assignment sheet Rylan gave me last week, plus the papers I drew out the answers on, and slide both across the table to her. "Here you go."

She pushes a paper back. This week's assignment, I'm assuming.

We must look like we're participating in some academic drug deal.

"Here's this week's assignment," she tells me. "Look it over while I grade this."

I nod, settling back in the chair and stretching my legs out. To the side, so I don't hit hers.

Rylan slides the paper back to me about ten minutes later.

"Ninety-one. Nice work."

She drew a little smiley face next to the two numbers, and fuck if I don't want to frame this. I'll stick it on the fridge for Conor and Hunter to admire, at the very least. Between the miracle of me managing an A on anything and the hat trick this past weekend, that should take care of the concerned glances I've been getting since the start of the semester.

"Thanks," I say, instead of the smug *Told you so* I had planned.

Nothing comes out about the three hours I spent on it or the teammate I had check it over, either.

We just stare at each other for a few seconds, and I'm startled the breath Rylan pulls in appears a little shaky, almost unsteady.

"Ready to start regression analysis?" she asks.

I'm ninety-one percent sure that I remember regression analysis just as well as I did summation notation and measures of variability.

But I don't say so. I just nod.

Because I'm wary of offending her again.

And...because I'm in no rush to leave.

CHAPTER TWELVE

RYLAN

I spot Isla standing by the hostess stand as soon as I step inside Gaffney's. It's busy and noisy inside the bar, which isn't surprising. The few times I came here in high school, all the summer before starting college, it was packed.

A relief then, since I was underage and felt less conspicuous because it was so crowded.

At age twenty-one, weaving through the crowd is more of an inconvenience.

"Hey!" Isla greets me once I make it over to her.

We hug, then head toward the back of the bar. Isla texted me yesterday afternoon, saying tonight was trivia at Gaffney's and asking if I wanted to go with her.

My Abstract Algebra class meets at nine a.m. tomorrow, and we have our first quiz of the semester. I should be reviewing my notes and getting a solid eight hours of sleep.

But I'm sick of being Responsible Rylan.

In Boston, I used school as an excuse anytime I was unsure or uncomfortable. Which was often, especially around Walker's friends, who didn't make much of an attempt to get to know me.

And I was determined to get perfect grades as reassurance to my parents Boston had been the right choice, especially when everything else about going to school there continued to feel wrong.

I'm determined for Holt to be a fresh start socially, not just a new school. If that means showing up to class tomorrow hungover, that's a college rite of passage, right?

Any awkwardness between me and Isla fades quickly as we catch up on each other's lives.

We weren't close friends when we were younger, for no reason except we didn't get to know each other well by age five and that's when our respective social circles were formed.

Up until running into her at the game, I hadn't talked to Isla since graduation. Conversation flows easily as we swap stories about our former classmates. We find a table and take seats on the stools, waiting for the blonde waitress to work her way over here.

I find out that Isla is majoring in computer science and that her parents moved from Somerville to Seattle a year ago because of a new job opportunity her mom was offered. She dated a guy for a few months freshman year but hasn't had a boyfriend since, so I share I haven't dated anyone since breaking up with Walker almost a year ago. I don't mention he cheated, because a part of me still feels ashamed about that detail. Like it was some failure on my part, not his. I know it's stupid and silly, but I can't seem to shake it whenever the topic of my ex comes up. Thinking about how Aidan looked at me when I was standing on his deck, pulling my clothes off, helps.

The waitress finally appears, and we both order beers.

"Did you do anything fun over winter break?" Isla asks.

"Uh…" The *fun* part involved the guy I'm working hard not to think about. "I was here, aside from a ski trip."

"Oh, that's cool. Where did you go skiing?"

"Vail. With a friend from abroad, her family has a house there."

"*Very* nice."

"Yeah. It was."

She takes a sip of beer, then laughs and wipes the foam mustache away after I smile and push the napkins toward her. "I've never been skiing."

"It was only my second time. Jess—my friend whose place we were staying at—takes it pretty seriously. I was ready to take a break after a few runs, but she was happy staying out there all day."

"Are you ladies playing trivia?" A smiling blond guy appears. He's tall—*very* tall—and good-looking—*very* good-looking.

"We are," Isla replies, glancing at me and lifting her eyebrows quickly.

One corner of my mouth lifts as he rests one elbow on our table.

"I'm Clayton."

"Isla."

"Rylan," I tell him.

"You guys know it's teams of four, right?" Clayton asks.

I didn't. No rules announcements have been made since I arrived. Last time I was here, there was no trivia-playing. We mostly just flirted with college guys so they'd buy the drinks and we wouldn't have to worry about getting carded.

But Isla smirks and nods. "Is that your way of begging for a spot on our team?"

"I don't know about *begging*, but I'm definitely interested." A second elbow lands on our table as he makes himself comfortable, the innuendo impossible to miss.

The waitress returns with our drinks, and I quickly pick up my beer glass to hide my smirk as Isla and Clayton continue to flirt.

More things I've missed, being out with a friend and banter with a cute guy. Easy, simple fun.

"Hey, Clayton," the waitress says.

"Hey." He gives her a nod, but his attention stays on Isla.

I get player vibes from him—in both senses of the word—but he doesn't seem like a douche. If I could do so inconspicuously, I'd flash Isla a thumbs-up.

By the time the waitress leaves, Clayton has taken a seat at our table. He's on the basketball team, so I pegged him right as an athlete. Or was on the team, rather—he's a senior and their season just ended.

"I went to a basketball game sophomore year," Isla tells him.

"And it was such a great experience you never went to another one?" he asks.

She takes a sip of her beer, her cheeks flushing pink. "I'm not a huge sports fan."

"Ri-ght," Clayton drawls. "Suppose you've never seen a hockey game, then?"

Isla blushes bright red. "All my friends like to go to those," she tells him. "It wouldn't have been my first choice." She glances at me. "Rylan's dad coaches the team."

"Really?" Clayton's attention lands on me for the first time since he came over.

Maybe I should be offended he's basically ignored me, but I'm not. I might be looking for fun, which Clayton has written all over him, but there's no spark between us. I think he's attractive, but there are no butterflies. No prickle of awareness from having his eyes on me.

I nod. "Yeah."

I wish Isla hadn't mentioned it, but I'm not going to deny it. She's probably used to our younger days, when my dad's job was just common knowledge. A known fact. I doubt she's considered the dynamics I've worried about since transferring, especially right now, when the spotlight on the hockey team is extra bright. I don't want anyone to treat me any differently—either better or worse—because of who my dad is.

"That's awesome," Clayton says. "The hockey guys always rave about Coach Keller. Almost make me wish I'd kept the skates on after middle school."

I smile, relieved by his response. "He loves his job."

"Trivia starting in five minutes," a guy who looks to be in his late twenties shouts from the corner. He's wearing a ball cap that has *Gaffney's* written on it.

"We need a fourth player," Clayton says. "I can go see if—"

"I'll play," a male voice volunteers. A *familiar* male voice.

Immediately, I stiffen, stripped of all ease. I'm hyperaware of nothing I was concerned about a second ago—my posture, my makeup, my hair, my outfit.

The way it looks like I'm third-wheeling.

"Phillips! Hey!" Clayton sounds thrilled to see Aidan.

I'm not surprised to learn Aidan and Clayton know each other. Aside from Clayton just mentioning he knows guys on the hockey team, they're similar. Both popular winter athletes who are seniors.

So Aidan's flat "Thomas" confuses me.

I've never heard him sound so abrupt and unfriendly.

Clayton looks puzzled too, so I don't think there's some ancient animosity that explains Aidan's behavior.

"Saw you guys won," Clayton comments cautiously. I think he's subtly trying to ask why Aidan seems to be in such a bad mood.

"Yep." Aidan takes a seat on the stool next to mine. His denim-clad thigh brushes my leg, and I almost jump from the contact.

His soapy, masculine scent surrounds me, and I fight the urge to breathe deeper. I pick up my glass and drain half my beer in one gulp, telling myself to chill the fuck out.

Our last study session ended on good terms, although I'm suspicious he knew what he was doing the entire time and our second session could have lasted five minutes, just like the first one did. Aidan got both practice problems right without taking a single note during my explanation.

Either way, we're fine. Good. Great.

Or at least, I thought we were...

"Hey, I'm Aidan." He introduces himself to Isla, his voice several degrees warmer than it was talking to Clayton.

She blushes, a brighter red than when Clayton was teasing her. I'm pretty sure Clayton notices, because the smile that greeted Aidan's arrival has totally disappeared.

"I know," Isla says. "I'm Isla."

"You a big hockey fan, Isla?" Aidan leans forward, flashing her a heart-stopping smile.

Now, Clayton looks like he swallowed something bitter. I pray I'm not about to end up in the middle of a jock pissing match and also wouldn't mind seeing him take a swing at Aidan. It's what I wish I could do, if I wasn't hiding my irritation much better than Clayton is.

And by hiding it, I mean chugging beer so I can't say anything.

Isla's cheeks are bright red now. "Of Holt hockey? Sure am."

"*Great* answer."

"Hey, Aidan. Awesome game. Can I get you a drink?"

The blonde waitress who served us earlier has appeared. Much faster than she showed up when Isla and I first sat down, I can't help but notice.

"Usual, please," he says. "Thanks, Stacey."

"You got it." Stacey winks at him before sauntering away.

"So what's your major, Isla?" Aidan asks.

His leg brushes mine beneath the table again, and I stiffen even more. My posture resembles a puppet's.

"Computer science," she tells him.

"That's cool. Do you know how to make your own app?"

Computer science is cool*, but math is amusing?*

"I could code a basic one, yeah," Isla answers.

"Awesome."

Stacey returns with his beer in record time, and Aidan flashes her another one of those priceless grins.

Priceless, because they seem to get him whatever he wants.

Attention, alcohol, praise.

My irritation, which he clearly doesn't care about.

"If I knew how to create my own app I would—"

"I'm grabbing another drink," I announce, cutting Aidan off mid-sentence before slipping off my stool and heading straight toward the bar.

I'm pissed, and I'm not sure why.

That he came over and commandeered my girls' night with an old friend, maybe. Possibly that he did it without directly acknowledging me *once*.

Clayton focusing on Isla didn't bother me. I was excited for her.

Aidan focusing on Isla annoys the shit out of me. He couldn't have bothered with a *Hi*? It's two letters. One syllable. A second out of his night.

I find an open spot along the bartop and lean against the scarred wooden surface, waiting for the bartender to work his way down to this end. Another drink isn't my best idea, especially considering how quickly I downed my first beer, but I really needed an excuse to escape that table. Plus, tonight I'm being Reckless Rylan, and this seems like something she would do.

Since the bartender is moving at the speed of molasses, I turn to survey the rest of the bar. Keeping my gaze far away from the back section.

Aidan isn't the only hockey player here, but the others I recognize are all clustered around a large table. He didn't come over to "play trivia" because he's here alone or has no one else to talk to, and I have no clue what to make of that. All I know is it irritates me. We're stuck together for one hour a week. He can't steer clear outside of those sixty minutes?

"They're passing out the answer sheets."

"Cool." I keep my eye on a group of guys by the pool table, debating if I have the guts to go over there and ask if they need another player. If Aidan is here, I'm sure Clayton and Isla have returned to flirting. And if Isla is occupied with a hot guy, I have no attachment to playing trivia tonight. Might as well take advantage of the buzz I'm experiencing to take another step out of my comfort zone.

"You mad at me about something?" Aidan asks.

I suppress the scoff that wants to come out. Still no *Hi*. Let alone a *How are you?* or a *Nice to see you.* "No."

He snorts. "Well—"

"Phillips!" A tall guy I've never seen before appears. "What the fuck happened to you?"

"I'm playing trivia," Aidan responds.

The guy laughs, once. "You're *what*?"

"Oh, good. Are you guys already waiting to order? The line at the other end is insane." A gorgeous redhead joins us. She looks vaguely familiar, but I don't think we've ever met. Unless I'm already tipsier than I realized and I'm forgetting faces.

"Get this, Harlow," Aidan's friend says. "Phillips is playing *trivia*."

Hearing her name solves the mystery. *She's Conor Hart's girlfriend*, I realize. She was at the hockey party I went to with Chloe and Malia.

"Really?" Harlow looks intrigued. "I didn't know Gaffney's had trivia."

"Where's Hart?" Aidan asks abruptly.

"Outside, on the phone with his mom," Harlow replies. "Which reminds me, game recap, please. I was supposed to watch it, but the meeting with my thesis advisor ran long and then Eve had this art project crisis, so all I know is that you guys won. Did Conor get a goal?"

"Yep," Aidan's friend says.

I'm gathering he's also on the team, but I don't recognize him. I do wonder if *extremely attractive* is a requirement for being on Holt's hockey team. Where the hell is my dad recruiting all these hot guys from?

"And an assist. But first star goes to this guy." He punches Aidan's shoulder. "Two goals and an assist. Phillips is making the rest of us look bad."

Two goals and an assist?

I was planning to check on the score of today's game. For my dad...and because I was curious about how Aidan played. But I haven't yet. And I'm oddly...relieved, knowing they not only won, but it wasn't the letdown Aidan was worried about.

"Been doing that for years, Morgan," Aidan replies. Then, surprisingly, he glances at me. "Don't look so shocked."

Harlow and Hunter—I remember a Hunter Morgan from the game I went to last weekend, so I'm assuming that's his first name—look at me, wearing identical expressions of surprise.

They obviously thought I was just randomly standing here

waiting to order a drink, not that Aidan was here because he was badgering me.

"I'm not shocked," I tell him.

And I'm not. I know he's capable of a lot more than he chooses to show the majority of the time.

Aidan holds eye contact, a furrow deepening between his eyes the longer we stare at each other.

His friend clears his throat. "Hey. I'm Hunter. I don't think we've met before…"

"Rylan," I supply.

"Rylan," he repeats. There's no spark of recognition on his face, just confusion.

"I'm Harlow," the redhead says, flashing me a friendly smile. "Nice to meet you, Rylan."

"You too," I tell her.

"Rylan studied abroad at Oxford last semester," Aidan says.

I glance at him, totally taken aback. First of all, I never specified *which* school I attended in London. Either that was a lucky guess or he looked me up on social media to find that out. And secondly, why is he mentioning it now?

I get the answer a few seconds later, when Harlow lights up. "Really? That's amazing! I would *love* to study in London. I was just in Ireland for part of winter break. Some of my dad's family lives just outside of Dublin."

"My program did a trip to Galway," I tell her. "It was gorgeous."

"I haven't been to Galway, but it's on my list. I've heard amazing things." Harlow is fully turned toward me now, her expression animated. "Where else did you go?"

"In Ireland? Cork. And we did some trips around Scotland and Wales as well. Edinburgh was my favorite."

Harlow nods eagerly. "Was the weather terrible?"

"Not too bad, actually. And I'm used to rain, from growing up here."

"You grew up in Somerville?" She looks—and sounds—surprised.

That's been the typical reaction from most of the people I've told, but there hasn't been any of the derision or scorn I was worried about. The *You stayed here?* look.

"Yeah. My dad got a job here when I was five. We've lived here ever since."

"What does your dad do?" she asks.

I resist the urge to look at Aidan. "He, uh, he coaches the hockey team."

"Oh, *fuck*," Hunter says, which is encouraging. "You're Phillips's freshman tutor?"

I raise both eyebrows, then glance at Aidan. "I'm a junior."

"Coach told me you were a new student," Aidan explains. "I just assumed that meant—"

"What are you guys doing over here?" Conor Hart appears, his dark hair visibly wet. It must be raining out, which sucks because I was planning on walking home.

"Meeting Phillips's tutor," Hunter answers.

Conor focuses on me, his eyes a stormy blue. Despite his intense gaze, the smile he offers is friendly. "Oh. Hey. I'm Conor."

I smile back. "Nice to meet you. I'm Rylan."

An awkward pause falls.

It's obvious Conor has put together I'm his coach's daughter, same as Hunter did. Neither of them seem to know how to navigate that.

"What can I get you guys?"

Finally, the bartender appears.

"Two—" Hunter stops talking.

I glance at Hunter to figure out why, but he's looking at Aidan.

"What are you getting?" Aidan asks me, ignoring his friend.

"I can order my own drink."

"Yeah, that's what I'm asking you to do."

We have another uncomfortable stare-off. Extra uncomfortable because I feel multiple sets of eyes on us.

"Vodka cranberry," I decide.

I don't care that they're common and considered basic. They taste good.

"Didn't you already have a beer?" Aidan asks.

"Did I ask for your input?" I snap.

"*Beer before liquor, never been sicker* is a saying, is all."

More staring.

Aidan sighs. "She'll have a vodka cranberry, and I'll take a pint of whatever you recommend on tap."

The bartender nods, then disappears.

"You're not getting your *usual*?" The snide question is out before I can swallow it.

"A pint of whatever is on tap is my usual, Alice."

"*Don't* call me that."

"Sorry," he says, not sounding the least bit apologetic.

I huff.

More uncomfortable silence.

"What do you think of Holt so far?" Harlow asks me.

I send her a smile that I hope conveys my gratitude. I'm stuck here until my drink arrives and I'd rather talk to Harlow than argue with Aidan or stand around in awkwardness. "It's been great."

"I can't believe that this is my last semester." Harlow's voice is wistful. "I'm jealous you have a whole year left."

"Why? Your junior year sucked," Conor says.

"How would you know?" Harlow responds. "You were ignoring me back then."

Conor grins. "Exactly."

Harlow rolls her eyes, but she's smiling.

"How long have you guys been together?" I ask.

Harlow says, "About a month" at the same time Conor says, "Twenty-four days."

Then he whispers something to Harlow that has her blushing.

"I have extra earplugs, if you need them," Aidan tells Hunter.

"Shut up, Phillips," Conor says.

The bartender returns with our drinks, mine maroon and Aidan's amber. He pays before I even have the chance to pull out my card.

Any other guy, and I'd say *Thanks*.

But that seems to be a harder word to tell Aidan.

I don't know why. Something about feeling uneven in comparison to him. He throws me off-kilter effortlessly, and so I'm always struggling to keep the balance. Trying to prove I'm unaffected, so I overcompensate into aloofness.

And Aidan turns to talk to Hunter before I can say anything at all. Maybe buying my drink was his idea of an apology for ignoring me earlier.

"Do you, uh, do you know those guys over there?" I ask Harlow, nodding toward the pool table.

She follows my gaze, looking away so quickly she might as well have just been casually glancing around. Way more suave than I could have managed.

"A couple of them," she tells me. "You interested?"

"I had a rough break-up, and I'm at a new school where I know about ten people. So...maybe."

Harlow smiles, then steps closer and lowers her voice. "I had Gen Chem with the guy leaning against the wall. Ninety-five percent certain his name is Ryker." She makes an apologetic face. "Sorry, I'm not always great with names. And then the one shooting right now is Finn...Ashford, I think? He's on the soccer team."

"Okay. Thanks." I chew on the inside of my cheek, debating whether I have the nerve to go over there or not.

"You want a wingwoman?"

"You don't have to..."

"I'd *love* to. Hanging with the same hockey crowd gets old. Plus..." She leans closer. "It'll piss Conor off, and I like to keep him on his toes."

"Bring my drink over to the pool table, Hart," she calls out, then links our arms together and pulls me in that direction.

There's some commotion behind us as we walk away, but I don't look back as Harlow leads the way. The guys notice our approach one by one, a combination of interest and apprehension obvious on their faces.

"Hey, Harlow." The guy Harlow said she had a class with—Ryker—glances behind us. "Would you happen to know why half the hockey team is glaring at me right now, by chance?"

"They're intense guys, Ryker. Just ignore them," Harlow tells him.

He doesn't correct her, so it seems like she was right about his name.

"Should I also ignore how Hart is walking this way, looking like he'd love to murder me?"

"Definitely," she replies. "He's just delivering my drink."

"Oh-kay," Ryker says, then glances at me. "Hey. You wanna play some pool?"

I nod. "But I have no clue how to."

"That's cool. We're just fooling around. C'mere, I'll show you."

Harlow gives me an encouraging look, then holds out her hand. "I'll watch your drink."

"Thank you." I take a large gulp of crimson liquid, then hand it over.

Ryker holds out a hand as I approach. "I'm Ryker."

I shake it, smiling. "Rylan."

He smiles back. "Cute. We kinda match."

Alice and Aidan. We're adorable.

I ban his voice from my head, where it doesn't belong.

Instead, I force the grin to remain on my face. "Just a warning. Not only have I never played pool before, but I'm generally uncoordinated."

Ryker laughs. "We'll make it work. Okay, to start…"

I make the mistake of glancing up right as Ryker starts to explain the rules. Conor has reached this corner, so Harlow is now double-fisting two drinks. She's also looking up at the hockey player hovering protectively over her like he's oxygen and stardust. Necessary and magical.

"Sorry," I say, interrupting Ryker. "Do you mind if I run to the bathroom before we start playing?"

"Yeah, no problem," he tells me. "I'll be here."

"'Kay. I'll be right back."

I pass Harlow, mouthing *bathroom* when she quirks a brow at me. She nods.

Isla is sitting at the same table when I walk by the back section. Clayton is still seated next to her. I catch her eye as I pass by, pointing toward the restrooms in case she wants to talk.

For once, there's no line in the women's restroom. I pee quickly, and am washing my hands when Isla walks in.

"Hey," she tells me. "Everything okay?"

"I wanted to ask you the same. There was a huge line at the bar and then these guys at the pool table…"

"Not much of a girls' night, right?" Isla says, smiling.

"We can still make it one. It seemed like you were into Clayton, so I wanted to give you guys some space, if you wanted it." I keep my selfish motivations of getting away from Aidan to myself.

Isla blushes. "I want it. As long as that's okay with you?"

"Of course. We can get lunch or coffee sometime soon, finish catching up."

"I'd love that." She hugs me, then quickly glances at her reflection in the mirror. Releases a giddy sigh that I'm jealous of. "Night!"

"Night," I reply, even though she's already halfway out the door. Dry my hands as slowly as possible, then pat my nose and forehead with a dry paper towel to get rid of any oil.

I'm stalling.

Because I'm attracted to Ryker, but I'm not giddy around him. There were no butterflies. I didn't wonder what he thought of my outfit. If he showed up somewhere and ignored me, I doubt I'd care.

Basically, my body doesn't react to him the way it responds to Aidan Phillips, and that pisses me off. But the only solution I can come up with is to go back out there and fake it.

Sulking in here about whatever weird chemistry attracts me to Aidan isn't going to fix anything.

I open the bathroom door and swallow the swear that wants to spew out.

It might not have fixed anything, but remaining in the restroom would have avoided this.

Aidan is leaning against the wall opposite the restrooms, his arms crossed casually. The pose seems deliberate, the rest of his body humming with tension. "That's your type?" he asks me. "*Pool* players?"

My chin tilts defiantly. "Maybe."

"Which game do you prefer? Blackball or eight-ball?"

I have no idea what the hell he's talking about, and that's probably obvious on my face. I'm buzzed, my cheeks warm and my reactions slow.

Aidan scoffs, then shakes his head. "Is this about your ex? You're trying to get over him?"

I got over Walker a year ago—when we broke up—but I don't say that. "It's about *me*. I might have grown up in Somerville, but everything else is new to me. New school, new people. I'm trying to fit in. To finally have some *fun*, which I thought you, of all people, would get."

"Me, of all people? What the hell is that supposed to mean?"

"You know *exactly* what it means."

He shoves away from the wall, towering over me and blocking the way back into the bar. I'm five eight, not exactly short. But with an angry, six-three Aidan inches away, I feel tiny.

"What *exactly* does it mean, Rylan?"

Stubbornly, I hold his gaze. "Six girls, Aidan. And I know you weren't a virgin when we hooked up. Are you really going to judge me for *playing pool* with a guy when we both know you've fucked most of this campus? What kind of sexist double standard is that?"

"I'm not judging you. But good to know that *you're* judging *me*." His tone is sharp and annoyed.

"Stick your little dick wherever you want. Doesn't make any difference to me."

Okay, I'm drunker than I thought. But I don't take any of it back.

Aidan's eyes flash like they're lit with green fire as he reaches out and runs his thumb along my bottom lip, the rough pad igniting all my sensitive nerves.

I quiver, everything that was missing with Ryker rushing in. All the giddiness and dizziness and awareness. The butterflies and the weak knees. They drown out my annoyance that it's all happening with *him*, of all people.

"This *fucking* mouth." He growls the words with a fierceness that settles low in my belly. I resist the urge to shiver.

Instead I step back, out of his reach. "Get out of my way."

"No." He remains in place, blocking the exit.

My jaw sets. "I mean it, Aidan. The overbearing asshole act might work on some girls, but not on me."

"It's not an act," he tells me. "You want to hook up and *have fun*? Fine. Do it with me."

I'm tempted. Very tempted. But my pride—plus the small part of my brain that's thinking logically—won't let me give in.

It was one thing before I knew who he was. Now, I have no excuse. I'm tutoring him. He's on the hockey team. And…he's in a different league. An experienced player who has slept with more people since we hooked up a few weeks ago than I've ever been with.

I lift my chin, glaring at him. "I told you—I'm *not interested.*"

"Bullshit," he says.

"You're one of my dad's players."

"So? *I'm* not going to tell him anything."

I scoff. "You're not worried he's going to find out and kick you off the team?"

My dad wouldn't do that. But I doubt Aidan knows that for certain.

"Do I look worried?" Aidan leans closer, erasing the small amount of space I put between us. "I haven't told anyone what happened in that hot tub. I can keep a secret."

"I'll see you on Tuesday." I push past him, relieved when he lets me pass by. And a little bit disappointed, which I quickly quash.

He'll lose interest soon.

Move on to someone else.

I'm not interested in standing in line behind all the other girls on this campus who want to fuck him.

At least, that's what I tell myself as I head for the pool table.

CHAPTER THIRTEEN

AIDAN

I'm jealous.

Jealous.

Because of a girl.

I didn't realize what this simmering annoyance was right away. Not until I was already over at the table talking to Rylan's friend, trying to figure out why Thomas sitting across from my tutor pissed me off so much. To the point that I ditched my teammates and signed up to play trivia.

Until I experienced the rush of relief, discovering I'd misread the situation and Clayton was interested in Rylan's friend.

Fucking idiot.

I'm fully on board the *Fuck Thomas* train now, right next to Hart. I don't see any more buddy-buddy bathroom chats in our future.

And I'm *still* jealous. The aggravation has only gotten worse, watching her laugh at something a guy with slicked back hair holding a cue stick says. I have no clue who he is. If I did, I would have come up with a better reason to warn Rylan away from him than that he plays pool.

I stand and head for the bar again, ignoring the guys who call out to me with drink requests. When the bartender reaches me, I just order water.

As much as I'd love to get wasted, I drove here. And Conor said it's pouring out, so I'd rather not have to walk home. Plus, who the hell knows what I would do drunk. I cornered Rylan by the restrooms after one beer, basically begging her to hook up again.

I don't do that shit. If a girl I hooked up with moves on to another guy, I'm relieved. That is, if I even notice she has.

I don't sulk or mope or fantasize about bodychecking a guy whose name I don't even know into the boards.

Even more pathetically, my eyes keep ending up on her as if there's some magnetic attraction to the spot where she's standing. Each time I hope she's ditched the guy, instead of being glad she's moving on from her asshole of an ex. Rylan's right—I've hooked up with plenty of girls. I'm in absolutely no position to dictate how she spends her Thursday night.

Still...I keep glancing over there, hoping something's changed. That she'll look upset or uncomfortable, and I'll have an excuse to go over and start shit. Start *more* shit, I mean.

Nope. She's waving her arms around, and the guy's grinning at her like he just won the goddamn lottery.

"Did you already order?" Harlow appears, shoving into the small space between me and the girl next to me, who keeps glancing over here.

"Yes." My response is short.

I'm irritated at Harlow, for no reason except she was the one who initiated the introduction with the guy currently checking out Rylan's tits.

So what if she's smiling at another guy?

So what if she's pissed at me again?

I. Don't. Care.

Except...I do.

"No problem. I'll wait." Harlow remains beside me. "Everything okay?"

I paste a smile on my face as she glances this way. "Of course. Just tired from the game earlier."

"Conor said you're headed home this weekend?"

"Yeah." I clear my throat, sneaking another glance at Rylan. Still standing by the guy. Still smiling.

"Not looking forward to it?"

I exhale. Shake my head. But I don't offer more details.

Both because I don't feel like talking about it and because I know Harlow's parents passed away, so complaining about my awful yet alive ones feels insensitive.

And I'm not used to having conversations about anything important with a chick. I don't have friends who are girls. Another thing Parker ruined.

"Conor told me you spent break telling him to talk to me."

The abrupt conversation shift captures more of my attention.

"He was listening, huh? It was like having a conversation with a brick wall," I tell her. "But yeah. I'm happy you guys worked it out."

"Me too." Harlow leans closer. "And I'm only mentioning it because I don't want you to think I'm sticking my nose in your love life for no reason."

I snort. "What love life?"

Harlow glances in the direction I keep looking. "You like her. Rylan."

"Sure, I like her," I say. "She's my tutor."

Harlow rolls her eyes. "No, I mean you *like* her. You're into her."

"No, I'm not."

"And you're mad at me for introducing her and Ryker."

Ryker. What a dumb name.

And Harlow's annoyingly perceptive. Neither Hunter nor Conor would have worked that out so quickly.

"I'm not mad at you," I lie.

I shouldn't be, at least. No question it's totally misplaced.

"Ask her on a date," Harlow advises me.

I scoff. "I don't do that shit."

Harlow shakes her head. "Do you hockey players all attend the same commitment-phobe class?"

Probably. It's called easy pussy. Tying yourself down to one girl when dozens want to fuck you is just dumb decision-making. But I can't tell Hart's girl that.

"I'm not interested in a relationship," I say instead.

"Why not?"

"I'm just not. And…bad experience," I admit.

Harlow's expression softens. "I'm sorry."

"It's fine. She's marrying my brother."

I haven't told anyone at Holt about my fucked-up romantic past. And it's worth the impulsive confession just to see Harlow blanche.

"Fuck."

I laugh. "Yeah."

Harlow recovers. "That doesn't seem like something Rylan would do."

"*Could* do," I correct. "I only have the one brother."

She shakes her head, looking vaguely disappointed.

"How are classes going?" It's all I can think to ask her about, and I'm eager to stop discussing Rylan.

Harlow raises one eyebrow. "You're asking me about school?"

"Yep."

Most of what I'd normally talk to a girl in a bar about doesn't work when the girl in question is my best friend's girlfriend.

"They're good. I'm stressed about my thesis, but…"

"What's your thesis about?"

All I know is that Harlow is a marine biology major and loves whales. Hart was watching a documentary on humpbacks one night, and I ended up staying for most of it. It was way more interesting than I was expecting.

"I think I've settled on the influence diet quality has on divergent population trends in local harbor seals."

"That's cool," I say, pretending I have any clue what that means.

All I really heard was seal diet. So, what they eat? Her thesis is about fish?

Harlow cracks a smile, then nods in the direction of the door. "She's leaving."

I spin around to look.

Sure enough, Rylan is moving toward the crowd headed in the direction of the door. There's no sign of the guy she was with—thank fuck—or her friend from earlier. She isn't looking this way, the tilt of her chin in the opposite direction of the bar so severe it looks purposeful.

I'm positive she's still pissed at me. Still wants nothing to do with me.

"I'm going to head out," I say, pretending not to notice Harlow's knowing smile. "Tell Conor I'll see him at home?"

"I'll tell him," Harlow says, before I follow Rylan.

I never got my water, but whatever. Maybe Harlow will want it.

Rylan is fast. I'm hustling to catch up, weaving around people trying to get my attention. I ignore them all, my focus on the brunette slipping out the door.

It's raining out, steady sheets falling from the black sky.

After just a few steps, my hair is plastered to my forehead.

"Rylan!" I call.

She keeps walking, so I jog after her and grab her elbow.

Rylan spins, her hand cocked in a fist. It falls when she realizes it's me. I'm half-surprised she doesn't follow through on the swing.

"Easy, slugger," I say.

"What did I tell you about sneaking up on me?" she snaps.

"You're planning to walk home in this?" I ask.

Her silence answers for her.

"Let me drive you." I shout the offer, basically, over the pounding deluge of rain.

"No."

"Then I'm going to walk with you, possibly get hypothermia, and we'll definitely lose the championship. You want that on your conscience, just because you're stubborn?"

Rylan's expression doesn't change, not even the slightest glimmer of amusement.

Yeah, she's definitely still pissed at me.

I exhale. "I'm sorry about earlier, okay? I was out of line."

"You think?"

At least she's talking to me, even if it's drowning in sarcasm.

"I won't say a word in the car, I swear. Even if you start ragging on my stats again. It's just a ride home."

"There's less to rag on now," she tells me.

Practically a gushing compliment, coming from her.

"Please?" I plead.

Rylan hesitates, the indecision visible on her face even through the falling rain.

Then there's a loud clap of thunder in the distance, and she caves.

"Fine."

I nod, then start walking toward where my truck is parked before she can change her mind.

"*This* is your car?" She literally stops, despite the rain, to stare.

If Hart were here, he'd be bent over laughing.

"Yep."

Technically, we're not in the car yet. And she asked me a question, so it seems better to answer than to keep my vow of silence going.

I unlock the truck, then climb into the driver's seat.

A few seconds later, Rylan climbs into the passenger side and slumps back against the seat. Her wet clothes squeak against the leather.

I start the truck, then turn the heat up to the maximum so warm air blasts out of the vents. Carefully, I back out of the spot and then pull out of the lot onto the main street that runs through downtown Somerville.

Between the screech of the wipers as they work to clear the windshield and the blare of air, it's not silent in the car, even though neither of us is saying anything. I also reach out and flip on the stereo, so the radio starts to play. My phone normally connects automatically, but it hasn't, and I'm not going to play around with it while Rylan is in the car.

At the end of the block, she asks, "Did something happen during the game earlier?"

I guess we're talking.

"Yeah. I kicked ass."

She snorts. "You've spent tonight acting like you lost."

I can't tell her the real reason for my bad mood—it has way too much to do with her. So instead I say, "I'm going home tomorrow."

A pause, like she's deliberating whether to keep the conversation going. "Where's home?"

"LA," I answer.

"You grew up there?"

"Yeah. Palm Springs."

"Sunny."

I smile. "Yeah."

"You're not close with your family."

She says it as more of a statement than a question, but I shake my head anyway.

"So…why are you going home?"

I didn't plan for it to go this far. Didn't expect her to ask. But she did, so I tell her.

"My older brother is getting married this summer. The engagement party is on Saturday. My parents care a lot about appearances, so they're insisting I be there for the whole happy family act."

"That sounds awkward."

I flick on the blinker to turn onto her street. Wish Rylan didn't know Somerville so well that she'd notice if I circled the block a few times to extend this trip. The whole cab smells like her shampoo or perfume, something floral and feminine. It's nice, whatever the scent is.

"Not as awkward as my brother marrying my ex." I keep my eyes on the road instead of watching her reaction. This feels very different than telling Harlow.

"Anti-hot tub sex girl?"

I snort a laugh as Rylan manages to surprise me once again.

I was expecting to spend this ride in uncomfortable silence, not laughing as we discuss Parker. "Yeah."

"Her loss."

I don't ask if she means choosing my brother over me or missing out on hot tub sex.

I'd like to think it's the former, but who knows? That night, Rylan made it clear she was only looking for a rebound from her ex. If Jameson had been the one in the hot tub when she wandered into the yard instead of me, maybe she still would have climbed in.

She doesn't ask me any more questions, but the quiet doesn't feel uneasy. More…comfortable.

A few seconds later, she starts humming along to the song on the radio. I glance at the screen to see the song name. It's "Brown Eyed Girl" by Van Morrison.

Rylan catches the movement. "I love this song," she confesses softly. "My dad used to sing it to me when I was little."

"Coach K sings?"

"Not well, but yeah." She's angled toward me now, her head resting back but tilted in my direction.

I don't think she's realized we're parked in front of her house. It looks like a brown blur from here, the rain still coming down heavily.

Any other girl, I'd think about leaning in. But she's shot me down twice now. I'm not making another move unless she does first.

"Do you have any good memories with your dad?"

Any other person, I wouldn't answer. "He took me to my first hockey game."

"How old were you?"

"Eight."

"And you loved it right away?"

I nod. "Yeah. Surest I've ever felt about anything. I'm not obsessed with it the way Hart is. His dream would be to only take skates off to sleep and to fu—" I cough, and she smirks. "I like skating. But my favorite thing about hockey is being part of the team. It's not like anything else. Hunter and Conor are my best friends, but we're way closer because we're teammates too."

"Did your brother play hockey too?"

I snort. "No. Too lowbrow for him. No one makes business deals between knocking teeth out. He played tennis in college. Golfs now."

"Lame."

"Agreed."

She holds my gaze. The air around us seems to thicken, transparency gaining shape and substance.

Rain keeps coming down as a man's voice croons about sunlight and rainbows.

Rylan breaks eye contact first, glancing out and startling when she realizes we've stopped. That we've *been* stopped.

She reaches toward her seat belt, fumbling with the buckle. I reach out to help her, my fingers brushing against her knuckles. As soon as we touch, she freezes.

The seat belt unsnaps with a loud *click*.

"Thanks," she says.

"No problem."

She tugs her sleeves down, covering her hands.

I take a deep breath. "I *am* sorry about earlier. Won't happen again."

"It's fine."

I can't gauge anything from her tone. If it's *really* fine or if she's just saying that.

Another deep breath. "I won't be around this weekend, but if you're wanting to have fun… There will be a hockey party next weekend. I can introduce you to a few decent guys, if you want."

The offer burns like acid on the way out.

But if she's looking for a hookup, I'd rather it be with a guy who will treat her well. I hear most of the gossip on this campus, stuff Rylan wouldn't necessarily know.

Instead of responding, she asks, "How long will you be in LA for?"

Rather than tell her the truth—that my dad arranged for my trip to last less than twenty-four hours, I say, "Sorry to disappoint, but I'll be back for tutoring on Tuesday."

"I'm not disappointed," she says. Then opens the door and hops out. "Night, Aidan."

She's running through the rain toward her house before I can say "Night" back.

Or ask her what the fuck *not disappointed* means.

CHAPTER FOURTEEN

AIDAN

This is even worse than I was expecting.

I knew my parents would go all out tonight. My mom has dreamed of snagging Parker as a daughter-in-law since she knew her best friend was having a girl.

Lucky for her, my mother had *two* sons for her best friend's daughter to choose between. And I'm sure she's happy Jameson is the one Parker settled on.

I can't picture myself in his place anyway, standing by the stage that contains an eight-piece orchestra. *If* I get married, which is a big if, this isn't what the engagement party will look like. Doubt I'd even have an engagement party. As far as I can tell, it's totally unnecessary. Just an excuse to spend a bunch of money on flowers and food and clothes before spending even more money on flowers and food and clothes for the wedding.

I tug at the constrictive collar of my shirt, then take another swig of scotch. The only reason I'd ever be excited about dressing up is if it was for an away game.

The open bar is the one upside I've discovered about this

evening so far. And I'm remaining close by it, because I have a feeling I'll need to.

I arrived in LA a couple of hours ago, and I'm ready to leave. Even the sunshine and dry air aren't enough of an enticement to stay. I had to miss afternoon practice to make my flight and my phone has been buzzing incessantly with messages about parties taking place tonight. All places I'd rather be.

Somerville is home now.

Not...this. Even if I wasn't here for the reason I am, I'd be just as miserable. All of my friends are away at school, so there's no one in town I want to hang out with.

I had an awkward reunion with my parents, which was expected. My dad was on a work call when the car they arranged from the airport dropped me off at my childhood home, and my mom was with two stylists having her hair done for tonight.

After showering and eating a snack, I changed into the tux I'm wearing. Most of the long trip here was my parents coordinating on who they'd talk to tonight, while I stared out the window at the standstill traffic. A five-mile drive took almost an hour.

I haven't spoken to Jameson yet. Or Parker. Just observed them from afar, playing the part of the happy couple. I know them both well enough to see through the fake smiles.

"Aidan! How are you?"

I straighten to shake the hand of my father's friend. "I'm good, thanks. Nice to see you, Mr. Mitchell."

"Michael, please." He smiles before ordering a drink from the bartender, then turns back to me. "How's school going?"

"Fine, thanks."

Not a lie for once, thanks to my recent studious streak. I caught up with all my reading on the three-hour flight here.

"And hockey?"

I grin. "Great. We should have a shot at a championship."

"That's fantastic. Lincoln mentioned you were having a great season."

I could have quit the hockey team freshman year and my father would have no clue. He's never been to a game or asked me about the team. As far as he knows, they've all been "great seasons."

But I'm here to play a part too, and it's not the role of a resentful son complaining to one of my father's friends and business associates that my dad doesn't give a shit about what makes me happy and considers hockey a waste of time.

"We are."

"Have you given any thought to what you'll do after graduation?"

I shake my head instead of bullshitting an answer like I probably should.

Michael Mitchell is a big deal, according to my father. If my dad was standing here, he would be flashing his widest, false smile and making something up about how I have so many opportunities to choose between but am keeping my options open.

"I'm always looking for new talent. Just say the word and I can put in a good one for you." He winks, pulling a business card out of his pocket and passing it to me.

I'm not sure exactly what Michael does, but I do know he's quite successful at it.

I also know I don't want to use my family's connections to get ahead.

"Appreciate that, sir," I say, tucking the card into my pocket.

"I should go say hi to the Andersons," he tells me. "Good luck with the rest of your season, Aidan. I'm sure I'll see you at the wedding."

I nod and force a smile, unable to muster a more enthusiastic response to the reminder.

Once Michael leaves, I ask the bartender for a refill. Drop a hefty tip into his jar and then abandon my spot, heading for the terrace that overlooks the ocean. I get stopped several times by friends of my family's, but finally make it to the door.

The party is at some fancy restaurant that's a favorite of my parents. I'm not a fan of the food here, which is filled with weird, exotic ingredients, but the view from this place is incredible. The sun set over the sparkling water a while ago, the lights from the restaurant now reflecting off the waves.

I step outside, pulling in a deep inhale of salty air as I walk toward the railing. It's warmer here than it was when I left Washington this morning, hovering in the high fifties. And still, I can't wait to get home.

I stare out at what little I can see of the water, entertaining the idea of going for a swim.

Enjoy imagining the looks on my parents' faces if I returned to the party with wet hair, smelling like seaweed.

"You lost me a hundred bucks, you know."

I turn, my fingers automatically tightening around the glass I'm holding as I watch Parker stroll toward me.

She looks absolutely stunning, her blonde hair styled elaborately and her makeup flawless. The pink gown she's wearing literally glimmers, only outshined by the massive diamond dwarfing her ring finger.

But something about her beauty bothers me in a way it never did before.

It's all manufactured, even the white fur wrapped around her shoulders suggesting pure innocence.

Her tone is calculated instead of unfiltered. Soft and melodic, meant to entice.

I can't recognize the pretty girl who used to chase me around my parents' backyard laughing and barefoot anywhere in her appearance, and it adds some sadness to the resentment.

Without asking, I know what she bet on.

"You should know Lincoln better than that," I tell her. "I could have been dying in a ditch somewhere and he would have dragged me out, shoved me into this tux, and ensured I ended up here."

"You look good for being grievously injured."

I don't pay her any compliments, just sip some scotch.

"It's nice to see you."

Again, I don't respond.

Her head tilts strategically as she studies me. "Jameson said you had fun in Vail."

I scoff, then take another drink. At this rate, I'll need another refill in a few minutes. "So did he."

I'm sure she knows he's fucking around on the side.

Sure enough, Parker's expression doesn't change. "How's school?"

"Can we skip the small talk?"

"Sure. What are you doing after this?"

"Flying home."

"Your mom said you're not leaving until tomorrow morning."

"Yeah, so?"

"So, what are you doing *tonight*? We could meet in the pool house…"

I stare at her, sure I'm misunderstanding. That she's not suggesting what I think she's suggesting.

But I'm not reading her wrong.

Parker takes a step closer, the look on her face one I've seen many times before.

"You're delusional," I tell her.

"I'm *practical*, Aidan. Marrying Jameson makes sense. But I'm not in love with him. It would be just like before—"

"*Nothing* is like before, Parker. Little tip? If you want to hook up with a guy, don't break up with him, then get engaged to his brother. What the fuck is wrong with you?"

"It was more complicated than that," she tells me.

I shake my head. "Maybe you want to remember things differently now, but that's what happened then."

"So I messed up. Is that what you want me to say?"

"I don't want you to say *anything* to me. I wish I could never see you again, but you made damn sure I'd have to, didn't you?"

Parker moves closer. More of her mask falls. Or maybe she's just swapping it for a different one, biting her bottom lip and fluttering her eyelashes. "Remember how good it was between us?"

Jesus. I was not prepared for this. I was expecting to have the happy couple act shoved down my throat, same as it's been every other time I've been forced to be around Parker and Jameson since they started dating. Not for her to start walking down memory lane and expect me to follow.

"You're marrying my brother," I remind her. "We're at your engagement party."

"I know."

"*Do you*? Because it kinda seems like you forgot."

"I just…you came." She looks young, all of sudden. But not happy, like in my memories.

"Because of *Jameson*, not you. And yeah, it was good between us. We were kids, and it was easy. You ended it, Parker. *Years* ago. Get over it, because I did. I'm never going to touch you again. If you're miserable, that's not my fault or my problem."

I step back, adjusting the buttons of my jacket the way Jameson always does before dismissing someone. Based on the way Parker's left eye twitches, she doesn't appreciate the reminder of her fiancé.

"I'm not miserable," she snaps.

"Great," I drawl. "Is Nicole single? She's one of your bridesmaids, right? I always thought she was hot."

"I have no idea," Parker replies airily.

Lies, I'm sure.

I leave her standing alone and walk back inside the restaurant, draining the rest of my glass in one gulp.

I *should* find Nicole. She hit on me a lot back when Parker and I were together, which is why I mentioned her name specifically.

Hell, any hot girl here would be a welcome distraction from this shitty evening.

But instead of searching out company, I decide to head straight for the exit.

"Aidan!"

I swear under my breath, my steps barely slowing as my father calls out my name.

His footsteps sound a second later, his dress shoes slapping a sharp staccato against the marble floor.

I sigh and turn, stuffing my fisted hands into my pockets.

"Where are you going?" my father demands.

We look a lot alike, my dad and I. Same light brown hair. Same green eyes. Same height. I'm practically a carbon copy of him, whereas Jameson is more a mix of our parents. Ironic, considering Jameson is identical to him in every other way. I've seen the same polite scowl my dad is aiming at me on my brother's face before.

He already knows the answer, but it's not a rhetorical question.

"I'm leaving," I respond. "Gotta get a good night's sleep before the early as fuck flight your assistant booked me on."

"We're hosting tonight," he tells me. "It's rude to leave before the guests."

"I showed up. I wore the tux. I ate the gross food. I laughed at all the stupid jokes. What else do you want from me, Dad?"

"Leaving early wasn't the deal, Aidan."

"Negotiate the terms better next time then. I'll see you at the wedding. Assuming you and Mom won't make it to graduation, since none of your snobby friends will be there to judge your parenting."

"Watch your mouth," he snaps. "You are part of this family, and tonight is about supporting your brother."

"He's marrying my ex-girlfriend. You don't see how that could be kinda awkward?"

"You and Parker dated as children. She and Jameson are a serious couple."

Based on the conversation we had out on the terrace, I'd be willing to bet my trust fund that my *childish* relationship with Parker was a hell of a lot more serious than hers and Jameson's is. As far as I know, she never cheated while she was dating me.

But I know that's an argument I'll never win with my father, and I don't care enough to have it. I meant what I told Parker—I'm over her. I just resent how she's affected my relationship with my family. How I've heard some variation of what my dad just told me from my parents ever since they started dating and how it's a reminder they always prioritize Jameson over me.

"If you say so. I'm still leaving."

"Don't be selfish, Aidan."

"Coming from the man who threatened to cut me off if I didn't show up tonight. Who were you thinking about then, Dad? Not me."

His fake smile falters. He clears his throat, then adjusts his cufflinks. "You're making a scene, son."

"If I stay, I'll make a bigger one. Bar is still open, and I haven't met all of Parker's bridesmaids yet..."

My father clicks his tongue with disgust, then turns away. "Fine. Take the car, send the driver back after he drops you off."

Part of me wants to reject the dismissal and stay anyway. Do exactly what I just threatened to.

But I don't care enough. Riling up my dad is no longer the fun time it used to be. It seems like a waste of one now. I'd rather have none of his attention than more disappointment and disapproval. And I'm not petty enough to hook up with one of Parker's bridesmaids just to piss her off. Having sex with a random girl would be about trying to get Rylan out of my head.

"Yes, *sir*," I say.

My dad shakes his head at my sarcastic tone. "Grow up, Aidan," he says. "And roll down the windows on the drive home. You reek of scotch. I don't want to ride home in a car that smells like a distillery."

Before I leave the restaurant, I order one last glass. I drain half, then take it with me to the car and spill the rest in the footwell. Slump back against the soft leather seat, staring out at the city lights as we crawl down the street.

Tomorrow, I'll stop being spiteful.

Tomorrow, I'll grow up.

CHAPTER FIFTEEN

RYLAN

I 'm leaning against a computer terminal, talking to one of the girls in my Number Theory class, when I spot him strolling into the library.

There's a ripple in the air that maybe I'm imagining, but I don't think I am. A charged presence that I'm only aware of when he's near.

He spots me and heads this way, prompting a silly little flip in my stomach. Callie's eyes grow wider and wider as Aidan approaches us, his backpack casually slung over one shoulder and the Rockies cap he sometimes wears on backward.

"See you later, Rylan," she tells me, then scurries off.

I remain in place, resisting the urge to play with my hair or fiddle with the zipper of my jacket.

I've started putting more effort into my Tuesday outfits and stopped changing into sweats after my last class of the day. Today, I'm wearing my tightest pair of skinny jeans tucked into boots and a knit sweater that I bought in Scotland.

Aidan's eyes skim over my outfit as he nears, but there's no change in his expression.

He looks…subdued, wearing joggers, a gray Holt Hockey sweatshirt, and an exhausted expression. Even with dark circles under his eyes, he's annoyingly gorgeous.

Without asking, I know his trip home went as poorly as he expected it would go.

"Hey," I say when he reaches me.

He clears his throat. "Hey."

"Kinda busy down here. You good going upstairs again?"

"Sure."

Neither of us says a word as we walk over to the elevator.

I press the button, then chew on the inside of my cheek as I wait for the doors to open.

It's all fizzing inside of me—everything I was trying to feel over the weekend. I went out on Saturday night, taking advantage of knowing Aidan was in another state and there was no risk of running into him at a party.

Talked to a dozen guys.

Kissed one.

Went home alone.

And part of me has been in denial since Thursday night, thinking my reactions to Aidan at the bar and in his car were because of the booze.

But I'm stone cold sober now.

He's not looking at me. Not talking to me. I'm not even sure if he's happy to see me.

And it feels like fireworks are going off inside of me. Like the nerves under my skin are raw and exposed. Like my deep, even breaths aren't pulling in enough air.

My heartbeat is erratic, my palms sweaty.

Basically, I'm a mess.

At least Aidan appears oblivious to it. He waits for me to step into the elevator first, presses five, and then goes back to staring into space.

As soon as the elevator doors close, I ask, "How was the trip home?"

Partly to distract myself from the way my body's freaking out about being this close to him again. Mostly because I really want to know.

He sighs, cracking his knuckles. "Shitty. Highlight was the open bar and the view. My folks rented out a restaurant right on the water."

"Was it sunny?"

"Yeah. Weather was good."

Don't ask. Don't ask. Don't—

"Your ex was…there?"

Dammit. I asked.

"At *her* engagement party?" Aidan smirks. "Yeah. Parker was there."

That's all he says.

Since I've come this far, I prompt, "How was that?"

"Underwhelming," he replies.

I have no clue what to make of that answer.

Thankfully, he elaborates this time.

"She's changed. We grew up together. Our moms were—are—best friends, so Parker was always around. We played in the yard as kids. Got into trouble on vacations together. She used to be…" He shakes his head. "She used to hate all the fancy shit, same as me. They had an eight-piece orchestra at the party." Another head shake. "Fucking ridiculous."

"Did you talk to your brother?"

"Nope." He pops the P. "That was another highlight of the night, actually."

"What about your parents?" I ask as we step out of the

elevator and head for the same table as last time. "Did it go okay with them?"

I'm overstepping. He's here for tutoring, not a therapy session.

But I'm curious, and Aidan doesn't appear annoyed by the questions.

"We didn't talk much. My mom was so busy with the party, she barely noticed I was even there. Got into it with my dad when I left early, but I held up my end of the deal. He won't cut me off."

"Your dad said he'd *cut you off* if you didn't go to the party celebrating your brother marrying your ex-girlfriend?"

"Yeah." Aidan grins unexpectedly. "Bet your family's looking pretty normal right about now, huh?"

I mean…yeah.

His smile grows, like he knows what I'm thinking. "Don't worry, I know it's fucked up. If you ask my parents, it's my fault Parker dumped me, so I have no right to be upset."

"*She* dumped *you*?"

"Uh-huh." He's not looking at me, pulling his textbook out of his backpack and flipping through the pages. "After I picked Holt over Stanford."

"You got into Stanford?" I ask, stunned.

Aware that's a little harsh but also…he failed a class here. I'm doubting his high school grades were stellar.

Aidan looks up and smirks. "Ouch."

"Sorry. I didn't mean…"

"Money can buy most things," he tells me.

"I wouldn't know. My family doesn't have a ski chalet in Vail."

I hide the wince that wants to appear. I didn't mean to bring

Colorado up. Neither of us has mentioned it recently, and that's how it should stay.

"Your friend does, though," Aidan says, appearing unbothered by the mention.

"That was probably my only visit," I tell him. "Jess and I hung out a lot in London, but we've barely talked since break. She goes to school down in Georgia."

"What about your friends in Boston?"

"I've kept in touch with some of them. But it's awkward. I met most of them through Walker, my ex."

"The cheater?"

"Yeah. And his 'drunk mistake,' as he called it, was with a girl his friends were all friends with too. That added to the awkwardness."

"Is that why you transferred?" he asks.

"No. I was already unhappy in Boston, just too stubborn to admit I'd made a mistake going to school there. My parents did a lot to even make it an option...so transferring felt ungrateful, I guess."

"Are you happier here?"

I swallow, then nod. "Yeah."

"I think they'd be *grateful* for that."

I know he's right. My mom has been texting me at least once a day, asking for updates I'm sure she passes along to my dad, who's less communicative. Especially via technology. He rarely remembers to charge his cell phone.

They're thrilled I'm enjoying my classes and making new friends.

Telling Aidan that—bragging about how amazing my parents are after just establishing how shitty his are seems insensitive, though.

So I just nod.

"How was your weekend?" he asks.

"Uh...okay."

His gaze sharpens. "Just okay?"

"Uh-huh." I reach down, pulling the folder from Professor Carrigan out of my backpack and opening it. "Today is measures of variability and—"

"What'd you do?"

I play with the edge of the paper, avoiding his eyes. "Not much. Homework, went to the gym, laundry."

"Anything *fun*?"

I stiffen, not missing the emphasis. "I hung out with my roommates. We went to a party."

"You hook up with anyone?" he asks casually, like he's asking what I ate for dinner beforehand.

I glance up. Hold his gaze. "None of your business."

Aidan's jaw flexes. "Was it the party at the soccer house on Fore Street or the brick place on Transit Street?"

I don't respond, knowing exactly what he's doing.

He's proving he knows everything that happens on or off campus, even when he isn't here.

But the party we went to was on Lake Avenue, so he's clearly not as omniscient as he thinks...

"Must have been the one the tennis guys on Lake hosted. I heard that party was mostly juniors."

I glare at him before remembering I wasn't supposed to react.

"Party on Lake." Aidan nods, then leans forward. "What happened?"

It's hard to think—to even inhale or exhale—when he's studying me this closely. I look away, out at the lights illuminating the campus green.

It *is* none of his business, but he didn't tell me that once when I was the one asking the questions.

And…I like that he cares. Enough not only to ask, but to push for an actual answer.

"Nothing, really. I kissed a guy, and it was bad." I suppress a shudder, recalling the soft lapping. He was way drunker than I was. "I told him I had to use the bathroom but actually snuck out the back door."

Aidan leans back, one corner of his mouth curling upward as he drapes an arm over the back of the chair next to him. He looks…amused. "Sounds like you didn't try very hard to *have fun*."

"What do you consider trying hard?" I snap. "Should I have kissed every guy there?"

He lifts one eyebrow. "You're asking me how to have fun?"

"Guess so. I've heard you're good at it."

Aidan stares at me.

I stare back.

This silent moment seems important, somehow.

His fingers tap against the back of the chair as we continue studying each other, instead of anything related to Stats.

"I think that a girl who talks about her pussy as part of first introductions isn't looking for a drunk fumbling at a party. I think that a girl who wanders around the woods with a condom while she's trespassing wants something less predictable. I think that you were in a boring relationship with an asshole who didn't appreciate what he had. I think you're desperate for fun but don't know what you'll actually enjoy." Aidan shrugs, his heated gaze a total contrast to his casual posture. "But maybe I'm wrong."

He's not.

We continue looking at each other across the table, neither of us breaking eye contact. It feels a lot like when I first saw him in that hot tub.

What happens next is up to me.

None of the anxiety or uncertainty I experienced at the prospect of hooking up with the guy on Saturday night appears as I hold his gaze.

He's giving me an excuse to take what I want under the guise of preserving my pride. To show him I'm capable of being that girl he described. Of having fun and using him to do it, just like he told me to in the hallway at Gaffney's.

I've kissed two guys since Aidan, and neither experience was very enjoyable.

Even if it's half as good as it was in the hot tub, it'll be an improvement on anything else I've experienced.

We're on the fifth floor of the library, which most students don't bother to come up to. I haven't seen anyone else since we sat down.

I push my chair back to stand, part of me disbelieving I'm actually doing this—after promising myself it was a onetime thing—and the rest of me overwhelmed by excitement.

This is a bad idea.

I know it, passing ten aisles before turning down one.

He's a hockey player. The guy I'm tutoring. Experienced and noncommittal.

Not my type at all, and yet I haven't been able to stop thinking about him. Maybe this will shove him out of my head.

At the very least, I'll have another memory to recall the next time I worry I've wasted all of college being responsible and cautious.

I lean back against a shelf, watching him approach me. My entire body is tingling with a combination of anticipation and nerves.

There's no triumph on his face, but there is some surprise.

And that's a thrill—knowing that *I* surprised him. That I'm showing him Alice was a different name, not a different person.

Aidan's green eyes are bright, his lips tilted up into a devilish smirk as he stops and leans back against the shelf of books opposite me. Relaxed but ready.

We face off the same way we did at the table. The same way we did in the tub.

Except, some of my high ground is sinking. Since I found out some important details—where he goes to school and what sport he plays—I've pretended not to want this. An act he's seen through. But this is me admitting it was an act. That I *am* interested. That I *do* want him, despite the reasons I should stay far away.

"What's the plan, Rylan?" he asks.

His pose is casual and easy, like this is just another Tuesday evening for him. It probably is. He does this all the time. The thought is reassuring. This might matter to me, but it's simply another hookup for him.

"This was as far as I got," I admit.

I couldn't just keep sitting there.

But now… Do I kiss him? Touch him? Is he going to kiss me? Touch me?

Aidan smiles but it disappears quickly, his expression brimming with burning intensity that makes my stomach clench. "You wanna do this? Take it out," he tells me.

This is happening.

I push away from the book spines I'm leaning against and close the distance between us, reaching for his crotch and deliberately rubbing a palm over the bulge of his erection before I lose my nerve. He stiffens beneath my hand. At least I know he's not unaffected, no matter how laid-back he looks.

And he's so, so close. Smelling amazing and radiating more heat than a furnace.

I suck in a deep, fortifying breath, then slip my hand into the elastic waistband of his pants and close my fist around the heavy weight of his cock. Shiver, when my grip tightens but my fingers don't touch. Tug, so his cock juts free from the confines of the cotton.

The black boxer briefs Aidan is wearing underneath his joggers are generic.

But he's not.

He's *huge.*

I already knew that. I've seen it before. But this is different. There's no barrier of water or steam. We're standing beneath fluorescent, buzzing lights that expose everything. Even the pulse of the vein that runs the length of his shaft is visible under the harsh lighting.

I trace it with a finger and he hisses, thickening in my grip even more.

Aidan's dick is beautiful. I'm not sure that's the proper adjective to describe a penis, but his is. Straight, thick, and long, it looks like it should be the model for vibrators everywhere. I'm getting hot and achy just looking at it. He hasn't touched me, and I'm already so aroused I feel like I'm drugged. Anticipation is a powerful aphrodisiac.

"*Little,* isn't it?"

I smile at the annoyance in his voice, some of my nerves disappearing as I recall our conversation outside the bathroom.

He wants this—wants it from *me*—and he hasn't been shy about saying so. I'm not the only one who's been thinking about this happening again. That helps me shove away the insecurity about all the other blowjobs he's undoubtedly received. The worry I won't measure up.

"Suck."

It's a command, not a suggestion. And I like his bossiness far more than I'd ever admit to Aidan.

I sink down onto my knees, the rasp of gray carpet against denim the only sound that registers.

Then guide his cock to my mouth, slowly licking around the flared tip before sucking him in a few inches. There's an intimidating amount left, a lot more than I've had to accommodate before. I try to remember comments I've heard friends make about deep throating, inhaling through my nose as I flatten my tongue and try to take him deeper.

I want to please him, for Aidan to enjoy this.

He groans my name. My real name this time—Rylan—not Alice, which is what he called me during our last hookup.

I didn't realize there would be a difference until right now.

I'm doing this. Not some reckless version of myself who's in a strange place with a stranger, play-acting at being a girl who can act first and then think later.

The pulse between my legs turns into a painful throb. I've never gotten that turned on by giving a blowjob before. But I get a glimpse of the way he's looking down at me—eyes hooded and expression slack with pleasure—and it's an extreme high. A ridiculous rush.

The wet *pop* as I release his dick from my mouth sounds far too loud in the silent library. It seems to echo around us, noisy enough for anyone on this floor to hear. Adrenaline buzzes in my blood, the possibility of discovery adding a secret thrill.

I flick the slit at the tip with my tongue, then take him into the back of my throat, hollowing my cheeks so he feels the suction. Aidan's hips jerk forward, and I know he's fighting the urge to fuck my mouth. His hands are fisted at his sides, the sexy V between his hips clenched tight.

My hands land on his thighs, memorizing the feel of tensed muscle strained to stay still. I suck harder and Aidan grunts, his features tightening like he's in pain.

"I'm going to come," he warns.

I could pull away.

I've *always* pulled away at this point. Never seen the appeal of swallowing. It's always seemed gross. Unnecessary. He gets off either way.

But I don't move. I reach up to play with his balls, appreciating he's one of those guys who grooms and that there's not a bunch of coarse hair in the way.

Warm, salty spurts start to fill my mouth, startling me. His cocks swells even more, which I thought was impossible.

And I swallow, fighting the urge to cough, the ache between my legs growing worse as Aidan watches me with an intoxicating combination of pride and possessiveness.

Arousal courses through me, knowing I'm responsible for that satisfied look on his face.

And then, the distinctive *ding* of elevator doors opening registers. The thrill of getting caught gets replaced by the terror of that actually taking place.

Reality rushes in.

I'm on my knees in the library for the campus playboy.

Those are facts.

My position. The location. His reputation.

What the fuck am I doing?

It was one thing before I knew who he was. When I was looking for a rebound.

But I let Aidan goad me into a situation that was a win-win for him. Either he was right or he got off.

Lose-lose for me.

I quickly stand, staggering back a step and wiping my mouth with the back of my hand.

Aidan watches me closely, appearing unconcerned by my reaction as he tucks his dick away.

Hooking up in a public place is obviously no big deal to him. But until that night in his hot tub, I was strictly a sex in bed girl. And the thrill of giving in—of showing him I can let go—is gone, leaving me wondering, again, what the hell I'm doing.

I'm supposed to be *tutoring* the guy. Explaining statistical processes, not sucking his cock.

A low hum of voices becomes audible. Whoever just arrived on the elevator is headed this way.

I turn and walk away, my muscles shaky and my head spinning.

That just happened.

I have the lingering taste of him in my mouth to prove it. Blood is rushing south past my knees now that I'm no longer in a kneeling position.

But part of me can't believe it did.

I return to the table in a daze. Two girls have settled in the armchairs closer to the window. I don't recognize either of them, thankfully. Don't have to make any small talk.

I just send them quick smiles as I hastily pack up my backpack.

We never even started our tutoring session. All I did was ask him questions I shouldn't want answers to.

There's no sign of Aidan, which I'm relieved about.

I feel guilty for just taking off, but staying feels impossible. I can't talk to him right now.

And not tutoring him isn't even the least professional thing I've done tonight.

I leave the assignment for the next week on the table next to his textbook before practically sprinting toward the stairwell.

Maybe running down the ten flights will help clear my head.

CHAPTER SIXTEEN

AIDAN

Hunter is waiting by the front door when I walk downstairs, his hockey bag slung over one shoulder and a knit hat pulled down low over his ears.

"Where's Hart?" I ask. The plan was for the three of us to carpool together.

He raises one eyebrow. "Where do you think? Harlow's."

"Jesus. Guy deserves a getting laid trophy." I grab my Holt Hockey jacket from the kitchen, pull it on, then follow Hunter outside.

"Maybe you should offer him the one on your shelf," he suggests.

I flip him off. Then say, "I don't have *that* much sex," for some unknown reason.

Morgan snorts as we climb into my truck. "Words I never thought I'd hear you say."

"And so what if I do? I'm single."

"Phillips, you're having this conversation with yourself. I don't need or want to discuss your sex life."

I back out of the driveway, then start driving toward the rink.

Our first playoff game is tonight. It's away, but not far. Only about an hour's drive.

And one we'll likely win.

But if we don't…it's all over.

"Been meaning to ask, how was your weekend?" Hunter asks.

We've both been crazy busy this week, and Conor has been totally absent. Since the start of the semester, we haven't hung out, just the three of us, once. And I've barely seen either of my best friends since returning from LA on Sunday.

I shrug. "Wasn't great. Whatever."

I know Conor has a complicated relationship with his dad. A close one with his mom.

Hunter is more of a mystery. His dad came for the winter sports banquet a few weeks ago, but Hunter has never mentioned his mom, so I have no clue what the story is there.

"Was quiet around here without you," he tells me.

I grin. "Aw. Did you miss me, Morgan?"

"No. It was peaceful."

I roll my eyes. Drive another block. We're almost to the rink.

"Have you ever had a weird end to a hookup?" I blurt.

If I don't discuss this with someone, I'm going to lose my fucking mind.

And probably play like crap tonight.

My gaze remains on the road, but I can feel Morgan looking at me.

"What do you mean by weird?"

"Like…she just took off. At the end."

"You're asking me for *girl advice*?"

"Forget it," I mutter. I should have known he'd make a thing about it.

Before he got with Harlow, Conor was usually with a different girl at every party. Hunter's more discreet than either of us. He prefers to pass out his disgusting Jell-O shots than flirt with anyone. I've seen him make out with chicks, but they've been rare occurrences. He mostly focuses on school and hockey and considers having more than one drink a wild night out.

"Maybe you were off your game," he suggests.

I snort. "That doesn't happen. Besides, she was blowing me."

"Did you come?"

I side-eye him. "What does that have to do with anything?"

"You asked for my advice, Phillips. I'm trying to gather information about what happened so I can give you some."

I sigh. "Yes, I came."

"Did you thank her?" Hunter asks.

"*Thank* her? I swear, if you suggest sending her a card or something…"

He snorts a laugh. "I mean reciprocate, you idiot. Did she get off?"

"I was planning to. We got…interrupted. It sounded like someone was coming over. Then she took off before I could say or do anything."

"Wait, where was this?"

"The library."

Hunter makes a face. "Guess I'll be studying at home from now on. Wouldn't want to walk in on you and…" He tilts his head. "Who was the chick?"

"Why do you care?"

"Why won't you tell me?" He taps his fingers against the door. "I swear, if it's a professor and you get kicked off the team and out of school—"

"Relax, Morgan, she's a junior."

Too late, I realize I should have just said student. Specifying her year was totally unnecessary.

"Holy fuck. It's Rylan Keller, isn't it?"

"No," I answer with no confidence.

Hunter groans. When I glance over, he's rubbing a palm across his face. "Goddammit, Aidan."

"What? She's twenty-one. Age appropriate."

His hand drops as he pins me with a flat stare. "She's also Coach's *daughter*, Phillips."

"So?"

"So, if he finds out—"

"He's not going to find out. But even if he does, she's an adult and she can make her own decisions."

"*And* she's not going to have to face any consequences. You're the one on probation. Coach went above and beyond to keep you on the team and on track to graduate, and this is how you thank him? Seducing his daughter?"

I snort. "If anyone *seduced* anyone, she seduced me."

Shocked the hell out of me too. I didn't think she'd follow through—on any of it.

"End it, Aidan. Seriously. If you've run through the entire senior class, there are plenty of other juniors whose last names aren't Keller."

I chew on the inside of my cheek, knowing Hunter is right.

Even ignoring the whole coach's daughter thing, there's the tutoring aspect. Not the fun instructions I gave Rylan, but my college degree being on the line.

Our last session didn't involve *any* tutoring. She just left me the assignment sheet.

If I don't graduate, I'll be the fuckup my family thinks I am. And as fun as pissing my father and brother off can be, there comes a point when it's not enough. Antagonizing them isn't a career. I know I'm very lucky to have a trust fund that basically guarantees I'll never have to worry about money. But I don't want to be *that guy*, the rich prick who lazes around and does nothing.

Jameson's self-importance might be overly inflated, but he's the one with the corner office.

Which means I should leave Rylan alone.

Hook up with someone else, like Hunter is suggesting.

Focus on hockey.

Show up to my tutoring sessions on time and leave with a dry dick.

"Holy shit," Hunter says suddenly.

I glance at him, startled. "What?"

"You like her."

"I don't hook up with girls I *don't* like."

"That's not what I mean, and you know it. You're seriously into her. She's not just sex to you."

He's the second person to tell me that, and I didn't need one to.

If I just wanted to get laid, I have lots of other options. If I just wanted to have sex with her...well, I already did that.

"It's complicated."

"Yeah, no shit it's complicated, Phillips. Feelings always are. Remember what Hart was like after things ended with Harlow?"

"*Remember*? I was stuck on vacation with him. The whole trip was me, Hart, and the wet blanket Hart threw on everything. I would never act like that."

Hunter rolls his eyes. "I'm sure Conor would've said the same thing. I'll give you the advice I gave him—wait 'til the end of the season. Then you won't have to worry about Coach, and you can pass your redo and be on track to graduate with us."

"Yeah..."

He sighs. "You're gonna ignore my advice just like Hart did, right?"

"Not *ignore*. Just probably not listen."

"Same outcome, Phillips. If this comes out, I'm going to pretend I knew nothing about anything."

I exhale as I pull into the rink's lot and park, cracking my neck before climbing out of the truck.

I need to focus on tonight's game, not a girl.

We're ranked first headed into the first round of playoffs. But going forward, every game counts in a different way. If we lose, it's all over.

And the guys are looking to me tonight. They're expecting a goal, ideally more than one. For me to continue the impressive scoring streak I've been on lately.

I grab my hockey bag out of the bed, slinging the strap over one shoulder before heading toward the cluster of guys already waiting by the bus. Hart is standing right by the door that leads on board with Sampson and Williams, so I drop my bag in the pile of others and head for them. Hunter follows me.

Halfway to them, I spot Coach walking out of the rink's front entrance.

And he's not alone.

I haven't seen Rylan since she left me in the library.

I don't have her number, and sending an email to her school address asking if she was okay after swallowing my cum felt way too weird. Showing up at her house was an option, I guess, but I didn't know how that would go over.

She took off, which seemed like a clear *I don't want to talk to you* message. So I have no idea what to expect from our next tutoring session. I was planning to show up and follow her lead. If Rylan wants to pretend it never happened, then I'll do the same.

I just wish I'd known that ahead of time.

I would have kissed her, at least, if I'd known how brief our hookup was going to be. And how it was going to end.

But I thought it was a Tuesday problem, at least.

Today, surrounded by my teammates and in front of her dad, is not how I would have chosen for our first encounter post-blowjob to go.

Rylan isn't looking this way. She's talking to her dad, and he's nodding in response.

As curious as I am to learn more about their relationship, I avert my eyes before she catches me staring.

Hunter and I reach Conor and the guys he's with, me fighting the urge to glance over at Rylan the entire time.

"Ready to kick some Barnett ass?" Robby asks, knocking fists with me and Hunter.

His enthusiasm is contagious, and I feel my focus start to sharpen. Puck drop is only a few hours away.

"Fuck yeah," Hunter replies, nodding.

He looks totally normal, no trace of our conversation in the truck obvious on his face, and I hope I appear just as unbothered.

But maybe not, because Conor is watching me with a worried wrinkle on his forehead. "Phillips? You good?"

"Yeah. I'm great." I manage a nod, keeping my eyes straight ahead and trying to ignore the prickling sensation along my skin that makes me think Rylan might be looking over here.

I'm trying so hard to ignore her proximity—I'm probably just paranoid.

She took off on Tuesday, so why would she be paying me any attention now?

The driver appears and unlocks the bus, so guys start filing on board.

I'm one of the first to get in line behind a couple of juniors, eager to get on the bus, put on headphones, and get in the zone for our approaching game.

Conor, Hunter, and Robby join the line behind me, their

chatter not loud enough to block out the conversation in front of me.

"Who's that girl with Coach?" Andy Pierce is asking.

"His daughter, I think. I heard this is her first semester on campus," Jake Brennan replies.

"Damn, that's Coach's daughter? She's hot."

"I have a class with her," Brennan boasts. "I'll tap that before the end of the season."

My hands are shoved into my pockets, so no one can see my fingers curl into fists.

"You're blocking the door," I bark.

Conor gives me a weird look. Hunter sighs behind me.

"Sorry, Phillips," Andy says, quickly climbing up the steps.

Brennan looks me over instead of moving. "Dude, did you forget to get laid last night or something? Because you're wound up—"

"Phillips!"

I glance over one shoulder.

Coach Keller is standing with Coach Zimmerman by the pile of our hockey bags. And Rylan is still right next to her father, studiously avoiding eye contact with me.

"Yeah, Coach?" I call out.

"Come here."

Fuck.

I avoid Hunter's concerned look and Conor's confused one as I split from my spot in line and walk over to where Coach is standing.

Rylan noticeably tenses as I approach, but Coach is focused on me.

He takes a few steps forward to meet me, his furrowed forehead comically similar to how Conor's looked earlier. I call Conor Coach Jr. during our off-season dryland practices, which Coach

Keller rarely attends. They're usually us fucking around while Hart reminds us how many days until the season starts.

"What's up, Coach?" I ask.

"You were off at practice yesterday," he tells me. "Everything okay?"

Your daughter is messing with my head.

I shut that train of thought down—hard. I'm distracted enough I'm worried I'll accidentally say something I shouldn't, during which is undoubtedly the worst possible time.

And my mistakes at practice weren't just about what happened with Rylan on Tuesday.

"I'm good, Coach. Just a little nervous."

Both of Coach's bushy eyebrows fly upward at the admission. "You know what I've thought, Phillips? Since you joined the team as a freshman?"

I shake my head.

"That I'd never met a player with more untapped potential. You're worried the way you've played these past few games has been an anomaly? They're *average* games for you, Phillips. There's not a damn thing limiting you out on the ice, except yourself. Today could be the last game you ever play. Leave it all out there and take the shot."

I know I've avoided expectations. Responsibilities. I'm reliable about showing up, and that's about it.

"What if I miss?"

"Then at least you took the shot. Not a thing wrong with trying and failing, Phillips."

Lincoln Phillips would strongly disagree with that statement.

If you ask my father, it's better to bench yourself than embarrass yourself.

"I'm not afraid to fail," I tell him.

Maybe myself too.

"Good," Coach replies. "Because you're starting tonight."

My stomach flips. "Wh-what? Why?"

"Because you earned it, Phillips."

"But Conor—"

"It was Hart's suggestion, Phillips. He's seen the same thing I have—you deserve it. He's looking out for the whole team, which is what a good captain does."

"But Hart *is* the captain. He should start."

If we lose, this could be Conor's last game too. I can't take that moment from him.

"Any team would be drooling over the number of goals one of my centers has scored this season. Let alone two. Barnett is expecting Hart to start. You'll be a surprise, Phillips."

I relax some. "It's a diversion tactic, then?"

I can handle being part of a ploy if he thinks it'll help us win.

Coach appraises me. Shakes his head. "It's me having you take that first face-off because that's most likely to win us the game. Statistically speaking." One side of his mouth lifts. "Need me to call your tutor over here so she can explain those odds to you?"

"No." My response is fast, maybe too quick. But an awkward interaction with Rylan is the last thing I need right now.

"You're ready," he tells me.

"I hope so."

"I know so." Coach Keller jerks his chin toward the waiting bus. "Grab a seat, Phillips."

I nod, then turn and head back that way. The rest of the team is already on board.

Before climbing the stairs, I glance back once.

Coach isn't looking this way, but she is.

Our eyes meet. Instead of looking away like I'm expecting, Rylan holds my gaze.

Kick ass, she mouths.

I nod.

Then climb onto the bus, determined to do exactly that.

Conor's seated about halfway back. I drop down across the aisle from him, spreading my legs out as far as the seats will allow.

"What did Coach want?"

"To tell me I'm *starting*." I raise one eyebrow at him. "Which you apparently recommended me for."

Conor nods. "I wanna win."

I snort. "You're ten times the player I am. We both know that."

"*We* don't know that. You *think* that because it gives you an excuse to party more and practice less."

I shake my head. "If we lose, it's over."

"I'm aware of how playoffs work, Phillips."

"You're the captain. You should start."

"I'm the captain, so I decide who starts."

I lean my head back against the cold glass of the window. "You wanna break that news to Coach, or should I?"

Hart rolls his eyes. "I suggested it. He agreed. How much longer do you want to argue about it?"

"I don't want to argue. I want you to—" I pause, then lean forward. "What are you doing?"

I swear Conor blushes. "Nothing."

"Bullshit. You're making *jewelry*?"

"It's just some beads."

"Beads that make jewelry."

"One of the kids I coach—Cody—his sister kinda has a crush on me. She brought this"—he holds up the plastic container that was in his lap—"last week as a gift because I told her I liked her bracelets. For me to make one of my own, which she'll be inspecting tomorrow."

"Wow." I grin. "Does Harlow know about her competition?"

"Yes," Conor grumbles. "I asked her to make it for me. She refused, told me to do it while I was sitting on the bus. So…" He shrugs, then rummages through the container again.

I deliberate, then lean toward the aisle. "Give me some."

"What?"

"Give me some beads so I can make a bracelet."

He rolls his eyes. "Phillips…"

"What? I'm serious. Give me some. Better than staring out the window."

Hart appears unconvinced but passes the container over for me to rifle through. I grab a section of string, a random assortment of beads, plus a three and a four for my jersey number. There are letters too, but I don't bother with those.

"Maybe this'll be my lucky charm," I tell Hart as I start threading the beads with the string.

He snorts, but his reply is serious. "You don't need a lucky charm, Phillips. You need to accept you're good, and that the team is relying on you to play well tonight. That you're an asset, not a benchwarmer."

Hearing *The team is relying on you to play well tonight* would normally spark some panic.

But I think of Rylan mouthing *Kick ass*.

Coach's encouraging expression when he told me to take shots.

Hart deciding I should start.

They all think I can do this.

So maybe…it's time I start thinking that too.

CHAPTER SEVENTEEN

RYLAN

To: aphillips@holt.edu
From: rkeller@holt.edu
Subject: *Tutoring*

Hey Aidan,

I'm sick and can't make tutoring tonight. Attaching this week's assignment from Professor Carringan for you to look over. We'll review it next week.

Best,
Rylan

I gnaw on my bottom lip, rereading the email I drafted to send to Aidan for the twentieth time. I'm aiming for a casual yet professional tone, something that doesn't suggest I spent a ridiculous amount of time writing and reviewing this.

Or that I'm feeling uncomfortable about how our last tutoring session ended.

And most of all, I'm trying to ensure he doesn't think this is a lame excuse to avoid seeing him.

I'm annoyed I'm sick, and not just because feeling crappy sucks. Because I'd like to get this awkwardness out of the way as soon as possible. But short of attaching a photo of me mid-cough with a red, dripping nose, I have no clue how to prove to Aidan this email isn't an excuse to evade him.

I add *Congrats on the win*, delete *Congrats on the win*, and then hit send.

Quit out of my email before a response could possibly come through, and slump back against the pillows. I started feeling stuffed up last night, then woke up with a sore throat and a cough. Dragged myself to my morning class, then came home before lunch and changed into sweatpants.

I've been in bed ever since, chugging sports drinks packed with electrolytes and nibbling on some crackers I found in one of the cabinets. I feel too shitty to make myself a full meal and am quarantining in my room to avoid getting my roommates sick, since that's a certain way to become the least popular person in the house.

I'm planning to take some cold medicine in an hour and hoping a solid night's sleep will mean I feel better in the morning. If not, I'll text my mom and take advantage of the fact she only lives ten minutes away now to have her come take care of me.

After scrolling on social media for a little bit, I attempt to do the reading for my Philosophy class. Give up, after only a few pages, and start watching a comedy on my laptop.

The opening credits are still rolling on the small screen when I hear a knock.

Not on my door, on my window.

I sit up in bed, sniffling before I climb off the mattress,

keeping my blanket wrapped around my shoulders. Creep over to the curtain and pull it back.

Aidan is outside.

I stand, stunned. Then mouth *Go away.*

He shakes his head.

I glance over one shoulder at my shut door. I texted all my roommates to let them know I was sick. Chloe has already tapped on my door twice, asking if I need anything. I really don't want them overhearing this conversation, and I wouldn't put it past Aidan to walk around to the front door if I refuse to let him in this way. Surprised he didn't do that in the first place, actually.

Reluctantly, I flick the lock on the window open and tug the sash up an inch. Shiver, when a gust of frigid air invades my warm room. There's no screen on the window, which might become an issue in May.

I step back, tightening my grasp on the blanket wrapped around me.

Aidan opens the window as wide as it'll go and climbs inside like he's done it a thousand times before, quickly shutting it behind him.

"What the hell are you doing here?" I ask.

I feel awful and am well aware I look terrible, and I'm irritated I care he's seeing me like this—in ratty sweats, wearing no makeup with a runny nose.

Aidan glances down. "Oh, shit," he says. "I left it outside."

He turns and reopens the window. Leans low, treating me to a spectacular view of his muscular ass, and then returns with a brown paper bag in hand that he sets on my desk before closing the window once again. "I know you're supposed to bring sick people chicken noodle soup, or whatever, but I don't know where to get that from and I was already getting Mexican."

I stare at the bag. "You brought me dinner?" I ask, just as shocked as when I saw him outside my window.

Aidan nods. "You said you were sick."

I don't miss the thread of suspicion in his voice as he looks me over, one corner of his mouth lifting as he takes in my bedraggled appearance.

"I *am* sick," I tell him.

His small smirk turns into a full, wide smile. "Yeah, I know. Your nose looks like Rudolph's."

"Shut up." I grab the bag off my desk and open it, my stomach grumbling at the delicious smells wafting from it.

I recognize the logo printed on the side of the bag from the Mexican place in Loughton. One of my favorite restaurants.

He has good taste in food.

"What are you watching?" Aidan asks, pulling off his Holt Hockey jacket. He drapes it on the back of my desk chair and nods toward my open laptop. He's wearing an unbuttoned flannel with the sleeves rolled up underneath.

I pause, mid-unwrapping my food. "You're staying?"

"Do you want me to go?"

"I'm definitely contagious. It's a terrible time for you to get sick, right when you're finally contributing to the team."

Holt advanced from the first round of the playoffs, mostly thanks to him. Aidan scored two goals in the team's four-one victory over Barnett.

Aidan grins. "Just following your instructions, tutor."

I'm not sure what possessed me to tell him to kick ass. I was planning to ignore Aidan—ignore all the hockey players looking at me like I was a zoo animal as they waited to board the bus to their first playoff game—uncomfortable and annoyed with myself for not getting to my dad's office earlier. I'd wanted to quickly wish him luck before the team left, that was it, but all the guys showed up at the rink a lot earlier than I thought they would.

Aidan's flannel gets stripped off next, leaving him in a cotton T-shirt. "Your room is sweltering."

I guess…he's staying.

"I know." I turned up the thermostat when I got home, after shivering all morning. "I'm sick," I remind him.

"Thought maybe you were avoiding me."

I focus on my food, pulling the foil off the burrito so carefully it comes away in one piece without a single tear. "No, I wouldn't…" I exhale. "I'm sorry I took off last week. I know you're busy and that you have a lot riding on passing the retake. I shouldn't have left without reviewing the assignment with you. That was really unprofessional, and I—"

"You think *that's* what I care about? That you never reviewed the assignment?"

"I mean…yeah. You're taking your *responsibilities seriously*, remember? So far, you've aced everything I've given you, so I don't think you actually need to worry about passing the second time. But I want to make sure that you do, and I shouldn't have left. So I'm sorry. I just…freaked out a little."

I tell all of that to the burrito he brought me, unable to meet his eyes.

"I was worried you were avoiding me because I was worried you were avoiding me, Rylan. I wasn't worried you were avoiding me because I'm mad you left or worried about re-failing the final."

"Oh. Okay."

In my tiny room, Aidan's presence is overwhelming.

I can smell his cologne mixed with a whiff of laundry detergent every time I sniffle. The scent saturates the air surrounding me. And no matter where I look, I can feel his gaze fixed on me.

Finally, I muster the courage to look up and make eye contact. He's leaning against the side of my mattress, which is a strange enough sight. But the look he's giving me is weird too. There's no playful smirk or easygoing grin. His gaze is intense, bordering on searching. He's serious and focused—on me.

"*Best in Show*," I tell him.

Now he looks puzzled. "What?"

"You asked what I was watching. *Best in Show*. You wanna watch?"

"Yeah, sure."

I nod, using one hand to keep my blanket wrapped around my shoulders and carrying my burrito in the other as I climb back onto my bed. The mattress dips as Aidan settles beside me, tucking one arm behind his head. His T-shirt rides up, flashing a very distracting view of the few inches above the low-riding waistband of his joggers. The sight heats me more effectively than the blanket I'm basically swaddled in.

"What's this movie about?" he asks me as I take a seat cross-legged beside him so I can lean over the wrapper while I eat.

"A dog show," I answer.

His only response is a hum.

"Do you have one?"

"A dog? No. Well, I guess I did, sort of. We had a golden for a little bit, but my dad gave it away to one of the housekeepers when he got sick of it. Said it wasn't contributing anything to the family. My dad's *big* on contributing." He scoffs, then shifts on the bed, revealing more of his abs.

"Every time you tell me something about your dad, I like him less."

Aidan snorts. "Yeah. Join the club." Then he sobers, tapping his fingers on his chest. "He's not a bad guy. Just…selfish. Detached. He worked his ass off to make certain we had the best of everything, didn't inherit any of his money. My mom was the rich princess with a trust fund."

"How'd they meet?"

"College. I don't know where exactly. I'm sure my mom was the queen bee on campus and my dad was a tech nerd with a lot of big ideas. Doubt they crossed paths a ton."

Sounds like us.

Except he's the popular one and I have no big ideas. I'm just trying to make it to senior year.

I swallow the last bite of my burrito. "Thanks for bringing dinner. You really didn't need to do that."

Rather than acknowledge my appreciation, he asks, "Have you gotten food from that place before?"

I nod, balling up the wrapper and setting it on my bedside table. "A bunch of times."

I lie down next to him, grateful for the barrier of my open laptop between us as I hit Play and resume the movie.

Aidan doesn't talk during the film, which is a relief because that's a pet peeve of mine. But he does laugh a lot, and at most of the same parts I do.

When the screen goes dark and the credits start to scroll, I'm disappointed.

I wait for him to get up and leave.

Instead, Aidan rolls his head to look at me and asks, "What the hell happened on Tuesday?"

My fingers find the hem of my blanket and start playing with it nervously. I thought we were past this. We acknowledged it happened, I apologized for taking off. The end.

"I didn't think I'd need to explain the concept of a blowjob to the campus playboy. That's *what happened*."

A muscle in his jaw twitches. "So I'm the campus playboy, huh? Is that what you meant by *knowing* me? You're judging me for enjoying myself, Rylan?"

I quickly shake my head. "No, I'm not judging you. I just meant you're more experienced. And I, uh, it was…" I swallow. Glance away, busying myself with closing the laptop screen. "We don't need to talk about it. It happened, and I said I was sorry for leaving right after. If you want to switch to working with a different tutor, then I'm sure that—"

"*Rylan*." He grabs my chin, forcing me to look at him.

Heat spreads from that one spot where he's touching me, throughout my entire body, warming me for the first time all day.

"Forget about the tutoring shit. It has nothing to do with this. There's nothing for you to apologize for. And I *want* to talk about what happened."

"Why? So you can leave a review or something?" I fight the urge to break eye contact. It's overwhelming, having him here, in my bed, close enough to touch. "Is that what you do with all your girls?"

"All my girls—" Aidan shakes his head. "Will you stop talking about other girls? I'm talking about *you* and *me*, no one else. And what the fuck does *leave a review* mean?"

"I'm sure you've gotten a lot of head, is all."

A tiny bit of vulnerability sneaks into my voice. I was in no way prepared to actually talk about this with him. I just assumed we'd both move on, pretend it never happened.

Now, he looks amused. "Wait, you think *it wasn't good*? That I'm bringing it up to give you *pointers*?"

I cover my face with my hands. Exhale, worried I might suffocate from humiliation. "Can you just…go? Please? I don't feel well, and I don't get why any of it matters."

There's a long pause, during which I wish I could see his face. "Can I make you feel better?"

I don't lower my hands. "If you want to bring over the bottle of cold medicine on my desk before you go, that'll help."

Aidan laughs, low and husky. "That's not what I'm talking about."

I'm too curious not to look at him.

When I pull my hands away, he's rolled over onto one elbow, *way* too close to me.

I can make out the lighter shades of green flecked in his eyes. The few freckles on his nose. The thin, faded scar in one corner of his lip. An old hockey injury, probably.

"I didn't get to touch you."

I shiver, and not because I'm cold. Because of the way he says that, like it's a privilege. Like it's a treat he missed out on. A gift he didn't get to unwrap.

"Can I?" he asks.

Slowly, I nod. I'm having trouble pulling in enough air all of a sudden, and it has nothing to do with being congested. My thighs clench together, trying to alleviate the ache there that's started throbbing.

Aidan's touch is light as his hand lands on my hip, gently tugging the blanket away and revealing the hole-y pair of sweatpants I've had since high school. His thumb slips inside the elastic waistband, rubbing back and forth lightly.

I exhale as every nerve ending sparks to life.

And...I forget.

I forget about my stuffy nose and sore throat.

I forget he's a hockey player.

I forget I'm tutoring him.

I'm only aware of his touch, of needing more of it and needing it lower, everything else fading to the background.

"Okay?" he asks.

"Yeah," I breathe.

He shifts so he's hovering above me, one quick tug taking care of the drawstring holding up the soft material of my sweatpants and another pull removing them entirely. I'm left in a pair of boring cotton underwear, not what I would have chosen to wear had I known he was going to see me like this.

And striped fuzzy socks, another unfortunate, unsexy choice.

But Aidan hasn't looked that low. He's focused on the wet spot I can feel rubbing against my swollen clit.

"You want that review now?"

"What?" My voice sounds a million miles away.

He's dragging my underwear down my legs *so* slowly, and each inch is an erotic torture. My breathing is already embarrassingly fast and I'm sure my face is bright red.

"The review of your blowjob." Shockingly, he keeps a straight face through that sentence.

I manage a scoff. "Are you seriously—*fuck*."

He's pushing a finger inside of me. My entire body arches, enjoying the sweet relief of finally getting filled there. Trying to get closer to his touch. He's playing my body like I'm an instrument and he's an expert musician, applying pressure to the perfect spot.

I haven't hooked up with anyone since Aidan, but there was a much longer dry spell before we met in Colorado. So I think it's *him*, not that I'm eager for an orgasm.

"Location was an interesting choice. There was a metal shelf digging into my spine and the fifth floor smells kind of musty. It was super quiet, which I thought I'd hate, but was actually kind of hot. I liked how I could hear you sucking, not just watch. Especially when you made those breathy little sighs. I could feel them in your throat but then also hear you."

I don't know if I should look horrified or start laughing. He's actually doing this, fingering me while reviewing our last hookup.

And if I wasn't already so wet, he'd be able to tell how much it's turning me on.

"Only downside is that I'm not sure how I'll be able to study there again without thinking about it. Not that I studied there much before, or at all really, but still. We might need to relocate our tutoring sessions if you want me to be paying attention to anything you're saying instead of thinking about your mouth on me. And then the way you took off when it sounded like someone was coming was disappointing. Since it was before I could do this."

He leans down, replacing his fingers with his tongue.

I can't control the "Fuck" that explodes out of my mouth at the first swipe.

As far as my roommates know, I'm in my room alone and sick. I'd really rather they don't wonder why I'm in here moaning. I bite down on my bottom lip hard enough to taste blood as he licks me again, my fingers fisting the comforter and my heels digging into the soft fabric. My hips lift in a shameless attempt to get closer to his mouth.

"You taste so fucking good." He presses a wet kiss to the divot inside my hipbone, then returns to tonguing my entrance.

I writhe, barely recognizing the needy sounds coming out of my mouth when he pulls away. He's stripped me down to the most primal of urges. I don't care about anything except coming.

"So, overall, I'd give location a four out of five," Aidan continues in a conversational tone.

I whimper as his fingers trail up the inside of my thigh, leaving a trail of goosebumps behind. My hips jerk involuntarily, silently begging for him to move higher. This intensity is new and overwhelming. Fooling around has always felt good. But it's never been this consuming urge, never been this torment of feeling like my world might end if he stops touching me.

His fingers trail down instead of up, drawing light circles on my skin that feel like being brushed by feathers. Soft and stimulating.

My growl is annoyed as I open my knees so wide I can feel the inside of my thighs protesting the stretch. I'm so turned on it feels like the pulse in my pussy has spread throughout my entire body.

I'm close. *So* close. Teetering at the edge, craving that final push.

"Is the library a favorite math major spot?" Aidan teases.

I'm too desperate for release to manage a coherent conversation. Or get annoyed he's teasing me about my major again.

"Shut up," I groan.

"I thought you wanted a review, Rylan. Something you'd rather I do with my mouth?"

Breathlessly, I nod, moving my head to the side so I can see him better. Most of my hair has come out of the bun I had it pulled back in earlier, now a messy halo spread across the comforter.

"And take your shirt off," I tell him.

The sight of his head between my legs is hot. But his shirt is blocking my view of his shoulders and biceps tensing as he touches me.

Aidan's eyes dance with arrogant amusement at the request—whatever, it's not like he had no clue I'm attracted to him—but he says nothing as he rises up onto his knees, then smoothly tugs the cotton shirt up and over his head. He's just as ridiculously ripped as he was in the hot tub weeks ago. And this is better, because I can see him more clearly, just like in the library. A faded, green-gray bruise stretches across part of his side.

I lift my foot, lightly tapping the old injury with my sock. "What happened?"

"Hockey." He leans over, treating me to a look at his impressive muscles in motion.

I clench around nothing, tempted to tell him to ditch his pants so I can admire his cock again too.

Aidan lies down beside me before I can say a word.

I don't move, not sure what's happening. He knows I haven't finished yet, and my impatient body is making it impossible for me to forget.

"Come sit," he says, tapping his chin.

My eyes widen when I realize what he means. A reaction I know Aidan doesn't miss, because his attention is laser-focused on me. He doesn't laugh or tease me, though. Just waits patiently as I sit up and crawl toward him, new bursts of arousal pumping through my system. Every experience I have with Aidan is going to include firsts, I guess.

"Other way," he instructs when I reach him. "So you can appreciate my abs."

I have no smart response to the mirth in his voice.

I lower my hips slowly. Aidan is having none of it.

He positions me exactly where he wants me, and then starts licking. With each swipe, more of my uncertainty disappears, until I'm grinding and rubbing against his mouth. The only thing that feels better than touching his hot, firm chest is his talented tongue between my thighs.

This angle is...too much. I'm spread open, completely exposed and at the mercy of his mouth. Aidan's grip is tight on my hips, holding me in place as the pleasure and pressure continue to build.

I can see the outline of his erection through the joggers he's wearing. And I moan, registering that's a reaction to me riding his face.

I want to lean forward and take him in my mouth, but it's

another thing I've never done before. I'd rather Aidan didn't find that out. Maybe if he thinks I'm selfish in bed, he'll lose interest in hooking up again.

Except…I'm not sure that's what I want.

There's no relief when I think about him leaving me alone.

Pleasure flares hotter and pressure winds tighter and then I explode, my entire body contracting as I come with a loud cry, harder than I ever have before.

And my mind goes blissfully, beautifully blank.

CHAPTER EIGHTEEN

AIDAN

> RYLAN: Did you look at the assignment?

> AIDAN: Look? Yeah.

> RYLAN: Did you *do* the assignment?

> AIDAN: I'd rather *do* you.

S he doesn't respond.

After staring at my phone for a minute, I turn it over so the screen is facing down and doesn't distract me.

I left Rylan's bedroom shortly after she came on Tuesday night. I could tell she wasn't sure what to do or say, and was maybe embarrassed about the hot as fuck way she rode my face. So I made a joke about me providing dinner and her being my dessert, handed her the cold medicine she asked for, and convinced her to give me her number for "academic purposes" so we could reschedule our tutoring session. Then climbed out of her window, giving myself a couple of shin bruises in the process.

I want to have sex with her. Badly.

But I don't know *how* to, and anyone I know would find that absolutely hilarious.

Yeah, I have a reputation. And yeah, I've hooked up with a lot of girls.

Rylan is different for a whole bunch of reasons.

For one, we already slept together. I'm not just assuming the sex will be good; I know it will be incredible.

Two, she's my tutor. And she's good at it. The only part of Stats I actually like. She apologized twice about leaving early last week. I don't want her to think she's a distraction or to feel uncomfortable during our tutoring sessions because of anything *unprofessional* that happens between us.

Three, she's Coach Keller's daughter. Up until he told me he'd arranged for her to tutor me, he'd never mentioned Rylan before. I don't think he's the old-fashioned, brandishing a shotgun kind of father, but I also doubt he'd be happy to find out Rylan and I have done more than discuss math. Now that playoffs have officially started, it's an especially terrible time to upset the team dynamic and piss off my coach.

This isn't suggesting to a girl we go upstairs at a party and then probably never talking to her again. It's actually pursuing a girl, which I've never done before. Parker was always around, and she made all the first moves toward me. Aside from our tutoring sessions, Rylan has mostly avoided me. And the only time she's initiated anything sexual was in the library, which was obviously impulsive and I kind of dared her into.

When I check my phone, because my willpower is shit, she still hasn't responded to my most recent text. I'm sure she's seen it by now.

I've never cared about coming on too strong before. Or worried about a girl thinking I lost interest. Both are concerns with Rylan.

So…I don't know what to do.

I refocus on the paper I'm working on for my Leadership in Organizations class.

There's a knock on my door a few minutes later.

"Yeah?" I call out.

Hart walks in. He's dressed to go out, in his hockey windbreaker and a backward baseball cap.

"You're doing homework?" He gasps dramatically.

I lean back in the chair and stretch. "Figured I'd mix it up a little."

"You're trying to impress your hot tutor, you mean. I know how you operate, Phillips."

"Is she hot?" I ask innocently.

Conor rolls his eyes. "Bullshit you didn't notice."

"And *you* did? I thought you were locked down tighter than Fort Knox."

"Just because I'm in love with Harlow doesn't mean I'm blind," he tells me.

I shrug, weirdly bothered by the knowledge Conor thinks Rylan is attractive. Even knowing he's in a serious relationship and would never do anything about it, there's some strange instinct to shout "She's mine!"

Conor tilts his head, studying me closer than I'd like. "She's Coach's daughter."

"I know that," I respond.

"Just reminding you. I know how you love to think with your dick."

I roll my eyes.

"Although I doubt you're her type. She's probably averse to hockey players, thanks to Coach."

Not to me, I think smugly. If I focus hard enough, I can still taste her on my tongue.

Rylan may not want to be attracted to me, but I'm positive she is. Maybe our first time, when I was just a random guy, could be written off as meaningless. But we've hooked up three times now, and twice she knew I'm one of her dad's hockey players. So I'm no longer buying her *not interested* excuse.

At least Hunter kept his mouth shut this time. Although I'm guessing it was more out of self-preservation than anything else. He didn't want to be the one Conor blew up at after finding out I've hooked up with our coach's daughter. Hart is teasing right now. If he knew I was *actually* trying to impress Rylan, actually interested in her, this would be a different conversation.

"You wanna go get food?" Conor asks me.

I shut my laptop. "What's Harlow busy with tonight?"

Hart rolls his eyes. "Do you wanna get food or not?"

"Oh, she's coming with us, then?"

"Phillips, c'mon."

"Ah, she's busy. Got it."

"I know I haven't been around at all lately, okay? Don't be a dick about it. Let's go get dinner, and you can catch me up on all of your latest hookups."

Excluding Rylan, there's nothing to tell.

I stand, pulling on a sweatshirt before grabbing my phone and wallet. "I've been focusing on hockey," I tell him.

Conor nods, turning serious as we head downstairs. "It's paying off, man. This is the best I've ever seen you play."

There's the same twist in my stomach whenever anyone has complimented me about hockey recently. But it's less panicked than it used to be. Maybe I'm getting better at playing under pressure after several games with expectations.

Expectations I've exceeded, even.

"Thanks. Is Hunter coming?"

"Nah, he's got a study thing for one of his classes."

I nod. "You driving?"

He usually prefers to, because of his weird issue with my truck's color. "You can, if you want."

"Really?"

"Yeah. As long as we go somewhere at least an hour away, so no one sees me riding around in the Eyesore."

I roll my eyes as I head into the kitchen and fish my keys out of the pocket of my hockey jacket. "We're getting burgers at Gaffney's. I haven't eaten there in a while."

"Okay, fine," Conor agrees.

I missed hanging out with my best friend. I think this is his way of telling me he missed me, too.

Once we're in my truck headed toward downtown, he asks, "How's that going, by the way?"

"How's what going?"

"The tutoring. You've skipped the past four wing nights. Can't you do it another night? It's messing with team morale. Table's too quiet without you."

I snort. Now I know he missed me. "No, I can't move it. She's busy."

"Busy *every* other night except Tuesday?"

"Yeah. I mean, no. I don't know. She's helping me. I don't want to be an inconvenience, or whatever."

A beat of silence. "Phillips, you fucking love being an inconvenience. It's your way or the wrong way."

"Well, maybe I'm evolving."

"Evolving…like finally talking about whatever's been bothering you the past few months?"

My hands briefly tighten on the steering wheel.

I should be grateful to have friends who care so much.

And I am. Conor and Hunter are brothers to me in a way Jameson never has been or will be. Even before all the shit with

Parker, we were never close. We bickered like siblings as kids, then grew up to fight like enemies. As much as Parker's betrayal stung, it was a paper cut in comparison to the knife in the back from my brother. He's never asked for my forgiveness, but I doubt I'll be able to offer any if he ever does.

"Remember my older brother?" I ask. "He showed up in Vail?"

"Yeah, of course."

"And remember the wedding he mentioned?"

"Yep, I remember. He's kinda young, no? Only a few years older than us?"

"Two years. And his age isn't the issue. It's that he's marrying my ex."

I wasn't sure if Harlow mentioned our conversation to Conor. I didn't ask her not to say anything. Didn't tell her Conor didn't know the real reason I returned to LA. I told him and Hunter it was for a family thing, not an engagement party, and neither of them pushed for any details.

I'm pleasantly surprised when I glance over and see the obvious shock on Hart's face.

Conor having a girlfriend has been a different dynamic. Realizing Harlow kept our conversation in confidence feels good. It makes me feel like she's a friend, not just his girl.

"You have *exes*?" Conor asks. "I thought you've never dated anyone."

"I only have one ex. We dated in high school. She ended things before I started at Holt. I never mentioned her because I wanted college to be a fresh start."

"So, what? She broke up with you and then started dating your brother?"

"Pretty much."

He shakes his head, incredulous. "Dude, that's fucked up."

"I know. I thought I was over it, but they announced their engagement in November. That got into my head, I guess."

"Fuck, Phillips. I'm so sorry."

We're in Gaffney's parking lot now, but neither of us moves to climb out of the truck.

"Thanks. I just haven't wanted to talk about it. Not a damn thing that'll change it, so I've been trying to just forget it's happening."

"You think it'll actually happen? The wedding?"

"Yeah, I do."

"She might just be trying to get your attention."

I'm positive that's how their relationship started. Parker always had a scheming streak. But Conor has no clue about the pretentious world my parents are a part of. Parker's family too. There's no way she would have said yes to Jameson's proposal unless she was planning to follow through on marrying him. The scandal of jilting him at the altar would horrify her mother and mine. She cares too much about their approval—now, she didn't when we were younger—just like Jameson does.

"Are you still in love with her?" Conor asks when I say nothing.

I shake my head. "Definitely not. I hate how it affected my relationship with my family. How Jameson thinks he won. It has nothing to do with her anymore."

"Won?" Conor nudges my arm with his elbow. "You're the one who's about to be lifting a trophy."

"We haven't won anything yet, Hart."

This is a weird role reversal. Usually I'm the optimist and he's the one pulling me back to reality with reminders of all that could go wrong.

"We will." Conor's voice is as confident as I've ever heard it. "You've been playing on a different level lately, man."

"There aren't many games left to play in," I remind him. "Might as well go out with a bang."

He nods, but I catch the spasm of unease in his expression. Realize I just reminded Conor they could be his last games too.

My stomach grumbles. "C'mon," I say. "I'm starving."

We head inside, snagging a high-top table toward the back of the bar with a prime view of one of the flatscreens. Basketball's on, which is not a favorite sport. And reminds me, I owe Thomas an apology. I haven't seen him since the last time I was here, when I acted like a jealous dick. Not even acted like—I was one.

It's not as packed in here as usual, but it's still busy. And plenty of people call out as they pass by our table, recognizing us. I wonder if we'll be as popular on campus once the season is over. Especially if we lose.

Coach's comment about my best not being an anomaly has stuck with me. I had no clue he thought that of me. Conor said almost the same thing, how I've never put my all into hockey so I could prioritize partying.

I haven't gone out as much lately. Haven't been distracting myself with a bunch of girls. If I'd focused sooner, would we be after our second championship? Our third? I started a playoff game, and we won. I didn't crack under the pressure.

Maybe I would've, as a sophomore. As a junior. Who knows, and there's no point in speculating. Our season isn't over yet.

I don't even bother glancing at the laminated menu on the table. I know exactly what I'm ordering.

A waitress appears only a few minutes after we sit down, the usual quick service I always experience here that has nothing to do with how crowded or slow Gaffney's is.

"Hey!" Her voice is as perky as the swing of her high ponytail as she glances between us with a wide smile.

I don't recognize her...but that doesn't mean much.

"Hey." Conor's smile is polite.

I've gotten used to the way he acts around girls now. The quick drop of eye contact, the lack of emotion in his tone. His body is angled toward the table, instead of toward her.

She's eyeing both of us but she focuses on me after picking up on Hart's indifferent vibe. "What can I get you guys?"

Hart raises one eyebrow, waiting for me to hit on her. It's the perfect opening.

I could lean forward, smirk, and say any number of things that would basically guarantee us hooking up later. Ask her what she recommends. Say what I want—her—isn't on the menu. Compliment her shirt while checking out her tits.

Instead, I'm doing the same damn thing as Hart.

"Burger, cooked medium rare. No tomato. And a pint of whatever draft is on tap." I hold out my menu. "Thanks."

The waitress nods, not quite managing to hide the disappointment in her expression before she turns toward Conor. He orders the same thing as me, except he opts for tomatoes on his burger and a Heineken.

"Are you feeling okay?" he asks me as soon as the waitress walks away.

"Yeah, why?"

"Because the waitress was hot, and you didn't hit on her. I thought you had to be in a coma for that to happen."

I roll my eyes. "Fuck off, Hart. Figured you'd be proud of me for focusing on hockey, not give me shit about it."

I doubt he'd be as proud if he knew my recent stretch of celibacy is because our coach's daughter will barely give me the time of day and she's the only girl my dick is currently interested in.

"I am. Just...surprised." His expression is more incredulous, and it's annoying.

Yeah, I like sex. Find me a guy who doesn't. And yeah, I've never had a girlfriend in college, so there have been a lot of girls.

Fuckboy, playboy, player.

I'm sure they're all words that have been used to describe me. I don't see anything wrong with enjoying my college years.

But I'm sick of that being all people associate—or expect —from me.

Conor pulls his phone out. It's buzzing with an incoming call.

"It's my mom," he tells me. "She must be on a break during her shift. I'll be right back."

I nod.

The waitress passes him by with our beers as Conor heads outside.

"Here you go," she tells me, setting a glass down in front of me and a bottle at Conor's empty spot.

"Thanks," I reply, rubbing my thumb against the condensation gathered on the outside of the beer. It squeaks, something I've loved doing since I was a kid with any chilled drink.

"Try it," she encourages. "New brew we just got in."

I take a sip, then wipe my mouth with the back of my hand to clear the foam. "It's good," I say.

Her tongue darts out, wetting her lower lip. "Do you taste the pine?"

"Uh…" I take another sip. "Maybe?"

She smiles. "What about the lemon and white pepper?"

I'm undecided if she's fucking with me or not.

"There are some peach and mango notes in there too."

"You know a lot about this beer."

"Because I brewed it. You're the first person who ordered it."

"You made this?" I ask, impressed. And a little concerned, because can people just *do that*? Brew beer and serve it to people?

"Yeah. It's my fifth brew. Took me a year to talk Arlo into

232

carrying it here."

"That's really cool."

"Thanks. The dream is to open up my own brewery one day."

"I'd drink there," I tell her, taking another sip. The beer is good. I can't taste any of the stuff she mentioned, but it's way better than the warm piss we have at parties.

"I'm Zara," she says.

"Aidan."

I study Zara more closely. Conor was right—she's hot.

She has a tattoo on the inside of her wrist I can't quite make out. It's writing in some fancy script. Despite the cold temperatures outside, she's wearing a tank top that's tight enough to show off her tits.

"Your boyfriend must love that he has a free beer supply," I say.

She leans closer, the end of her ponytail almost brushing the top of the table. "I don't have a boyfriend, Aidan."

Zara licks her bottom lip again, and it's a hot move. My dick reacts, thickening as I imagine her tongue on it.

We're facing Mulbridge in the quarterfinals, and their defense is packed with bruisers. I'm not looking forward to the beating I'll be taking, and it's been a while since my body felt *good*. The whole time Rylan was sucking me, I was in a state of disbelief it was really happening. Then uncertainty, when she immediately bailed.

"I get off at eleven," she prompts. Again, giving me the perfect opening.

But…I can't take it.

I'd be fucking Zara's mouth, but I'd be pretending it was Rylan on her knees. And I've done a lot of stupid shit in my life, but I've never hooked up with a girl and thought about someone else.

"I'm busy later," I tell her.

"That's cool," she says, but I see the disappointment flash across her face. "Maybe another time."

She's gone before I can decide how to reply.

I exhale, scrubbing a palm across my face and then downing a large gulp of beer.

What the hell is the matter with me?

Zara was hot. Here. Interested. She's not my tutor and although I don't know her last name, I'm positive it's not Keller.

Rylan isn't here. But I'm still thinking about her. Still remembering how her candid *less* when I asked what she thought the number was hit me in the center of my chest and why I was so fucking relieved when she told me she hasn't hooked up with anyone else since me.

I'm acting like I'm in a committed relationship with her, while she's kissing random guys at parties.

My phone buzzes in my pocket. I pull it out to see a text from…Rylan Keller.

There are fucking flutters in my stomach as I rush to unlock the screen.

> RYLAN: I'm calling bullshit on you asking for my number for "academic purposes."

I smirk, then text her right back.

> AIDAN: If I agree with your bullshit call, are you going to block me?

> RYLAN: IDK. Agree and find out.

> AIDAN: I'm calling bullshit on you believing I wanted your number for "academic purposes."

She doesn't respond right away this time, so I send her

another message.

> AIDAN: I need help.

RYLAN: With random variables and discrete probability distributions?

> AIDAN: What's that?

RYLAN: Your latest assignment, Aidan.

> AIDAN: I don't need math help.

> AIDAN: I need help with you.

> AIDAN: Because I'm not sure if we're good or not.

> AIDAN: Did Tuesday freak you out again?

RYLAN: I'm not freaked out.

RYLAN: We're good.

> AIDAN: You haven't blocked me.

RYLAN: How'd you know?

> AIDAN: Smartass.

> AIDAN: Are you feeling better?

RYLAN: Yeah, thanks.

> AIDAN: My tongue is available, if you relapse.

> AIDAN: Or just want to get off.

RYLAN: That was a one-time thing.

> AIDAN: Two-time thing.

> AIDAN: Three, counting Colorado.

RYLAN: So...you don't need math help?

RYLAN: Just assistance getting laid?

AIDAN: I don't need help getting laid.

AIDAN: I want *your* help.

RYLAN: Go hit up another girl on campus.

RYLAN: Problem solved.

AIDAN: I've discovered a problem with every other girl on campus.

RYLAN: If I ask what the problem is, will you stop texting me?

AIDAN: Dunno. Try it.

RYLAN: What is the problem with every other girl on campus?

AIDAN: They're not you.

No response again.

I exhale, then run a hand through my hair and toss my phone down.

I thought Tuesday was a turning point. That I hadn't heard from her since then because she was still feeling under the weather.

Guess not. She literally just told me to go hook up with someone else.

"Sorry. That took longer than I was expecting." Conor takes the seat across from me again.

"No worries," I tell him. "How's your mom?"

"She's good. Hoping to visit again soon. I want her and Harlow to get to know each other better."

I nod. "Do you think she'll make it to a game?"

"I'm not sure. Probably not. Her work schedule is insane."

Conor takes a pull from his beer. "My dad has been coming."

I smirk when I see the colorful bracelet on his wrist. Hart has been wearing the bracelet he made himself since our first playoff game, even after showing it to the little girl who gave the kit to him. I have yet to put mine on. But I don't tease him about it, knowing Conor usually avoids discussing his dad. Him bringing his old man up is a big deal.

"How's that going?"

Hart shrugs. "I haven't decided. He said he'd show up just to watch me. We haven't talked or anything."

"Here are the burgers." Zara reappears with two plates.

My stomach rumbles as soon as I smell the grilled meat and fried potatoes.

"Thanks," I say as she sets mine down.

"No problem. Want ketchup, Aidan?"

Conor smirks at me from across the table, catching on to the fact I chatted with her while he was gone.

"I'm good, thanks."

Zara nods, then leaves without offering Hart any.

"I love ketchup," he grumbles.

"Shut up." I flick a fry at him.

"Do I need to text Hunter for a ride home?"

"No."

I can only imagine the complaining from Morgan if he did. One, that his study whatever got interrupted. Two, that it was so I could hook up.

Or maybe he'd be relieved, thinking I've moved on from our coach's daughter like he told me to.

I take a big bite of burger, then glance down at my phone screen.

Still stubbornly black.

I haven't moved on. But I obviously should.

CHAPTER NINETEEN

RYLAN

I tighten the scarf around my neck, my watering eyes focused on the stone pavers of the path as I walk across them as quickly as my leather riding boots will allow.

I'm headed in the direction of the sports complex, which happens to be the same way the wind is blowing from. It feels like walking toward a fan blowing frigid air. Icy blasts comb through my hair and burn my cheeks.

All of the athletic buildings are located on the far edge of campus.

A long walk in nice weather. A miserable one during the cold snap Somerville is currently experiencing.

The usual dampness in the air has been replaced by a bitter bite. And since I looked awful the last time he saw me, I've dressed up extra this week on the off chance I run into Aidan. I haven't, which I thought would be a relief. Instead, I'm scanning the rink's parking lot for his truck, disappointed when I don't spot the distinctive bright shade.

I should have worn sweatpants instead of this cute, impractical skirt.

My dad's old SUV is one of the only vehicles in the lot. I'm having dinner at my parents' tonight, and my dad is giving me a ride from the rink.

There's no sign of my dad, just his car, so I keep walking toward the main entrance.

The double doors open right before I reach them, and Conor Hart walks out. His dark hair is damp, and he has a hockey bag slung over one shoulder.

The first thing I do is glance behind him to see if anyone else is coming out. He's alone, and I quickly snuff out the disappointment that appears again.

Conor smiles. "Hey."

"Hey," I echo.

Both of us pause, neither saying anything.

"I'm Rylan," I remind him.

"Right. I remember. Aidan's tutor."

Better than being called the coach's daughter, I guess.

But I don't like being referred to as Aidan's anything. Or rather, I like it too much. It's the possessive way he pulled my hips down onto his mouth in verbal form.

"I usually just go by Rylan," I say. "Team captain."

Conor smirks. "Touché. You here to see your dad?"

I nod. "You here for extra practice?"

The team's practice ended a couple of hours ago. I know the hockey team's entire schedule now, thanks to Aidan. He sent me his so we could reschedule the study sessions we've missed lately. Sent me his *entire* schedule. Classes, practices, games. Basically a map of his whereabouts, but I haven't orchestrated bumping into him.

"Yeah," Conor replies, adjusting the strap on his shoulder. "Can't prepare too much before the next round. Or if you can, I am."

I smile. "Well…good luck." I'm nervous around Conor, and it's not the awkwardness of him being one of my dad's players or a really hot guy. He's Aidan's best friend.

"Thanks," he says.

I smile again before continuing toward the doors.

"Rylan."

I still with surprise, then turn back around.

"I just wanted to say thanks."

My forehead wrinkles. "For what?"

"For tutoring Phillips. Knowing him, it probably hasn't been the easiest job in the world. He loves to fuck around and to stir shit up, but he's one of the best guys I've ever met. I don't want to win a championship without him, and you're why he's still on the team. So, thanks. I've walked in on Aidan actually studying at least a dozen times this week."

"That's all him," I say, almost defensively.

It's nice of Conor to credit me, but I'm a terrible tutor. I haven't responded to Aidan's email with his schedule because I know the conviction about staying away from him will disappear as soon as we meet. When I woke up on Wednesday morning, well-rested and clear-headed, all the uncertainty his presence chased away reappeared.

I couldn't think past pleasure when he was in my bed. When he was touching me.

But since then, all I've done is second-guess what happened. And it's not just the complications that Aidan is on the hockey team or the guy that I'm tutoring. Hooking up with Aidan didn't just happen because I'm insanely attracted to him.

I like him.

He's not just the confident, gorgeous guy I encountered in the woods. Or just the carefree, popular player who sauntered into the library for our first tutoring session.

He's considerate and funny and intriguing.

All good things.

Too good.

I'm not concerned about his connection to my dad or the dubious ethics of hooking up with my tutee, even if Conor's praise makes me feel way worse about how I've handled that.

I'm worried Aidan is going to break my heart. I've spent way too long staring at his *They're not you* text, and those are just words on a screen.

"If you say so," Conor says. "See ya 'round, Rylan."

"Bye, Conor," I reply, watching him head toward the lot.

He's wearing the same Holt Hockey jacket Aidan often wears. Aidan's hair is a lighter shade of brown, but he and Conor are about the same build.

It's easy to imagine that's Aidan walking away from me.

Which is exactly what he will do, at some point. Either because I give in and he gets bored or because I don't give in and he gets bored.

I need to be prepared for that outcome either way.

Aidan's not a relationship guy.

Walker seemed like one. We started out as friends. Got drinks, then drinks turned into dinner. We were officially dating for a month before we had sex for the first time.

In some ways, Aidan Phillips is an ideal candidate for a fling. The perfect way to regain my confidence and to try new things. To just *have fun*.

Him playing hockey and failing Stats complicated it.

But he had to *ruin* it by walking me home. Paying for my drink. Bringing me dinner.

You're not supposed to have feelings for a fling.

And I have feelings for Aidan.

Another cold gust of wind convinces me to head inside rather than continue standing here.

Stepping in through the double doors is a relief. It's not warm inside the building, but it's *warmer*.

I walk through the lobby and toward the ice, gazing around in awe. It's bigger than I remember, maybe because it's the first time in years I've seen the rink when it's completely empty.

The ice is flawless, gleaming beneath the bright lights. And it's church silent, so quiet I can hear my footsteps as the bottoms of my boots hit the rubber mats.

It's very different staring out at the rink when there's no one on it. It's just an endless expanse of white. Smooth and pristine, such a sharp contrast to the clashes that were taking place on its surface the last time I was looking at it.

I haven't skated in years.

And I miss it, I realize suddenly. It's one of those things I worked to outgrow simply because that seemed like what growing up was at the time.

The weightless glide. The proud way my dad would watch me. The constant fear of falling.

"Hey, honey."

I turn. My dad is walking this way with a couple of binders tucked under one arm.

"Hey, Dad."

He reaches me, squeezing me against his side the same way he did when I was little. "You're feeling better? Your mom said you came down with a cold."

"Yeah, I'm much better. Just needed a few good nights' sleep."

"Good. Have you been waiting long? You should have come back to my office."

"I just got here," I assure him. "I haven't been waiting at all."

"Oh, all right. Are you ready to go?"

I nod, then blurt, "Were you upset when I stopped playing hockey?"

Wondering that has stuck with me, ever since Aidan brought it up. I thought not choosing Holt was the first time I let down my dad, but maybe that happened a lot earlier. He just nodded when I told him I wanted to do gymnastics with my friends instead, and that was that.

Both of his eyebrows rise. "Upset? No."

"Disappointed, then?"

"Of course not. I only wanted you to play if you loved it, Rylan."

"I mean, I liked it."

He chuckles. "Where is this coming from? You haven't talked about hockey in years. You *playing* hockey, in a decade."

"I just…" I look at the ice again. "You and Mom were right about Holt. You said I should give going here a chance, and I never did. I dug my heels in about going to Boston, and it was a mistake. I'm just…worried about what other ones I've made."

"Well, you weren't going to be a gold medalist. I wouldn't worry."

"Dad!"

He laughs loud enough to echo off the high ceilings. "Rylan, nothing's a mistake unless you decide it's a mistake. I'm proud of you for deciding hockey wasn't your path, not upset or disappointed. Just like I'm proud of you for flying across the country for college. Just like I'm proud of you for transferring."

I nod, my throat suspiciously thick and my nose tingling from more than just the cold. "Thanks, Dad." I glance upward at the lone banner decorating the rafters. "Are you ready for the quarterfinals?"

"I think so. Hart hasn't wavered. Willis has been strong in net.

Morgan is always reliable. And Phillips has really stepped up recently."

I force my expression to remain impassive. I've heard my dad talk about his players before. But those were meaningless names.

It feels—sounds—different, now that I've met most of the guys he just mentioned.

Now that it matters to me if Aidan wins a championship.

I'm not just rooting for Holt to win because of my dad.

"How has tutoring him been going?" he asks.

My eyes remain on the ice. "Good," I tell him.

"Great." My dad sounds relieved.

I wonder what he would say—how he would sound—if I confided I'd discussed a lot more than math with Aidan.

That he's been the highlight of transferring.

That when I'm around him I feel special and *seen*, in a way I've never experienced before.

But I'm not brave enough to say any of that out loud. I've never talked boys with my dad; those have always been conversations with my mom. And this isn't a crush on a random guy in one of my classes. This is one of his players. He's known Aidan a lot longer than I have. He cares enough about him to make the effort to keep him on the team and to ask me to tutor him. I don't want to risk upsetting their relationship by disclosing my feelings, especially when I'm planning to do nothing about them.

"You hungry?" he asks. "Your mom started cooking before I left this morning."

I smile. "Yeah. Let's go."

One last look at the ice and then I follow him back toward the lobby.

———

My dad drops me off at my house just before ten. I basically have to roll myself out of the car, I'm so full. I'm a decent cook, but nothing compared to my mom. She made all my favorites, and I ate way too much tonight.

"Hey!" Chloe greets me when I walk into the kitchen to store the leftovers my mom sent me home with. Her tone is as upbeat as ever, but there's a tightness to her expression I'm confused by.

Mystery solved, when I see a guy slouched next to Dakota on the couch.

He's fully focused on his phone, not even taking his eyes off the screen as he reaches out and grabs his can of beer to take a chug. Dakota is either unbothered by his behavior or used to it, painting her toenails purple between bites of pizza.

This must be her boyfriend, Mason, and I can see why Malia and Chloe aren't his biggest fans.

"Hey," I reply, focusing on Chloe as I walk over to the fridge and set the glass containers on the shelf.

"How was dinner with your parents?"

"It was good. If you're hungry, my mom sent me home with a ton of extra food."

"We just ate." Chloe reaches up, storing a pot in the cabinet next to the stove. "But I'll take you up on that tomorrow. I'm sick of cooking."

"You're the new Emily?"

I glance toward the couch, where Mason has finally looked up from his phone.

"Uh, I guess so. I'm Rylan. Nice to meet you."

Rather than respond, he stands and walks this way. His eyes are focused on my legs, which makes me glad I still have my winter coat on. "I'm Mason."

"Nice to meet you, Mason."

He walks over to the fridge and pulls another can of beer out. "How ya liking Holt?"

"Good, thanks."

"Heard your dad coaches the hockey team."

Only a matter of time, I guess, until that became common knowledge.

I nod. "Yeah, he does."

"Does that mean you have a thing for hockey guys, like the rest of the girls at this school?"

My stomach roils unpleasantly when he winks.

Chloe makes a face, possibly taking the question as a personal insult. Dakota snorts, still focused on her nails.

"It means my dad coaches the hockey team," I say cooly.

I'm liking Mason less by the second. At least he takes the hint and heads back to the couch with his fresh beer.

"Gonna go study," I tell Chloe.

She nods, then tilts her head toward the couch and mouths *Ignore him.*

I nod back, then head down the hallway to my bedroom. Change into comfier, warmer clothes before settling at my desk to get some work done.

Instead of starting on any of my assignments, I unlock my phone.

Stare at Aidan's latest message, in what's become a familiar routine.

He hasn't texted since, and I don't know what that means. Has he already lost interest? Is he annoyed at me for not replying? Is this a game to him?

I shut my phone off and open a textbook, focusing on this week's problem set. Abstract Algebra seems less complicated than thinking about Aidan Phillips.

CHAPTER TWENTY

AIDAN

The pain intensifies as soon as I move my arm.

I hiss, shifting so that the ice pack is back in place before attempting to text her again.

> AIDAN: Can't make tutoring tonight.
>
> AIDAN: Sorry.
>
> AIDAN: LMK about rescheduling.

The last message I sent Rylan was *They're not you.*

A text she never replied to, so I try to strike a more detached tone this time around rather than that of a desperate dog begging for a pat.

I've never worked harder for anything in my life than a scrap of Rylan Keller's attention, and maybe that's my whole damn problem.

I wouldn't want to hook up with a lazy underachiever either.

Although my track record is pretty good where the hooking up part is concerned, so I doubt that's why she hasn't responded.

I've just started dozing off when my phone buzzes on my chest. It's another painful process to lift it up.

I wish that I'd taken Coach up on his offer to leave practice early right about now. I feel like I got hit by a truck and my ribs look like they did. I had a nasty collision with Williams earlier—bad timing when neither of us were looking—and I took the worst of it, right in the same spot that Pierce knocked a few weeks ago.

Unfortunately, it's not Rylan answering.

It's my mom calling.

I debate not picking up, but that'll only earn me a lecture from my dad in the next voicemail he leaves.

My phone has been mercifully absent of calls from family members since Jameson's engagement party, but I know that'll change as the wedding creeps closer.

"Hi, Mom."

"Oh, honey, I wasn't sure you'd answer. You must be so busy with your final semester."

I tamp down the snort that wants to come out. "Hockey practice just ended and the kegger I'm hosting doesn't start for an hour. You caught me at the perfect time."

Her sigh is exasperated. "Aidan."

"What's up, Mom?" I shift, flinching when the cold pack brushes a bit of unnumbed skin.

"I just wanted to see how you were doing. I hardly saw you during your visit."

"So you waited *two weeks* to call me?"

Another sigh. One that will result in my father chastising me for upsetting my mother and Jameson gloating about having favorite child in the bag.

"I'm fine, Mom. My classes are going well."

For once, it's not a lie. The worse I've scored on one of Professor Carrigan's assignments is an eighty-six. I'm carrying all

Bs and one A in my other classes, my new studiousness paying off across the board.

"What about hockey?"

I'm...stunned. My mom has made it clear on multiple occasions how she views hockey as a low form of entertainment. Nothing more than grown men running into each other on ice for fun.

"Hockey's...good," I say cautiously.

"We were thinking of coming to the championship game."

I'm so surprised, it takes me a good minute to respond. "In *Cleveland*?"

Each year, the NCAA chooses a neutral location for all college championship games to take place. This year the Division III matchup is set to take place in Cleveland, Ohio. Even if the game were taking place in LA, I wasn't expecting my family to come. Seeing as they've *never* attended a Holt hockey game.

"Right. Cleveland, yes."

"We might not make it that far," I tell her. "There are two more rounds to get through first."

Two rounds my ribs might not let me play in. Thank God we only have a film session tomorrow.

"Well, if you do, we'll be there."

"Who's *we*?" I ask, increasingly suspicious.

There's no way my mom developed an interest in hockey or a desire to visit Ohio overnight.

"Oh, just me, your father, and Jameson. Plus Parker and her parents."

"Why the fuck would the Maddens go?"

"Language," she chides. "And they, uh, their nephew plays for Fabor."

Our expected opponent.

All the pieces come together. Their future in-laws are going to support their nephew, so my parents feel obligated to come see me play for the first time.

I'm pissed—at them and at myself.

I'd rather they continue to make snide comments about me spending time pushing a rubber circle around the ice than feign any interest. And I hate how, for a few seconds, I thought that maybe they were coming for *me*.

There's a soft knock on my bedroom door.

"Come in," I call out, figuring it's Conor or Hunter.

They've seen me scowling on the phone before, so who cares if they witness this?

But when the door opens, Rylan is the one standing in the doorway.

"I have to go, Mom," I tell her, then hang up and sit up, tossing my phone away onto the mattress.

"Hey." Rylan's expression is all uncertainty as she takes a step forward, playing with the strap of her backpack. "I didn't mean to, um, interrupt…"

"You're in my bedroom," I say stupidly.

Obviously, she's in my bedroom, and I'm too shocked to do anything except state that fact.

"Yeah. Um, I saw your texts, and I just…you're okay?" Rylan scans me over like she's looking for a defect.

"I had a rough practice, and I'm sore as shit, but otherwise, yeah. I'm good."

"And we're…uh, good?"

"This is about the texts."

She's here because she thinks she hurt my feelings.

My irritation spikes, right along with my pain level as my side protests sitting upright. "I told you nothing else that happened between us would affect tutoring."

"Yeah, you said that. And *then* you canceled tutoring the week after you…"

"The week after I what, Rylan?"

She holds eye contact. "The week after you went down on me."

That's my girl.

Well, not *my* girl.

"I meant what I said. Me rescheduling had nothing to do with eating you out last week or you not answering my texts. I'm having a shitty fucking day and I knew I wouldn't be able to focus tonight. That's it."

Rylan studies me for a minute, then nods. "Okay."

She tugs the zipper of her jacket an inch higher.

She's leaving, I realize.

"How'd you know where I live?"

"You told me, remember? And it's 'common knowledge on campus,' right?"

I smirk, mostly at her use of air quotes. A little because I really like having her in my room and it's hitting me more that she's actually *here*.

"And you just invited yourself inside?"

Her cheeks flush pink. "No one was answering the door, and it was unlocked."

"Team went to Gaffney's after practice. It's wings night."

"Why didn't you go?"

I lie back down, then tug my shirt up. My side looks worse than it did an hour ago, sections darkening to a mottled purple.

Rylan sucks in a sharp breath, then steps closer to my bed. Closer and closer, until her cool fingers are brushing my ribs. "That happened at practice?"

"Yeah." I relax into the mattress, her light touch more

soothing than the cold ice pack was. "I was playing sloppy and Williams wasn't looking where he was going. Bad timing."

"Sorry."

"You weren't the one who tossed me into the boards." I shift, then wince. Massage my shoulder, which also hurts. "Tomorrow's an easy day. Some sleep and a few painkillers, and I'll be fine."

She's silent and standing still. Then the sound of her coat's zipper fills the room again. Except instead of going up, it's coming down.

I watch like it's the most fascinating sight I've ever witnessed.

And honestly? Rylan taking her clothes off in my room is absolutely up there.

Unfortunately, the strip show ends with her sweater still on. Rylan tosses her jacket on the opposite side of my bed, then pushes her sleeves up to her elbows. She's wearing a gray skirt that hugs her hips, and a pair of black tights. If I could move with any sort of ease right now, I'd absolutely be tugging both down and repeating last week's tutoring session.

"Roll over," she tells me.

I raise an eyebrow. "What? Why?"

Moving is the last thing I feel like doing, and I'd be lying if I said I'm not holding out hope for a blowjob, even if it's a pity one. Oral seems to be as far as Rylan is willing to take our hookups, and I'll take whatever she's willing to give. Her telling me to lie dick down snuffs out any hope of that happening.

"Just trust me, Phillips."

My teammates and Coach call me by my last name a lot, but no girl ever has.

It's a reminder we're friends, or something similar to that. Something more than tutor and student. Something different than just sex, even though I'm dying to get that from her.

I roll over, smushing my face into the pillow and exhaling

through my nose as I wait for the pain in my side to subside. It feels like someone just slid a hot poker into my ribs.

The mattress dips, and I turn my face to the side so I can try to see what Rylan is doing. I can't see shit, but I can feel her straddle my lower back. Feel the heat of her against the base of my spine.

"Fuck," I groan, as my dick twitches unhappily.

"Too hard?" There's a worried note to Rylan's voice as she shifts her weight, only succeeding in torturing me more.

"You're not what's hard."

"Oh." Then another "*Oh*" as she registers my meaning. "Really? Me sitting on your back is turning you on?"

"It's a new kink for me too."

"Does that mean you haven't had any *fun* recently?" she asks, slowly tugging my shirt up.

I shouldn't have even bothered putting one on after my shower. I just didn't want to look at the bruise blossoming on my side.

I wish I could see her face. Tell if she's as nonchalant about me hooking up with another girl as she sounds.

"No."

And it's been a hell of a lot longer than a week since I had sex, but I don't tell her that. I clear my throat, hoping my "You?" sounds casual.

"Just you."

I like the way that sounds way too much. It's even better than hearing *Zero*.

Rylan's hands reach my shoulders, tucking my shirt out of the way, and then her thumbs are pressing into the skin just below them.

I groan—loudly—as she starts to rub my sore muscles, exerting the perfect amount of pressure. My entire body relaxes, going limp with relief. Even the pain in my side eases, overwhelmed by the wave of pleasure. Instead of distracting me, it feels like she's fixing me.

I groan again as she works her way down. Whatever the long muscles that stretch on either side of my spine are called, they're knotted and tight.

"Should I be worried that you weren't this loud when we had sex?"

I huff a laugh. "I was this loud. You were just distracted."

She hums, her hands moving up to my shoulders and then down my biceps. It actually feels like I'm floating away from my body, melting down into the mattress as her magical hands work me over.

"We could have sex again," I suggest. "So you have a more recent comparison?"

"Nice try."

"I meant it, you know."

Her grip loosens for a second, but that's the only reaction before she continues massaging.

"I want to have sex with *you*. I'm not just wanting sex."

She's silent, and I'm both grateful and relieved I can't see her expression.

"I'll stop mentioning it. Since you're, you know, *not interested* and all. I just wanted to make sure that was clear."

Rylan doesn't respond. But she doesn't stop rubbing, and she doesn't move away, so hopefully I didn't fuck it up too badly.

"That was your mom on the phone?" she asks.

"Yeah." I sigh, a little of my earlier irritation filtering through the bliss of having her on my bed turning my muscles into jelly. "She wanted to tell me they're coming to the championship game. Assuming we get that far."

"That's…nice?"

"Best part is they're showing up because Parker's parents are

254

going to support their nephew. He plays for Fabor. If Glendale beats them, I'm guessing they won't show."

"Aidan…"

"It's fine. Whatever. I shouldn't have been surprised."

"It's not fine."

"Yeah. It sucks. But it is what it is. I am who I am; my parents are who they are. Even when we got along, we were never that close. We'll never be that open, loving family, and I accepted that a long time ago."

"You don't think people can change?"

"I think people have to want to change, to change. And no one in this equation does, so…nothing will change."

"I'm sorry."

I roll onto my back, sick of not seeing her face. Rylan ends up straddling my lap, my shirt twisted between us. "Stop apologizing for shit that isn't your fault."

"What do you want me to do, then?"

"Kiss me," comes out embarrassingly fast. "I didn't have a chance to in the library and last time you were a Petri dish of germs."

Rylan smirks. "Petri dish? And *I'm* the nerd?"

"I probably wouldn't have failed biology if you'd been my tutor," I tell her.

"I don't believe you failed biology."

"You doubted I got into Stanford."

"I'm glad you didn't go to Stanford."

"So glad you're going to kiss me?"

Her smile grows, which I take as a positive sign. "I'm thinking about it."

"Any questions I can answer first? Technique? Tongue or no tongue? Timing between breaths? Head tilt?"

She leans closer. Close enough I can smell her shampoo, the

same scent that lingered in my truck for a few days after I drove her home in the rain.

"I'll just give you a review later."

I'm still chuckling when she closes the small distance between our lips.

Electricity races through my body.

Even after our two hookups since, part of me thought that kissing Rylan the night we met was one of those memories that ages well. That improves over time, warping the original until you're reminded of the reality. Like a movie you watch and love as a kid but then is actually terrible when you rewatch it as an adult.

But kissing Rylan? This is just as good as I remember. Better, maybe, because she's no longer a stranger. I know that she loves having her hair tugged because she let out a breathy whimper every time I pulled while she was blowing me in the library. And it's ridiculously satisfying, when she reacts the same way to me wrapping the strands around my fingers now.

It starts out slow and skilled, like we're two competitors trying to outdo the other. I nibble on her bottom lip. She sucks on my tongue. Then gradually, it grows more desperate. More about getting as close to each other as possible than showing each other up. Like we're on the same team, united by the same goal.

I'm not sure how far she's planning to take this.

There's no way Rylan is oblivious to my massive erection digging into her ass. And I've made it clear I want to fuck her. My body is in rough shape, but I'll rally if she gives me the green light.

"Is this what tutoring looks like? Sign me up."

Rylan pulls away, panting, as soon as she hears Hunter's voice.

He's standing in the open doorway with his arms crossed, wearing an amused smile that doesn't reach his eyes.

And Rylan won't meet mine, sliding off the bed with her coat clutched in one hand.

Without her saying a single word, I know tonight is over. She's already pulling on her jacket and smoothing her hair.

"How was Gaffney's?" I ask Hunter, trying to act like this is a normal situation, even though all of us know it's anything but.

"Usual. Brought you back some wings, if you're hungry."

I nod, tugging my T-shirt back down. "Thanks, man."

Rylan picks up her backpack from my floor, still avoiding eye contact. I can't tell if she's embarrassed or annoyed or upset, and I can't ask in front of Hunter.

"I should go."

"Okay," I say.

"Nice to see you again, Rylan," Hunter says as she passes him and heads down the hallway toward the stairs.

He remains in place once she's out of sight, pinning me with a serious look, complete with his judgmental eyebrows. "What the fuck are you doing, Phillips?"

I lean back against my pillows, rubbing a hand across my face. "Would it be better or worse if I said I have no clue?"

"Hart would have been right behind me if he wasn't dropping Harlow off. Just saying, making out with your tutor with the door wide open was one of your dumber moves."

His eyebrows lift again before he leaves.

"Can you bring the wings upstairs?" I call out.

No response.

Guess not.

CHAPTER TWENTY-ONE

RYLAN

I have a problem, and his name is Aidan Phillips.

That's all I can think about as Theo talks about the grad program at MIT he's hoping to get accepted into. He asked me if I wanted to grab coffee after our shared algebra class, and I didn't see any reason to say no at the time.

Now, I've realized a reason. Aidan was right. Theo *does* like me, is viewing this as a pseudo date, and I can't stop thinking about a six-three hockey player.

When I first found out Hot Tub Guy was a hockey player on my dad's team who I'd have to see on a weekly basis, I was mortified.

Somehow, Aidan erased that embarrassment.

I've never met someone so comfortable in his own skin, and maybe some of that confidence has rubbed off on me.

He didn't tell me to keep what happened between us a secret. He didn't freak out about the fact my father is his coach. He didn't ask for a different tutor.

And the immediate attraction I experienced when I first saw him, sitting in that steaming tub staring up at the stars and sipping whiskey, hasn't gone anywhere.

No matter how many times I try to convince myself it's a terrible idea, it remains. It's expanded and grown, turning into a force I have no control over.

I think of him at stupid, inconvenient times like right now, when I'm sitting and talking to a guy I *should* like. I've never experienced flutters of nerves around Theo, let alone the burning need I fled Aidan's bedroom with, but maybe I could.

I'm *trying* to, unsuccessfully.

"What did you think of Boston?" Theo asks me.

I resist the urge to make a face.

My distaste has nothing to do with the city. Or the university. It has everything to do with who I was there, how I accepted the bare minimum.

After living with Chloe, Malia, and Dakota, I'm aware of how checked out my other roommates were. After having classmates like Theo, who's made an obvious effort to familiarize me with Holt's mathematics department, I'm aware of how cutthroat my old classmates were. And since meeting Aidan, I'm aware of how lackluster my relationship with Walker was.

"It was nice," I tell him. "I didn't explore as much as I wish I had. It's easy to take it for granted while you're there. But the science museum is amazing. And I used to study on the Common in the warmer weather. Great restaurants."

"Do you miss it at all?"

"No," I reply, then take a sip of my coffee. "I just fit here better, I guess."

Theo chuckles, running a hand through his hair. "Yeah. My folks are pushing for me to consider University of Iowa. They thought Washington was far. Massachusetts sounds like a different planet to them."

"That's nice, though. That you're so close to them."

He nods, his expression serious. "Yeah. They're the best. My dad took out a second mortgage on the house to send me to the best high school in the state."

"Do you have any siblings?" I ask.

"Yeah, I…"

The rest of Theo's answer is drowned out by the rush of blood in my ears.

Aidan is walking in with two guys I don't recognize. One of them is wearing a Holt Hockey hoodie, so I assume they're all teammates.

He's grinning in response to what one of them is saying, his expression nothing like the defeated, exhausted one he was wearing on Tuesday night.

I'm still not sure what possessed me to climb on his bed and act like his personal masseuse. My mom used to get terrible migraines when I was younger, and I got used to seeing my dad rubbing her temples regardless of whether she was experiencing one or not. Aidan said he was sore, and a back rub was just the thing that occurred to me to do. But I feel weird about it now, just like I'm embarrassed Hunter walked in on us.

I showed up to make sure things between us weren't weird, and then I managed to make it more awkward.

"What about you?" Theo is asking.

Since I missed most of what he just said, my response is a gamble we're still on the same topic. "Nope. Only child."

Theo says, "Lucky," with an exasperated eye roll that makes me think I missed some funny story about his siblings.

I could tell him that my mom had two miscarriages after me, but I don't.

Those trips to the hospital feel too personal to share with a guy I hardly know. Never mind that I told Aidan about Walker cheating on me the first time we met. Maybe there's some thin line between not knowing someone at all and not knowing them well enough, and that's the zone Theo and I are in.

"I'm going to grab another muffin," Theo tells me. "You want anything?"

"No. I'm good, thanks."

I glance down at my open notebook as soon as Theo leaves the table. We were comparing answers on this week's problem set earlier. Now it's a convenient way to look busy while I'm sitting alone.

My phone buzzes on the table.

> AIDAN: You look bored.

I keep my eyes down, fighting the urge to look up at him and react.

I didn't think he'd noticed me. Theo chose a table tucked in the back corner.

> RYLAN: I'm studying math. According to you, that's boring.

His response is immediate.

> AIDAN: I never said that.

> AIDAN: Looks like you're on a date.

I gnaw on my bottom lip, then stop when I remember he might be watching.

> RYLAN: You've implied it.

> RYLAN: And so what if I am?

Two minutes pass before he responds.

AIDAN: When are we rescheduling tutoring for this week?

RYLAN: You tell me. You're the one who canceled on Tuesday.

As soon as I send it, I regret it. I would have had trouble *breathing* with a bruise like his, let alone studying.

As far as excuses go, I've definitely heard worse.

RYLAN: We both know your schedule is busier than mine.

AIDAN: Just pick one of the times that's open on it, then.

AIDAN: Or send me *your* schedule, and I'll do it.

RYLAN: Fine. I'll email you tonight.

AIDAN: Text me.

AIDAN: I only check my school email once a month.

RYLAN: Please tell me you're kidding.

AIDAN: I prefer talking in person.

AIDAN: For example, you showing up in my bedroom instead of just texting me back? A plus plus, tutor.

This is when I should stop texting him. I can feel our conversation veering into dangerous territory.

RYLAN: How's your bruise?

AIDAN: If you wanted a shirtless pic, you just had to ask.

When I don't reply, he texts again.

> AIDAN: If I say it looks awful and feels worse, will you rub my back again?

> > RYLAN: No.

> AIDAN: Worth a shot.

> AIDAN: I'll live.

> AIDAN: Thanks for asking.

I wonder if anyone else has.

Do guys talk about injuries with each other or is it all macho, tough guy shit? I know his parents aren't checking in on his health.

"Sorry. Long line."

Theo returns to his spot next to me.

"No problem." I fix a smile on my face, then finally give in to the urge to glance over at Aidan.

He's with the same two guys, plus a group of four girls who've materialized from somewhere. The one standing closest to Aidan is currently getting glared at by the girl working the espresso machine. I recognize her from the last time I was in here at the same time as Aidan, and it appears the torch she's holding for him is still blazing.

Aidan glances at me before I can look away, catching me staring. His expression is unreadable.

The girl grabs his arm, then rises on her tiptoes to whisper something. Aidan glances down at her, grinning in response to whatever she said.

I know he's a flirt.

I've told him—multiple times—to hook up with someone else. Part of me thought that would be a relief. A door slamming closed. Temptation removed.

So I'm totally unprepared for the hot flare of jealousy.

For the strong urge to stand up and walk over there and push the manicured hand off his arm like I have any claim to stake.

For the realization that I'm even more screwed than I realized.

I force my attention away from Aidan and back to Theo.

Successfully, until my phone buzzes ten minutes later.

I don't check it for another twenty minutes, on the way to my next class.

Aidan sent me three texts.

The first one is a photo. He didn't take it, and I smile at the thought of him asking one of his teammates to snap it. One of the guys he was with is in the background of the main parking lot, laughing.

Aidan's pulling his shirt up with one hand. He's holding his coffee cup in the other. Strategically, so I can't actually see the bruise on his side. That makes me think it looks just as bad as he was joking about.

Beneath the photo, he's sent two messages.

> AIDAN: Since I know you like looking at them.
>
> AIDAN: BTW, I'm still waiting on that review...

CHAPTER TWENTY-TWO

AIDAN

There's something about being unhappy amidst a group of really happy people that's incredibly isolating. Misery loves company, I guess. My misery is all alone at a rager that's maybe the wildest party I've attended in college.

I should be having a good time tonight.

No, an *amazing* time.

We beat Mulbridge five to three. One more win, and we'll be headed to Cleveland. Playing for a championship. Which has been the goal all season but has always seemed unlikely. I'm in a state of disbelief, I think, about how likely it's suddenly looking.

A hot blonde pulled me into a dance shortly after I arrived with Hunter and Conor and grinded her ass all over my dick. I made up an excuse as soon as the song was over and ended up in the kitchen, watching Hunter pass out his Jell-O shots and Conor standing with his arms wrapped around Harlow. Guys keep slapping my back or punching my shoulder, shouting congratulations. Girls keep trying to catch my eye or "accidentally" brushing up against me.

Something about it all just feels…empty.

It's like I forgot what I liked about this.

Like drinking and flirting was a form of denial, but I've accepted reality, so it now seems ineffective. Unnecessary.

I walk out of the kitchen, stopping to talk to a couple of my teammates before heading into the bathroom. Not the half bath off the kitchen, but the one attached to the downstairs master. Pierce's room, I think. Or maybe Brennan's. Who the fuck cares? All I'm concerned about is that it's empty, with no line.

I take a piss, wash my hands, then lean against the tile wall and pull my phone out of my pocket.

She never responded to my last text asking for a review.

I don't need one. Rylan kissed me first, and I know she was into it. If Hunter hadn't showed up, we probably would have had sex.

Her lack of reply isn't a subtle hint. But I saw the annoyance on her face when she spotted the girls swarming me in the coffee shop. A hell of a lot more emotion than was in her expression looking at Coffee Shop Guy.

So I haven't given up, as stupid and as pointless as it might be. If she were here, I'd be enjoying this party a hell of a lot more. I run a hand through my hair, debating.

I pocket my phone without messaging her.

Maybe after a few more shots I'll ask her to send me a photo back, but I'm not drunk yet.

There's a brunette lying on the bed when I walk out of the bathroom. There's a leap of excitement in my chest that dies when I register her face. The odds of Rylan showing up at another hockey party seemed slim anyway.

"Hey, Aidan." She sits up, a coy smile curving up her lips as she crosses her legs, drawing the bottom of her skirt up so high she's practically flashing her panties at me. "Saw you head in here…thought you might want some company."

A line I've heard before.

Most of my hookups have involved girls following me into bathrooms or bedrooms, actually.

Tonight, it does nothing for me. It's been weeks since I had sex, and playing through how this would go is like watching a movie. Undressing her...talking to her...touching her... I can picture each step.

There's no motivation to make the effort, even when it's being tossed right into my lap.

I know it'll feel good in the moment, and I know I'll feel just as empty when it's over.

"Not looking for any company tonight," I tell her.

Her expression is a mixture of shocked and embarrassed, which I feel bad about.

I'm not known for turning girls down, but I'm not going to fuck her just to spare her feelings.

I settle on "Have a good night" before heading out of the bedroom.

Sampson is standing in the hallway, smirking in my direction. His grin widens, and I'm guessing the girl left the bedroom right after me. Know exactly what it looks like. My hair is even messed up from my own irritation.

"Party just started, Phillips," he tells me. "Pace yourself."

"Did you guys get shots?" Hunter appears before I can respond to Robby, holding a tray of wiggling cups. They look disgusting but don't taste terrible.

I down one, since I'm currently sober and probably the person enjoying this party the least. Maybe the girl I just turned down is feeling worse.

"Hell yeah!" Robby slaps my shoulder as I swallow, nearly causing me to choke. "Phillips just scored again," he tells Hunter.

"Oh, yeah?"

I avoid eye contact with Morgan as I crush the cup in my hand, then toss it back on his tray. He hasn't brought up Rylan since he saw her in my bedroom, and I'm relieved.

I don't know what there is to say.

Yeah, I like her. Yeah, I'm attracted to her.

I have no clue if she likes me. And any attraction to me seems to vary on a day-by-day basis.

"Some brunette," Robby is saying. "What was her name, Phillips?"

"No idea," I say, tempted to reach for another shot.

Sampson whistles, then shakes his head.

"See you guys later." I continue down the hallway, heading toward the living room instead of back into the kitchen. Chances are there's a drinking game going on in there by now.

I push through the crowd of bodies, my elbow accidentally knocking into someone's shoulder. I turn, an apology already on my lips. "Shit. I'm sorry…" I blink, but she's still standing in front of me.

This time, it's really her. And she looks hot as fuck, wearing jeans and one of those drapey tops that shifts and shows flashes of cleavage if you look hard enough. And I'm *definitely* looking hard enough.

"Goal and an assist," Rylan tells me, smiling. "Not terrible." She looked up my stats from the game earlier, not just the final score.

It makes me wish I'd managed a second goal so they were more impressive.

"High praise." I step closer, rewarded when her chest lifts with a rapid breath. Her shirt inches to the left, revealing the curve of her left breast.

We're just inside the doorway, close to a corner of the room, so it's easy enough to isolate ourselves, to block her off with my body.

It's dim, and everyone around us is drunk and distracted.

"What are you doing here, Rye?"

I'm close enough to catch the bob of her throat as she swallows. At least I know she's affected too.

"I, um, I came with Isla. She thought Clayton might be here."

"I didn't ask why your friend came. I asked why you're here."

"To have fun."

God, what I would've given for her answer to be *You*.

"Oh, yeah? Too bad there's no pool table for you to hang around."

Her brown eyes flash with annoyance. "You can be a real dick, you know that?"

Yeah. I know that. What I don't know is why I'm physically incapable of leaving her alone. I should have said *Hi* and kept walking.

"I'm here to have a drink and hang out and maybe kiss a guy, if there was a moment," she continues.

Fuck me.

I don't know if I should laugh or punch the wall behind her. The one girl I can't get out of my head, and she showed up at my team's party to *maybe kiss a guy, if there was a moment*.

"Great. Have fun."

I turn around and walk away, heading toward the front door instead of remaining in the living room like I was planning before I ran into her. I'm in a worse mood than before, and don't feel like being around anyone.

The guys will all assume I snuck off to have a threesome or something.

I'm halfway across the front yard when I hear her calling my name. I debate whether to keep walking, because there's a chance

I'll say something worse than *Have fun* if we have another conversation. And I don't want to hurt Rylan. Seeing her upset affects me differently, triggers some protective urge that's been there ever since she told me her ex had cheated that first night.

"Aidan!" She shouts my name again, loud enough for the whole block to hear, and then I have no choice but to turn around.

I spin to face her. If I was in a better mood, I'd be tempted to smile at Rylan's light jog to catch up. Puffs of air trail behind her.

It's colder than usual out, a frigid night that reminds me of Colorado.

"Where are you going?" she asks, crossing her arms and rubbing her biceps.

I hook a thumb over one shoulder. "Home."

She gnaws on her bottom lip. "Why?"

"I'm tired. Long day."

"The rest of the team seems to be rallying just fine."

"Yep. Go celebrate with them."

She grabs my sleeve before I can turn away, anticipating the movement. "You're mad at me."

"Nope. Go have your *moment*."

A little of the confusion clears from her expression. "That's going to be tricky, since you're leaving."

"Oh," I realize.

"Yeah. *Oh*." A smirk appears on her face. "You were jealous."

"Obviously. I thought you'd moved on before giving me your review."

"You really need to drop the review thing—"

Since she's already holding on to me, it's easy to tug her closer and kiss her. When I pull back, she has wet lips and a dazed expression.

Fuck, she's so beautiful. Breath stalls in my chest.

"All I need is a star rating."

"Out of five? Or out of ten? Are half stars allowed? Or if not, do I round up or do I round down?"

"All you really needed to say was 'perfect score,'" I tell her.

Rylan smirks. "How about thumbs up or thumbs down?"

I sigh. Roll my eyes. "Sure. Which one did I get?"

"Let's go for a drive, and I'll tell you."

I lift an eyebrow. "Go for a drive. In your imaginary car?"

"No, in your obnoxiously red truck." She points across the street.

"Did Hart bribe you to say that?"

Rylan shakes her head. "It's the same color as a fire engine, Aidan."

"Men like red cars, okay?"

"Only if they're trying to compensate for something."

"Well, there goes your theory, because…" I gesture toward my crotch.

Rylan scoffs before holding her hand out. "Keys."

"What?"

"You've been drinking. I'm sober."

"I had one shot," I protest. "And it was one of Hunter's gross Jell-O ones, which are ninety percent sugar and ten percent alcohol."

I've never let anyone drive my truck. Not many people have asked, but still. Picking it out was a rare perfect day with my parents, and red has always been my favorite color. The list of items I'm attached to besides that truck is pretty short.

"Please."

I cave like a house of cards. "Fine."

Then follow her across the street, intrigued as fuck about where she's taking me.

Tonight is finally looking up.

CHAPTER TWENTY-THREE

RYLAN

There's a tremor in my hand as I shift into park and turn off Aidan's truck.

Showing up at the hockey party was an impulsive decision, one I'd probably be regretting if it hadn't ended up here. As soon as Isla texted me, I hoped this would happen.

But I braced myself to walk in and see Aidan kissing another girl. He wasn't supposed to immediately focus all of his attention on me, then leave when I suggested I'd showed up for any other reason than him to avoid coming off as desperate.

Him kissing me in the yard tore apart the remaining shreds of my willpower.

I'm giving in. Having fun. Forgetting about consequences.

I want to have sex with him.

So I drove to the town landing that overlooks the Sound, the de facto make-out spot back when I was in high school. The parking lot is empty tonight.

"How scenic," Aidan comments.

I huff a laugh as his headlights automatically shut off.

There are a few lamps lighting the perimeter of the parking

area, but past the asphalt, all you can see is inky darkness. If the windows were down, we could hear the crash of waves across the shore, but it's way too cold for that tonight. The heat that blasted through the vents during the drive here is already dissipating. Hopefully some remnants will last long enough to keep me from getting frostbite in unpleasant places.

"We're not here for the view, Phillips."

"No?" He didn't ask any questions about our destination as I drove, just fiddled with the music and stared out the window.

"No." I pull my top off, hoping Aidan doesn't notice the way my fingers tremble as I do. Not from cold, from nerves.

All of this is new to me, which makes it thrilling...and terrifying.

I've kissed guys here before, but that was it. I've never had sex in a car, but I'm guessing he has.

Aidan's eyes darken to the color of pines as he stares at my boobs. The shirt I was wearing is one of my favorites, but it cuts too low in the back to wear a bra with it.

I unbutton my jeans, then shimmy out of them in the least embarrassing way I can manage, considering they're tight and there's a steering wheel in the way.

And then I'm left in a pink lace thong, the most colorful, least practical pair of underwear I own.

Aidan slides his seat back as far as it'll go, which makes me certain I was right and he's hooked up in here before. The thought bothers me less than seeing him with the girl in the coffee shop did. He's here with *me*, his expression so heated I'm no longer aware of the cooling air in the cab.

"Come here." He spreads his legs and opens his arms, his voice a deep, commanding rumble that immediately gets me wet.

A steady buzz of excitement thrums through my veins as I climb across the center console. It goes about as gracefully as sliding out of my skinny jeans did, but my clumsiness seems irrelevant once I'm straddling his lap.

His hands immediately cup my breasts, his thumbs rubbing my nipples into sensitive points. I moan, rocking my hips harder into his as he leans forward and circles my left tit with his tongue. A flash of heat creeps across my chest.

"I fucking love your boobs," he says, moving to the right one.

My eyes flutter closed as I dig my fingers into his soft hair, arching my back.

It feels *so good*. The graze of his teeth. The confident way he swirls his tongue. The ridge of his erection pressed right against my center.

Even the rub of lace against denim.

All of it mixes with the relief of having this decision made. Of jumping, and no longer worrying or wondering what the landing will look like. Just enjoying the fall.

No matter how Aidan and I end—if this mysterious attraction to him fizzles out in a week or a month, if the only times I see him after this are for his Stats tutoring—I know I won't regret tonight.

I fully let go for the first time since I climbed into that hot tub, totally surrendering to him. My hands slip from his hair, tracing his neck and shoulders before sliding down his chest until I find the hem of his shirt. The taut skin is a startling contrast to the soft cotton, his body heat searing directly into my skin.

His mouth releases my nipple and then his tongue slips back into my mouth like he's dying for another taste, while his hands continue to massage my breasts.

I keep waiting for him to move things along faster. To unzip his jeans and just *fuck* me.

But he doesn't.

Aidan continues brushing and teasing, running his fingers

down the bumps of my spine. Covering the cheeks of my ass and grinding my pussy against the denim covering his erection. Palming and playing with my breasts until my nipples are aching, pointed and begging for more attention from his mouth. Fisting my hair, pulling the strands gently to the side as his tongue drags down the column of my neck.

I was wet before I climbed into his lap. I'm a quivering mass of need now, wearing nothing except a soaked thong. Humping and whimpering and panting, while he's fully clothed and composed.

I could come from his hands running all over me, it feels like.

But I want more. I want him, and not this patient version.

I want the guy outside the bathroom at Gaffney's. The guy who told me to "take it out." The guy who tapped his chin.

Finally, I crack. "*Please.*"

"Please what, baby?"

That *baby* settles right between my thighs, adding to the ache there.

"I brought you here to have sex."

He chuckles, low and the consistency of gravel. "Yeah, I figured that out."

"So…" I move my hips again, urging him along.

Something shifts in his expression, but it's not bright enough for me to tell what it is. "That's what you're looking for? A quick fuck?"

Yes seems like both the right and wrong answer.

"I need more," I tell him instead, grabbing his hand and guiding it where I want his fingers.

Aidan grunts when he reaches the drenched lace, his Adam's apple bobbing. One finger slips beneath my underwear and pushes inside of me, then it's two. I cry out, not even caring how loud I am. This time, there's no one around to hear it. It's like being back in the Colorado woods.

"Fuck, you're tight."

I whimper as his fingers work, bearing down on his hand as hard as I can. Reach down and tug the hem of his Henley up as far as it'll go, gently grazing my fingertips against the bruise on his side. It's faded some, but still appears purple and painful.

"You never responded to the photo I sent," he says.

"I was too busy getting myself off to it."

The look of pure shock on his face makes me laugh. He seems cocky enough to consider I've fantasized about him, so I'm guessing his surprise is more me admitting it. The impulsive confession startled me too, but I don't play it off. I want him to know this isn't a lapse. That I've been thinking about this as much as he has. Maybe more.

Shock ebbs away into pure heat. "Show me," he demands, lifting my hips off his lap.

My knees are spread on either side of his legs, his broad thighs holding mine open. His eyes are on my center, a secret spot no one else has ever inspected so hungrily, making me squirm with a mixture of arousal and vulnerability. He's still fully dressed, so I'm the only one exposed. But it's exciting, too, since Aidan's often casual and relaxed. I imagine the intense focus on his face is how he looks on the ice, beneath the barrier of his helmet's cage.

Slowly, I lift my hand and touch my clit. It doesn't feel the same as when he was the one rubbing me, but the approval in his expression is thrilling. He watches my fingers move like he's memorizing each motion.

Aidan's expression becomes more strained with each passing second, the tendons in his neck fully visible. And then he's ripping his fly down and reaching inside his jeans. Wrapping a thick hand around his cock, the tendons in his arms flexing as he strokes himself. I watch his erection grow until he's fully hard, swollen and thick.

I gasp, my fingers moving faster.

"You close?" he asks.

I nod. Then nod again.

I could come right now, easily. I've never done this before—touched myself in front of a guy. The thrill is exciting and erotic, but I fight the pleasure.

I'm holding back, not wanting to come until it's around his cock.

His hand is moving slower than mine, slow tugs as he stares at me. "Look how hard I am for you."

Jesus. And he thinks *my* mouth is distracting.

I scooch back as far as I can go, which is not far, so I can maneuver enough to pull my thong off. The material is flimsy enough to barely be in the way, but I don't want any barrier.

Aidan reaches past me, opening the glove compartment. When he leans back against the seat, there's a foil wrapper in his hand. He tears the condom open with his teeth, pinches the tip, then rolls the rubber down his huge erection.

Maybe if we hadn't already hooked up once, the size of his cock would be more daunting.

But I know it'll fit. Remember how incredible it felt when it did.

I lean forward and kiss him, new nerves appearing as anticipation mixes with arousal. He guides the fat tip to my opening, grunting when he feels the slickness that's evidence of how worked up I am. It's practically dripping down my thighs. I shiver when I feel him *there*, hot and thick. But he doesn't push into me, just drags the head back and forth through the wetness.

My head falls into the crook of his neck, breathing heavily as

I inhale his delicious, masculine scent. Everything about Aidan is so *male*, the muscles I'm touching and the dick about to enter me, and it incites all these primal desires inside of me.

The steady beat of Aidan's heart pounds against my palm, rhythmic and reassuring. He's a hot, experienced guy. But he's also a human, just like me. Flesh and bone and blood, with insecurities and fears.

I press my lips against the hot skin just beneath his jawbone. "I might be bad at this," I whisper.

"Bad at what?"

"This." I sink down, both of us groaning when he slips in an inch.

"You're not bad at this." His tone says not to argue, so I stay silent. "*Rylan*. Who told you that you were bad at sex?"

"It's more that no one told me I was good at it."

Aidan's silent for a moment. Then he says, "I'm a few seconds from coming just from thinking about being back inside of you. I've jacked off thinking about that night in Colorado for *weeks*. Whatever some guy told you—or didn't—it says a lot more about him than you. Sounds like he couldn't handle you."

"And you can?"

I know he can. He has.

He smirks. "Fuck around and find out, Rye."

I'm totally unprepared for how it feels—sinking down. How he spreads and stretches me. How he *fills* me after the sweet eternity it takes for my body to readjust to his size.

"That's it. Good girl."

I exhale, the warmth of Aidan's hands on my hips spreading through my entire body. His praise heating me just as much.

"Look at you taking me." He sounds so proud.

I'm panting. I can feel him expanding inside of me, the sting of the first couple of strokes *almost* painful. But it's drowned out by everything else I'm experiencing. By the satisfaction of having sex with him.

He fucks me with slow, shallow strokes. We both watch as his hips flex, working his cock in and out of me.

Turns out I didn't have to worry about the heat in the truck. It feels like my entire body is on fire.

Aidan's hands slide up my back, tangling into my hair and tugging on the strands. Something I never realized I loved until the first time he did it. The spark of pain amplifies the pleasure. His lips are back on mine, his tongue tracing my lips gently before he nips my bottom one. Then he's demanding entrance, licking inside my mouth.

I forget how to breathe.

He's *everywhere*, making each nerve sing. I barely remember to continue moving my hips, the biological urge to feel the friction of his dick dragging inside of me overriding everything else. I grind down as hard as I can, and then my climax hits me with the force of a tsunami. My entire body quakes as I tighten around his cock. I can't see or hear or think. I just feel, drowning in a pool of pleasure.

Aidan coming is the sexiest sight I've ever seen. His features tighten, the same pinched expression he wore when he was in bed icing his bruise. Except this time, his face slackens a few seconds later. He fucks me through the aftershocks shuddering through my body, a mixture of masculine grunts and swear words spilling out of his mouth. And then he slumps against the passenger seat, his eyes still hooded and his breathing as fast and rapid as mine as he runs a hand through his hair, mussing up the strands even more than I did.

Neither of us moves, staring at each other. The truck is silent aside from our breathing, the scent of sex lingering in the air.

He's still inside of me, half-hard.

I'm not sure I can move. My entire body feels like a wrung-out sponge.

"It's snowing," Aidan says gruffly, glancing away.

I look out the window, remembering there's a world outside of this truck.

Sure enough, snow is coming down from the sky steadily, backlit by the lights surrounding the parking area. It's already coated the asphalt of the parking lot, covering the faded lines and the cracks with a fluffy sheet. Collected on the light posts that line the edge.

It's a beautiful sight. Ethereal. Mesmerizing.

I look at him.

Aidan isn't watching the snowfall.

He's studying me with a small smile curving up the corners of his mouth. When our eyes meet, he reaches forward and brushes a piece of hair away from my face, tucking it carefully behind one ear.

"We should go before the roads get too bad," he says softly.

I nod. "Yeah. We should."

There's a lurch low in my stomach when his gaze stays on mine. He doesn't look at the snow. At my naked body or the spot where we're still connected. He just studies my face, like he doesn't want to look away. Like he wants to stay in this special moment as much as I do.

And it feels like I'm falling as fast as the flakes around us.

CHAPTER TWENTY-FOUR

AIDAN

The locker room is an eerie silent as Conor stands.

Even more quiet than during Coach's pregame speeches, because Conor's are a rarer occurrence. No one's wrapping their stick or pulling on their game jersey.

We're all seated with our attention squarely aimed at our captain.

My knee bounces, impatient energy pinballing through me.

In ten minutes, I'll be out on the ice. In two hours, I'll know if we're playing in the final.

Today will either be my last hockey game—ever—or the final step before getting the chance to end my career as a champion.

No pressure.

It's not just up to me. We've won every game this season as a team, the same way we lost one.

But I can feel the burning desire to *fight*.

Not physically, although I'm usually happy to drop gloves.

I want this win. Want it for *me*, not just for Conor or for Hunter or for any of the other seniors on the team. Or for Coach Keller.

I want University of Worthington—our opponent today—to be worried every time I'm on the ice. The guys are expecting me to play well today, after my consistent contributions recently. But I want to exceed those expectations, not just meet them.

"You good?" Hunter asks in a low voice from his spot beside me.

I glance over, the grin coming automatically. "I'm great."

His eyes widen slightly, like he was expecting a less enthusiastic answer. Then Hunter matches my grin with one of his own. Nods.

Conor clears his throat once he reaches the center of the locker room. "I wasn't sure we'd get this far, to be honest," he tells us. "We all know games can be unpredictable, and wanting a win is never enough. We've got a better record than Worthington. We're focused, we're ready, we're prepared. I see a group of guys that I wouldn't want to play against. We've been the underdogs for years, and now we're the team everyone is worried about. I've never played with a more supportive team. The way you've all stepped up this season…" He shakes his head. "If we lose, I want you guys to know it's been an honor being your captain. No matter what that scoreboard says at the end of the game, you're all winners."

I love Hart, but his motivational speeches need some work. Usually he just reminds us which players to worry about and then ends it with a "Hit the ice!"

So I stand. "Save the *I love losers* speech, Hart. You're never going to need it. Because we're going to make Worthington wish Pendelton had beat them. Right, boys?"

There are rumbles of agreement through the locker room.

"They're going to pray they lost in the quarterfinals, because that would have been better than having to face us. Right, boys?"

Louder agreement, this time.

"We're going to embarrass them. Fucking *humiliate* them. Make them look like a team Hart's PeeWee kids could beat. *Right, boys?*"

The cheers bounce off the walls, mixed with some laughter. Robby bangs his stick against his metal locker. Jack Williams wolf whistles.

"You think you're tired? Sore? I have a bruise the size of Washington on my ribs. I can't remember the last time some part of my body didn't hurt. Suck it the fuck up. You're playing for a school that hasn't won a hockey championship since before cell phones were invented. We don't get to sit back. To wait until the last period to wake up or to think there's another season if we lose. You think getting this far was hard? Getting this far again will be *harder*. You wanna skate around for another year looking at that old, sad banner hanging from the ceiling? I'll be gone, off doing something amazing." All the guys laugh. "Most of you won't be. And all I've heard since November is what an amazing season we're having. Bullshit. This is an *average* season for us."

I glance at Coach Keller. He's leaning against the doorway, holding one of his binders. His expression is impassive, like usual, no indication of what he's thinking. But he doesn't look disapproving, so I keep going.

"We're capable of more than they think. They're worried about how many goals we're going to score? Don't even let them touch the puck. Let Willis enjoy a mini-vacation between the pipes. Whether we win tonight is up to all of you. Not Worthington. They think they're here to play us. We're here to play *them*. One day, those guys will tell their grandkids about the semifinal game they lost to a Hall of Famer." I glance at Hart. "That cover it, Captain?"

Conor is staring at me, shocked.

I've never interrupted one of his speeches before.

Partly because they were better than today's. Mostly because I wasn't paying close attention. I was texting or eating a snack.

"Guess so," I say, when Hart says nothing. There are a few snickers. "Let's fucking go, boys!"

The entire team clambers to their feet, the hum of energy in the air similar to a live wire exposed to water. Dangerous and electric.

"Where the fuck did that come from?" Hunter asks me as we walk down the hallway.

"What?"

"Your little speech."

"What the fuck was little about it?"

Hunter rolls his eyes. "It was good."

"What was good?"

"Your *big* speech, Phillips. If we win this, it'll be because of you."

I glance at him, shocked.

Hunter looks serious.

"It's the whole team. I'm not—"

"Conor can't carry the whole team, Aidan. You just launched them all out there. If we win this, it'll be because of you. If Hart's slapshot was enough to win that trophy, we'd be chasing our fourth championship."

He steps onto the ice and skates away before I can respond.

I follow, slower than usual, as I turn his words around in my head. I know I've been contributing more, yeah. Taking responsibility instead of shirking it. But Conor's the captain. I'm the guy on the team underclassmen text if they're wondering where a party on campus is or to ask for a spare condom. I'm the team mascot, the party animal.

"Phillips!"

I finish my first lap around our end of the ice, then skate over to the bench.

Coach Keller is standing with his arms crossed. Coach Zimmerman is at the opposite end of the bench, rearranging a few extra sticks.

"That was quite a speech," he tells me. Nothing in his expression indicates if *quite* is a good or a bad thing.

"Sorry for not keeping it, uh, clean," I say.

Technically, Holt's athletic program has an anti-profanity policy. Not a well-enforced one, and Coach has never reprimanded us for language during practice. But I've never heard him swear, and most of the guys make an effort to clean it up whenever we know he's in earshot. I lost track of how many f-bombs I dropped earlier.

"I'm proud of you, Phillips," he says.

It's a sucker punch to my stomach.

I stare at Coach, certain I heard wrong. "Uh, what?"

"Sixteen seasons, and I remember every player I've coached. As soon as I met Hart, I knew he'd have an impact. You? Never occurred to me until your sophomore year. Our last game of the season. Hart sat in the locker room for two hours after the rest of the team left. Remember where you went?"

I shake my head.

"Old friend of mine was at Gaffney's. Texted me, saying a bunch of my players were there drinking."

I remember it now. Or parts of it, before I got wasted and went home with some random girl. That was a tough loss.

"Hart was the logical choice as captain. But you were on my short list, ever since I saw that message. And you reminded me why, just now. You're a leader, Aidan. One people follow because they *want* to, not because they're supposed to. Stop underestimating that. Letting people underestimate you. Believe you have two games left, but play like this is your last one."

I've never noticed before, but Coach's eyes are the same warm brown as Rylan's, the color of melted chocolate.

She's here, somewhere. Maybe.

We haven't talked since I dropped her off after our snowy trip to the Sound. I'm supposed to meet her for our rescheduled tutoring session tomorrow, and have no clue what to expect.

I force myself to focus. To nod. "Yes, sir."

Coach nods back.

And then I turn around to finish my warm-up.

———

We won.

Conor's on his phone, and I'm certain he's texting Harlow.

For the first time, there's someone I feel like talking to who isn't in the locker room.

And she already messaged me.

RYLAN: Congrats!!! :)

Suddenly, simply texting her doesn't seem like enough. I want to see her. Touch her.

I rush through showering and changing, same as the other guys. We're all exhausted yet jubilant. No one will be partying tonight, not knowing that there's an actual championship on the line now. Our spot is guaranteed, it's no longer a hypothetical goal. No one wants to be the weak link who messes it all up, and getting drunk isn't going to help.

Most of the team is headed straight to bed. I'm certain Conor is going over to Harlow's. And I avoid looking in Hunter's direction as I grab my gear, glad we drove here separately earlier.

There aren't any other cars parked on her street, but it's late enough hopefully no one will notice my truck. Or call a tow truck, since I have no clue if you're allowed to park on the street overnight here.

I pull out my phone and respond to her text.

> AIDAN: Thanks.
>
> AIDAN: You up?

> RYLAN: Why does this seem like a booty call?

> AIDAN: Because it's a booty call.
>
> AIDAN: Wanna fuck? sounded worse.

> RYLAN: Window is unlocked.

> AIDAN: Be there in two minutes.

She doesn't reply.

I probably should have given her more warning, rather than rushing here as quickly as I could. I climb out of my truck, lock it, and then head toward the brown house four doors down. The wind is chilly, but my skin feels impervious to the cold after skating for the past couple of hours. My system is still flooded with adrenaline and the high of winning.

And there's a fresh rush of excitement when I slide open Rylan's window. It was pure dumb luck I guessed right last time, and I was fully prepared to dive into the bushes if some other girl had come to the window. This time, it's much easier to find the flat rock in the flowerbed and use it as leverage to swing one leg through and then pull the rest of my body up. I close the window behind me quickly, not wanting to let all the heat in her room out.

The lamp sitting on her desk is on, casting a subtle golden glow.

Rylan is lying in bed, turned toward me with her hands tucked under one cheek. Her smile is a little shy, and I think she's blushing, but it's harder to tell in the dim light. "Hey," she whispers.

"Hey." My voice comes out rough, so I clear my throat. "I didn't realize you'd already gone to bed. I can…"

"Get in bed, Phillips," she tells me, her voice closer to the way she normally talks to me.

Despite what Hunter thinks, I'm not an idiot, so I listen, stripping off everything. I leave my clothes in a pile on her floor, grab a condom out of my pocket, and walk toward her bed.

Rylan sits up as I approach, and I almost swallow my tongue.

"*That's* what you wear to sleep in?" I choke out.

I'm still having fantasies about the pink lace thong she had on in the truck.

This outfit is red silk, so low cut it might as well not be covering her boobs at all. And it's so short I can see the hem above where the sheets are pooling around her waist. I take a mental picture. If she ever sends me a photo back, this is what I'd request.

I crawl over Rylan, her familiar smell surrounding me. Dip my head down to kiss her, which feels as natural as breathing. Like *not* kissing her would be the strange thing to do right now.

She kisses me back, winding her arms around the back of my neck and then slipping her fingers into my hair. I grunt as she combs through the damp strands, tugging lightly and then scratching her nails against my scalp.

As hot as the truck and the tub were, I'm dying to fuck her like this.

No steaming water and frozen temperatures to contend with.

No small cab only allowing limited movements.

"I like this," I murmur, fiddling with a strap on her top before kissing a line down the center of her exposed chest.

"Yeah, I thought you might." Her laugh is low and breathy, turning into a moan when I tug the silk to the side so I can suck on her nipple.

I'm obsessed with her tits. They're full and perky and perfect.

"It's the same color as your truck," she tells me.

I didn't think I could get any harder right now. But knowing she put this on with me in mind? Yeah, that has me stiffening even more.

I strip the sheets back so I can see all of her. Slide a hand down to her knee, hiking it up over my hip and spreading her open. She didn't bother putting on any underwear, which is as sexy as the outfit she's wearing.

We both groan when my needy erection rubs against her bare pussy.

Rylan's hands settle on my shoulders, her nails digging into the same spot she massaged before.

This time, I don't tease her.

I'm too worked up. From the game earlier. From how the main thing I've thought about since stepping off the ice was *this*, watching her bite her bottom lip and lift her hips as if I need an enticement. From seeing the same desperation I'm experiencing written all over her face.

I rip the condom wrapper open, cover myself, and then thrust inside of her.

Wet, tight heat clenches around me as I push deeper, like a slick fist. I move my hand to the inside of her thigh, holding her open and thrusting as deeply as I can. I'm not going to last long. I'm incapable of lasting long with her, it seems.

And then I'm there, all the way inside of her. I exhale through my nose, trying to think about anything except how incredible it feels. I want to savor this, for it to last as long as possible.

Her inner muscles squeeze around me, deliberately. Pleasure zings along my cock in response to the hot friction, steadily spreading throughout the rest of my body.

"*Fuck*, baby." I don't mean to say it. The endearment slips out, just like last time.

My balls are heavy, the base of my spine tingling. Our mouths meet in a messy, enthusiastic kiss as her breasts rub against my chest. Rylan is making those breathy sounds that drive me insane, like she's too overwhelmed to take normal inhales. Her hands slip down my back until they reach my ass, her nails digging in like she's trying to physically pull me even deeper inside of her.

I'm barely hanging on. My hand moves between our bodies, finding the swollen bud of her clit right above where I'm pumping into her.

Then, *finally*, she's coming.

My steady strokes falter as her pussy constricts around my cock. The edges of my vision blur as my bloodstream swims with endorphins and relief and desire and something more intense than lust. I release with a long grunt, my dick jerking as I fill the condom.

We don't move for a minute, both breathing heavily. I don't *want* to move. I want to stay exactly where I am. The burning urge to fuck her has been sated, but I can still feel my skin buzzing from her proximity.

I have to force myself to roll away from her, grabbing a tissue from the box on her side table to wrap the condom in before tossing it in the trash.

I lie back down, but I'm not sure I should. Everything about tonight was impulsive, and I have no clue what she's wanting or expecting. She hadn't texted me since we had sex in my truck on Friday night.

I saw her message and reacted, high off the win and wanting to celebrate.

If she's wanting to go to sleep, I don't want to be that guy who can't take a hint and hangs around until it's awkward. But I don't want her to think I showed up here just for sex, that this was just about getting off for me.

Rylan turns toward me, her hand landing on my abs. Her fingers skim the ridges. "Any new injuries?" she asks conversationally.

I raise an eyebrow when she glances up at me. "Did I just fuck you like I was wounded?"

She rolls her eyes. "Sorry for caring."

Immediate regret.

I thought… I don't know what I thought. I assumed she was teasing. That she thinks I'm a slowpoke who can't evade hits. A wimp who can't skate through some pain.

As pathetic as it sounds, I'm not used to someone caring. If I mentioned an injury to my parents, they'd say it was my own fault for not quitting hockey like they suggested. Hunter and Conor get just as banged up as I do. Complaining to either of them usually turns into a competition of who can power through the worst beating.

"I, uh, I'm fine," I say awkwardly. "Worthington was slow."

Rylan says nothing, her hand stilling on my stomach.

Fuck. I'm so *bad* at this. Every time we've hooked up, I've had no clue what to do after one or both of us finished. I'm accustomed to being buzzed during this part, for there to be a party to return to or some other distraction drawing my attention away. In her dim, empty bedroom, there's nothing except us.

"How's your week been?" I ask, clenching my jaw as soon as

the question is out. I've come up with better small talk around strangers in my classes.

"Pretty good. I got dinner with some people from my algebra class last night. It was fun. Feels like I'm making some friends."

"That's great," I say, burying the urge to ask if the guy from the coffee shop was there.

"You excited?" she asks. "About the final?"

Her fingers start moving again, and it's incredibly distracting.

"Yeah."

"Nervous?"

"That too. We came this far, which is an accomplishment. But also…it's a hell of a long way to come to lose."

"It's a hell of a long way to come, no matter what."

"It is."

I meant everything I said to the guys earlier. But that's no guarantee we'll win the championship.

"I'm rooting for you," she tells me.

Not for Holt.

For *me*.

There's a swell of my warmth in my chest. And lower, when she continues tracing random patterns across my stomach. I pulled the sheets over us when I lay down, but she's going to notice my erection pretty soon.

I reach for her hand, threading our fingers together.

"You don't like that?"

"I like it too much."

It takes a second for my words to register. Then she glances at the tent I'm pitching.

"Seriously? You played a game tonight. And we *just* had sex."

I shrug. "I told you I liked the top."

But it has little to do with what she's wearing, except that she wore it for me. It's all her.

"It's a dress," she informs me.

"It doesn't even cover your ass. It's a top."

"Doesn't even cover my ass, huh? Maybe I should just take it off, then."

I stop breathing when she flings the sheet off of us and rises up on her knees, tugging the red fabric over her head and tossing it away. And as much as I liked—loved—her outfit, it doesn't compare to seeing her like this. My balls draw up tight. My thighs tense. And my dick is throbbing, rapidly inflating as Rylan lets me look my fill.

My fist finds my aching cock. Her tongue darts out, wetting her lips as she watches me stroke myself.

"You're so good at teasing me," I tell her. "So good at taking me. It's all I've been thinking about, Rye. Every time I fuck my fist, I pretend it's your tight pussy I'm filling."

Rylan swallows, her chest heaving with faster breaths. She's still on her knees, hand on her thigh, and I can tell she's toying with the idea of touching herself.

"Do it," I encourage.

I haven't forgotten what she said in my truck, and I want to help build up her confidence however I can. It's not like it's some hardship on my part.

"I'd rather you did."

My heart leaps. "Yeah?"

She nods, then lies down on her side with her back facing me. "I've never had sex in this position, and I've always wanted to try it."

It feels important, that she's comfortable admitting that to me. It's fuel, to the protective, possessive urges that keep flaring up around her. And I hate how I have to answer. "I only brought the one condom."

"There are some in the drawer."

I roll over and reach toward the table beside her bed. Something unclenches in my chest when I see the box is still sealed.

"You must not have been a Boy Scout," Rylan comments, glancing over her shoulder as I open the box and grab a condom out. "You're always *un*prepared."

I snort, sheathing my penis and then scooching behind her. "You thought I was a Boy Scout before that?"

"Nah." She grins. "I would've been shocked."

I slap her ass lightly and she moans, grinding back against me with no barrier between our bodies. It's so easy to find her entrance and notch the head of my cock, so right to wrap her hair around my fist before I start to thrust because I know she likes it.

And fuck if this—talking to her, touching her, just being near her—doesn't feel more important than winning the game earlier did.

CHAPTER TWENTY-FIVE

RYLAN

"Your résumé is very impressive, Rylan," Professor Nolan tells me.

Most students select their own advisor by the end of sophomore year, when they declare their major. Since I wasn't attending Holt then, Professor Nelson was automatically assigned to me because he's the chair of the Mathematics department.

"Thank you," I reply. My fingers twist anxiously on my lap. "But, you don't think it looks...indecisive? Holt is the third school I've attended, technically."

"Many students choose to transfer, and studying abroad is seen as an attribute. If anything, this showcases your ability to not only adapt to different academic institutions, but to thrive in each circumstance. I wouldn't worry it will limit your opportunities anywhere."

I nod, only partially convinced. I have no regrets about transferring to Holt. All it's done is convince me I messed up not coming here in the first place. But I'm worried it's a shortcoming. Proof I'm not as prepared as I pretend I am.

"Here's a list of companies math majors have interned with

recently." Professor Nelson hands me a piece of paper. "If you're interested in applying to any of them for summer opportunities, we should meet again before spring break. There might be a few tweaks we can make to your résumé, depending on where we're applying. But like I said, you're a strong candidate. I wouldn't worry."

"Okay, thanks," I say. "I'll take a look."

"Great. Anything else you wanted to discuss?"

I shake my head. "Nope. All good."

He smiles. "All right. I'll see you in class on Friday."

"See you in class." I stand, then head out of his office and down the hallway.

Once I'm outside, I pull my phone out of my pocket.

> RYLAN: You busy?

AIDAN: Yes.

AIDAN: Texting you.

> RYLAN: Can I come over?

AIDAN: I'll come to you instead.

AIDAN: A bunch of guys from the team are over.

I like his message, tug my hat down so it covers more of my ears, and then hustle across campus. When I approach my house ten minutes later, Aidan is leaning against his impossible-to-miss truck, looking hotter than any guy should.

He's wearing a tight athletic shirt that stretches across his ripped chest. If I focus hard enough, which I absolutely am, I can make out the definition of each individual muscle. It doesn't matter that I know what he looks like shirtless. That I have a photo I stare at way too much. That we've had sex four times now.

Once I'm close enough, he reaches out, snags me around the waist, and pulls me into his body.

He drops a scorching kiss on my lips, then pulls back like that's a common way to greet each other. "Hey."

"Hey." I'm a little breathless, eating him up with my eyes. He's here. He got here before me, even when he was hanging out with his teammates.

Aidan pulls a packet of papers out of his back pocket and hands it to me. "Brought you a present."

"Flowers? You shouldn't have."

Aidan smirks. "Thought you'd appreciate me handing in my second to last assignment early."

"Early is good. Thanks." I take the papers from him, scanning the rough pencil sketches.

We met for tutoring yesterday. He flew through these crazy fast.

"So were you thinking we'd head inside, or…"

"Oh. Uh, yeah."

Now that he's here, I'm second-guessing everything.

Meeting with my advisor freaked me out. Despite Professor Nelson's assurances about my résumé, I still feel like I'm floundering. Like I've bounced from school to school. I have no clue what I want to do this summer. No idea what my post-grad plan is.

I felt stressed, and Aidan's the person I reached out to.

Not Chloe. Not Malia. Not Isla. Not Theo, who was the logical, academic choice. Not my parents.

I texted Aidan.

He hasn't avoided me since the night in his truck. He sought me out, coming over here after Holt won the semifinals. It was a booty call…but it felt like more than a booty call too. We had sex —twice—but we also talked. Laughed.

We've barely seen each other since, me busy with classes and him preparing for the next round of playoffs. We haven't discussed whatever this is, and calling him for comfort feels very girlfriendy. Him immediately showing up seems very boyfriendy.

And now he's handing me his Stats assignment, reminding me that not only are we in a tutoring arrangement, we're in one that's about to end.

"Pretty sure some of my roommates are home," I tell him as we head up the front walk.

Aidan shrugs, appearing indifferent to that piece of information.

Sure enough, Chloe's making a smoothie in the kitchen. Dakota is sitting on the couch, and Mason is slouched next to her. This time his gaze is focused on the television screen instead of his phone's.

They're watching the replay of a hockey game, ironically. Professional, not college.

"Hey, guys," I say.

"Hey, how was—" Chloe glances up and immediately stops talking, her mouth snapping shut and her cheeks turning pink.

I strive for nonchalance as I walk toward the fridge and grab a can of soda out. "Want one?" I ask Aidan.

"Yeah, sure," he replies, leaning a hip against the counter.

"You remember Chloe?" I ask. "And this is one of my other roommates, Dakota, and her boyfriend, Mason."

"You're Aidan Phillips," Mason states, his normally indifferent expression more animated than I've ever seen it before.

"Yep," Aidan confirms. "Nice to meet you, man."

But he delivers it in a hard, flinty tone that sounds more like *Let's never talk again*. The last time I heard him talk that way, it was aimed at Clayton Thomas.

"Library was crowded, so we came over to study in my

room," I say, waving the papers Aidan gave me around like a Fourth of July sparkler. "See you guys later."

Aidan follows me down the hallway and into my bedroom without saying a word. Once the door is shut behind us, he asks, "Does that Mason guy hang out here a lot?"

"That was only the second time I've met him." I pause, watching Aidan toss his jacket away. "Why?"

"I don't like him."

"You can join the club." I hold the papers he gave me up. "Should I grade these now?"

Aidan shrugs, which isn't very helpful.

I was assuming he was coming over for sex, and he seems to be treating it like a study session.

I'm not sure what to make of that.

"What are these notecards for?" he asks, flipping through the stack on my desk.

"They're for a presentation next week."

"Is that what you're stressed about?"

He's more astute than I realized. That, or I'm more transparent.

"No."

Aidan drops the deck, then turns to face me. "You feel like talking about it?"

I shake my head. "No. Anything you wanted to discuss?"

He's fighting a smile now. "Nah, I'm good."

"Great."

I set the soda down on my desk. Then rise up on my tiptoes and kiss him.

Aidan reacts immediately, his hands spreading across the small of my back. They slide lower, cupping my ass and pulling our hips together.

I slip my hands under his shirt, exploring the impressive

topography of his back. He groans, his hands reversing course and sneaking under my sweater instead.

He pulls back, running his tongue along his lower lip as he studies me. Then he reaches out, pulling off my pink hat and tossing it toward my desk.

"This is my favorite hat," Aidan tells me.

It's the one I was wearing in Colorado, and I think he remembers that. He commented on it when we ran into each other in the coffee shop a few weeks ago too.

"Mine too," I say.

He tugs my sweater over my head next, his eyes darkening when he sees the light-blue bra I'm wearing underneath. I've retired most of my more comfortable cotton underwear since we started hooking up. Just in case.

His hands leave a trail of goosebumps in their wake as they move up and down my ribcage before palming my breasts. I bite my bottom lip as he cups them through the lace, the sudden burst of pleasure almost painful.

"You wet for me, Rye?"

I nod, sliding my hands up his shirt and over his abs. Yanking up until the tight fabric peels away, leaving him shirtless.

"Are you wearing a friendship bracelet?" I ask, the flash of color on his wrist drawing my attention.

"Yeah. It's a long story involving Conor, a crush, and a bus ride. Actually…" He tilts his head. "It's not that long. Conor had the stuff because the sister of one of his PeeWee players has a crush on him. He was making one on the bus, and I was bored. Hart's been wearing his ever since and kept asking why I wasn't wearing mine." Aidan rolls his eyes.

Stringing beads is *not* what I pictured my dad's players doing before games.

"Here," Aidan says, slipping the bracelet off his wrist and onto mine. "Better gift than homework, right?"

It's too big, slipping down almost to my knuckles. But as I finger the beads, smiling when I see the three and the four that must be because of his jersey number, I know there's no chance I'll be taking it off anytime soon. "Right."

I rise up again to kiss him. A steady throb starts between my legs when his hands land on my ribs, moving across my back until he finds the clasp of my bra and flicks it free.

We've had sex several times now, and it still feels different every time.

It's *him*, I guess.

My body reacts to Aidan in a way it never has to anyone else, and maybe that's how every girl he hooks up with feels. But he's in *my* bedroom right now, not anyone else's.

I reach for the waistband of his pants, but Aidan pushes my hand away.

"Nah, you're not touching my dick until you've come at least once."

I shiver at the way he says that. At the way he makes me feel like my pleasure is a priority, not a chore.

"Hang on," I tell him, turning on my Bluetooth speaker and picking a random playlist. The game wasn't on that loud, and they're probably all listening to our "studying."

Aidan tugs down my jeans roughly, leaving me in just my underwear. He slaps my ass hard enough to make me jump and loudly enough to make me glad I turned on the music. "Get on the bed."

"We're using a bed again? How boring."

He spanks me again, and I'm surprised how much I like it. The sharp sting fades into a glowing warmth that spreads, igniting my entire body.

When I still don't move, he picks me up and tosses me on the bed.

Breath leaves me in a rapid rush as I land spread eagle, sinking against the soft comforter.

"You should have turned the music up louder," Aidan says conversationally, then spreads my thighs and lowers his mouth.

CHAPTER TWENTY-SIX

AIDAN

Twenty-five expectant faces stare up at me.

When Hart asked me to step in for him at PeeWee practice this week, I didn't think agreeing would be a big deal. According to Conor, the team's actual coach, Josh Cassidy, handles all the logistics of drills and Conor's job is just to retrieve wayward pucks and help kids who are having extra trouble.

I'll never know if that was a lie or not, because when I showed up to assist, I learned that Coach Cassidy came down with a stomach bug and so the sole authority figure on the ice is…me.

When Hart gets back from wherever the hell he was going on his class trip—I was texting Rylan and not really paying attention at the time—he's going to get an earful. This is not what I signed on for.

But there's nothing I can do about it now.

It was either run the practice myself or tell a couple dozen little kids who already had several pounds of equipment on that they wouldn't get to skate today.

"Let's start with laps," I announce. "Just...yeah. Skate in circles."

One of the little kids raises his hand. "How many laps, Coach Aidan?"

"Um...I'll let you know when to stop."

I expect that answer to go over about as well as canceling practice, but the kids surprise me by not voicing a single complaint.

I'm even more surprised by their skill level. Better than I was at this age.

Hastily, I tug my phone out of my pocket and search *kids hockey drills*. I scan through the results, grimacing when the first five all involve using cones.

I don't have any cones, and leaving the kids unattended to go search the rink for some seems like a bad idea.

I try to think of the drills Coach has run us through during practice recently, but my mind is blank. It's like driving somewhere yourself versus sitting in the passenger seat. I remember certain details, but not the whole drive.

We practiced zone entry and stick handling yesterday. I don't think I can replicate that at a less advanced level.

I'm not keeping close track, but they've probably skated at least twenty laps by the time I decide they can't do that all practice.

I stick two fingers in my mouth and whistle, enjoying the awed looks as the kids skate over.

"We're going to play a game of three-on-three," I decide.

Playing a game is better than drills, right?

The kids seem undecided.

"Who is playing on first line?" one kid asks.

I have no clue what his name is. They all introduced themselves at the start of practice, but there was no way I was going to memorize names and faces in one go.

"What's your name?"

"Cody."

He says his name like I should know it. His confidence kinda reminds me of Hart.

"Why are you asking me which line you'll play on, Cody?"

"Uh…" He glances around at his teammates. "'Cause I wanna know?"

"The only thing you need to know is that I'm the coach today. Everyone on the center line."

They all skate toward the red streak instantly. Even Cody.

I pick up the bucket of pucks and skate after them.

"Change of plans. Make the shot, stay standing. Miss, sit."

I skate down the line, handing each of them a puck. Stop at the home bench and whistle.

"Go!"

The first player shoots. Misses, grimaces, sits.

The second player shoots. He misses too.

Third does too.

Maybe this was a bad idea. I'm trying to teach them an equalizer—it matters if you make the shot, not what line you're on when you take it—not decimate their confidence.

"That whistle looks good on you, Phillips."

I glance over one shoulder, shocked to see Rylan standing a few feet away. She's wearing her pom-pom hat, hands shoved deep into her pockets.

"What are you doing here?" I ask.

I wanna step off the ice and kiss her, but I'm guessing that'll set off a chorus of "Ews" from the peanut gallery, and I have no idea where her dad is.

Rylan's eyes are bright and sparkling as she glances at the ice. Takes in the scene. "You're coaching?"

I rub the back of my neck. "Hart helps out with the team but had a conflict this week. Asked me to step in. The usual coach got sick, so...yeah. Going terribly so far."

I glance at the net. Empty still, a quarter of the way down the line.

"You're being too hard on yourself," she tells me. "They look like they're having fun."

I'm used to hearing the opposite. That I'm too easy on myself, that I don't care about anything important. I thought Rylan believed the same thing. That I'm the *campus playboy* in her eyes, same as everyone else's. I don't know when that changed. I didn't know that *had* changed.

Impulsively, I say, "I missed you."

I haven't seen her since I went over to her house on Wednesday.

Before Rylan can reply, I hear a familiar voice.

"Hey, honey."

Immediately, I stiffen. I should have guessed she was here because of her dad, but it didn't occur to me. I have a tendency to focus on nothing except her, whenever she's near. I was just happy to see her, not wondering why she was here.

"Hey, Dad."

I swallow, turning to watch Coach approach the bench. His Holt Hockey cap is pulled low, shading his eyes and making it harder to read his reaction to finding me talking to his daughter.

"Phillips."

"Coach." I'm tenser than a wood board, and I hope he doesn't notice.

"You're running the PeeWee practice?" He sounds surprised, understandably.

"Hart recruited me. And the normal coach is sick."

"How's it going?" He looks out at the ice.

I wince, certain he's looking at a lot of misses. "Not great."

"Try two lines. Zig zag passes. Or have them race from one end. Goal line, blue line. Goal line, center line. Goal line, blue line. Goal line, goal line. That'll wear them out fast."

"I will, Coach. Thanks."

He nods, then glances at Rylan. "You ready to go?"

"Yep." She glances at me. "Good luck. I'll, uh, see you on Tuesday."

"For tutoring," I clarify. Unnecessarily.

Because I'm hoping I'll see her sooner, and that no math will be involved. And since we're nowhere I can actually say that, I'm overcompensating.

"Right. For tutoring." Rylan gives me a weird look, then follows her dad toward the lobby. I watch her until she's out of sight, wishing she would turn around the whole time. I want her to stay. To pull her around the ice with me after this practice ends, same as I watched Hart do with Harlow.

I push away from the boards.

They're halfway down the line now. By the time the last kid shoots, only two pucks have gone in.

I pick one up on my stick and skate back toward the center line. Skid to a dramatic stop, spraying a bunch of shavings toward the opposite end.

Then shoot.

The netting bulges from the impact.

"Two lines!" I bark.

They all scramble to listen.

And I skate after them, filled with fresh determination.

CHAPTER TWENTY-SEVEN

RYLAN

"Hey, Rylan."

I turn to see a guy I've never seen before standing with two other guys, one of whom looks vaguely familiar.

I got here ten minutes ago and have spent all of that time unsuccessfully looking for Aidan. So far, he's nowhere to be found.

"Hey…" I have no clue who he is or why he's talking to me. How he even knows my name.

Guess that comes through clearly in my voice, because there's a spasm of annoyance in his expression.

"Jake Brennan, remember? We have Intro to Philosophy together. I sit two rows behind you."

"Right," I say, although I still have no recollection of ever meeting Jake before.

Intro to Philosophy is my least favorite class this semester, one I'm only taking because it fulfills one of the Holt requirements I need to graduate. Maybe that's why I blocked Jake out.

That, or I can't seem to focus on any guy who isn't Aidan Phillips.

"Can I get you a drink?" Jake offers.

One of his buddies doesn't manage to fully hide his smirk behind his plastic cup.

"I'm good, thanks." I go to shove my hands into my pockets, then remember I'm wearing a skirt and can't. So I end up just rubbing my palms against the maroon-colored fake leather.

Finally, I place why the smirking buddy looks familiar. "You're on the hockey team," I say. He's the guy in the background of the photo Aidan sent me.

He nods, his grin widening. "Cole Smith. Nice to officially meet you."

"Officially?"

"Yeah, Brennan said your dad is Coach K, right?"

"Right," I say, a little annoyed that's my introduction.

I'm proud of my dad and his accomplishments. Doesn't mean I want to be reminded of them at a party. Be reduced to that association.

"Yeah, well, any friend of the guy taking us to a national championship is a friend of ours, or however that saying goes."

"She's his daughter, dickhead," the third guy chimes in with. "That's not the saying—at all."

"Ignore them," Jake says, stepping forward. "Sure you don't want that drink? Kitchen is right this way."

"Um, sure. Whatever," I reply distractedly, taking another look around the living room. I already checked the kitchen once, but maybe Aidan has showed up since.

"*Um, sure. Whatever.*" Cole laughs. "I take back everything I said about you being off your game, Brennan."

Jake flips Cole off before guiding me down the hallway toward the kitchen.

"Have you seen Phillips?" a tall guy with shaggy blond hair stops to ask.

I pause too, very interested in the answer. I couldn't come up with any casual way to ask Jake the same thing.

Jake smirks. "Of course not, Sampson."

Sampson groans. "Damnit. I was hoping he'd be done upstairs by now. I really need to talk to him."

A cold drip of uncertainty trickles through me like a leaky faucet. Aidan is *busy* upstairs, and I can easily extrapolate exactly what that means.

And it *hurts*, so much worse than I was expecting it to.

Way more than walking in on Walker did.

This time, I have no right to be mad. I *am* mad, but I have no right to be.

We're not in a relationship. Aidan never said he wasn't seeing other girls. Never asked me if I was seeing other guys.

Except, I thought there was something more between us than simply sex.

My fingers find the bracelet hidden beneath my sleeve. I haven't taken it off since Aidan slipped it on my wrist. It felt like some physical indication that I meant something to him. A signal that he *wasn't* hooking up with girls upstairs at parties.

I saw the signs with Walker. How he was often busy. How he'd take hours to reply to my texts. How we stopped having sex.

My *boyfriend* cheating on me wasn't a surprise.

But the campus playboy who constantly has girls hitting on him hooking up with someone else is as shocking as a slap.

He said he didn't want anyone else, and I feel foolish for believing him. I guess that changed after we fucked a few more times. He's already bored.

All of a sudden, the warm, smoky air is suffocating.

"I gotta go," I blurt, then spin around and head in the direction of the front door.

I didn't tell Aidan I was coming to this party, and now I'm

extra glad. He won't question why I wasn't here tonight, and he'll hopefully be too busy preparing for the championship to talk anytime soon.

Meaning I'm in fantastic shape to not see him until our final tutoring session on Tuesday, after which I'll never have to see him again.

Someone calls my name, but I don't turn around to see who it is or find out what they want. I'm too focused on getting the hell out of here as quickly as possible.

I reach the front door, yank it open, and freeze.

Conor and Harlow are walking up the stairs that lead from the walkway to the porch. Hunter is right behind them, followed by…Aidan.

The relief is staggering.

Another reminder I'm in way deeper with Aidan than I was supposed to wade.

I've made the predictable mistake of developing way too many feelings for the guy I'm sleeping with. Some of them felt inevitable. Unlike Aidan, I'm not used to separating emotion from sex. But I thought any feelings of mine were tempered by reality —that I could sleep with him and still know that our fling could end at any time.

I'm braced for him to lose interest, especially after what just happened. But there's no clear limit to my feelings, no line I know I'm not about to cross.

He's here, right in front of me. Not upstairs, talking to someone else. Laughing with someone else. Touching someone else. Fucking someone else. Doing all the things I want him only to do with me.

"Hey, Rylan." Harlow gives me a friendly smile, fracturing the awkward pause of me just staring at Aidan. "You leaving?"

"Hi, Harlow. I—um..." I'm still frozen. "No. I just needed some air."

She nods. "Good. It's nice to see you. I love your skirt."

"Thanks," I manage to say. Realize I'm blocking the doorway and finally unfreeze, stepping out of the way.

Predictably, there's a roar of noise as everyone in the living room realizes who just arrived. Conor flashes me a grin as he passes by. Hunter's smile is more reserved, but it's there. And then Aidan appears, looming in the doorway.

My mouth goes dry at the sight of him.

He's wearing my favorite flannel—when I memorized his wardrobe, I'm not really sure—a dark green and black checkered print that emphasizes the color of his eyes. And that green gaze is aimed directly at me. He's ignoring his friends. Ignoring the people shouting his name as they register his arrival.

I swallow twice, my tongue thick and useless in my mouth. He crowds me to shut the door, his smell intoxicating.

"You okay?" There's a concerned wrinkle between his eyes as he studies me, like I'm a puzzle he's trying to decode.

"Yeah. I'm okay."

"Didn't think you'd be here. Seemed like you were hanging out with your folks tonight."

"My dad goes to bed by ten, so..."

"You should have texted. I could have picked you up."

"It's not a far walk."

His gaze sharpens. "You walked? By yourself?"

I like his annoyance way, way too much. Love that he cares.

"Yeah. How did the rest of the PeeWee practice go?"

Aidan deliberates, obviously deciding whether to let the topic of me walking go. Finally, he answers, a smile creeping across his face that tells me the answer before he does. "Not bad, actually."

"I'm glad."

Someone bumps into him from behind. Aidan doesn't even glance to see who. He acts like this is exactly what he wanted, invading my personal space until all I can see is him.

"You want a drink?" he murmurs.

I shake my head, then head for the stairs.

I'm already drunk on him.

CHAPTER TWENTY-EIGHT

AIDAN

Rylan turns into the bathroom at the top of the stairs. By some miracle, it's unoccupied. Guess it's early enough in the evening that most people aren't drunk enough to need a toilet yet.

A few people greet me as they pass by, but my focus is on the brunette ahead of me.

I duck into the bathroom behind her, then close and lock the door behind us. She's leaning back against the counter that surrounds the sink with her arms crossed, a knowing smirk on her face as she watches me ensure we won't get interrupted.

We haven't talked, not really, since she texted me on Wednesday and we ended up having sex in her room. She was clearly upset about something, something she didn't want to talk about. And I wasn't expecting to be as annoyed about that as I felt. I've dumped plenty of my shit on her. The least I could do was listen to her talk about whatever was bothering her. But she didn't want to that, and so I rolled with it.

I didn't think she'd be here tonight, since she left the rink with her dad earlier.

And I have no idea why she was heading toward the door as I arrived, or why she looked so surprised to see me with my friends on the front porch.

"How was dinner with your parents?" I ask.

There's a flash of surprise on her face, like that's a shocking question for me to ask.

"Fine. Good."

"You tell them what was bothering you on Wednesday?"

More surprise. "It was nothing."

I take that as a no.

"Something with your classes?" I press.

"It's just math."

I step closer. "It's not *just* anything, Rylan. You can talk to me."

"I didn't come up here to *talk* to you, Aidan." She takes a seat on the edge of the counter, the sexy red skirt she's wearing riding up higher on her thighs as she spreads them.

A hot girl—a hot girl I can't stop thinking about—wants to have sex with me. And I'm *disappointed*. I'm hurt that she doesn't trust me. Won't confide in me.

But I don't know how to tell her that. If I should tell her that. I can't force her to talk to me, to view me as someone worth sharing worries with.

And I'm used to girls only wanting one thing from me. What I'm not used to is wanting more than sex from them.

Rylan pulls her top off. My eyes immediately go to her tits, which are practically spilling out of the lacy bra she's wearing. But then I spot the bracelet on her wrist, the one I put on her. The one with my jersey number amidst a bunch of beads.

I step between her spread thighs, deliberately brushing my thumb against her wrist before sliding my hand into her hair and using it to tug her head back so she's looking straight at me.

There's a flush to her cheeks that wasn't there a few seconds ago.

"Nice bracelet," I say.

"Thanks," she replies. "It was a gift."

I smirk before I lean down and kiss her. My head might be confused about how to handle things with her, but my body thinks it's straightforward. See her, kiss her, touch her, fuck her. Doesn't matter where we are. How recently we hooked up. I always react like it's the first time.

She whispers, "I want you," against my lips, and I'm instantly hard.

"Can't get enough, huh?"

"Are you complaining?"

"Definitely not."

I kneel between her parted legs, impatiently tugging down her tights as far as they'll go. I do the same to her soaked underwear before I lightly bite the inside of her thigh, then suck. Her knuckles turn white where her hand is clutching the edge of the counter, the colorful bracelet just as stark against her pale skin.

My mouth moves higher. Her taste floods my mouth, and my dick strains against the zipper of my jeans, desperate to join in on the fun.

Rylan rocks her hips, the breathy moans she's making sending bolts of heat down my spine. She whimpers when I wrap my hands around her thighs, pulling her closer and spreading her wider.

"Holy fuck," she says as more wetness soaks my tongue.

I move my mouth higher, sucking lightly on her clit as I curl two fingers inside of her. By now, I know exactly what she likes.

A few seconds later, she's coming, calling out my name. And I'm supremely satisfied, even though my cock is still making my pants uncomfortably tight.

That might have been a new record.

I straighten and kiss her.

Rylan makes a surprised sound when she tastes herself on my mouth, then relaxes into me. Her hands slide down my chest to the waistband of my jeans. I groan into her mouth as she works at the button and zipper, thrilled by this turn of events. We had sex two days ago, and that doesn't feel like recent enough.

I pull away when her hand finds my cock, mesmerized by looking down at the sight of her small hand working the engorged length.

Her nails are painted the same shade of red as her skirt, and it matches my angry-looking dick. The tip is already shiny with pre-cum. I grunt as her fingers spread it around.

"Do you have a condom?" she asks.

Thank God she's as insatiable as I am. Either is better than having to take care of this myself, but I'd rather fuck her than get a hand job.

"No, but…" I pull open the drawer next to her left leg and rifle through it. No luck, but the one below has a box of condoms. I grab one and rip it open, rolling the latex on as Rylan hops down from the counter, turns around, and leans over.

"You good?" I ask, tossing the condom wrapper into the trash.

"Yeah. My legs were just falling asleep."

Rylan's breath catches as I walk up behind her, her entire body jolting when she feels my erection brush the inside of her thigh. There's a mark where I sucked her earlier that will probably stick around a while, and I hope she's not pissed about the hickey when she notices it.

"Do you know what you look like when you come?" I ask her, kissing her neck. I rub my cock between her legs but don't enter her yet. I already know this will be the highlight of my night, so I'm in no rush.

Rylan shakes her head. Her lips are parted, watching our reflections.

I slip an inch into her, and she moans. Her cheeks are flushed, her chest heaving with ragged breaths. I drop my gaze to watch her take me.

"You look so good, baby. You always look good. But taking my cock?" I push in another couple of inches, hissing when she clenches around me. "It's the hottest fucking thing I've ever seen."

She whimpers, pushing back against me and trying to force me deeper.

Someone bangs on the bathroom door, but I don't react. It's locked, and having trouble finding an open bathroom at a college party is basically a canon event.

Rylan's still watching us in the mirror. Every reaction on her face, I feel spasm around me.

I've never experienced this overwhelming need with anyone except her. I've been turned on and horny many times before. But it's never felt this acute. Been this blinding urge. No matter how many times I fill her or how deep she takes me, it's never enough. I'm desperate to come, but I never want to stop thrusting into heaven.

My heartbeat hammers out a wild, adrenaline-fueled rhythm. It feels like flying down the ice.

"More," she begs, pushing back against me. "Harder."

I wish we were on a bed. It's much harder to angle her the way I want her in here, but I try. Her legs start to shake. I stop rubbing her clit and pinch it instead. She calls out my name again.

I glance down, savoring the sight of her bent over the sink and stretched around me.

She looks sexy.

She looks satisfied.

She looks like *mine*.

Skin slaps as I pound into her, totally losing control.

"Is this what you want, Rylan?"

A choked cry is her only reply. I wrap her hair around my hand, tugging it the way I know she likes.

"You're so fucking full of my cock, you can't even talk. Is that what you were begging for, baby?"

She makes a choked sound. "I'm-I'm going to…"

I know exactly what she's trying to say. I can feel her convulsing around me. She comes with a loud moan, and I'm right behind her. She collapses onto the counter.

Both of us are panting, coming down from the incredible high.

Rylan recovers first, pulling away. I take care of the condom while she pees, avoiding eye contact with me the entire time.

The same awkwardness from before I saw the bracelet on her wrist is back. I'm not sure what she wants or expects from me. Am I coming on too strong? Not strong enough?

I don't usually stick around this long.

Sex in the bathroom at a party is familiar, this part after is not.

I lean against the wall next to the shower and watch as she fixes her tights and skirt. Washes her hands and then attempts to fix the mess I made of her hair.

Are we going to avoid each other the rest of the night?

Are we—

"Do you know Jake Brennan?" she asks suddenly.

"Yeah, of course," I reply. "He's on the team."

Rylan nods, twisting her hair into a low bun. Immediately, I want to pull the elastic out and run my fingers through the strands.

"Why?" I ask, refocusing on the conversation.

More like demand, but whatever. I haven't forgotten his comments about Rylan by the bus before our first playoff game.

"Just wondering."

"*Why* were you wondering?"

"I was talking to him earlier."

"Again, *why*?"

She shrugs. "Because we were talking. He's nice."

Nice?

"Stay away from Brennan, okay?"

"Why?" she challenges.

"He's...he can be kind of..." I war with myself. I don't talk shit about my teammates. But I don't want Rylan around him, knowing he's interested in her and that he has a reputation similar to mine. And...I'm jealous. He's a junior, like her. He'll be here next year, while I'll be where the hell knows. "Are you into him or something?"

"He knew who my dad is," she says. I don't miss that she didn't answer the question.

"It's not that big of a campus." The whole team knows who she is, since she showed up at the bus before our first playoff game, but I don't tell her that.

Someone starts pounding on the bathroom door again. Whoever they are, they're more persistent than the last person was, continuing to hammer away when neither of us answers. Or maybe that is why they keep knocking.

"I think I need a drink after all," she says.

"I can grab you one," I offer.

"If everyone already knows who I am, then it's probably best we keep our distance downstairs. I'd rather not have the whole campus gossiping about us."

My jaw works as I force a nod. Technically, she's right. The guys all know who she is, and me hovering around Rylan would probably end up in the team group chat. Hunter knows about us, but Conor has no clue. There would be lots of speculation and maybe some backlash about me seemingly prioritizing sex over a championship.

But it feels wrong, watching her unlock the door and head into the hallway, knowing that we'll be acting like strangers downstairs after what just happened in here. I don't really give a shit what my teammates think about us, and I can't tell if she does or if she just thinks that *I* do.

I scrub a hand across my face before following Rylan downstairs.

Multiple people stop me in the living room. It takes at least ten minutes to make it into the kitchen.

I spot Rylan immediately. She's standing by the fridge, holding a red cup and talking to Harlow. I watch as Jake fucking Brennan approaches them, saying something that makes Rylan smile as he grabs a beer out of the fridge.

My jaw clenches so tightly I'm concerned it might snap as I walk past them.

Telling myself not to care accomplishes nothing as I head toward where Hart is standing by the sink, sipping what I'm assuming is water. Conor doesn't drink during the season. He looks bored, his gaze flicking in the same direction mine wants to go every few seconds.

Nothing like attending a party sober and celibate.

Then again, I've had sex tonight plus a beer I downed before coming over here, and I'm currently miserable.

"You good?" Conor asks, paying more attention than I'd like as I lean against the counter next to him and help myself to another beer.

I nod, then take a sip. Glance at Rylan. Brennan is still standing over there.

Hart's still studying me.

I didn't take the time to do much more than toss the condom

and fix my pants before leaving the bathroom, and it's probably obvious exactly what I was just doing upstairs. He has seen me look a lot worse, though.

"You're sleeping with Rylan Keller, huh?"

I choke on another sip of beer. Cough. Clear my throat. "Yes."

My candid answer surprises both of us. Conor clearly expected me to deny it, and I wasn't planning on discussing Rylan with him—ever. I didn't think there would be anything to discuss, and I was wrong.

He shakes his head. "Phillips…"

I glance at Rylan. Brennan is still over there. "Who told you?"

"I've had sex at a party before, man. You two disappeared when we got here, came back down around the same time. She cleaned up better than you, but you both look a little, uh, rumpled."

"I won't let it fuck up the championship."

There's a pause, then, "Do you like her, or it is just sex?" Conor's taking this better than I would have expected, considering I just admitted to hooking up with our coach's daughter.

I can tell myself Rylan is an adult all I want, but the truth is, I know Coach Keller would not be happy if he found out. Not only did he arrange for Rylan to tutor me so she could help me graduate, not get laid, but students aren't the only ones who gossip on campus. I'm any father's worst nightmare for his daughter. If Coach finds out, I don't think he could—or would—actually kick me off the team. We only have one game left. But it would result in some extremely awkward dynamics, ones that could cost the trophy.

I sneak another peek at Rylan, watching as she taps the fingers that were just wrapped around my cock against her red plastic cup. "It's not just sex."

"So…why are you over here scowling?"

I scowl more. Sip some beer. "I don't think it's more to her."

"Really?" Conor sounds surprised, which I guess I should take as a compliment. "What did she say?"

"What did she say about what?" I down more beer, because Brennan is still standing over there and it's slowly driving me insane.

"What did she say when you told her you like her?" Hart enunciates each word, like I'm an idiot.

"Nothing."

He whistles. "Ouch. Okay, never mind—"

"I mean, I haven't told her."

"Why not?"

"I don't know if I want a relationship, or whatever. I don't think that she does. Her ex was an asshole and—"

"Are you hooking up with other girls?"

I finish my beer, then tell him the truth. "No."

Conor nods, like that was the answer he was expecting for some reason. "Then you're basically already in a relationship, Phillips. Is she hooking up with other guys?"

"I don't know," I admit.

I would be surprised if she is. But *I don't know*. Brennan is still hanging around, so she hasn't shut him down.

"Tell her how you feel, Phillips," he advises. "Ask her to officially be your girlfriend. If you've stopped sticking your dick into every hot girl at this school and if *that*"—he nods in Rylan's direction again—"bothers you, then tell her how you feel. Or else forget about her and don't hold this against Brennan. She's not your girl; he can flirt with her all he wants."

I suck in a deep breath, studying Rylan. She's laughing and nodding along to something Brennan is saying, looking like she's having the time of her life.

I'm not sure how she feels about me. I know she loves the

sex, because the rest of her body can't lie to me the way her lips can. And I think she enjoys our banter, even if she's never admitted it.

But *me*, excluding my mouth and dick? I have no clue. It might make me a coward, factoring her feelings into my own. But it's also human, I think, to not want to get shot down. I've *never* asked a girl to be my girlfriend.

And I'm not even sure if I'm capable of a relationship, not just if I want one. With Parker, it wasn't a heavy conversation. It was hooking up, then going to dances together, then her calling me her boyfriend. I could have fought it, but I didn't, and then it blew up in my face.

Looking back, I'm not even sure if I loved her. Maybe I loved some version of her, or maybe we were just familiar and easy. Maybe what I thought was heartbreak was actually a bruised ego.

"I'm headed out," I tell Conor.

He appears disappointed, which surprises me. I assumed he'd be warning me away from Rylan, telling me to focus on hockey and my grades.

But he says nothing else, just nods and holds out a fist for me to tap.

I leave the kitchen and head down the hallway. Out the front door. It's not that cold tonight, hovering right around freezing.

I don't make it down the front steps. Our final practice before the championship game isn't until tomorrow afternoon. My final hockey practice—ever. Heading home and helping myself to some of the vodka in the freezer before crashing sounds very tempting.

But…she walked here.

And there's no way I'll be able to sleep—no matter how much I have to drink—not knowing if she made it home safely.

I lean against one of the porch balusters, debating what to do. Text her? Stand out here like a stalker?

Before I can decide anything, the front door opens, and Rylan steps out. She stills as soon as she sees me standing here, glancing behind her once before stepping outside and shutting the door behind her.

"I thought you left." She said the same thing to me after our first tutoring session. She looks as uncertain now as she did then, watching me with a wariness I'm not sure what to make of.

I shrug a shoulder. "You walked."

Emotions flash across her face too fast for me to register any one of them. Then she walks forward until our bodies press together, her floral smell surrounding me as she clutches the front of my sweatshirt and rises up to kiss me.

We make out for a few minutes, until we're both breathing heavily. And it feels so *right*. So reassuring, after watching her from across the kitchen. She's here, in my arms.

"I'm not into him," she whispers when our lips separate. "I had no clue who he was until he came up to me tonight and mentioned my dad."

"Okay," I reply, relief rushing through me.

That only solves one of my problems, though. Tonight, I realized I'm unsatisfied with our arrangement. That sex with Rylan isn't enough.

Conor made it sound simple—just tell her how you feel, ask her to be your girlfriend—but it's not simple. And I witnessed how badly he fucked up things with Harlow. He's not exactly a romantic expert to take advice from.

"Can I walk you home?" I ask. Maybe I'll come up with the right words during the two blocks.

It sucks when she shakes her head.

But then she says, "I'd rather you walked me across the street," and my heart returns from its trip to the porch floor.

I live across the street.

She's wanting to come back to my place. Back to my bed.

Hope sparks in my chest, contemplating that maybe she does care. Maybe this does matter to her. We already hooked up tonight, and she was leaving right after me.

"I mean, if that's okay," she says, and I realize she read into my silence. "If you don't—"

"Of course it's okay," I reply.

I grab her hand, and her expression looks startled. Have we held hands before? Maybe not, I guess. It's nice, though, having her warm fingers wrapped around mine. I can feel her bracelet where it's slipped down her wrist. I sized it for mine, so it's way too big on her.

But she's wearing it. She's been wearing it.

Hand in hand, we cross the street to my house. To the place where I never take girls.

And it feels just as right as kissing her did.

CHAPTER TWENTY-NINE

RYLAN

Someone's saying my name, but I'm too sleepy to open my eyes. I'm cozy and warm, snuggled underneath a thick comforter. Every time I inhale, there are happy flutters in my stomach.

"Rylan."

I groan, rolling over, expecting to encounter more soft pillow. Instead, I hit a firm chest. My eyes fly open, registering Aidan's smirk first. He's lying in bed beside me—in *his* bed. That's what the delicious scent is. I'm wrapped in sheets that smell like him.

"Wow. And I thought *I* was hard to wake up," he comments.

I roll onto my back, wiping my mouth with the back of my hand in case there's drool and running my fingers through what I'm sure is a bad case of bedhead. I'm groggy and Aidan looks like a male model. Whereas I'm barefaced and yawning. All his bathroom had was a bar of soap, so my skin is probably already breaking out.

"What time is it?" I ask.

"No clue. I forgot to charge my phone last night. It's dead."

I cover up another yawn. "Um, okay…"

We didn't talk much last night, after I invited myself over. We had sex, which I'm reminded of when I shift under the sheets. He was rougher than usual, and I loved every single second of it. He gave me one of his T-shirts to wear to bed. I don't remember anything after that, so I must have fallen asleep fast.

And now, he's just staring at me.

I feel my face flush under the scrutiny.

"I'll, uh, go."

Aidan grabs my forearm before I can move, calloused fingertips sliding down to my wrist until he reaches the bracelet I'm wearing. That seems to be his favorite spot to touch me now. "I don't want you to go."

"Then why'd you wake me up?"

Aidan shifts, his thigh brushing against mine under the covers, and I think the answer will be *sex*. Instead, he says, "Because I wanted to tell you something. I've *been* wanting to tell you something, and I ran out of patience when you weren't waking up."

"Jeez. Sorry for sleeping."

He doesn't crack a smile. I study his expression, shocked by the nervousness and seriousness I find there.

"Is something wrong?"

"That'll kinda depend on how you take this," he replies.

Now *I'm* nervous. "Okay..." I'm not sure what else to say.

He takes a deep breath. "After everything that happened with Parker, I didn't think I wanted another relationship. I wasn't sure if I was capable of it, honestly. If she hadn't pushed me for one, I'm not even sure I would've ended up dating her. It never made much sense to me. My parents fought a lot and half of my friends in high school were fucking around on the side. It seemed easier —smarter to just avoid the whole commitment thing."

His voice dips, down into a lower timbre that's overwhelmingly intimate.

"But then I met *you*, Rylan, and I realized it's not a choice you make—having feelings for someone. That it happens without you realizing. That one day you're driving a girl home from the library, and then all of a sudden you can't imagine touching anyone else except her. She becomes the first person you want to talk to after you win a game. The last person you think about before you fall asleep."

I'm frozen. Totally stunned.

Am I dreaming?

"You asked me the wrong question, that night on the porch. You asked how many girls I'd been with since you. You should have asked me how many girls I've been with since I walked into the library and saw you sitting there. Since I found out you were a student here, not at some school in England. *None.* I'm not interested in any other girl, and I really fucking hope you're not interested in any other guy."

My head is spinning. I reach for the crease of my elbow and pinch myself—hard.

Aidan's eyebrows knit. "What are you doing?"

"You have *feelings* for me?" I blurt.

"Did you seriously just pinch yourself?" He sounds amused.

"I was fast asleep five minutes ago, Aidan. I thought maybe this was a dream."

"Would it have been a good dream, or a bad dream?"

I suck in a deep breath, my brain still processing. I can't believe he just told me all that. That he feels that way. "Good."

The naked relief on his face is as startling as the nerves were. I'm used to Aidan appearing sure. Even when he told me he was anxious about playing well again, after his hat trick, he was confident about being nervous. Owned it with no hesitation. I'd never seen him look truly uncertain before.

But he wasn't sure what I would say. He just delivered that

shocking, romantic speech, put himself out there, and all I really managed was one word in response.

"I-I had no idea," I tell him. "I thought this was just sex to you."

"It's not." Aidan reaches out, tenderly brushing some hair out of my face. "Is that all it was to you?"

I shake my head. "Of course not. I realized I had feelings for you the night you brought me dinner. That's why I wasn't sure about having sex again. I knew I'd just get more attached."

"You've been into me for that long, huh? I knew *pool players are my type* was bullshit."

I roll my eyes, then reach up to brush his jawline. He leans into my touch.

"Yeah, I've been into you for that long. I'm crazy about you, Aidan. I freaked out about what to do with my life, and you were the first person I thought to talk to."

His expression softens. "That's what you were upset about, on Wednesday?"

"Yeah. But it was nothing, really."

"If it upset you, it's not nothing."

I think I'm in love with him. I'm absolutely in love with *this*, lying in bed beside him while he focuses on me like every word out of my mouth is the most interesting thing he's ever heard.

"I had a meeting with my advisor."

"Okay."

"He thinks my résumé is okay, but I'm still worried it's not. That it looks like I'm…flighty. That I don't know what I'm doing. And I *don't* know what I'm doing. I'm happy here, way happier than I was in Boston or at Oxford. But I… I don't know. I chose to major in math because it made sense at the time. It sounded smart and important. But Professor Nelson gave me this list of companies for internships. I looked a bunch of them up, and they all sound boring. I don't want to work in a cubicle, staring at spreadsheets all day. So now I'm worried I chose my major wrong too, but I can't possibly change that and I—why are you smiling?"

"Because I'm graduating in May with a two point something GPA and absolutely no marketable skills, and you're worried your math degree and four point oh are going to hold you back."

I chew on the inside of my cheek. "You're right. I'm being silly. It'll all be fine."

"You're not being silly. That's not what I'm saying. I get freaking out about the future, a little too well. I'm just trying to give you some perspective. You have amazing grades and you've had experiences people will see as impressive, not flighty. If you end up in a job you hate, then you find a new one. Go to grad school and study something that's not math. There will always be other options, Rye."

I exhale. Nod. "Yeah. You're right."

"Nah, I'm an idiot, because I just realized I never actually asked you."

"Asked me what?"

"If you'll be my girlfriend." He grimaces. "That wasn't a question either. Will you be my girlfriend, Rylan?"

"Are you...sure?"

Yes is the answer I want to shout. But the last guy who asked me that question changed his mind in the most painful way possible. Aidan's different from Walker in practically every way. I don't think he'd cheat on me. But the memory of hearing his teammates say he was upstairs last night is still a fresh, raw one. I haven't forgotten how hearing that felt. And I convinced myself Aidan wasn't a possibility. That he wouldn't ever want a relationship. I'm still absorbing that he does.

"I'm sure," he says. "I wouldn't have said anything if I wasn't."

Aidan doesn't sound mad I'm doubting him. Just matter-of-fact, like there's no question in his mind. His confidence bolsters mine. And I'd rather regret leaping than to never jump at all.

"Okay. Then yeah, I'll be your girlfriend."

He grins, wide and boyish, then rolls so he's hovering over me, holding most of his weight off me. All I can feel is the rasp of his strong legs rubbing mine, and the delicious drag of his erection against my inner thigh. My knees part automatically, spreading to accommodate him.

Aidan doesn't reach down, though. His mouth brushes back and forth against mine twice, the touch lighter than a feather floating past. Then he's kissing me, intense, overwhelming ones that make my mind go blank. That sear into my skin like a brand and leave my lips tingling, even after his move down to my neck.

"I like you in my bed, wearing my clothes," he tells me between kisses.

"I like being in your bed, wearing your clothes," I reply between pants, running my hands down his muscular back. "What time do you have practice?"

"Not until—" A phone rings, cutting him off. "Yours," he says. "Mine's dead."

I glance over the side of the bed, at the spot on the floor where I left my phone.

"It's my, uh, dad. I'll call him back."

"It's okay. Take it." He rolls away.

After a split-second of deliberation, I reach for it. My dad rarely calls and never this early, so something might be wrong.

"Hey, Dad."

"Hey, honey. How are you?"

Fantastic. I have a new boyfriend, and he's one of your players.

This isn't how I can tell him, though. And it's something I need to talk to Aidan about first.

"Um, fine. How about you? Is everything okay?"

"Yes, everything's great." He pauses, like something just occurred to him. "I didn't wake you up, did I?"

"No, I was up."

"Oh, good. I just wanted to call and say how excited I am that you'll be at the championship. Your mom spilled the beans last night."

I don't trust myself to look over at Aidan. I'm guessing he can hear our whole conversation. He's lying less than a foot away from me.

"It was supposed to be a surprise," I tell him.

My dad chuckles. "Your mother hasn't successfully kept a secret from me in thirty years, sweetie. She left the tickets in the printer."

"She didn't even need to print them. The airline scans it on your phone now."

"Really?" News to my dad, I can tell. I'm positive his plane ticket is printed somewhere. "Well, it means a lot I'll have my girls there."

"Good, I'm looking forward to it."

"Me too. I just wanted to check in. Everything okay?"

"Yeah, everything's good."

"Great. Talk soon, honey."

"Okay. Bye, Dad." I hang up, then toss my phone onto the bed.

He speaks first. "You're going to the game?"

I nod before glancing over. "Yeah. My mom wanted to surprise my dad by showing up and asked me if I wanted to go too. I haven't done much to support him, especially before I transferred here, so I thought it would be nice. Plus…"

"Plus what?"

"Plus, I wanted to watch you win."

"You think we will, huh?" He's not fishing for compliments. He's really asking.

"I do, yeah." I suck my bottom lip into my mouth. "And…I think we should wait to tell my dad. About us. He's waited even longer than you guys for this. I don't want him distracted or—or for it to affect things between you two."

Aidan's expression doesn't change, giving me no indication on whether he's relieved or offended I want to keep us a secret for now. "How do you think he'll take it?"

"I have no idea. He's usually good about letting me live my own life, but he didn't like Walker and wasn't shy about saying so."

"Something we have in common."

I snort. "He might think it's a conflict, because of the tutoring. So we should probably wait until after you pass the retake too."

One corner of his mouth curves up, creasing his cheek like a comma. "Sounds like you want me to be your dirty little secret," Aidan tells me, smirking.

I smirk back. "Do you have a problem with that, Phillips?"

"Nope." He pops the P. "Should we come up with code names? Secret meeting spots? Or maybe—"

I crawl on top of him, and that quickly shuts Aidan up.

CHAPTER THIRTY

AIDAN

The hotel we're hopefully spending our last night in before becoming champions is kind of a dump.

It's *fine*, I guess. No pool, slow WiFi, and the food tastes worse than Holt's dining hall, but it's clean and the television works.

I'm lying on my bed, flipping through cable channels, when Hunter walks out of the bathroom. Coach assigned rooms randomly on the flight, and we reassigned them on the ride from the airport to here. Hart is bunking with Sampson next door, and Morgan and I are sharing.

"We gotta go," Hunter tells me, pulling on a sweatshirt.

I glance at my phone, realizing he's right when I check the time. No texts from Rylan, which is disappointing. She and her mom took a later flight than the team did, so they might not have landed yet.

I stand, stretch, and follow Hunter into the hallway. Other guys are filtering out of their rooms, and I knock fists with several of them. Lots of forced smiles get tossed around too.

We're all nervous.

Tomorrow is a big day. Up there with all the major life events, especially for the seniors on the team. We all know it's our last chance. The rest of the guys are simply assuming it is, that the way we got here won't be replicated.

It's as far as we could possibly come. The peak at the top of the mountain.

If we lose, we all know it'll be a long, painful fall down.

As many of us as possible squeeze into the elevator, then Sampson hits the button for the lobby. We're eating dinner at the hotel, which I have low expectations for after lunch. But you can't beat convenience, and I think the hotel is giving the university a discount since we're such a large group staying here. Based on the size of Holt's athletic budget, I'm guessing the cost couldn't be beat either.

Coach Keller is standing with Coach Zimmerman by the small seating area right next to the front desk. A few other guys from the team are already down here, waiting with them.

I glance at Coach Keller first. He meets my gaze, giving me a small nod.

I can't enjoy his recent approval of me. The way it feels like I've finally found my place on the team. I feel guilty as shit, knowing I'm secretly sleeping with his daughter. Even if she is my girlfriend now.

So far, I haven't told anyone that.

I would trust Hunter and Conor to keep it to themselves, but they're both totally focused on the game tomorrow. And I don't trust any of the other guys on the team to keep that I'm hooking up with our coach's daughter to themselves.

I'm not planning to tell my parents I have a girlfriend now, even though it'd be very easy to do. They're here, in Cincinnati, since we're facing Fabor tomorrow.

My dad called me three days ago, letting me know they'd

booked plane tickets and were coming to the game. Staying some-where way nicer than this, I'm sure.

Once everyone's downstairs, we head into the restaurant attached to the lobby.

Dinner is mostly silent, which is rare for what's usually a rambunctious group. There's the occasional joke or tease, but the majority is filled by the clank of metal utensils against china.

Anxious energy hums through the air, electric and tangible. Willis's knee is bouncing so much it's a miracle the whole tabletop doesn't get knocked over. Hopefully he'll have better control of his limbs in goal tomorrow. Otherwise, we're screwed.

The tension around the table reaches a fever pitch when the meal ends.

Coach Keller stands and clears his throat.

Silence falls. The only other people in here are an elderly couple, and they haven't made a sound since we arrived.

"I'm no Kurt Russell," he starts.

"Holy shit. Did Coach seriously just make a pop culture refer-ence?" Hunter whispers to me.

"*Miracle* came out over a decade ago. Doesn't count," Sampson says from this spot across the table.

"I don't believe in luck or happenstance or fate," Coach continues. "I believe in hard work and drive and determination. You get what you earn. You boys…you're unlike any team I've ever coached. Not only because you're the first team to reach this point. For the past three years, I've watched Hart work harder than any one player should to keep this team afloat. The rest of you rose to the challenge this season. That's not to say other teams I've coached haven't tried to. Truth is, Division III sports are a crapshoot. We're the teams no one cares about unless they compete against us. This season, you made people care. People think they love to root for the underdog. The truth is, they only love to do so if the underdog wins. And that is exactly what we're going to do tomorrow, boys. We're going to win. Because we're the better team. Because you've earned it. Because we're prepared and we're ready. I'm proud of you all, no matter what. Play a game tomorrow that you're proud of too."

Coach Keller looks around the table with a stoic expression.

"I'm headed to bed. Any of you choose other ways to spend the evening hours, and I'll have some words for you in the morning. I imagine Hart will as well."

He leaves the restaurant, Coach Zimmerman following right behind him.

There's not much to say after that.

We're at a hotel near an airport in Middle of Nowhere, Ohio. There's nothing to do except go to bed, and I know that's what the whole team is going to do. No one wants to be skating sluggish tomorrow.

Once we're back in the room, I change into sweatpants and a clean T-shirt. Brush my teeth, then flop on the bed to channel surf again.

Hunter has a short conversation with his dad, then reads in the armchair for about an hour.

When he goes to bed, I turn off the TV. Scroll on my phone for about twenty minutes, until I'm sure he's asleep.

Then, I text her.

CHAPTER THIRTY-ONE

RYLAN

> AIDAN: What's your room number?

> RYLAN: Aidan…

> AIDAN: You're right.

> AIDAN: It'll be more fun if I go around knocking on doors and wake the whole team up.

> RYLAN: 520.

I climb out of bed as soon as I send the message. Run on my tiptoes to the bathroom so I can brush my teeth again, then readjust the tank top of the matching silk sleep set I'm wearing. The only upside of having my period is that my boobs are bigger and more sensitive than usual.

There's a low knock a few seconds later.

I head for the door, quickly glancing through the peephole before unlocking it.

"Hey." Aidan steps into my room, giving me a quick kiss before immediately pulling off his shirt. "How long have you been here?"

"About an hour. My mom and I stopped for dinner on the way."

He glances past me, at the empty bed with the covers pulled back. "I didn't wake you up, did I?"

Like I'm the one who should be well-rested tomorrow.

"No. You didn't wake me up."

He nods, then pulls off his sweatpants too, standing in my room in just a pair of black boxer briefs. My mouth goes dry as I focus on the sizable bulge tucked inside the fabric, cursing my menstrual cycle. My mom is staying in my dad's room, two floors down. Judging by how long it took Aidan to get here, he's not staying on this floor, which means his teammates aren't either. We have a hotel room with a queen-sized bed to ourselves, so of course this is the day my period came.

Aidan walks over to the bed and climbs in on the opposite side. I turn off all the lights except the lamp on my side, then climb in too.

The warm weight of his arm wraps around my waist, pulling me into him so we're spooning. He nuzzles my neck, making a throaty, contented sound deep in his throat. We've only slept in bed together once before, but it feels natural to have him on the mattress next to me. I could definitely get used to this.

Aidan says nothing, his breathing even and rhythmic. But I don't think he's asleep. I can feel the restless energy humming around him.

"Are you nervous?" I whisper.

"Yeah. But whether we win or lose tomorrow, nothing will change for me. May will still look the same, whatever the hell that turns out to be. It's a big deal, but I'm trying not to psych myself out."

"Your parents came?"

"As far as I know. My dad told me they were."

For a few minutes, we're both silent.

"You're hard," I finally state.

"Duh. You're like two inches away." He kisses my shoulder before pulling the covers back and sitting up like he's climbing out of bed. "I'll go take care of it. That'll be faster than running through hockey stats."

"I want to do it," I tell him.

Aidan pauses. I see the heat in his eyes, but there's also hesitation. "That's not why I came here, Rylan. I just wanted to see you. Hold you. It wasn't about sex."

There's a gooey, warm sensation in the center of my chest.

"I know. We're not having sex. I'm on my period. But..." I reach out, tracing the waistband of his boxers with my fingertips. "I'm considering giving you a blowjob."

He lies back, his abs clenching deliciously. Tucks his hands behind his head. "Considering, huh?"

"Uh-huh." I slip one finger beneath the elastic, running it back and forth between his hipbones.

Aidan looks like he's in serious pain, the tendons of his neck standing out as his jaw clenches tight. The front of his boxers are tented now.

"Anything I can do to help you make the decision?" he grits out.

I laugh, pulling my hand away and then tugging the comforter farther down.

"You can finish your review of the last one I gave you. You never made it past location last time. No musty smell or metal shelves this time, so I assume you have no complaints there?"

"I have no complaints *at all*."

"I mean it," I say, tugging down his boxers until his cock bobs free. It's swollen and totally erect, pre-cum beaded at the fat tip. I wet my lips. "Tell me what you like."

"Your mouth, sucking."

"Details, Aidan. Do you like your balls touched? Or ass play? I don't think I can deep throat you, but I can—"

"Baby, stop talking. I'm about two seconds from shooting my load just because of how you're *looking* at my dick. If you keep talking, I'm going to..." He pinches the bridge of his nose. "Just *please*, put your mouth on me."

I want to laugh, he looks so tortured.

"Fine. But we're discussing this another time."

"You really think I'm going to argue with—*fuck*."

He groans—loudly—when I lick him from root to tip. Then suck him deep until he's brushing the back of my throat.

I like this angle better than kneeling. My knees are resting on the soft mattress instead of a firm floor as I lean down, moving my mouth up and down his thick shaft. My hair falls forward and Aidan immediately pulls it back, grunting my name along with a warning he's close.

And he wasn't kidding about coming fast. He chants my name as he fills my mouth, groaning louder every time he feels me swallow.

I sit up, trying to ignore the pulse between my thighs. He looks so sexy like this, sprawled out in bed with all his muscles on display and his dick out. Even satisfied, the size is impressive.

The arousal must be obvious on my face, because he asks, "Do you not want to have sex, or are you saying that because you think a little blood is going to freak me out?"

"It's more than a little blood."

"I don't care."

"I care. It's...gross."

"Okay. Your call. Wanna make out, at least?"

"Will you play with my boobs?" I ask. "They're really sensitive and—*oh*."

Aidan doesn't need any more instruction. He's already tugged my shirt down as far as it'll go, capturing one nipple into the warm, wet heat of his mouth and then releasing it. Blowing on it.

I squirm, feeling him start to harden again as he does the same thing to my other boob.

I arch my back as he continues to suck and lick and nibble, running my hands through his hair and down his back. He starts to thrust, humping me through my pajamas. His dick inflates even more.

"You're insatiable," I moan.

"Your boobs are out," he replies, like that's a full explanation. I guess maybe it is.

When he texted, I was feeling bloated and achy. Now, I'm so turned on I can hardly think straight.

I come with a loud cry, hoping there's no one staying in the room next to this one.

Aidan kisses me for a good minute before pulling away. I slip out of bed so I can clean up in the bathroom.

He's lying on his back when I return to bed, his boxer briefs back in place.

I snuggle into his side, starting to feel drowsy.

I'm *almost* asleep when I hear him say my name softly.

My heavy eyelids fight to stay closed. Before I can murmur a "What?" he whispers, "I love you."

I freeze, not that it matters since I'm already motionless. If Aidan can feel the sudden tension in my body, he ignores it, punching the pillow once and then tightening his grip on me.

I lie awake, listening to his quiet confession on a loop in my head. One I'm not sure I was supposed to hear.

Sometime during the endless echo of *I love you*, I fall asleep for real.

———

I'm in the bathroom brushing my teeth when there's a loud knock on my door.

I spit and then tiptoe out of the bathroom, glancing at my bed. Aidan is still fast asleep, a pillow pulled over his head and the covers pooled around his waist. All I can see are his abs.

Another knock.

I pull on a sweatshirt and then rush over to the door. Glance through the peephole, and freeze.

My dad is outside.

I swear under my breath before grabbing the keycard off the television stand and opening the door the smallest crack possible as I step out into the hallway.

My dad looks alert, like he's been up for hours, showered and dressed in a suit. He's holding a coffee cup in one hand.

"Morning," I greet, my voice filled with fake cheer. "Big day!"

He frowns at me, and I silently pray I don't have a hickey on my neck or something equally incriminating. "Disastrous day, so far. The bus didn't start this morning. And Phillips is missing."

Fuck.

"What's wrong with the bus?" I ask, like a coward.

"If anyone knew that, it would be running. The company is working on sending a replacement, but we're supposed to leave for the arena in forty-five minutes. Have you seen Phillips?"

I swallow. "Uh, yes."

"Well you—wait. *Yes*?" Obviously not the answer my dad was expecting. "Where the hell is he? I've got hotel staff and the entire team searching every floor."

I shove my hands into the front pocket of my sweatshirt.

"He's, um, he's in there." I tilt my head to the left, toward the closed door I just exited from.

Shock. Uncertainty. Disbelief. Uneasiness. Awkwardness. Annoyance.

They all scroll across my dad's face as he absorbs that answer and registers what Aidan being in my room means.

"I didn't mean for—"

"We'll discuss this later, Rylan. Tell Phillips to get his ass downstairs. *Now.*"

My dad turns and strides away without another word.

CHAPTER THIRTY-TWO

AIDAN

"Where the hell were you?" Hunter asks.

I got down to the lobby about five minutes ago, and that's the twentieth time he's asked me that. I'm busy digging through my bag, trying to clear my head enough to make sure I have everything I need. At least the essentials. Granola bar, stick tape, blue Gatorade…

"Where the hell were you?"

Twenty-one times.

"Don't worry about it," I answer, trying to concentrate.

I packed in a mad rush after a white-faced Rylan shook me awake to tell me her dad had the whole team and most of the hotel looking for me. Setting an alarm didn't occur to me, which was just dumb. Hunter's an early riser, and he apparently freaked the fuck out when he woke up and found my bed empty.

"I *am* worried about it, Phillips. I woke up, all your stuff was there, and you were gone. I must have texted you fifty times!"

He's not exaggerating. My phone shows six hundred unread messages.

"I'm here now, so it seems irrelevant."

"Hey, Phillips. Is it true?"

I glance at Brennan, who's approached with Collins and Sampson. The rest of the guys are already on the new bus that just arrived.

"What?"

"That Coach found you in his *daughter's* room?" Jake's voice is a mixture of disbelief and awe.

Hunter looks at me so fast I hear his neck crack.

"We're playing in the fucking championship today," I say. "Worry less about where I spent last night."

"Doesn't seem like *you're* worried about the championship game," Brennan tells me. "Just concerned with getting your dick wet."

My jaw clenches so tight a muscle might snap.

Sampson's eyebrows are almost up to his hairline. "*Coach's daughter*, Phillips? How the fuck did you manage that?"

I'm seconds from losing my shit.

"And how the fuck are you still on the team?" Collins asks. "Coach didn't string you up by your balls?"

"How was she?" Brennan asks eagerly.

I turn so fast he takes a hasty step back. "Shut your mouth or I'll shut it for you, Brennan."

He rolls his eyes, not taking me seriously. "C'mon, Phillips. You fucked Coach's daughter the night before the championship and you're not going to share details? Guess I'll have to see for myself—"

I lunge.

Hunter grabs the back of my jacket just in time, pulling me back a few feet and then yanking the fabric again for good measure. "Phillips! Are you fucking kidding me?"

"She's my girlfriend," I growl at Jake. "Stay the fuck away from her."

Brennan looks shocked, and Collins and Sampson appear just as taken aback.

Then they all straighten in unison, looking behind me.

And I know, without turning around, who's standing there.

"Get. On. The. Bus," Coach Keller barks.

Hunter lets go of my coat, following Brennan, Collins, and Sampson as they all speed walk toward the automatic doors that lead outside.

I hoist my bag on my shoulder to follow them.

"Not you, Phillips."

Hunter glances back, an annoyed, concerned expression on his face. The rest of the guys keep walking. Jake is gloating, I'm sure.

I spin around slowly.

Coach's expression is stony. I'm guessing he heard the girl-friend comment. Even if he didn't, he knows I spent the night in his daughter's bed.

"If it wouldn't make winning today harder for every player on this team—guys who've worked hard all season and who deserve this trophy and who bothered to obey the room assignments last night—you'd be warming the bench today."

I swallow. I wasn't the only one who switched rooms, but I was the only one who got caught.

And there's the *where* I got caught, which I know is what Coach is really bothered by. If Sampson and I had switched, I doubt Coach would care I bunked with Hart.

"I'm disappointed in you, Phillips." That's all he says, and it's all he has to.

I've heard that a hundred times from my father, and it stings every time. And not only is this coming from my coach, it's my girlfriend's dad saying this to me.

An anvil of guilt lands in my gut. "It's not what you think," I manage to say.

"I think you spent the night before the biggest hockey game of your life somewhere you shouldn't have been. In a room I paid for with my daughter, who didn't use to lie to me."

Okay, so it's what he thinks.

"It's not just fuc—fooling around. I care about her."

I love her.

But I haven't told Rylan that. Not while she's been conscious, anyway. I'm not saying it to her dad first, even if it means he thinks I snuck into her room just to get laid last night.

Nothing in Coach's expression softens. "Get on the damn bus, Phillips."

As soon as I step on board, all the chatter dies down. No one will make direct eye contact with me.

Not Hunter, sitting in the second row.

Not Willis, whose knee starts bouncing faster when I pass.

The only one who meets my gaze is Hart, and I wish he hadn't.

He's sitting halfway back, his flinty glare more painful than a puck to the face.

Deliberately, Conor turns his head away to look out the window right before I pass. Giving me the cold shoulder.

I flinch, then keep walking toward a seat in the back of the bus.

I get why they're all pissed. It doesn't matter that I slept better next to Rylan than I would've listening to Hunter's snoring all night. That I'm well-rested and raring to go. That I'm ready to play—to win.

Most of them don't know Rylan's my girlfriend. Many of them won't care. Hart didn't bring Harlow along. We're supposed to be focused, not flirting.

Last night, I snuck out like a high schooler disobeying curfew

349

to fool around with our coach's daughter. And then they all got pulled out of bed early to look for me.

I'd think I'm selfish and stupid too.

Coach is visibly incensed when he climbs on board and starts calling out names. I feel the ripple of anxiety through the whole team, hearing the steel in his tone. He's clear-headed and even-tempered most of the time. I've seen him in a better mood after bad losses than he looks right now.

I take a seat and pull on my headphones.

I can't do a damn thing about last night. All I can do is play the best hockey game of my life.

CHAPTER THIRTY-THREE

RYLAN

My nails are biting into my palms so hard I'm worried I'll draw blood.

Forty minutes of play, and the game is scoreless. Tied at zero.

There have been plenty of chances. Penalties. Close calls.

No goals.

I'm a ball of anxiety, my entire body vibrating despite the numbness of sitting in the same spot on hard plastic for two periods. My muscles are clenched so tightly they're trembling.

If they lose…

Even my usually upbeat mom is stressed, picking at a stray thread on her jacket as we watch the players return to the rink for the third period. For the final period. Holt's faces are severe and stressed as they step on the ice and skate by, heading toward their bench.

"It's not over yet," my mom murmurs, almost to herself.

No, it's not over.

But it's not looking good either, and I feel partially responsible.

I could have told Aidan to leave last night. I could have set an alarm or woken him up sooner. I could have told my dad how I felt about Aidan sooner. I could have lied to my dad in that hallway, so at least he didn't find out I was sleeping with one of his players right before the game.

I did none of that.

And now, they might lose.

Maybe they would have lost anyway. Maybe a victory today wasn't meant to be. The worst part of sports, in my opinion? Someone always has to lose. Someone will lose, when the twenty minutes on the clock tick down to nothing. Championship games can't end in a tie. There has to be a winner, which means there must be a loser.

"There's still twenty minutes," I say. "Plenty of time."

My mom glances at me, her expression a mixture of concern and uncertainty.

My dad told her what happened. Who was in my room last night.

My mom's never managed to surprise my dad because they don't keep secrets from each other. They're honest about the hard stuff along with the easy things. I remember too much of those two hospital visits. But what stands out most vividly is how I felt safe, not just sad, watching my mom cry into my dad's shoulder after each miscarriage. I knew that they really loved each other, that they were there for each other. It was a standard to strive for, one I feel like I've finally found.

I glance over, catching the crease on her forehead before she quickly smooths it out. The only thing worse than watching Holt miss opportunity after opportunity is doing so with my mom's troubled gaze on me, worried about what I'm doing.

She hasn't asked yet, but I know she will eventually.

Since the officials are having some discussion and the third period hasn't started yet, I decide to get it over with.

"I'm dating him."

She looks at me, shock visible on her face. "You…are?"

I nod. "It's new. And I was waiting to tell Dad until after the season had ended. I didn't want it to affect how he treated Aidan, or anything else with the team." I look over at her. "He's a good guy, Mom. A great guy. We weren't—" I blush. I haven't talked about sex with my mom since she gave me The Talk back in middle school. "We weren't doing anything." If anything is defined as actual sex, which I'm definitely not going to clarify. "He came over to talk and to sleep. That was it."

My mom studies me, then sighs. "Honey, it was still irresponsible. Whether you're in a relationship with him or not, we trusted you. This trip was supposed to be about supporting your father, not sneaking around with a boyfriend neither of us knew you had."

"I know. And I *did* come to support Dad, so I'm sorry what happened might have ruined today for him. Disappointing him… disappointing you, I hate it. I'll apologize to him as soon as I can. But…there are *two* guys I love on the team. Aidan needed me last night, and I wanted to be there for him. That, I'm not going to apologize for."

My mom nods, her expression softening as she reaches over and squeezes my knee. "Okay."

My dad's always been the disciplinarian parent. My mom's a romantic.

"I'm excited to meet him, sweetie."

"I'm excited for you to meet him too."

She's going to *love* Aidan, I'm sure. Walker was standoffish with my parents, trying to impress them by talking about the research he was doing and how much grant money he was getting. Aidan charmed *me*, and I'm way more similar to my gruff dad than my easygoing mom. My mom will probably be planning our wedding after their first conversation.

The third period begins.

The whole game has been physical. Desperate, both teams fighting for puck possession. This is another level. Every few seconds, it seems, there's a loud bang as bodies collide with boards.

I'm tenser than a statue, as time ticks down to ten minutes remaining. If this game goes into overtime I might need to do a shot or something. The arena is huge and packed. And I've seen other people walking around with cups of beer, just like at professional games. There's got to be a bar in here somewhere.

Aidan's line is out on the ice. I watch as he says something to one of his wingers, who shakes his head, and then skates into position for the face-off.

Aidan wins it, passing to the player he was just talking to. They hustle up the ice, the other guy entering the zone with the puck first.

"Come on, come on, come on," I chant.

Ambient noise swallows it up. The chatter of the crowd, the scrape of blades against ice, the sharp tweet of a whistle.

One winger passes to the other winger, who passes it back. Then Aidan has the puck again.

He shoots...and the siren screams for the first time all game.

I sit, stunned, for a second. After waiting most of the game for a goal, it's a shock to finally see one. But the scoreboard changes and the loudspeaker crackles to life and it registers.

"Holt University goal scored by number thirty-four, Aidan Phillips..."

I leap to my feet, hugging my mom.

Aidan's at the bench now, talking with a few teammates.

Their huddle breaks, and then play resumes.

Fabor is desperate now, as minutes continue to tick down. They barrage Holt's goalie, Willis, with shot after shot, but he blocks them all. And Holt is reenergized by their lead, keeping up with every play Fabor throws at them.

Two minutes are left on the clock, and Aidan's goal is the only one on the scoreboard.

Fabor pulls their goalie, gaining a man advantage.

One minute left.

Thirty seconds.

Willis deflects another shot, and a blue jersey picks up the puck. Then zooms toward the opposite end of the rink, Fabor's red jerseys fighting and failing to keep up.

The Holt player shoots...and scores.

Another siren.

Another announcement.

This time it's "Holt University goal scored by number fifteen, Conor Hart..."

Ten seconds.

Five.

Four.

Three.

Two.

One.

The buzzer sounds.

I scream, hugging my mom as we both jump up and down.

Blue jerseys swarm the ice.

And Holt's hockey team are champions.

CHAPTER THIRTY-FOUR

AIDAN

W e won.

We *won*, and it hasn't fully sunk in yet.

I don't know if I'll *ever* process what this feels like. It's a feeling I've never experienced before. Standing on unfamiliar ice in front of a sold-out crowd, knowing that months—years—of work are culminated in this one moment. Early practices and weight sessions and long bus rides. Literal blood and sweat. Bruises and sore muscles. The grind of showing up hungover or tired or simply not in the mood to skate. My dad's voice, telling me to go to Stanford and get a fancy degree and to forget about the pointless exercise of playing hockey. All the film sessions in the creepy back room and the speeches from Coach K and the inside jokes with my teammates.

The last competitive hockey game I'll ever play just ended, and I'll be stepping off this ice as a champion.

We won, and a large part of me was convinced we'd lose.

My body is humming with residual adrenaline, thinking there's more. Another shift to skate. Another puck to chase. Another goal to score.

This is the view from the top, and it's strange to stop climbing. To realize there's nowhere else to go from here.

It's pandemonium around me. The ice is littered with the helmets and gloves and sticks that got tossed when the remaining time hit zero and that haven't been picked up since we shook hands with Fabor. We lifted the trophy and took a team photo, and these are the last few moments before we head to the locker room.

I stare at the scoreboard that registered one of the goals that I scored. When it mattered more than ever before, when I needed to, I came through for my teammates. None of the guys who've hugged me so far have mentioned this morning.

Conor is so choked up he can barely talk as he skates toward me. I'm so glad he got a goal too. So relieved he won't have to wonder if losing this game lost him his shot at the pros. He wraps his arms around me, neither of us saying anything as we hug in the midst of our jubilant teammates.

If I'd missed that goal, I'm not sure I ever would have forgiven myself.

If he'd missed that goal, I'm not sure he ever would have forgiven himself.

Those are the opportunities you never get back.

"I love you, Phillips," he tells me, slapping my back twice. "That was a hell of a goal."

My throat thickens. I'd do a hell of lot more than win a hockey game for Hart. He's my brother in every way that matters. I wanted this win for me. But I wanted it for him even more.

"I love you too, man," I say. "Yours wasn't awful either."

He pulls back so I can see his grin. "Empty netter? If I'd missed, I would've told the scouts not to sign me myself."

I snort. "Must have been your lucky bracelet." He's still wearing it.

Conor rolls his eyes, then glances around. He runs a hand

through his dark hair, shaking his head. "I can't believe it. I can't fucking believe it. We actually won."

"Only because I saved your speech last round," I tell him.

He guffaws, shoving me. "Well, it definitely wasn't your wayward dick helping anyone focus."

I turn serious. "I know. I'm sorry—"

Conor holds up a hand, silencing me. "We're good, Phillips. Don't apologize. We both know you'd do it again." He smirks. "I heard you called her your girlfriend in front of Coach. Assuming he doesn't toss you under a Zamboni, maybe we can double date sometime."

I surprise us both by agreeing. "Yeah, that would be fun."

"Happy for you, man." Hart punches my shoulder, then skates away to hug Willis.

I hug Hunter next, who's so stunned he's hardly speaking, and then after that it's a blur of celebrations that eventually moves into the locker room so we can all shower and change. The high of winning has fully erased any awkwardness with the team. I don't try to apologize to any of the other guys. My goal said it all, I hope. I don't owe any of them an explanation or justification.

Coach is another story, but this isn't the time or the place to have a serious conversation with him. He's talking to Willis, nodding along to something our goalie is saying with a rare smile on his face.

Rylan is in this arena somewhere. But I doubt I'll get to see her before boarding the bus, and we're headed straight to the airport from here. This arena is five times the size of Holt's, and no one's lingering around in the locker room. Everyone's eager to get back to Washington, where we can *really* celebrate.

I wonder if news has spread across campus yet. Probably. There were a bunch of watch parties planned and most of the guys are on their phones, likely posting on social media. Conor has his pressed to his ear, talking to his mom. Hunter's texting his dad.

And me?

I forgot my family was coming, until I find them waiting in the hallway outside the locker room.

They stand out among the other Holt fans who made the trip to Ohio, my mom in a sleek fur coat and Parker in a pink puffer jacket. My dad and Jameson in their designer suits. There's no sign of the Maddens. Maybe they're off commiserating with Fabor.

I chew on the inside of my cheek as I walk over with my hand shoved deep into my pockets.

Them coming here to see me play for appearances' sake was cold. Walking right past them without saying a word would be colder.

And I don't *want* to be always arguing with my parents. I'm sick of it. I'd rather they either leave me alone or stop bitching about my choices.

"That was a good game." My dad speaks first, buttoning up his wool coat.

I snort at the understatement. We just won the Division III championship. "Yeah."

"Not a bad way to end the season," Jameson chimes in with.

I'm tempted to snort again, but I don't. "I should go," I say instead, hiking a thumb over one shoulder. Most of the guys are halfway down the hallway by now. "Got a bus and a flight to catch."

That seems to wake my mom up. "I'm so happy for you, Aidan," she says, stepping forward and giving me a hug.

The sweet, floral scent of her expensive perfume fills my nose. I don't love the smell, but it's nostalgic. The same fragrance she's worn since I was a little kid.

"Thanks, Mom," I mumble.

They came, I guess. Regardless of the reason they made the trip, they were here to see me win. It doesn't mean as much, but it means something. And maybe...maybe this is the only way they knew how to come.

My mom doesn't even complain about the wet drops from my hair landing on her fancy coat. Impressive, since it was passed down from her mother and I've been personally subjected to a lot of lectures about how carefully the heirloom needs to be handled before.

"I'll see you guys at the wedding, I guess," I say, readjusting my bag on my shoulder.

My mom's eyebrows rise. "We'll be at your graduation, Aidan," she tells me. "I already made a dinner reservation at that Italian restaurant we ate at before. It wasn't too terrible, and I couldn't find any better options."

"Oh," I reply, genuinely taken aback. My parents haven't visited Holt since freshman year. Neither of them mentioned attending my graduation, so I just assumed...they wouldn't. "Okay, then. I'll, uh, see you then."

My mom nods, then steps back.

My dad holds out a hand next. We shake, his expression somber as he claps a second hand around mine. "Most exciting hockey game I've ever been to."

Considering he hasn't been to many, it's not the highest of praise. But he's trying, so I do too.

"Probably never would have started playing if you hadn't taken me to one. So...thanks, I guess."

There's a glimmer of a smile on his face. "You're welcome, son. Safe travels back to Washington."

I glance at Jameson, but neither of us says anything. Parker hasn't spoken a word, and I don't even look at her. She's not part of my family, yet. And it's the best congratulations she could give me, staying silent. Letting me have this moment with my mom and my dad and the guy who's technically my brother, even if he stopped acting like it a while ago. I'm startled—and relieved—by the emptiness I feel toward Parker. No regret or resentment or anger. She's just a girl, standing next to Jameson.

My eyes return to my mom. "Can you add one more to the dinner reservation?" I ask her. "I'd like you guys to meet my girlfriend."

Her eyebrows arch, showing her surprise. That I'm dating someone or that I care about them meeting her, I'm not sure.

She recovers quickly. "Of course."

I nod. "Great. I really gotta go."

The rest of the team is long gone. At least that means they didn't witness this whole awkward reunion with my family, but I've caused enough problems today. I don't need the guys all annoyed I delayed departure. If we miss our flight, or something, I'll never hear the end of it.

I say goodbye, kinda sorta including Jameson and Parker in it, and then hurry down the hallway and through the double doors that lead into the rear parking lot where the bus parked. I spot it ahead, the profiles of my teammates visible through the tinted windows. Everyone else is already seated. My steps quicken.

I'm halfway across the lot when I hear her voice.

"Aidan!"

I look to the left.

Rylan is running toward me. Sprinting, really, from the direction of one of the few cars parked in the special access lot. A dark-haired woman is standing by the sedan, talking on her phone. Rylan's mom, I'm guessing.

As soon as she reaches me, Rylan kisses me for the whole

team to see. Arms around my neck, legs around my waist kind of enthusiasm.

My world narrows down to her. Her smell. The heat of her body as she clings to me. The pride visible on her face as she pulls back to beam at me.

I'm pretty sure I can hear the hollers on the bus from here. Hopefully that means Coach isn't on board yet, witnessing me make out with his daughter.

"That was an amazing goal," she says, giving me one more peck before she lets go of me.

I grin. "Thanks. It was the *good luck* blowjob you gave me last night."

She shoves me for that comment. "It wouldn't have done shit if you got benched today."

Coach K wouldn't have done that. And that's the reason the disappointment he voiced earlier stung so badly. Because he's a good man—a fair man—and I let him down.

I wince. "How mad is your dad?"

Rylan's lips press together in a subtle grimace. "Mad. Mostly at me, for not telling him. I talked to him after the game, and I'm sure we'll have more conversations about my 'irresponsible behavior' on this trip. But he'll get over it. He wants me to be happy. And you—" She smiles. "You make me *very* happy, Aidan Phillips."

The three words are right there, waiting, on the tip of my tongue.

But I don't want to tell Rylan I love her for the first time in a parking lot, breathing exhaust fumes.

So I kiss her again, instead, trying to convey how I feel about her wordlessly.

Until a bus horn honks.

"Is your dad on the bus?" I ask Rylan.

362

"Yeah, the whole team's been on there for a few minutes," she says. "My mom and I were about to leave, but then I saw you walking over."

I drag a palm down my face. I would have still kissed her, sure. But probably for a little less longer and with a lot less tongue.

Rylan nudges me. "I thought you didn't care my dad's your coach?" she teases. "He's not anymore, technically."

"I know," I groan. "It's worse. He's my girlfriend's dad."

She laughs. "I gotta go. I'll see you soon, okay?"

I nod. Kiss her again, because what's one more at this point?

Then head for the bus.

The whole team starts clapping when I board, which is a massive improvement from this morning's reaction. But I don't think they're cheering because of my goal on the ice, and a risky glance at Coach's impassive expression suggests he's surmised the same.

I sink down in the seat next to Hart, who grins and elbows me, then pull on my headphones.

And start listening to "Brown Eyed Girl" as we drive toward the airport.

CHAPTER THIRTY-FIVE

AIDAN

"Hey. How was your night?" I ask when Hunter walks into the living room. He was gone when I got home earlier.

I'm sprawled out on the couch, wearing sweatpants and mindlessly scrolling through my phone.

"It was fine." Hunter shrugs out of his jacket, revealing the sweater and button-down he's wearing beneath.

I whistle. "Damn. What's with the fancy clothes?"

"I was out on a date."

I choke a little. "A *date*?"

"Yeah, it's when you take a girl out to dinner and talk to her."

I roll my eyes, then sit up. "I know what a date is, dick. I just didn't know *you* were dating."

"Yeah, well…" Hunter sighs, tugging at his tie before sprawling in the armchair. "It didn't go that great."

I'm still caught up on the fact that he's dating, but Hunter clearly isn't in the mood to elaborate. So all I say is "Sorry."

Hunter nods. "Thanks."

The curiosity is too much.

"So how long have you been, uh, dating this girl?"

He grunts, tossing the tie on the coffee table piled with the homework I was planning to get done tonight. "Tonight was the second date. I don't think we'll make it to a third."

"Bummer. Isn't that supposed to be the best one?"

"This isn't about sex."

"Then what is it about?"

Hunter slouches back in the armchair, staring at the hockey game I've got muted in the background. "You and Hart have both settled down. I thought it might be nice to meet someone. I was never crazy about the party scene, so I thought I'd try dating."

"I have not settled down. I'm twenty-two—still a wild stallion."

He snorts—loudly. "Please *never* say that again. And call yourself whatever you want. It's a Friday night, and you're on the couch, sober, waiting for Rylan to text you. You've changed, and it's a good thing. So has Hart. If he and Harlow don't get married, I'll be shocked."

"Did you mention marriage on the second date, Morgan? Because that might have been where you went wrong."

Hunter flips me off. "You hear about your retake yet?"

"No." I glance at my phone, resisting the urge to check my email again.

I had my second Stats final yesterday. If I pass, I'll graduate on time. If I don't, I won't.

No pressure.

I think I did well. I actually studied this time, and Rylan reviewed all the assignments with me at the beginning of this week. But until I see the results, I won't know for sure. And Professor Carrigan said she'd grade it "as soon as she could" but didn't elaborate any more beyond that. So I'm stuck in a state of limbo, waiting for the final number.

"I had this weird moment earlier," Hunter tells me.

My attention returns to him. "What do you mean? What kind of weird moment?"

"I was talking to this girl, and it was just…I dunno. Weird."

"Dude, you're going to have to come up with another adjective. Weird *how*? She was staring at your dick the whole time? She was bleeding? She was on a date with you, and you mentioned marriage?"

"No, I…" He shakes his head. "Never mind."

I open my mouth, right as the front door opens and closes for a second time.

Conor's eyebrows lift when he enters the living room. "Wow. You're *both* home."

"Phillips is waiting for girls' night to end."

"Morgan had a shitty date."

"Oh-kay." Hart drops down onto the couch next to me. "I got none of that."

"Hunter just got back from a bad date that involved a weird moment," I say.

"Phillips is waiting for his girlfriend to invite him over," Hunter states.

"How'd you know that?" I ask.

"Because you told me Rylan had a girls' night on Friday two days ago."

"Oh." I glance at Conor. "What are you doing home?"

He left for Harlow's less than an hour ago.

"He got kicked out." Hunter answers before Conor can. When we both look his way, he shrugs. "Right?"

"Yeah," Hart grumbles.

"Shit. What'd you do?"

"Nothing. Eve had some emergency and Harlow went to pick her up."

"What kind of emergency?" I ask. I've only talked to

Harlow's best friend Eve a couple of times, and both were entertaining experiences.

"Something about her boyfriend, I think. I dunno. I only heard
Harlow's end of the conversation."

Morgan has a strange expression on his face, like he wants to
say something but isn't sure he should.

"Huh," I say. "Well, since we're all home, sitting around like
losers instead of champions, why don't we—"

My phone buzzes, and I dive for it.

Conor snickers. Hunter sighs.

RYLAN: Hi.

RYLAN: Boy ban has been lifted.

RYLAN: Please come fuck me.

"See you guys." I stand, then hustle toward the door.

"You're a fucking tamed stallion, Phillips!" Hunter calls
after me.

CHAPTER THIRTY-SIX

AIDAN

I pull in a deep breath, already knowing I'll regret this. Knock loudly.

"What?" Conor calls.

I tighten my grip on the silky fabric, then open his bedroom door. Hart is sitting at his desk, typing on his laptop. He spins around, a smirk spreading across his face as he registers what I'm holding.

I exhale, then hold the ties up. "Which color?"

Conor stares at me for a few seconds, then bends over, laughing.

"Cool, thanks for nothing." I turn to go.

"Wait! I'm sorry, I just—" The asshole I call my best friend is still wiping tears of laughter from his eyes. "I just was not expecting you to show up in my room asking for *fashion* advice. Let me see the options again."

I deliberate, decide I've come this far, then lift them up again.

Conor starts laughing again.

"Hart! For fuck's sake, just pick one."

"Okay. Blue, I guess."

I glance at the navy tie. "I'm wearing black pants. Aren't you not supposed to wear black and blue together?"

"Why? Because you'll look like a bruise?"

I glare at his grin.

"Phillips, I'm the wrong person to ask."

Probably true. Hart mostly wears a collection of Holt Hockey gear. But Hunter isn't home, so he's my only option.

Conor reaches for his phone. "I'll call Harlow."

"No, don't—" I groan when it starts ringing. Chances I'll ever hear the end of this just plummeted to zero. And she'll probably tell Rylan, since they're besties now.

"Hey, Hayes," he says when Harlow answers. "Fashion question for you."

Whatever Harlow replies with, it makes him smile.

"Not for me. Aidan needs help picking out the outfit he's going to get buried in."

I roll my eyes.

A pause.

"No, he's feeling fine. But he's going over to Coach's house for dinner, and we're not sure he'll make it back alive."

Asshole. As if I'm not nervous enough about tonight already.

Harlow says something.

"What are the choices? Um, blue or—" Conor squints. "Darker blue?"

"It's green," I tell him.

"Blue or green," he relays to Harlow. Then asks me, "What else are you wearing?"

"What do you mean, what else am I wearing? It's what I'm wearing."

He looks me up and down, then tells Harlow. "Navy pants. White shirt."

"They're *black*, Hart. I *just* told you they were black."

"Jesus, Phillips, calm the fuck down. You asked me for help, remember?"

Yup. And I knew I'd regret it.

"Harlow wants to know if you have navy pants," he relays.

"What's wrong with black pants?"

"Aidan wants to know what's wrong with black pants," Conor tells Harlow.

This is the most ridiculous game of Telephone ever.

I step forward. "Just give me the phone."

Conor hands his cell over.

"Hi, Harlow," I say.

"Hi, Aidan." She sounds supremely amused. "I hear you're getting dressed for your own funeral."

"Yeah. And your boyfriend has been absolutely no help."

Conor flips me off.

"He considers dressing up jeans instead of sweatpants, so you should have known that," Harlow tells me.

True.

"Okay, so I have a green tie or a blue one."

"Conor told me that much."

"So, which one do I wear?"

"With black pants and a white shirt? Either way, you'll look like a waiter."

I groan, glancing down. This was the one part of my outfit I had decided on.

"And why are you wearing a tie? Rylan said you guys were going to her parents' house."

I rub my temple, feeling a headache coming on. "I'm trying to make a good impression."

"Then you should go back in time and *not* sneak into their daughter's hotel room."

"That's helpful, Harlow. Thanks."

She laughs. "Wear jeans and a nice sweater. Something you're more comfortable in."

I exhale. "Okay, thanks."

I hand Conor back his phone and then head toward the door.

"Phillips," he calls after me.

"What?" I glance back.

Conor grins. "Good luck."

I roll my eyes, then continue to my room to finish getting ready.

———

Rylan's roommate Chloe is the one who answers the door.

"Hey, Aidan," she says, greeting me with a smile.

"Hey." I step inside the front hallway. "How's it going, Chloe?"

"Not bad." She glances toward the couch, where one of Rylan's other roommates is sitting on the couch with her boyfriend. I can never remember the guy's name, but I can't stand him. Both times I've been around him, he's checked Rylan out. "You?"

"Pretty good," I reply.

Rylan appears a few seconds later, wearing one of those short skirts that drive me insane. She kisses me, says bye to her roommates, then pulls me down the front path toward where I parked my truck on the street.

I tug her to a stop before she reaches toward the door handle, caging her between my body and the bed of the truck.

Rylan quirks an eyebrow at me before running a hand down the center of my chest. I changed into jeans and a sweater, per Harlow's advice.

"Something wrong?" she asks.

I shake my head, fishing my phone out of my pocket and pulling up the screenshot I took earlier before handing it over to her.

She scans the lines of text, her lips moving silently. "You passed?"

"I passed."

More like *decimated*. I scored a ninety-three on my retake of the final.

Rylan perches up on her tiptoes, wrapping her arms around my neck. "I'm so proud of you," she murmurs.

I'm proud of me too. Relieved, even though me graduating will actually complicate our relationship.

I take a deep breath, inhaling her scent. "Thank you," I whisper.

"This was all you, Aidan. You knew the material already. You just needed to, you know, show that."

"I wouldn't have showed anything, if not for you."

She rolls her eyes.

"I mean it. You encouraged me. Believed in me. That meant everything."

Her expression softens before she kisses me again. "C'mon. We're going to be late, and you already didn't make a great first impression." She smirks, then climbs into my truck.

I roll my eyes and head for the driver's side.

CHAPTER THIRTY-SEVEN

RYLAN

I've never had a guy come over to my parents' house for dinner before. Visit the house I grew up in, that's filled with reminders of my childhood. My cement handprints are on the front walk. The walls are covered with photos I took and elementary school art projects. Several of my school photos are attached to the fridge with magnets.

My parents met Walker once, the one time they came to Boston during my sophomore year, and it did not go that well. After about ten minutes, I could tell they didn't like him, and Walker never made much effort to sway their opinion toward the positive.

Everything about tonight feels different, from the moment my mom opens the front door and points out the handprints. I avoid Aidan's amused gaze as she tells the story of how excited I was to make them.

She beams at our clasped hands as we enter the house, then fawns over the bouquet of flowers Aidan brought her. Launches into a series of questions as soon as we're seated in the living room.

My mom adores him, just like I knew she would.

My dad isn't the stern presence I thought he'd be either. He doesn't say much from his seat in his favorite armchair, but he's not scowling or grumbling. He mostly watches us, taking careful note of Aidan's hand on my knee. He rests his hand there every time we drive somewhere too, and it's become natural. And my dad's expression isn't disapproving, just assessing. Just like he seems to notice how Aidan gets up to refill my drink as soon as I finish it.

My dad and I haven't discussed Aidan beyond the awkward "Sorry about this morning," delivered by me right after Holt won the championship. I think my conversation with my mom helped a lot more. I'm sure she passed along everything I told her.

I figured tonight's dinner invitation was a result of my mom twisting my dad's arm. But my dad accepts Aidan's offer to help with the grilling readily enough, and I can see their lips moving while they're standing on the back patio so they're not standing in silence. Hopefully they're discussing hockey, not me.

It's rainy and cold out, but they seem determined not to let it impinge on the barbecue efforts.

My mom and I end up in the kitchen, her tossing the salad while I sip on wine.

"You like him?" I ask.

She nods. "He's very charming. Polite. Good-looking." I make a face, and she smiles. "But you know what my favorite thing about Aidan is?"

"What?"

My mom points the salad tongs she's holding at me. "That smile on your face."

I take a sip of wine, pretty sure I'm blushing. "Do you think Dad'll be okay with it?"

"I think having your kid grow up is bittersweet. We're both so proud of you, Rylan. But…you're his little girl." My mom smiles. "And I'm positive it didn't occur to him this is how the tutoring arrangement he set up might go. Between that and the way he found out…it threw him for a loop. Just give him a chance to readjust."

I nod, then glance toward the patio. They're still talking, which is hopefully a good sign.

"Do you think I made a mistake?" I ask my mom. "Me not starting at Holt as a freshman?"

"Do *you* think it was a mistake?" she counters.

I lift a shoulder, then let it drop. "I don't know. Part of me thinks so, since it's felt right being here in a way it never felt in Boston. I thought I just needed time to get comfortable there, that everything would start to make sense, and it never did. Then I came here and everything was so much easier, from the start. I hate thinking I missed out on that for two years. But then part of me thinks…maybe I *needed* to go to another school to appreciate Holt. Does that make any sense?"

"It makes a lot of sense, sweetheart. And I think instead of focusing on how you got here, just enjoy that you are. Don't look back at the paths you could have taken. Focus on what's ahead."

I nod. "I am. Or I'm trying to, at least."

"Good."

The sliding door opens and my dad steps inside. "We need an offload tray, Miriam."

My mom nods, then turns to rummage through one of the lower cabinets.

I glance at my dad. "Everything…okay out there?"

His neutral expression doesn't change. "Phillips isn't terrible with a grill. Picked it up faster than penalty kills."

"His name is *Aidan*, Dad. Which you know."

"I know, honey. And if I ever call him that, you'll know that things are *not* okay."

I take that to mean my dad is still claiming Aidan as one of his players, who he always refers to by their last names. That there's some affection there, buried beneath his obligation to interrogate any guy I date.

"He's…important to me," I say.

My mom hands my dad a metal tray. "Here you go, Anthony."

My dad hands it to me. "Take that out to Phillips. He should be able to handle it."

It sounds like another tiny endorsement.

After I take the tray, my dad doesn't let go.

"No guy will ever be good enough for you," he tells me. "Not my stubborn, brilliant, beautiful little girl. But…" He smiles. "You could do worse than Phillips. A lot worse."

I swallow. Nod. "Thanks, Dad."

He nods back. There's still a lump in my throat as I head outside with the tray clutched in one hand.

I feel so lucky. So loved. So much like I'm exactly where I'm supposed to be.

Even the chilly, damp air doesn't extinguish my good mood.

"I flipped everything again, so…" Aidan glances over, registers it's me, and then straightens from the grill. "Oh. Hey. What happened to Coach?"

"He sent me out here. I think it's a vote of confidence in your barbecuing skills."

"Oh. Okay. Cool." He lifts the lid of the grill to survey the cooking meat. "Is there a thermometer somewhere? I think it's done, but I really don't want to fuck this up by feeding your parents anything raw."

The only other time I've ever seen Aidan this nervous was the morning he asked me to be his girlfriend. He was rambling and fidgety the whole drive here, talking about going bowling with Harlow and Conor next weekend. Mentioning the voicemail his dad left him and the paper he has due on Monday.

And now? Fiddling with the burners and frowning at the food? He looks vulnerable. So far from the suave guy lounging in that stone hot tub, staring up at the stars like a fallen god.

"I'll grab a thermometer," I say.

"Great, thanks."

I turn to go, then turn back. I've spent the past week debating when, where, *how* to say this to him. Maybe he didn't mean it, that night. Maybe it will freak him out.

But Aidan has a talent for pushing me out of my comfort zone, so I let him draw me out once again. Even if he doesn't feel the same way, I want him to know this is how *I* feel.

"Hey, Aidan?"

"Yeah?" he replies, still studying the grill.

A light mist has started to fall, backlit by the light attached to the rear of my parents' house. All it illuminates is the patio, the rest of the fenced yard lost in the night. All that's visible is Aidan, the grill, and the empty pots my mom will replant in the spring.

"I love you."

Immediately, he tenses. I can see his shoulder muscles contract beneath his sweater.

Aidan turns to face me, the intensity in his expression severe as he studies me.

"You do?" There's something tentative and hopeful in the question, so unlike his usual confident self.

I nod. I think part of me realized loving him was inevitable from the moment I saw him standing outside my window. Or maybe it was the way my stomach dropped when I saw him sitting in steaming water. How something shifted irrevocably in that moment to accommodate this overwhelming emotion that's only expanded.

"Yeah. I do."

Aidan abandons the smoking grill and walks over to me. He touches me slowly—reverently—his hands landing on my hips before they slide around to my back. And he stares at me, somehow seeing all of me. I feel stripped raw in a safe way, holding his gaze as he just *looks* at me. Looks at me like he never wants to focus on anything else. Examine anywhere else.

His right hand lifts, his thumb brushing across my cheek and leaving a tingling trail in its wake before he twirls a piece of my hair around one finger.

"I said it first," he tells me.

"I know. I heard you that night, in the hotel room. But I wasn't sure if I was supposed to, and then with all the craziness after the game I just…" I exhale. "Even if you didn't mean it, or if you're not ready to say it, I mean it. Whenever you're—"

Aidan smiles, shaking his head. "I meant it then, and I mean it now. I love you, Rylan Alice Keller, even though you lied about your name the first time we met and had the audacity to insult me the second time."

I roll my eyes. "Can you please let that go?"

Aidan laughs, then kisses the top of my head. "Never. Both are fond memories I'll never forget. Now, can you grab the thermometer before I burn the meat I spent the past twenty minutes bragging to your dad I know how to cook perfectly?"

I roll my eyes, then head for the door.

"Rye?"

I glance back. "Yeah?"

"I've never loved anyone the way I love you. It terrifies the shit out of me, and it's the best thing I've ever experienced. You make me want to do better. Be better. So…thank you. For making me *want* to change."

"Thank you for changing," I tell him. "Because I would have fallen in love with you anyway, and you would've broken my heart."

"It was the pink pom-pom hat that pulled me," he tells me seriously.

I shake my head. "Should I share that tip with the rest of the girls on campus?"

"Sure. But it wouldn't have worked with any other girl on campus. Just you."

EPILOGUE

RYLAN

I smooth the front of my dress, brush a flake of mascara away from under my eye, and take a deep breath.

"Rye!" Aidan calls. "We're going to be late."

Another deep breath, and then I open the bathroom door.

He's leaning against the opposite wall, looking hot as hell in his custom tux. Jameson asked Aidan to be his best man, which is kind of fucked up if you ask me, but no one did. Aidan said he doesn't care, that he's happy to go along with whatever, and he seems to mean it.

Ever since we arrived at the fancy hotel on the Pacific where his brother is getting married, Aidan has been totally relaxed.

We lounged on the beach yesterday until we had to get ready for the rehearsal dinner, and Aidan smiled through all of it.

Me, on the other hand? I'm a bundle of nerves.

Part of it is that Parker is even more gorgeous than I pictured —perfect hair, perfect skin, perfect smile—and it's intimidating to know she's the only other girlfriend Aidan has had. The rest is that despite Aidan's troubled relationship with his family, I want them to like me. I'd only met his parents once before this weekend, when Aidan graduated in May. It went okay, but it was also awkward.

I'm used to being the girl parents love—studious and reliable. A positive influence. Yet I'm totally out of my depth in Aidan's world. Or his parents' world, rather. I'm positive Aidan doesn't care about any of the things his mom talked my ear off about last night, but she obviously does. And I barely followed any of it.

His whistle, long and low, is what jerks me out of my stress spiral.

This is the first time Aidan has seen the dress I bought for the wedding. It was the most money I've ever spent on an outfit before, and worth every penny to see the look on Aidan's face. The saleswoman told me it was giving Hollywood starlet, which seemed appropriate for the occasion. It's glitzy and glamorous and low-cut, the detail that Aidan is most focused on. It's like he's never seen my boobs before.

"You look…" He exhales. "*Wow*. There aren't words, Rye."

"What a compliment," I drawl.

I'm mostly teasing him to alleviate my own nerves. The look on his face is already inflating my ego.

"You want compliments?" He stalks closer, toying with the strap on my left shoulder currently holding half the dress up.

I bat his hand away. "You said we were going to be late."

"I don't give a shit. They can wait."

"So can you. We had sex last night."

I grab my clutch off the dresser, then head for the door. After a lot of grumbling, Aidan follows behind.

"Last night was a long time ago," he tells me as we walk down the hallway.

I roll my eyes but don't respond otherwise. A few seconds later, I'm tugged to a stop so abrupt, I almost fall in my heels. At least I know Aidan has excellent reflexes and will probably catch me.

"What's wrong?" he asks, his green gaze searching.

"I'm...nervous," I admit.

His eyebrows knit together. "You don't have anything to be nervous about."

"We're going to your brother's wedding to your ex-girlfriend, which your entire family is attending. This is different from the barbecue at my parents', Aidan."

He winces, rubbing the back of his neck. "Your dad was my coach? So that was weird?"

I scoff. "Nice try. This is more awkward, and you know it."

"I know. If you want to skip it, you can stay in the room. Order room service, go down to the spa."

As tempting as that sounds, I shake my head. "I'm good. Let's go."

He studies my expression, nods, then grabs my hand and pulls me toward the elevator.

———

The ceremony itself is a blur. It's held out on a terrace, with the dazzling backdrop of the aquamarine Pacific behind. Then all the guests migrate into a ballroom where the reception is being held.

Uniformed waiters start moving through the crowd, passing out appetizers and glasses of champagne.

I help myself to both as I people watch, waiting for Aidan to appear. He got pulled into photos with his family, and he's literally the only person I know here. Eating and drinking gives me something to do, at least.

"Hi. I'm Parker."

I turn to face the blonde woman, trying to mask my

surprise. I force a smile, swiping a napkin across my lower lip to make sure I caught any crumbs. I have no idea what half of the hors d'oeuvres are, but everything I've sampled has been delicious.

"Rylan," I say. "Congratulations, on the wedding."

"You could tell I'm the bride?" Her tone is teasing, but her gaze is sharp as she looks me up and down.

"The white dress was a bit of a giveaway."

"Right." Her tone is still light as she tucks a piece of blonde hair behind one ear. The huge diamond on her left hand sparkles under the twinkling lights. "You're here with Aidan?"

I don't buy the question she turns the statement into. She saw us sitting together at the rehearsal dinner last night.

"Yes." I sip some champagne, holding her stare.

Parker stiffens, like she's realized I know a lot more about her than she knows about me. "Did you go to Holt?"

I don't miss the sneer as she says the school's name. I would have guessed she attended a university with a single-digit acceptance rate even if Aidan hadn't told me so.

"I *do* go there."

Parker smiles. "Ah, a younger woman. Aidan is more like Jameson than he thinks."

My polite expression starts to feel like hardening cement. "I don't see any similarities." I pick up my appetizer plate. "I'm sure you have a lot of other guests to greet. Congratulations, again."

Ex or not, she's Aidan's sister-in-law now. If he and I end up having a future together—and I'm really hoping we will—making an enemy of Parker won't help anything.

I turn to continue down the buffet table.

"Rylan."

I spin back around.

It looks like the mask has fallen from Parker's face. I'm

suddenly reminded she's only a year older than I am. There's an earnestness to her face that wasn't there before.

"He's…special. Don't take that for granted—the way I did."

"I won't," I tell her, then continue walking.

———

After dinner ends—a six course meal—the wedding cake gets cut up and distributed.

More drinks.

The dance floor opens up.

Aidan gets sucked into a long conversation with one of his father's friends. Dances with his mom, and then Parker.

I decide to hit up the bar for a fresh drink.

I'm not annoyed Aidan is dancing with his ex, more impressed. I don't think I could move past everything that happened between them as entirely as Aidan seems to have. I can see the strain in his expression from here, though. I know today hasn't been easy for him. That he's eager to have it all over with.

The bartender passes me another margarita. I take a long sip, then glance at the dance floor again.

"I love her, you know."

I startle, glancing to the left. Aidan's brother Jameson—the groom—has appeared. Holding a tumbler of scotch in one hand as he watches Aidan and Parker waltz together. The only words we'd exchanged up until now were simple, brief pleasantries. Jameson talking to me at all, let alone what's he's saying, is a shock.

"I'm sure my brother has told you the whole sob story, and that I was the girlfriend-stealing villain in the tale. But truthfully? I saw my shot and I took it. Parker wanted him to be me, but Aidan was never going to end up at Stanford or working for my dad. She thought he loved her enough to change, and she was wrong. So…I took my shot."

"You fucked over your brother, you mean?"

Jameson's eyebrows rise when I swear, but his only other reaction is to swirl the liquid in his glass. "I asked her to get coffee on campus to ask her to give Aidan another chance. My parents were worried…he was going off the rails. We spent four hours talking. I asked her out on a date the next day. Took me until she insisted on going to my parents' place in Vail for Christmas to realize she was trying to make Aidan jealous."

"So, of course, you proposed."

He smirks, the similarity to Aidan's uncanny. "Not for a couple of years. Not until she accepted it was over between them. We all grew up together. I have no clue how she didn't realize Aidan doesn't forgive. He's one hell of a grudge holder. Aside from cheating on him, dating me is the worst thing she could have done."

"Why are you telling me all this?"

Jameson's gaze remains on the dancing couple. "Because this is the happiest I've seen Aidan in a long time. He graduated and got a good job. I looked up that company he's working for in Seattle. Their market capitalization is decent."

Aidan started working at a marketing firm in June. He seems to enjoy his job, and he's undoubtedly the most popular employee in the office. I'm just relieved he's living only an hour away from Somerville. He could have ended up a lot farther away.

"And because…our relationship sucks. It's always been bad, but it barely even feels like I have a brother any longer. I had no idea he was any good at hockey—I thought it was just a hobby—until we went to that game and thousands of people were screaming his name. I have no idea how to fix things with him, to make it better than this mess it is now. And I figured…having you not hate me might be a decent start. So…I wanted you to know I'm not a prick who went after his little brother's ex-girlfriend just because he could. If you want to feel bad for a Phillips brother… the woman I just married doesn't look at me the way you look at Aidan."

"If we get married, please come up with a better best man speech," I tell him.

Jameson laughs. "Like Aidan would ever ask me to stand up with him. He'll ask one of his hockey buddies."

Probably true. But Jameson looks morose enough, I don't say so. I guess part of his plan worked, because I do feel a little bad for him.

I take a sip of margarita, not sure what to say.

The music changes to a tempo I recognize. One that's noticeably different from the dramatic, sweeping melody that was just playing.

"I love this song," I tell Jameson.

He half-smiles. "Do you want to dance?"

"Oh. Uh…"

"I got it from here, Jameson." Aidan appears. The look he gives his brother isn't hostile, but it's not friendly either.

"Did you do this?" I ask him as he pulls me out onto the dance floor.

"Maybe." He grins, then spins me.

We dance through "Brown Eyed Girl" and then the music switches to a slower song. He pulls me against his chest, basically just rocking us back and forth.

"What were you and Jameson talking about?" Aidan asks.

"You, mostly."

"Hmmm."

"He was nice."

"He better have been."

I lean back and interlock my fingers behind his neck. "What did you and Parker talk about?"

"How dry the cake was."

"I thought the cake was good," I say.

"So did I. I mostly just nodded along." His lips brush my cheek. "Were you jealous? Because if you need a reminder of who I belong to, I'd be happy to fuck you for a few hours…"

"Aidan…" I half-moan, half-reprimand as his mouth moves to the side of my neck.

The dance floor isn't crowded, but it's not empty either. There's an older couple five feet from us.

"Let's go swimming," he suggests suddenly.

"What?"

"We're right by the ocean. Let's go swimming."

"*Now?*"

"Why not?"

I can think of a dozen reasons. We're at his brother's wedding reception. I spent an hour on my hair and makeup. It's dark out, and there are no lifeguards.

But then I decide…*fuck it.*

I grab Aidan's hand and pull him toward the nearest exit.

"Really?" His voice is high and excited, like a little kid's.

I don't answer. I just head for the red sign.

It's warmer out than I was expecting. The sun went down hours ago.

Maybe it's because I've spent all day inside the air-conditioned hotel.

At the edge of the stone patio, I pause, reaching down to pick up my heels after I step out of them. Aidan waits for me, tugging at his bowtie and then the top button of his shirt. If we go back to the reception after this, everyone is going to think we snuck off to have sex.

Which is kinda what I wish he'd suggested. The closer I walk to the crashing waves, the more ominous they look. The only light is what's spilling out of the hotel windows, and it ends about ten feet into the sand. Past that, everything is shadowed shapes. No lifeguard. No spectators. If we get swept out to sea, no one will ever know.

"Second-guessing?" Aidan teases. The wind is ruffling his hair, and my breath stalls in my lungs as I look over at him.

I can't believe he's *mine*.

And he knows me too well, the quirk of his eyebrow telling me he'll tease me about this later, but he'll also turn right around if that's what I decide to do.

"I need you to do my zipper."

I tuck my hair to the side and out of the way, then turn so my back is facing him. The warmth of his hands appears a few seconds later, finding the tiny closure at the top and then tugging down the zipper. He doesn't stop after a few inches. He pulls it down as far as it'll go, then kisses the top of my spine before stepping away.

"Thanks," I murmur, stepping out of the dress and folding it carefully before dropping it onto the sand.

"*Fuck*, Rylan."

I smile before straightening, knowing he's spotted the lingerie I splurged on to wear under the dress. I paid a lot of money for practically nothing. The black scalloped lace is totally transparent, the same consistency as a veil. I was terrified it would tear, pulling it on. "What?"

"You know what." His hands find my hips and then tug me back into him. "You've been wearing *this* the whole time?"

"No. I changed into it on the way out here," I say sarcastically.

He spanks me and I moan, shamelessly grinding my ass against his growing erection.

"I love you so fucking much, baby." His mouth finds the sensitive spot just below my jawline, sucking gently as he palms my tits roughly.

I sink back against Aidan, drunk on his proximity. As soon as he touches me, I have a tendency to forget there's a world beyond him. He's intoxicating in the best way.

The first fireworks scare the shit out of me.

The sound echoes like a gunshot, the explosion of color turning the sand and the water pink in addition to the sky. I glance up, wishing I hadn't left my phone at the table so I could snap a photo.

Aidan looks up too. "Fucking typical," he grumbles. "The wedding wasn't enough of a spectacle?"

I pull out of his grasp and run toward the water, knowing he'll follow. I splash through the shallows, the salty water stinging my skin.

I'm not even waist deep when I hear him behind me.

A strong arm wraps around my waist and then I'm spinning, colliding with his bare chest. Getting naked fast is a talent of his.

"I'll always chase you," he tells me gruffly.

Impulsively, I kiss him.

Fireworks are still going off overhead, and this feels like one of those rare, romantic moments to take advantage of.

Aidan growls, his hands cupping my ass and lifting me so my feet are no longer on the sandy bottom. I wrap my legs around his waist, digging my fingers into his shoulders as I fuse our mouths together.

Aside from our underwear, we're both totally naked. His lips leave my mouth to work their way down my neck. I'm pretty sure he's going to leave a hickey.

"You want to?" I ask.

"Rye, don't ever ask me if I want to fuck you. The answer is always going to be yes."

I feel him then, peeling the wet lace away from my pussy and pushing inside of me. He goes slow, letting me adjust to the awkward angle and different surroundings.

Waves are rolling past us.

Another burst of fireworks lights up the sky overhead.

"This is a first," he tells me.

I smile. "Yeah?"

"Uh-huh."

"Tell me your review tomorrow."

His laugh vibrates through his chest.

We're back in the water, under the stars, just like the first night we met. But I could be anywhere in the world with Aidan, and I know it'll feel like this.

Like home.

THE END

ALSO BY C.W. FARNSWORTH

Standalones

Four Months, Three Words

Come Break My Heart Again

Winning Mr. Wrong

Back Where We Began

Like I Never Said

Fly Bye

Serve

Heartbreak for Two

Pretty Ugly Promises

Six Summers to Fall

King of Country

Rival Love

Kiss Now, Lie Later

For Now, Not Forever

The Kensingtons

Fake Empire

Real Regrets

Truth and Lies

Friday Night Lies

Tuesday Night Truths

Kluvberg

First Flight, Final Fall

All The Wrong Plays

Holt Hockey

Famous Last Words

Against All Odds

From Now On

ACKNOWLEDGMENTS

This was the most fun I've had writing a book in a long time. I wasn't planning to continue the Holt Hockey series until this summer. But Aidan's story kept stealing my attention from other projects, until I decided to sit down and get out the scenes stuck in my head. I figured it would be a few chapters. It was an entire book. And I'm so fortunate to work with a team of incredible women who jumped on board enthusiastically when I asked if they could maybe, possibly squeeze this project in.

Mary Scarlett, thank you for this beautiful cover. And for being so gracious and accommodating about every change and detail. I adore working with you.

Tiffany, I say it every time and I always mean it—this book is a thousand times better for having your eyes on it. You have an incredible talent for enhancing a manuscript's feel and not just tidying the words on the screen. I am so grateful for your wisdom and your work ethic. I swear, this was the last crazy deadline!

Britt, your excitement for this book and about this series was contagious. Reading through your comments put the biggest smile on my face and made me so eager to have this book out in the world. You're such a joy to work with and I can't wait to hear your thoughts on Hunter's book.

To my family, thank you for understanding why I was working over the holidays and for taking care of absolutely everything so I could finish this book on time. You're the best.

And finally, to any readers who made it all the way to the Acknowledgments! Thank you so much for reading. I hope you loved Aidan and Rylan's story, and I'm very grateful for your support.

ABOUT THE AUTHOR

C.W. Farnsworth is the author of numerous adult and young adult romance novels featuring sports, strong female leads, and happy endings.

Charlotte lives in Rhode Island and when she isn't writing spends her free time reading, at the beach, or snuggling with her Australian Shepherd.

Find her on Facebook (@cwfarnsworth), TikTok (@authorcwfarnsworth), Instagram (@authorcwfarnsworth) and check out her website www.authorcwfarnsworth.com for news about upcoming releases!

Made in United States
Orlando, FL
02 February 2024

43186931R00240